ALL I WANT IS FOREVER

Talia stared into his eyes. Without thinking, he pressed his lips to the back of her hand. His gaze traveled down her face and neck to the small spot of skin exposed by the V-neck blouse. He took in the luscious curve of her full breasts outlined by the delicate fabric. Her lips parted. She clasped her long, elegant fingers around his wrist, then drew him closer. Derrick's pulse beat like a drum when she tenderly kissed him.

They kissed on and on, each savoring the sensation. Both sighed when they finally parted. Derrick breathed heavily, his mind fogged with a lust so powerful he shook. The clink of dishes brought him back to where they were in the nick of time.

"How long will you be in town?" she whispered.

"Two days. I can stay longer," Derrick answered in a raspy voice.

"No promises."

"No promises," he repeated.

Also by Lynn Emery

GOTTA GET NEXT TO YOU
TELL ME SOMETHING GOOD

LYNN EMERY

All I Want Is Forever

HarperTorch
An Imprint of HarperCollins*Publishers*

This is a work of fiction. Names, characters, places, and incidents are products of the author's imagination or are used fictitiously and are not to be construed as real. Any resemblance to actual events, locales, organizations, or persons, living or dead, is entirely coincidental.

HARPERTORCH
An Imprint of HarperCollins*Publishers*
10 East 53rd Street
New York, New York 10022-5299

ISBN: 0-06-008928-8

First HarperTorch paperback printing: November 2002

Printed in the United States of America

Visit HarperTorch on the World Wide Web at www.harpercollins.com

10 9 8 7 6 5 4 3 2 1

prologue

∞

Talia breathed a sigh a relief as she walked home from school. The day hadn't been quite as bad as it could have been. Only a few girls had made fun of her clothes. No one had mentioned Monette. She clenched her teeth and hugged the tattered book sack to her worn pink shirt. There was always tomorrow. Each day was an obstacle course. No different from all the days she'd experienced in her fourteen years.

A lanky boy the color of nutmeg strolled out of a trash-strewn dirt alley and onto the cracked sidewalk. Derrick Guillory wore a blue T-shirt under a denim jacket and a pair of faded blue jeans. He folded his arms across his chest. At fifteen, his body showed signs of developing into a well-muscled adult male.

"Hey, wait up."

Talia stopped and turned around. Derrick and she had been buddies since elementary school. She'd been with her second foster family at the time. Now that she was back with her mother again, the last thing she needed was for him to follow her home. There was no telling what she would find. Monette might be high again, hanging out with her no-good friends or in one of her paranoid fits.

"I've got to get home fast." Talia tried to go around him, but he blocked her path.

He grinned at her. His topaz eyes sparkled with mischief. "No problem. I'm on the track team, remember?"

"Sure, you braggin' every chance you get. Now go home." Talia covered her anxiety with sarcasm. She prayed he'd get insulted and leave.

His dark eyes narrowed for an instant in anger. He studied her for a second until his expression changed into one of concern. "What's wrong? I better go with you."

"You bein' real dumb today, ain't ya? Okay, I'll spell it out. Leave me alone." Talia glared at him with her chin up. She whirled around and hurried off. *Please don't follow me.*

"Sure. I'll see you later," he called after her.

Talia did not answer him. She ran around a corner and down Laroux Lane, a fancy name that did not fit the dusty road. She climbed up the steps of the house. A couple of cheap chairs from a discarded dinette set sat on either end of the back porch. She was grateful none of her mother's so-called friends were perched on them today.

"I'm home." Talia let go of the broken strap and dropped the book sack down on the breakfast table.

When there was no answer, she swore softly. Once again Monette had walked off, leaving the door open. They had little to steal, but Monette's no-good pals would take anything not nailed down. Still Talia felt relief mixed with anger. At least she might actually get homework done. Then she heard a thump.

"Monette?"

She went through the kitchen and into the living

room. Talia was halfway across the room when the man stood up from the sofa. She spun around, then froze. Earl Glasper leered at her. He'd been her mother's lover off and on for the last three years and he was trouble. Dressed in Tommy Hilfiger jeans and white shirt, he still had the look of a street thug in expensive clothes.

"Your mama stepped out a minute." Earl walked toward her. The chunky gold bracelet on his nut brown wrist and matching necklace flashed as he moved. "Sit down. I was just gonna watch some television."

"I'm going to spend the night with a friend." Talia backed up. "Just tell her I'll call later."

Earl nodded slowly. His gaze swept her from head to toe. "Got you a boyfriend already, huh? Ain't surprised. You one fine little lady."

Talia tugged at the short plaid skirt she wore. Earl always had a way of making her feel exposed. "See ya."

Earl's slow, easy manner vanished. He crossed the space between them in two long strides and caught her wrist. "Why you runnin' off? I got more than any kid can give you."

"Let go of me!" Talia tried to yank free, but his grip tightened. She gasped when his free hand rubbed her thigh and went up her skirt.

"You a younger, sweeter version of your mama." Earl pulled her against his chest. "I've seen you hangin' 'round that little chump Derrick. You ready for a man, baby."

Talia struggled to get free. Earl only seemed amused by her attempts. When he pressed his wet lips against her neck Talia shrieked. The hand he stuck under her skirt fingered the fabric of her panties.

"What the hell goin' on here?"

Monette stood in the door leading to the kitchen, one hand on her hip. She wore a dark red knit dress that clung to her voluptuous figure. Her long auburn hair was swept up.

Earl let go of Talia abruptly, causing her to stumble. "Hey, girl. I was just—"

Talia sank to the floor and covered her ears with both hands, trying to block out the ugliness. She wanted it all simply to go away. Monette and Earl took no notice of her muted sobs as she huddled in a corner.

"Don't bother lyin'." Monette took a small gun from her purse. "Now I got another reason to shoot your ass."

"What you talkin' 'bout, baby? Stop actin' crazy." Earl backed away with both hands raised. "I was just playin' with the kid."

"Uh-huh. Like I believe that." Monette pointed the gun at him and walked closer.

"Look, she's almost grown and knows how to tease a dude. What you expect? You was the same way at her age." Earl lifted a shoulder. He smiled at Monette. "Now come on, sugar. Don't be like that."

"I got your sugar right here, you bastard. I know you been sellin' folks out, Earl." Monette glared at him.

"What?" Earl blinked hard at her.

"Yeah, I found out." Monette spat out the words.

"Stop talkin' crazy. I ain't done nuthin' like that." His chest rose and fell faster as he spoke. Yet he continued to gaze at her as though they were having a simple chat.

"Maybe I'll just tell Carlo and the other dudes on the street. Let them handle your ass."

"You don't know what you sayin', girl." Earl didn't lose the smile, but it seemed to stretch tight across his broad features.

"You ain't dealin' coke to get those fancy clothes and gold chains." Monette panted, her face twisted with anger. "You the reason I spent eighteen months in parish prison."

"Don't be stupid. Somebody been lyin' on me." Earl's hand shot out, and he grabbed for the gun.

"Get off me!" Monette tried to jerk back, but Earl clamped a beefy hand around her wrist. She screamed when he slammed his fist against her head with his other hand.

"You got nerve pullin' a gun on me," he said through clenched teeth.

Monette raked her long acrylic nails down his neck. Earl howled in rage. The two twirled around in a circle, fighting for control of the gun. Talia shrank against the wall, her eyes wide with horror. She jumped when the gun went off. Earl yelled a profanity and punched Monette again. A second shot sounded, this time muffled. Both of them seemed suspended for a second. Then, in what seemed like slow motion, Earl fell to his knees. He bent double until his forehead touched the hardwood floor.

They both stared at the motionless figure. The violent man looked like a helpless child. His blood formed an oval that grew by the second. Talia knew the rough times she'd been through already were nothing compared to what would come. Monette and Talia started when the front door flew open. Derrick looked at them, then at Earl.

"I heard the shot. Lemme help," he said.

Monette scooped up her purse where it had fallen on the floor during the struggle. She stuffed the gun inside it. "You saw anybody else out there?"

"No, but—"

"Get her down to Miz Rose's house on Kingfish

Street. You know where I'm talkin' 'bout?" Monette said to Derrick.

"Yeah."

"Then get back here. I can't move him by myself," she ordered.

Derrick rubbed his hands together. "But—"

"Get goin' before somebody show up, boy!" Monette barked.

He led Talia out of the house, murmuring reassurances to her. Neither of them looked at Earl as they left. The fifteen-minute walk to her former foster mother's home seemed to take forever. Talia trembled each time a car approached, sure the police had tracked them down. Derrick squeezed Talia's hand hard at the sight of Miss Rose's cheery yellow wood frame house. Miss Rose came to the door, wiping her hands on a dish towel. When she saw Talia's expression, Miss Rose unlatched the screen door fast.

"My Lord, child. What's happened now?"

"Miss Monette ain't feelin' too good," Derrick said. "Can Talia—"

"Come on in here, baby. I got some clothes that oughta fit you. Doggone shame the way that woman lives," Miss Rose muttered to herself. She started toward a back bedroom.

"Wait!" Talia called out, as Derrick started to leave. She followed him onto the front porch, glancing over her shoulder to make sure they were alone. "What's going to happen?"

"Don't worry," he said quietly. "I'll take care of it."

"But what if—"

"Just go on and let Miz Rose get you somethin' to eat." Derrick took off his jacket and put it around her shoulders. "It's gonna be alright."

Talia shivered, but not because of the brisk fall evening. Derrick gave a quick nod of encouragement before he strode off into the gathering dusk. They had shared many secrets since childhood. They would never dare to whisper this secret again. Not even to each other.

Chapter 1

∞

"I have an appointment with Senator Collins," Talia said crisply.

"I'll let him know you're here, Ms. Marchand," the young blond secretary said with a professional smile.

Talia did not sit down. She waited another twenty minutes before she was shown into his office. With no trace of the irritation she felt in her expression, Talia extended a hand to him and smiled widely. Senator Collins, his hair silvery gray, was a tall man. The senior senator was known to be ultraconservative. He was also famous for his acerbic wit, mainly aimed at feminists and minorities. Both in private circles, of course. She had her work cut out for her, but Talia was ready. Half the battle was knowing your opponent much better than he suspected. Though leaning toward the right on a number of issues herself, Talia found him hard to stomach.

"Senator, I very much appreciate your taking time to see me," Talia said.

"Nonsense. I'm here to serve the people of my district, Ms. Marchand. Sit down, please. Drink?" Senator Collins nodded to his chief aide. Felicity Allgood stood at attention, waiting to do his bidding.

"Bottled water is fine. Thanks." Talia accepted the bottle of Kentwood Spring Water Felicity handed her. "Congratulations on getting funds for the highway project." Pork barrel project was a more accurate description.

"Thank you. I'm very pleased that my esteemed colleagues saw the light." Senator Collins wore a crooked grin. They both knew he'd called in political favors to get what he wanted.

She smiled back at him. "Yes. Which of course means much needed jobs."

"Nonunion jobs so hardworking people can feed their children," he replied in his best politician's tone.

"Exactly. Putting children first is the reason we need child welfare reform. A substantial percentage of juvenile and adult offenders are products of a flawed foster care system." Talia performed a neat segue into the reason for her visit.

"The government interferes in family life too much, Ms. Marchand. Speeding up the process of separating biological parents from their children—"

"Parents who have consistently shown an inability or unwillingness to make a safe home for their children, Senator. We're not talking about railroading parents," Talia cut in smoothly.

"Throwing money at the problem is a liberal failing. I would have thought your outfit wouldn't advocate such an approach." Senator Collins took a sip of pineapple juice from the bottle Felicity provided.

"The National Council of Juvenile and Family Court Judges address that issue as well." Talia nodded. She gave a concise summary of costs as calculated by a council task force.

I see." Senator Collins waved a hand at his aide when the young woman pointed to her wristwatch. "I'm sure you brought a report for me."

Talia took out a blue folder with the council's justice scales logo on it. "Yes. Please don't hesitate to give me a call if you have questions."

In short order she made one last pitch, inquired about his wife and kids, and made her exit. She removed her cell phone from the leather briefcase. Talia glanced around. She found a spot away from a clump of people.

"Hi, I just left his office. Pompous as usual. Yes, call the good senator and remind him he needs help on the farm subsidy bill. Thanks."

She flipped the tiny phone closed and put it away. Talia smiled to herself as she proceeded on her way. Lobbying Congress for nonprofit advocacy organizations was part of her atonement. She made a substantial salary as a highly paid political consultant for three large insurance and pharmaceutical companies. Not that she was at all ashamed of her work for them. Still, taking on the cause of foster care reform had hit close to home. She'd shunned any kind of social work or social services profession. Instead she'd taken business and public policy courses in college. Talia had always meant to follow the money. Yet influence and control were just as important to her. As she walked purposefully down the halls of the Capitol Complex, she mentally ran through her list of appointments for the day. As usual she made time to schmooze with congressional staffers along the way. A tall man the color of mahogany waved to her. Jarrod Thompson worked in the Department of Justice, one of a legion of sharp young lawyers. He was ahead of the pack since he had an MBA and spoke four languages. All her friends said they were the perfect power couple.

"Hello, Ms. Get-things-done. Got time for me?"

"Sure, I've always got time for you." Talia beamed at him. Jarrod had helped her out more than once.

"I'm talking purely social. No pumping me for inside tidbits to help your clients." Jarrod wagged a long forefinger at her.

"Agreed. Besides, I don't need anything right now," Talia added with an impish grin.

"Sure, sure. You only lust after my mind," Jarrod quipped.

"Don't forget those killer contacts," Talia shot back.

Jarrod put a hand on her elbow as they exited one crowded hallway into another. "So how has your day been so far?"

"Packed, but I'm on schedule." Talia glanced at her Seiko sterling silver watch. "I've got a two o'clock with Representative Westin. The honorable House member from Montana is being difficult."

"I'm sure you'll handle him. What about B. Smith's?"

"Perfect. I—" Talia stopped short. "It can't be," she murmured.

A tall, imposing figure rose head and shoulders above the crowd around him. His smoky topaz eyes gazed straight into hers. With at least twenty feet between them, she felt the impact of his presence. She hadn't seen him in at least five years. Distance in neither space nor time had lessened his effect on her. Six feet four inches tall, Derrick Guillory radiated power. His hair was longer than she'd ever seen it before. The tight dark bronze curls lay in waves combed back from his face. He wore a light tan suit and crisp white shirt, with a silk tie the color of vintage burgundy. The suit coat stretched across a broad chest and shoulders. Derrick stood against the wall allowing the flow of humanity to pass him by. More than a few women turned to give him a second look. Derrick caused a stir without noticing. His electric gaze never left Talia's face.

"Whoa, what's up with this?" Jarrod stared at her, then followed her gaze. "Talia, you look like a ghost just popped up in the crowd."

"He's real enough," she whispered.

Talia could have added an unwelcome one. Except that the tingle spreading up her spine felt pleasant. Derrick brought the good and the bad with him, as always.

"What?" Jarrod looked at her.

"Nothing," Talia mumbled low. She brushed a hand across her brow.

Jarrod frowned as he continued to scan the crowd. He moved closer to her protectively. "If it's someone you don't want to see, then let's get out of here."

As if he sensed what was about to happen, Derrick strode forward. He moved with the grace of a seasoned running back, easily shortening the distance between them.

Jarrod caught sight of Derrick seconds later and walked in front of Talia.

"Okay, this brother obviously doesn't see me. I'll make sure he does," Jarrod said.

"Wait, I know—" Talia tried to moved around him, but a large woman bumped into her.

"Hello." Derrick's basso voice rolled out like quiet thunder. "Talia," he said simply.

Talia stepped from behind Jarrod a bit breathless, but not from being jarred by the solid, fleshy woman. "Hello, Derrick."

"You know each other?" Jarrod said in a flat voice.

"From home, in Louisiana," she said slowly. "Derrick Guillory, this is Jarrod Thompson."

Talia stared at Derrick. The strong line of his jaw made him look like a man both dangerous and exciting. The muscular frame encased in expensive fabric made him look like a beautiful African warrior prince dressed in Western clothes.

"Hi." Jarrod did not look pleased, but he stuck out his hand anyway.

"Hello." Derrick shook it briefly. Both men seemed eager to break contact.

"An old friend from home, huh?"

Derrick looked Jarrod straight in the eyes. A slow, easy smile spread across his face. "We go back a long, long way."

"Is that right?" Jarrod tightened his hold on Talia's arm. "What brings you to the big city?"

"Business," Derrick said shortly, then glanced at Talia. "Your office said you'd be with Senator Collins. I took a chance I would catch you before you left."

"Oh." Talia could not stop looking into his eyes.

"We're on our way to another meeting," Jarrod put in.

Talia snapped out of her reverie. "Let me catch up with you later, Jarrod."

"But you know these folks don't like to be kept waiting," Jarrod said with an edge to his tone.

"I'm sure you can answer all their questions. I'll call you," Talia said pointedly.

"Fine, I'll call you later. Tonight. Remember, we have plans later this week." Jarrod strode away, looking back over his shoulder at them.

Talia watched him leave through narrowed eyes. His possessiveness rubbed her nerves raw. She'd set him straight soon enough. "Right," she tossed after him.

"I get the feeling your friend was talking about more than a meeting," Derrick rumbled. He wore an impassive expression.

Talia faced him. "How did you find me so easily?" She swept a hand out. "This place is like a maze."

"I'm an investigator. I'm good at finding people." He smiled, revealing dazzling white teeth against his smooth, brown skin.

The effect of such a stunning contrast made Talia gasp. She looked away from his face to recover. "I see."

She didn't really see at all. Talia struggled with conflicted emotions. Part of her wanted to ask more about him and why he had made it a point to find her. At the same time she didn't want to know. She'd run from him and Louisiana years ago. Yet no one had made her feel safe and cared for the way Derrick could. The only exception had been Mama Rose. Between the two of them they'd brought her through a dark and scary period in her life.

"I talked to Miss Rose last week. I'm glad she's doing better."

Talia looked at him sharply. She trembled from the chill that spread through her. Like Mama Rose, he could read her.

"I'm sorry I didn't get to see you when you visited three months ago," Derrick added, when Talia didn't speak.

"I was really busy." She looked away from his gaze.

They both knew she'd had no intention of looking him up.

"I need to talk to you," Derrick said, and closed a large hand over her wrist.

Talia looked down at the way his long fingers wrapped around her flesh. His touch sent heat up her arm and into her heart. Memories rushed in on her.

"Please," she murmured, her thoughts far from talking with him. "Not here."

"Of course not here, Talia," Derrick replied. "Come on. We can go to B. Smith's." He pulled her gently, yet firmly along with him.

"No, I—" Talia stammered, her voice barely audible to her own ears above the noisy crowd.

She didn't want him bringing Rougon or the past into her life in Washington, D.C. Yet his hold on her was more than physical. She'd avoided him for years for this very reason. Now Talia realized how foolish she'd been in her confidence. She'd convinced herself her adolescent need for protection and love explained his potent effect on her. After all these years she wanted to lay him down, burned to feel his lean, hard body stretched atop hers. Once they were outside, Derrick hailed a taxi. They were inside and pulling away from the curb before she knew it.

"I hear you've practically conquered this city. At least that's what Miss Rose says." Derrick stretched one arm across the seat behind her.

Talia cleared her throat. She resisted the urge to snuggle in the shelter of his embrace. "Well, you know Mama Rose likes drama."

"She's just proud of her baby girl, and with good reason. You've got a great reputation. My boss kept hearing your name in meetings."

"Really?" Talia inched away from him to further clear her head. "What are you doing here anyway?"

"We—" Derrick broke off when the taxi came to a stop. "Here you go, keep the change." He handed the fare to the driver.

Talia followed him inside the elegant restaurant. A handsome young man greeted them with a big smile.

"Hello. Table for two?"

"Yes," Derrick replied.

He led them through the large dining room to a smaller, more intimate section. They were seated at a table with fresh Louisiana irises. B. Smith's boasted the finest nouveau soul cuisine in the city and featured Louisiana-inspired entrées.

"Tony will be your waiter. I'll give you time to look over the menu. What would you like to drink?"

Talia ordered diet soda and Derrick ordered sweetened iced tea. "You're still hooked on sugar."

"Yeah, I guess I should cut back in my old age." Derrick grinned as he opened his suit jacket. He patted his flat stomach. "Gotta keep fit."

Talia took in the outline of his hard body beneath the fine cotton shirt. "I don't think you have to worry just yet."

Tony appeared with their drinks. Talia felt absurdly grateful for the interruption. She gulped down the cold soda, hoping it would cool her off. *Okay, try to remember you're not a horny sixteen-year-old now.* After they ordered, Derrick blasted her attempts by turning on the full strength of his presence. He gazed at her with an expression of intense, caring interest.

"How are you doing?" He leaned toward her, one hand on the back of her chair.

She glanced away. "Not bad. I don't exactly run the nation's capital. The president and Congress have some say," she joked, hoping to deflect the real question in his eyes.

"At least they think they do, again according to Miss Rose." Derrick's sensuous lips curved up.

"I divide my time between chasing a dollar and helping a few folks who don't have big money muscle." Talia lifted a shoulder. "Makes me feel less guilty about helping low people in high places."

"Bull, you care about people. You always have," Derrick said with quiet force. "I thought you'd be a nurse or a social worker."

"And take a vow of poverty? Not hardly. I had my fill of being poor and downtrodden, thank you very much," she said bitterly.

Derrick closed a large hand over one of hers. "You made it out, baby," he said softly. "It's okay."

Talia stared into his clear, dark eyes and almost got lost. She pulled back with great effort. "I've got a good life," she said too quickly.

"You've got a lot of friends to stand by you. That Jarrod guy for one." Derrick let go of her hand and picked up his glass.

"Jarrod was one of the first people who helped me in this town. He's a real nice person," Talia said. She shot a sideways glance at him.

Derrick nodded. "I like the way he jumped to protect you. He's alright. But you don't need to be protected from me, Talia."

"I never told him anything, just that I'm from Louisiana and a little about Mama Rose." Talia swirled the straw around in her glass.

He sighed and put down his glass. "I'm not talking about him. I've been in town three days. I debated looking you up."

"Derrick, it wasn't you." Talia's voice trailed off.

"I know. You needed a clean break." Derrick stared at his strong hands clasped together. "Things were rough."

"But we both made it through," she murmured. "All that is behind us now."

"Is it?" He looked at her.

"Yes," Talia said vehemently. "Over and done with years ago."

"Lately I've been thinking about those days."

"Don't," she said. "You're not responsible."

"Monette wrote to me four months ago, Talia. She's got a new lawyer."

"She's always getting a new lawyer. Another scam, a new scheme. Same old Monette."

"I thought you two didn't keep in touch." Derrick looked at Talia steadily.

"I get a letter now and then from my half sister." Talia frowned. "I tried to tell her about Monette. She's too young to remember. Her adoptive parents are great people. But Alyssa had this need to find her biological parents."

"And you. She wanted to find her sister and brother," Derrick said.

"Yeah, finding Karl was easy since he was always in jail," Talia retorted.

"He had it bad, too," Derrick said.

"So have other people. They didn't hold up convenience stores because of it." Talia wore a hard expression.

"Okay, you've got a good point. But, Talia—"

"I really don't want to talk about him, or anything connected to that part of my life." She glanced around as she cut him off.

"I only wanted to spend time with you before . . . Let's have dinner tonight. There's something you need to know before it hits the newspapers."

"Here we are!"

The waiter stood at the table with two large dinner plates on a tray. He set them down in front of Talia first, then Derrick. Talia had completely lost her interest in lunch. A sick queasy feeling of dread lay in her stomach like a rock.

"Enjoy. Need anything else? Are we good?" Tony smiled at them.

"We're fine, thanks," Derrick said. He watched the waiter leave, then turned back to Talia.

The grave expression on his handsome face gave Talia chills. "Why the big mystery?"

"I've been talking to Monette for the past six months. I think you need to know what's going on. And no, she didn't ask me to tell you."

Talia gave a small, cynical laugh. The rock in her stomach crumbled. She was on familiar ground. "Like I said, one of Monette's schemes. Okay, dinner it is then."

"Good." Derrick nodded and lowered his voice as he leaned even closer. "But it's not what you think. I'll tell you this much, there's a good chance Monette will get out of prison. It may take another five months, but it'll happen."

"I've heard that before, but whatever," Talia replied. She picked up her fork. "I refuse to let her ruin a great lunch."

Despite her words, Talia did not eat much of her spinach salad. She glanced at her watch. Before she spoke, Derrick got the waiter's attention. Within minutes he'd paid for the meal, left Tony a generous tip, and escorted her out of the restaurant.

"There's a great Chinese restaurant called City Lights of China. I'll meet you there at about—"

"You don't want me to know where you live." Derrick gazed at her with sadness in his dark eyes.

"I just thought it would be easier with both of us having a long day and . . ." Talia's voice faded, and she sighed.

"It's okay. We can meet there," he said quietly.

Talia fumbled in her purse for a business card and pen. She wrote on the back of it. "Here's the address."

Derrick didn't take it. "I said it's okay."

"I didn't mean—" Talia stepped closer and placed the card in his hand.

"I'll meet you at seven-thirty tonight." Still Derrick closed his large hand around hers and took the card.

Talia swallowed hard. The years rolled away, and she could see them together, two teenagers seeking comfort from a harsh world. The scent and sound of the bayou rushed back to her. She could almost hear the musical blending of crickets and cicadas in the sultry Louisiana summer twilight. A strong memory of the smell of gardenias in bloom hit her. They had sat on Miss Rose's gallery many a night staring at the stars for hours in silence. Then suddenly he would wrap an arm around her. He would always be there to protect her. No one and nothing could change what was between them. Yet the fear and embarrassment her mother caused had only grown. At seventeen Talia had gotten her way out. She won a scholarship to a high school in Natchitoches, Louisiana, for academically gifted teens. Derrick had known the day she got on the Greyhound bus to leave Rougon that she was running away from him as well. He never said a word, but he knew. She'd seen it in his eyes as he stood watching the bus pull away. The next year Derrick had left town to attend a community college.

Derrick got into a cab and waved once. He gazed at her as it drove away. Talia tried to push down the rise of an old fear. She should have known this day would come.

Three hours later she sat in the conference room with six other staffers of Gallagher and Associates. Even on a Friday afternoon they were hard at it. Peter Gallagher liked to start out every week with a strategy session and pep talk. He ended the week with a postmortem. Both were prime reasons his firm got results on the Hill. Eileen Vargas rattled off figures she'd discussed with congressional aides. The petite brunette slapped her leather portfolio closed.

"I think it's dead in the water. Hell, you've seen the news stories. Television stories that show little old ladies taking long bus rides to Mexico for cheap medicine." She shrugged. "I'm good, but I'm not *that* good." Her remark brought laughter.

"I hear ya. Our clients already look like a bunch of callous money-grubbers," Bill Elliot chimed in. His Texas drawl, though softened after years in Washington, was still evident.

"Big insurance companies *are* callous money-grubbers," Jasmine Hellinger spoke up. She was the firm's liberal conscience. She tossed her long, intricately braided auburn hair. Her cocoa brown face was pretty despite her deep frown of distaste.

"Yeah, but it's our job to convince people they're not," Eileen replied with a wink.

"Real nice," Jasmine muttered.

"Let's be fair. The Association of Insurers donates a lot of green to charities. And their employees are number one in volunteerism," Bill said.

"Sure. After they help people become homeless, they serve them warm gruel at soup kitchens around the country. How giving of them!" Jasmine retorted.

"We all need insurance, Jas," Eileen put in, and took a sip of kava juice from a bottle.

"Right, right." Jasmine waved a hand.

They went on to another subject. Talia moved the swivel chair in half circles and paid token attention. She did manage to jump in with her own report of the week when it was her turn. Peter listened intently as she spoke. The others asked a few questions. Talia finished up with a summary of her meeting with Senator Collins. The others went on discussing strategy and the latest political rumors that might affect their lobbying efforts. Talia tried to take an interest. Instead she stared out the window, her thoughts hundreds of miles and a life away.

"What's got that faraway look in your eye, Talia?" Pete rocked back in his chair. His green eyes gazed at her over long fingers that formed a steeple. "You should be on top of the world."

Talia snapped out of her trance and blinked at him. "It's been one heck of a long week. Guess the fallout is catching up with me. Too little sleep and too much bad coffee."

"Maybe you want to take time off. If you need to go home again, let me know." Pete studied her with a concerned expression.

"I'm fine." Talia shook her head. "Thanks anyway."

"Glad to hear it. But you might still get a trip home. You'll be interested in our new clients." Pete wore a wide grin. "The Louisiana Association of District Attorneys, the Louisiana State Police, and the Louisiana Association of Trial Lawyers."

"So that's why he's in town," Talia said in an undertone.

"What?" Pete blinked at her curiously.

"Nothing, nothing," Talia said quickly.

Derrick worked as an investigator for the Pointe Coupee Parish District Attorney. He'd been with that office for at least six years. Pete described how they'd contacted him. Talia didn't listen. All she could think of was Derrick's collusion in Monette's latest plot. The last thing Talia needed was Monette messing with her life again. Derrick had a misplaced need to rescue women in distress. In this case the woman in question had a long rap sheet, a drug problem, and enjoyed using people until their lives were ruined. Talia clenched both hands into fists.

"Damn him!" Talia whispered.

Chapter 2

∞

The words "new clients" had gotten the attention of her colleagues. All were young, ambitious, and loved jumping into new assignments. Jasmine's hazelnut eyes sparkled with interest. Eileen stopped in the middle of teasing Bill and leaned both elbows on the table.

"Defense attorneys usually fight whatever the other two want," Jasmine put in. "Strange bedfellows as the old saying goes."

"Yeah, what's up with that?" Eileen looked at Pete.

"They're interested in changing mandatory drug-sentencing laws, but for very different reasons," Pete said. "District attorneys want to ease prison crowding and clogged court dockets. The defense attorneys feel the law targets minorities and is therefore discriminatory."

"Touchy issue. President Bush certainly doesn't want to be accused of being soft on drug dealers." Bill rubbed his jaw.

"Neither does Congress," Eileen added.

"Long shot," Jasmine said tersely.

While Pete continued talking, Talia's mind spun with the new information. Derrick knew more about her mother's push to get out of prison than he'd let on.

Monette had been arrested with over a kilo of high-grade cocaine six months after that awful night. Talia had been in the courtroom as they read the sentence. While her maternal aunts wailed at the forty-year sentence, Talia showed no emotion. In truth she'd been numb for six months. Still she restrained herself from showing how she really felt, that Monette was finally getting what she deserved.

Jasmine leaned over to her. "Girlfriend, you look like someone just put a big fat bug on your salad plate and asked you to taste it. Tell me what's going on," she said quietly.

Talia massaged her temples. "I've got a headache. Nothing a couple of Advil won't cure."

She'd grown as close to Jasmine as she had to anyone in her life. Yet there was a part of Talia no one could share. Not in this new and improved life of hers. Derrick had ridden into town like a Creole cowboy dragging trouble with him.

"So that's about it. Okay, Marchand. This is right up your alley." Pete swung his chair to face her. "And I'm sure Jasmine is eager to lend you a hand."

"You know it," Jasmine said promptly.

"What?" Talia said sharply. "I've got my hands full, Pete. Besides, I don't care if scumbag drug dealers rot in prison." She could not keep the bitterness from her tone.

Her stomach twisted as she fought the darkness that threatened to swallow her up. Sometimes at two in the morning she still had nightmares from her childhood. Except these dreams were based in reality. Suddenly she would be five years old again and shivering in the cold on a filthy mattress. Talia's hand shook as she massaged her temples again.

"Hey, babe. It's okay." Eileen poured her a glass of cold grapefruit juice. "Drink up."

Talia glanced around to find them gazing at her in surprise. "Sorry," she said in a strangled voice, and took a long drink.

"If you feel so strongly about the issue, then I'll hand it off to someone else."

Pete stared at her hard. Despite what most people thought they knew about Gallagher and Associates, their boss was moderate in his political views. He liked to think of himself as a commonsense conservative, not slavish to the party line. In fact he infuriated many conservatives by landing too far left for their tastes on certain issues. Which explained their eclectic client list. Talia knew what he was thinking.

"I should keep an open mind until I hear all the facts. Well, I know them already."

"Really? Read this first. I made copies for everyone." Pete liked his top staff to know about every assignment. He believed it made them a better team. "Look at those examples and tell me if you feel the same."

Jasmine flipped open the first page of the blue folder. She tapped a forefinger on the photocopy of a newspaper article. "I read about this kid. She gets hooked up with the wrong boyfriend in college. When he gets caught with drugs, he rolls on her. Result?"

"Here we go," Bill muttered as he rolled his eyes. "She gets to rant about men and conservatives."

"Even better, conservative men," Eileen said with a grin.

"He gets off with a slap on the wrist and she gets a life sentence for drug and gun smuggling." Jasmine slapped the table hard. "Low-down dog!"

"Excuse me, but little Miss Debutante knew he was dealing on the side." Talia held up a hand to stop Jasmine's protest. "I'll save my tears this time, okay?"

"She shouldn't serve a life sentence for being young

and stupid." Jasmine leaned forward. "Most of these cases involve poor, minority kids."

Talia glanced away from the intense young woman's gaze. Mama Rose had said the same thing about Monette time after time. "Go to it then. Save all those little idiots from themselves."

Pete sat straight and looked Talia in the eye. "Certainly Jasmine will help on this one. But it's *you* they want, Talia. The DA from your hometown specifically mentioned your reputation."

A nasty suspicion took root as Talia drummed her fingers on the leather chair's arm. "I don't know the man," she said in a curt tone.

"He knows you or at least your work," Pete replied. He flipped through the report. "And he wants help dealing with the state legislature as well."

"Louisiana isn't known for being liberal on law and order issues. The legislature defeated a bill just this year to reduce sentences for several nonviolent crimes." Talia frowned.

"Is that right?" Pete propped both elbows on the table.

Talia nodded. "In fact, this is a reversal of their position. But then it might make sense."

"How's that?" Eileen asked.

"A number of legislators, even some hard cases, have said building more jails isn't the answer." Talia lifted a shoulder. "I have to say they surprised me with that one."

"Lock 'em up, and let 'em rot? Is that really how you feel?" Jasmine asked.

"No, but—" Talia cleared her throat. "Look, maybe this young woman needs a break."

"She's one of many," Jasmine said.

"I'm really busy. Besides, Jas here is damn good. She can handle it." Talia smiled at her.

"Hell yeah I can." Jasmine nodded. "But you know Louisiana politics and all the nuances."

"I haven't lived there in over ten years." Talia tapped a forefinger on the smooth surface of the conference table.

"But you've obviously kept up on what's happening in the state," Pete said. "Jasmine is right on target. That kind of insight is invaluable."

Talia pressed her lips together too late. *Nice going, big mouth!* She was backed into a corner. Her colleagues would wonder if she continued to fight on this one.

"Fine," Talia said with a tight smile.

The others went on talking about the weekend. Talia spun her favorite Cross pen in a circle. She couldn't wait to see Derrick. He would get a piece of her mind for the neat little setup he had engineered.

Derrick stood in the foyer of the Chinese restaurant. He glanced several times at his watch. *Relax. You're early*. Still, a knot of tension in his neck muscles wouldn't listen to logic. She'd run from him before. Maybe she wouldn't show.

They'd grown up and not seen each other in more than five years. The last time was in the hospital when Miss Rose suffered a mild heart attack. He hadn't expected to see her. Derrick shook his head. Not true. He'd known eventually they would meet if he kept going to visit Miss Rose. Talia would never have stayed away knowing her foster mother was ill. She hadn't been happy to see him then either. Or was she? Maybe the warm spark in her beautiful brown eyes when she first saw him was all in his mind. In any event she kept her distance then just as she wanted to now. Not that he intended to rekindle a teenage flame.

"I'm here," Talia said over his shoulder.

Derrick started at the soft, sensuous voice and turned quickly. Talia gazed up at him. Fire started at the base of his spine when he looked into her eyes. The lovely girl was now a heart-stopping gorgeous woman of thirty. At five-foot-six, the top of her head just reached his chin. She wore dark red lipstick that made her mouth look succulent and delicious.

Talia wore a lipstick red silk shirt tucked into a matching short skirt. The soft fabric draped her lush curves to perfection. A large printed scarf was draped over her right shoulder. Her thick dark bronze hair was swept up into a French twist. Derrick had a flash of slowly taking it loose until it draped her naked shoulders. Pure, simple lust seized him. He took a step close to her and brushed his mouth against hers. Talia gave a tiny gasp, but didn't move away. She stared into his eyes as though looking for the answer to some critical question.

Derrick blinked hard, unable to take his eyes from her. "You look fantastic." He swept both hands out.

"I-I'm a little late, sorry," she murmured.

"I hadn't noticed." Derrick lifted a hand to touch her hair. He stopped when Talia tilted her head away slightly.

The headwaiter, ready and efficient, moved up with a smile. "Table for two?"

She cleared her throat. "By the way, that's not your shade. Let's go to our table."

Derrick took a handkerchief from his pocket and wiped lipstick from his mouth. "Right."

"Nonsmoking," Talia said to the headwaiter.

Derrick watched her stroll with her head up, hips swaying. Men turned to look despite being with dates. Though obviously surprised by his kiss, she had quickly regained her poise. He burned in a way that told him he'd have trouble sleeping later. He was a fool stuck in an adolescent dream, he told himself.

"Is this okay?" The thin man looked at Derrick expectantly. He gestured to a table set against the wall.

"Sure," he managed to get out.

They sat down and ordered drinks when their waitress arrived. Talia asked for merlot while he ordered a glass of Chinese beer. Once the woman was gone, they avoided looking at each other for several moments.

"It's been a long time," Talia said finally.

"Over five years," he replied.

"Yes." Talia gave a slight nod.

"And here we are." Derrick glanced at her.

She gazed at him steadily, both eyebrows raised. They were the same dark, communicative frames above her eyes. He recognized the expression from their childhood days. She was about to pounce.

"Not by accident either."

"Your boss told you." Derrick sat back as though to dodge her first jab.

"Didn't think I'd go back to the office I suppose."

"No I—"

"When were you planning to tell me? And I'm sure this has something to do with that bit of news you shared about Monette." Talia stabbed a forefinger at him.

"Only indirectly." Derrick broke off when the waitress arrived with their drinks.

"Ready to order?" The young woman smiled at them.

Talia ordered chicken with broccoli and Derrick ordered Szechuan beef. The waitress darted off. Seconds later Talia scowled at him.

"You might try telling me the truth," Talia snapped.

"I've always been real with you, Talia." Derrick squinted at her. "Name one time I lied."

She lowered her hand. "You're right. It's just . . ." Her voice trailed off and she took a sip of wine.

"You think I'm trying to mess up your well-ordered world." Derrick shook his head slowly. "I only want the best for you. I tried to protect you back then and—"

"You don't have to say it." Talia drew in a shaky breath.

At that moment the confident, bold woman dissolved. Talia closed her eyes briefly, then opened them and took another sip of wine. Her smooth skin seemed pale with dread as though a ghost had sat down next to her. In a way that was exactly what he represented, a haunting reminder of something she'd buried long ago. Talia put down the wineglass and clasped her hands together. She seemed to pull inward to protect herself. He ached to take her in his arms, to caress away the fear.

"No one will hurt you if I can help it. That includes me, Talia. I wouldn't have come under other circumstances." Derrick clenched one hand to dull the pain. "I know how you feel."

Talia didn't speak for several seconds. Her expression softened when she looked at him again. "Sorry. Guess I haven't dealt with my issues very well."

Derrick smiled. "Hey, we go back a long way. Don't worry about speaking your mind to me. You never did."

"My mouth used to get me in all kinds of trouble." Her full lips lifted, a tantalizing hint of a smile.

His heart turned over at the sight. Derrick leaned close to her. "Got you out of a lot of trouble, too. Remember that time I almost got caught stealing Mr. Boudreaux's figs? He came out with that old gun loaded with buckshot."

"Oh yeah," Talia said. She tilted her head to one side. "You and that undesirable element you hung around with almost got shot that day."

Derrick grinned at her. "Poor old guy went crazy trying to keep us out of his fig trees. You popped out from the bushes with that wide-eyed innocent expression and charmed his socks off. Amazing the way he just swallowed that tale you told."

"You mean about the swarm of squirrels? Mr. Boudreaux's lightbulb was short a few watts, you know."

Derrick threw back his head and laughed hard. Talia laughed with him after a second. They were wiping their eyes by the time the waitress appeared with their food. The tension between them vanished. As they ate, they shared other funny stories of childhood exploits.

"Man, I never realized how bad we were until now," Derrick said. "We were always into something."

"Forget that 'we' stuff. *You* were always into something, Derrick Guillory." Talia poked his arm.

"Now that brings back painful memories. Mama would call my full name when I was in big trouble." He winced.

"How is your mama?" Talia's voice dropped to a gentle timbre.

"Pretty good. She's in one of those subsidized housing developments. She seems to really like it." Derrick stared at his plate without seeing the food on it.

"You've taken good care of her." Talia leaned across the table to make her point.

Derrick took her hand. "Thanks."

"For what?" Talia looked uneasy, yet she didn't pull away.

"You always stuck by me when things got tough. Actually we stuck by each other." Derrick searched her face.

Talia removed her hand and picked up her wineglass. "Who else was going to save your butt?" Her tone was light as she looked away.

"Most people said I'd end up in prison like my father. But not you."

"I know what it's like to be judged based on your parents," Talia said softly. "Even more reason that I owe you an apology."

"I should have given you warning that I was in town instead of showing up like that."

"It's okay, Derrick. I'm glad you came."

Derrick felt a rush that left him feeling dazed. Until that moment he hadn't realized how much she meant to him. He was ridiculously happy at the simple statement.

"I fought being assigned the mandatory-sentencing thing. I shouldn't base my work decisions on a bumpy childhood. Talking to you helped me work through that." Talia sat straight.

His spirits fell a notch. "Glad I could help."

"I did a lot to escape those days, but I left behind pleasant memories, too." Talia looked at him with emotion in her eyes. "Thanks for bringing them back."

When he took her hand again she seemed at ease. "Then the trip was worth it. Except—"

"I know, the real reason you're here."

"I'm sorry, Talia."

Derrick was more than sorry. He wanted to kick himself for waiting so long to visit Talia. Visions of a happy reunion flashed in his head. Now he had to bring news that was sure to upset her. She'd turn away from him for good. Still, he'd grown up and out of that schoolboy love thing, right? He'd moved on. Regret bit into him when her expression hardened.

"It's not you. It's Monette, but then it's always Monette!" she said bitterly. "What is she up to?"

"Like I said, she's trying to get out of prison on parole. But this time it's different. I hear she might have a chance." Derrick pushed his half empty plate aside.

"Got some rich old guy to bribe somebody?" Talia retorted.

"No, she has great legal representation. A project out of the Tulane Law Center is helping her. Professor James Rand and a group of law students take on select cases of inmates," Derrick said.

"So Monette has been able to con them. No surprise. She's that good."

"These people aren't gullible, Talia. You deal with lawyers."

"They're professional cynics," Talia said.

He nodded. "Professor Rand and his students thoroughly check out each story. I'm talking months of research, interviewing people involved and reading the trial transcripts."

"So they're taking on Monette's case because?" Talia's eyes held a spark of interest.

"Her court-appointed lawyer did a poor job from what I understand."

"That's it?" Talia grunted. "Half the prisons could be emptied on those grounds."

"Rand has a special interest in mandatory-sentencing cases. Also, this Tulane project takes on cases where there's evidence the person is innocent."

" 'Innocent' is one word I wouldn't use to describe Monette," Talia said.

"Monette says her conviction was funky, based on bogus evidence, and Rand knows it, whatever that means." Derrick lifted a shoulder.

"Classic Monette Victor speak for 'Hold on to your wallet cause I'm working a scam.' " Talia wore a smile empty of amusement.

"I don't think so this time." Derrick held up one palm to cut off another retort. "Okay, I know your mama."

"No, Derrick. You don't know her the way I do." Talia stared into her empty wineglass for several seconds. She waved down the passing waitress. "Another one please."

He watched her without speaking. There was no use arguing with Talia about Monette. The facts were not in Monette's favor anyway. Talia seemed to turn inward. She drew invisible circles on the red linen tablecloth. When the waitress brought a full glass of wine, she took a long drink from it. Derrick waited patiently. Finally, Talia squared her shoulders and looked at him steadily.

"I can't blame her for trying anything. LCIW isn't a resort," Talia said. The Louisiana Correctional Institute for Women held some of the toughest female offenders in the state, the country even.

"There must be something to what she's saying. Tulane Law Clinic doesn't take on cases just because an inmate talks a good game," Derrick replied.

"Fine, I wish her well. Thanks for telling me." Talia nodded as though filing it away neatly in a special mental and emotional compartment. "Now let's do justice to this wonderful meal."

"That's it? Your mother is fighting for parole on a forty-year drug sentence, and you just take the news and go on eating?" Derrick lowered his voice.

"If you were expecting me to book a flight and rush home for a warm family moment, get real." Talia folded her arms in a defensive posture.

"No, but after so many years maybe it's time for some kind of closure, some kind of resolution. If not for her, then for you."

"You've been watching too many talk shows. I can't count the number of times Monette let me down. Hell, kicked me down is more accurate."

"All right, I can't argue with you on that." Derrick took a deep breath and let it out. "The other thing is—"

"Oh, happy day. More good news from home," Talia mumbled.

"There might be some publicity, big-time. Monette is worried that you'll be hurt when all this hits the fan." Derrick held up both hands when Talia glanced at him sharply. "Like I said, she won't give more details."

"Typical Monette. No normal appeal for parole for her, no ma'am." Talia let out a sharp laugh.

Derrick wore a half smile. "Yeah. The day I visited her she was all made up. She dropped a few hints about maybe being on *20/20* or *60 Minutes*."

"My mother has always aspired to national fame. Notoriety on a local scale never seemed enough for her." Talia waved a hand. "I can deal with it if push comes to shove."

He gazed at her with skepticism. She was taking that last bit of news too well. "Really?"

Talia's eyes narrowed to slits. "No one will connect her to me."

"What about digging up too much history?" he murmured.

Talia's smile turned into a grimace. "If she says one word to hurt you, I'll personally help them throw away the key to that damn prison cell."

"She'd never do that."

"Monette would turn on anyone if it suited her purpose." Talia leaned across the table. "You tell her what I said!"

"Why don't you tell her? I think you should talk to her face-to-face. Maybe you wouldn't feel so angry."

"I know what you're trying to do, but it's too late."

"Your mama really wants to protect you." Derrick squeezed her hand.

"She's about twenty-five years too late." Talia lifted her chin. "I don't need her now."

"Maybe she needs you."

"Monette is good at manipulating men. Especially men with a soft spot for women in trouble," Talia said. "Don't fall for her line of bull."

"I'm even less gullible than an army of legal sharks. Remember, I grew up hard, too." Derrick held his own demons from the past at bay.

"Like I said, your one weakness is rescuing women. It can get you into deep trouble."

"I take care of myself pretty well. Don't worry about me."

They gazed at each other for a long time, in silence, without moving. Talia let out an audible sigh. "We have this habit of looking out for each other."

"Being apart for years doesn't seem to matter, does it?" he said quietly.

They'd met in elementary school on a dusty playground. At the time Talia was in the third grade and Derrick was in the fourth. They had recognized each other, two kids who hated going home most days, Derrick because of his father and Talia because of her mother.

Talia nodded, then sat straight again. The tough girl returned. "I can weather the storm. I'm established, so 'mama drama' won't affect my career."

"Monette will be relieved to hear that." Derrick smiled. "You're a lot more like her than you think. You've always got a Plan B when the stuff hits the fan."

Talia scowled at him. "I let you off easy for showing up unannounced. Don't mess it up."

"Calm down." Derrick wrapped his fingers around her wrist. "That was a compliment. You're a smart, talented woman who survived."

Without thinking he lifted her hand and pressed his lips to the back of it. His gaze traveled down her face and neck to the small spot of skin exposed by the V-neck blouse. He took in the luscious curve of full breasts outlined by the delicate fabric. Her full lips parted. She clasped her long, elegant fingers around his wrist, then drew him closer. Derrick's pulse beat like a drum when she tenderly kissed him. Heat licked at his pelvis when her tongue ran across his bottom lip. Without thinking, he traced a forefinger along the silky skin on her throat and was about to unbutton the blouse. The clink of dishes brought him back to where they were in the nick of time.

"How long will you be in town?" she whispered.

"Two days. I can stay longer," Derrick answered in a raspy voice.

"No promises." Talia stared into his eyes.

"No promises," he repeated.

They needed each other badly. Or at least Derrick realized how much he needed her. No one else could ease the special brand of isolation that came from keeping an unspeakable secret.

Chapter 3

"What's up, everybody?" Talia sighed and plopped down into an empty chair in Eileen's office. "One helluva day and it's only one o'clock!"

"Hey, road warrior," Jasmine replied with a smile.

"So take a break like us," Eileen said. She had her feet propped up on an empty file box next to her desk.

"Yeah, get some lunch," Jasmine added. She ate from a small cup of low-fat strawberry yogurt and read an open copy of *Time* magazine on her lap.

"I don't have anything. I couldn't make up my mind." Talia rubbed her eyes. "If I have to read one more fine print document in the Federal Register, some bureaucrat will die."

"Tell me about it. Those health rules are the worst." Eileen made a sour face.

"This town thrives on killing trees to print up single-spaced reports in tiny print." Jasmine smiled.

"There should be a law," Talia said with a laugh.

Eileen groaned. "Please don't say that outside this room. Some silly congressional aide will draft a bill! The liberals have shoved too much big government down our throats—"

"Don't start, Eileen," Jasmine said with a warning frown.

"Please! I came here for a breather from 'spirited debate,'" Talia added.

"Okay, okay." Eileen waved a hand at them both.

Talia patted her midsection. "I'm empty. Do we have anything here?"

"Go take a look. I brought sandwich and salad fixings for the long days." Eileen pointed to the door in the direction of the small office kitchen.

Talia kicked off her black Fendi pumps and padded down the carpeted hall. She found cheese, smoked turkey, and a package of small French bread loaves. Minutes later she'd made a sandwich and found a bottle of spring water to wash it down. Talia returned to Eileen's office.

"Bless your little 'be prepared' Girl Scout heart, Eileen," she said and sat down again.

"Even a conservative has some good points," Jasmine teased. She dodged a paper clip Eileen flung at her.

"I'm going to send you two to the principal's office in a minute." Talia shook her head at them.

Eileen dabbed her mouth with a paper napkin. "Tell us all the news that's fit to print. What's happening with your home state connection?"

"Forget that. Skip to the fine hunk from your old 'hood." Jasmine put down the empty yogurt container.

"Yeah," Eileen said with enthusiasm. She swung her chair around to face Talia fully. "I hear he's six feet four inches of the world's finest chocolate."

"Oh grow up, will you," Talia said, wearing a staid expression. "Don't the high-powered folks in this town have anything better to do than engage in petty gossip?"

Eileen and Jasmine looked at each other, then at Talia. "You're joking!" they said together. All three burst into laughter.

Talia wiped her eyes. "I plead temporary insanity."

"Okay, now that you've come to your senses," Jasmine began.

"Dish it, darlin'," Eileen picked up.

"Start with him being a private dick," Jasmine said with a smirk.

Eileen let out a howl of laughter. "I just got a mental picture."

"Derrick is not—" Talia started.

"Hmm, sexy name. Derrick Guillory. Suits the brother to a tee." Jasmine leaned over and tapped Eileen's arm.

"Sure does. Wait, I haven't seen him." Eileen looked at Jasmine.

"Tall, dark, and oh-so-handsome. Girl, he's one delicious Happy Meal!" Jasmine nodded vigorously.

"Since you know all about him, I can let you tell it." Talia pressed her lips together.

"Sorry. Go on." Jasmine waved at her.

"It's a short story. Derrick is primarily an investigator with the Pointe Coupee Parish DA's Office. He's also a licensed private *investigator*." Talia shot Jasmine a heated look before she went on. "He does a few jobs on the side. Civil stuff only, of course."

"Cool," Eileen said.

"So he's here with his boss trying to fix this mandatory-sentencing outrage. Good man." Jasmine gave a curt nod of approval. "Keep him."

"I hadn't looked at all the ramifications. Criminal justice resources are being used up on small fry. The big guns are tossing sacrificial lambs to the cops and getting away." Talia took a swig of water.

"An excellent point that may appeal to conservatives." Eileen smiled.

"I've been meeting with Pete mostly." Talia took the

last bite of her sandwich. "He's meeting with Perrilloux, not me."

"Right, and having dinner with sexy Derrick is part of the job." Jasmine winked at Eileen. "You were spotted, sweetheart. You know this is a small town."

Talia sighed. Her attempt to deflect Jasmine's probing into more personal areas had failed. "We knew each other in grade school."

"And?" Jasmine prompted.

"We're just catching up on old times. That's all." Talia tossed the paper napkin she held into a trash can.

Jasmine threw up both hands. "Oh come on. I'm a cynic. Make me believe in romance again."

"Buy a romance novel because there's nothing more to it," Talia tossed back. She stood, brushed crumbs from her skirt, and put on her shoes. "I've got a ton of things to do."

She grabbed her soft leather briefcase and strode out before they could say anything more. She went down the hallway, passed by Jasmine's small office, and turned a corner. The door to Bill's office was open. He waved at her as he talked into his phone headset. Talia waved back. Her corner office looked out on Wisconsin Avenue.

"Safe at last," she mumbled, and kicked the door closed behind her.

An interesting choice of words, she mused. Once again she'd danced around attempts to find out more about her personal life. Talia worked behind the scenes for that very reason. Gathering information to help others influence government suited her well. Those out front got the attention and the intense media scrutiny that resulted.

Talia dropped her briefcase onto her desk and sat down. Instead of following her routine of checking voice mail and e-mail messages, she sat staring out of the window.

Just what would happen between her and Derrick? They'd talked about old times, that much was true. She couldn't lie to herself. There was a strange chemistry between them. Derrick inspired a sense of safety with his solid, muscular presence. Not that Talia needed protection. The scared, lonely little girl was gone. Still she admitted that it felt good to know that he had her back covered. For years she'd relied only on her own survival skills. Just as he had when they were children, Derrick made her know she wasn't alone after all.

His appearance had awakened other memories. She remembered the strong, lithe body of the seventeen-year-old boy. They'd discovered the pleasure of love-making. Derrick had made up for a lack of experience with passion.

"As if you would have known the difference." She smiled to herself.

They'd talked about every aspect of taking the big step. Derrick had planned their first time down to the last detail and made sure she didn't feel pressured. His assured tender caresses had helped her relax immediately. After the first time, she'd been eager to repeat the experience. Then one bright summer day Talia experienced true ecstasy.

Talia let out a long shaky sigh at the potency of her memory. Somehow she'd have to fend off that feeling. Twisted up with that seductive dream was a ghastly nightmare.

"Knock, knock." Bill walked in with a smile.

She jumped at the sound of his voice. "Geez, Bill! You scared the crap out of me."

"Sorry, kiddo." His jovial expression faded as he studied her. "You okay?"

"Yeah, fine. What's up?" Talia took several deep breaths to shake Derrick's influence. She put on a smile.

Bill carried a thick folder under one arm. He sat down in one of two chairs in front of her desk. "You sure? You look rattled."

"I'm sure." Talia forced her smile wider. "Just deep in thought on how to kick legislative butt."

"Uh-huh. I was just talking to Pete about this Louisiana thing." He watched her closely.

Talia got up and took off her jacket to cover any reaction. "Surprisingly we might be making headway. Jarrod tells me there are some in the Justice Department who realize the problems."

"I know. I've been talking to a few folks myself. A pal of mine pretty high up feels it's a waste, too." Bill propped an ankle on his knee.

"Hey, I'm back." Jasmine strolled in with a can of diet cola in one hand.

"Hi," Talia said.

"Thanks for the help on that auto industry assignment, cowboy." She slapped Bill's shoulder and dropped down into the chair next to him. "Your buddy Ken knows his stuff, and we've got a date."

"Sure, I'm here to help your love life," Bill drawled.

"Ken Worthington? Wow, you reeled in the big one, Jas," Talia said with a grin. Ken Worthington was not only from an old-money Washington, D.C., family, he was a top Justice Department official with a bright future.

"Please! He's a nice brother, intelligent, and no cheesy come-on lines." Jasmine flipped a manicured hand at her.

"Keep him then," Talia quipped.

"We'll see," Jasmine said, with a sassy toss of her head. "Back to biz. Here are some notes I did last night on mandatory sentencing. Thank me for my unwavering dedication later."

Talia read the outline. "Nice job."

"Just making sure you keep that handsome hometown guy of yours happy." Jasmine grinned mischievously.

"What's this?" Bill glanced at Talia.

"Nothing," Talia snapped. She glared at Jasmine.

"Ahem, guess I'll mosey on to my office." Jasmine stood. "See ya." She beat a hasty retreat.

"We won't get Congress to change this session, but we can lay the groundwork for the next one. I think in a few months we might approach the Black Caucus staffers about drafting a bill." Talia read through the notes.

"Uh-huh." Bill continued to study her.

"We'll also need the Latino Caucus. There are a couple of moderate Republicans I can work on in the meantime." Talia avoided his gaze.

"Right. Can I say something?" Bill uncrossed his legs and sat forward, elbows resting on both knees.

"Sure. You've got good insight into these law-and-order issues. Of course we agree to disagree on most of them." Talia wore a slight smile.

Bill shook his head. "I'm not talking about politics now. Something's got you shook. Don't bother to deny it," he said quickly, when she opened her mouth to protest.

"Since when did you become my big brother?" Talia joked.

"Since the first day we started working together," he replied. "Us Southern folk stick together."

She felt a warm flush of affection. Bill had taken her under his wing even before she came to work for Pete. They'd met while she was still a grad student at Howard University. Their unique friendship grew, and he'd advised her on career moves since that time. He had become her big brother in a sense. She'd never quite understood why though. He was from a wealthy family with political clout in Texas. Yet they'd always had an easy, close working relationship.

"Lighten up. I'm tired and stretched thin is all." Talia glanced away from his perceptive gaze.

"Look, I left Texas for a lot of reasons. Mostly to get away from a control freak drunken father who beat the stuffing out of me every chance he got."

So that was it. Adults who were knocked around as kids seemed able to recognize each other. Rich or poor, black, white, or purple, it didn't matter. Talia had met enough kids from deep-pocket families to know hellish childhoods were equal opportunity. Or as Mama Rose would say, "The devil is always busy, child." Still she couldn't share her Louisiana past with anyone, not even Bill and Jasmine.

"Every once in a while he still tries to mess with my head. Old bastard is pushing seventy years old and just as crazy-mean. I know all about trying to escape." Bill sat back. "You've been jittery since this guy Guillory showed up."

"Don't worry about me, I'm cool. I mean it, Bill." Talia looked at him steadily.

Bill rubbed his jaw for a long minute, then nodded. "Okay. Remember you can call on me."

Derrick appeared in the open door of her office as though conjured up by a voodoo spell. A chill spread up her spine at the look in his dark eyes. The lightweight gray suit seemed tailor-made to fit his large frame. He wore a white shirt that made a striking contrast to his creamy brown skin.

"Sorry to interrupt. I met your colleague Jasmine,

and she said I could come back." Derrick nodded toward the front of the office suite.

Bill stood. "No problem. I'm on my way out. Bill Elliot."

"Derrick Guillory. Nice to meet you," Derrick said. The men shook hands.

"First time in D.C?" Bill wore an easy smile.

"No, I was here a couple of years ago on business." Derrick's gaze flickered to Talia for only a second before he looked at Bill again.

She worked on keeping a bland expression. So he'd been in town before without calling her. Well, she had it coming. Not that she wanted to see him, right? A worrisome tickle of anger lodged in her chest all the same.

"Then welcome back." Bill gave Talia a meaningful glance that said he sensed the undercurrent. "Good meeting you. Talia, I'll talk to you tomorrow." He closed the door on his way out.

"Bye, Bill." Talia lifted her chin and smiled at Derrick. "So what brings you this way?"

"Larry called your boss, and they agreed to meet. Since I hadn't seen your office, I came along." Derrick scanned the layout as though he were conducting an investigation. "Nice."

"Thanks. Sit down." Talia suddenly felt exposed. Of course he was conducting an investigation, of her.

"I've really enjoyed these last few days." Derrick folded his tall frame into the chair Bill had only minutes before vacated. He continued to examine the decor.

"Learning a lot down at the Justice Department I guess." Talia maintained a cool tone.

He turned his unsettling topaz gaze on her. "I meant being with you."

Talia felt a spike of pleasure at the deep, sultry timbre of his voice. The sound flowed over her like hot sauce, setting her body on fire. Her mind told her body not to be affected. Derrick's gaze drifted down to her chest. In the silence she could hear him breathing. Talia fought against the tide pulling her back to an old attraction. She cleared her mind of what they'd had. After all, that was years ago, right? Switching to the business at hand might help.

"So you guys must be wrapping up all your meetings," Talia said.

"I leave tomorrow." Derrick answered the question she didn't ask.

"Listen, about the sentencing laws. I've given Pete a complete rundown on how we should approach it. I can give you a copy." Talia swung her chair around and tapped the keyboard of her Dell computer.

"My boss gave me one, but thanks," Derrick said.

"Oh. Well, we can go over a few things Pete is probably discussing with him right now. For instance we've identified at least six congressmen who are on the fence." Talia switched to a screen that listed members of key congressional committees.

"Interesting. You've got a dossier on each congressman." Derrick rose and walked over to stand next to her.

Talia knew it was her imagination that she could feel the heat from his skin. Derrick put one hand on the back of her leather chair and the other on the desk. The spicy scent of his cologne snaked around her delicately. His muscular thigh moved close in a tantalizing way. She battled an urge to wrap both arms around it. Talia leaned to the left, away from him.

"We do keep a file on their views and track their votes." Talia turned her head in an effort to keep it clear.

"What's this?" He touched her arm, then pointed to an icon on the monitor.

"That switches to another report. I have the committees listed with the issues before them."

"I understand you helped customize this application." Derrick's voice deepened.

"I modified the database with the help of the group that designed it when we got it about a year ago. Keeping track of the major players on key issues is critical for us and our clients." Talia could hardly breathe with him so close. As if to intensify his assault, he moved closer.

Derrick smiled at her. "Long way from down the bayou, baby girl. You've got folks impressed in this town, and that ain't easy."

Talia rose and walked to the table in a seating area near the window. She poured herself a glass of water from an insulated carafe. To buy time to recover, she took her time taking a drink. In the interim her brain kicked back in. He seemed to know quite a lot about her.

"Sounds like you've put together a dossier on me."

"Not really. But you can't blame me for being curious. After all we've—"

"Right," she broke in. "I'm going to be working late."

"I see."

They stared at each other in silence. The only sounds were the hum from her computer and the muted horns from traffic below. Talia tried not to think of him as a tall serving of mocha latte. She didn't want to imagine his hips pressed against hers as they rocked together. Before she knew it he was across the room. When the phone on her desk rang, he paused, and she breathed a sigh of relief.

"Talia, line four," the receptionist said through the speaker.

She hit the button, happy to have a reason to stop

whatever was about to happen. "This is Talia Marchand."

"Hey, you. I hope your day has been easier than mine. But it'll end right if you meet me at our usual place." Jarrod laughed. "I've got one heck of a story to tell you about your favorite senator."

Talia blinked hard at Derrick, who retreated to the other side of the room. "Uh, let me get back to you. I'm really tied up."

"I know your old friend from Louisiana is still in town." There was a pause. When Jarrod spoke again the amusement was gone from his voice. "You want to tell me about it?"

She picked up the receiver. "I'm in back-to-back meetings. I don't have to tell you what that's like." Talia turned her chair around as she spoke lower. "I'll give you a call. No, Jarrod, that's not some kind of code. Let's talk about this later, okay? Good-bye."

"Look, if I'm causing a problem, I'll back off." Derrick avoided her gaze by looking out of the window.

"Jarrod and I have been dating, we're not engaged." Talia immediately wondered why she'd said that.

"Then let's go out tonight." Derrick's poised exterior cracked. He swallowed hard before he spoke again. "There's so much we haven't said, and I'll be gone soon."

She shook her head. "I don't think we should, Derrick. That's not true. I *know* we shouldn't."

"I'm not asking for much," he said quietly. "One evening."

He towered over her, but not in an overbearing way meant to impose his will. The raw emotion in his eyes and voice tore at her. She ached to move closer to him. Instead, she put more space between them.

Talia faced the facts. She wanted him, yearned for

the mind-bending sexual healing every nerve in her body sensed he could give. Yet even more dangerous was the emotional hunger he fed. He only wanted one night, but he'd leave her yearning for forever. She crossed her arms and turned her back to him.

"Why start something we can't finish?" she said.

"It's better than nothing."

"I'm not so sure," Talia said.

Derrick put his hands on her shoulders. His lips were close to her ear. "My flight leaves at three o'clock tomorrow afternoon. I won't call you or try to see you again."

"Derrick, I—"

"Please," he murmured, and tightened his grip.

Talia swayed against him. His need to be with her answered her own. "I'll be through by six-thirty."

He stepped back when male voices approached.

"Her office is right down here, Mr. Perrilloux," Pete said. "She's the lady who really knows this issue from the Louisiana angle. I'm just the cheering section on this one."

Talia brushed back her hair, hoping it didn't look as tangled as she felt emotionally. She assumed a businesslike pose only seconds before Pete entered with Derrick's boss. Larry Perrilloux looked to be in his early fifties. A few strands of silver sprinkled his black hair. He couldn't have been more than five feet eleven inches tall. Still, he had an air of quiet authority about him. His dark eyes were bright with intelligence. He gave Derrick a quick nod.

"Hello, Ms. Marchand. Glad to have your insightful report." He shook her hand. There was a trace of Cajun lilt to his voice.

"Thank you. I was just telling Derrick that change goes slowly, but there's movement." Talia moved farther away from Derrick as she spoke in a crisp no-nonsense tone.

"We talked to Representative Tauzin, and he told us making an appearance might help," Derrick said. His serious expression showed no trace of the fire that had been in his eyes moments before.

"I wouldn't have wasted money or time coming here otherwise. Crime doesn't take a holiday. Not even in a rural area," Perrilloux said solemnly.

"We're not saying it's going to be easy. You know the political fallout for those who look soft on crime." Pete crossed his arms.

"Which is why I like your approach, Pete. Hammer home the point about maximizing our resources to go after the real bad guys." Perrilloux slapped a fist into the palm of his other hand to make his point.

"I'm putting together dollar figures on the cost of incarceration versus treatment. I'm also getting data on the effect of removing violent big-time dealers off the street," Talia said.

"Decrease in crime rates, less costly overtime paid to police officers, more uniforms free to patrol," Pete put in. "That sort of thing."

"Excellent, just what we need. I look forward to hearing from you. Good-bye, Ms. Marchand." Perrilloux walked toward the door with Pete.

"Good-bye," Talia said. She smiled at him, then glanced at Derrick. "Good-bye."

"I'll see you later, Talia," Derrick said.

Perrilloux stopped and looked back at them. "That's right, you two know each other. Nice to renew acquaintances with hometown folks." His wide smile transformed the serious "tough on crime" man into an affable Cajun gentleman.

One of Pete's eyebrows went up. Two sets of keen

eyes gazed at them for several seconds. Both men seemed to expect an explanation.

"Sure is," Derrick said with a placid air. He walked toward the two men.

Talia let out a long slow breath once the door closed and the three men were gone. She sagged against her desk. "One more night. I can take it."

The pleasant buzz all over her body generated by the anticipation of his strong arms and full, sweet lips implied otherwise.

Derrick stole sideways glances at her as they strolled along the riverfront of Washington Harbor. The warm, humid night air reminded him of Louisiana. Twinkling lights reflected in the dark water. They'd talked through a dinner at Joe's Seafood on K Street. The spectacular view of the river seemed to ease the tension between them. For a crazy moment he imagined they were just two people attracted to each other out on a date. Then Talia began to talk about her mother in a quiet voice. He just listened. Pain, disappointment, and suppressed bitterness tinged each word. She'd been terse and unwavering. Monette was out of her life. Rather than upset the fragile control he sensed could shatter at any minute, Derrick changed the subject. Now they walked along with no particular destination in mind. They sat down on a bench when two couples, double-daters, got up. Talia stared off across the river.

"I'm never going back, not to stay," she said.

"I know." He wanted to put his arms around her but didn't. "I'm part of the reason."

Talia sighed, but waited before speaking. "Yes."

Derrick flinched at the hard truth. "I'm not going to lie either. I'd do the same thing all over again."

She turned to him. "I can understand the first time, Derrick. But you let Monette use you."

"Monette needed help, and if she'd been arrested—"

"She was arrested anyway later on," Talia broke in heatedly. "You could have gone to prison."

"But I didn't."

"No thanks to her! I have to hand it to her though. Monette is a genius at getting men to dance to her tune." Talia tensed, took a deep breath, then let it out. "All except one. Earl," she whispered.

He could no longer resist touching her. She only held back for an instant when he pulled her against his chest. His heart beat faster when she relaxed.

"I know," he murmured.

Talia looked into his eyes. "I hate going home. Everywhere I look reminds me of something bad. If Mama Rose wasn't there, I'd never go back."

Derrick wanted to smooth away the frightened expression. He tried to think of something he could say to reassure her. Instead, he settled for holding her tight and gently rocking her. Jazz from a nearby bistro flowed around them. They were silent for a good twenty minutes before he spoke.

"I can't be sure the press won't track you down, Talia. I'll do what I can to keep you out of it. Monette feels the same way. You're not part of the story. I might even convince them not to mention you." Derrick stroked her arm with one hand as he spoke.

"Thanks for coming to warn me. Sorry I acted like a bitch at first," Talia said softly.

"I wanted to tell you in person," he replied, and rested his chin on the soft cushion of dark hair.

"Why didn't you call me when you were in town before?" She went very still in his arms.

"Like you said, why stir up something we'd have to let go?"

Derrick ached down deep in his soul at the awful reality. He would forever be associated with violence and fear. Somehow he'd hoped that he could love the horror away. Then Talia fled, leaving him behind in stunned misery. Not that he blamed her. Such a wound could never completely heal.

"I don't know what to say." Talia sighed and moved away.

"You don't have to explain."

"No, I want to tell you." Talia turned to him. "Leaving Rougon wasn't easy. Once I got used to being in a whole new place things got easier. I was accepted for being me. I made real friends for the first time in my life. I learned new things about myself."

"I always knew you were smart and talented," he said quietly.

"But *I* didn't believe it until then. I was amazed at getting offered six college scholarships!" Talia tapped a finger on her chest. "Me, the girl with raggedy clothes and a crazy mama. But none of that mattered."

"I'm happy you were able to follow your dreams." Derrick managed to smile at her through the sadness that clutched at his heart.

They held hands in silence for a long time, just watching people pass by. A breeze from the Potomac blew a thick lock of hair across her face. Derrick smoothed it back before Talia reached up. She looked at him, her eyes shiny. A tear slid down one cheek. He pressed his lips to it and tasted the sweet saltiness of her skin. They embraced. He felt the farewell in her touch. Not rejection, but a silent message that they could never be.

"Don't you dare come here again and not call me," she whispered. Talia pulled away and gazed into his eyes. "I mean it."

He could only nod. The lump in his throat kept him from speaking. She let go of him. Derrick let out a long cleansing breath. In spite of the yearning still inside, he didn't feel grief. Talia had fashioned her own life free of the chaos and danger of her childhood.

"You're successful. That's all I ever wanted for you."

"And you?" Talia studied him.

"I'm good." Derrick said. "I only work part-time for the DA's Office. I've got my own investigative firm on the side."

"Terrible D working with the authorities. Wouldn't Mrs. Haywood be stunned?"

He smiled at the mention of their old principal in grade school. Mrs. Haywood had issued him dark warnings at least three times a week.

"I can hear her now. 'Son, there's worse places than a classroom!' " Derrick shook his head. "She helped me get my first honest job."

"Get out of here!" Talia's mouth dropped open.

"We're pretty close now." Derrick laughed again at the look of astonishment on Talia's lovely face.

"I thought you'd hate each other until the end of time!" Talia threw her head back and laughed hard. "Now I really do believe in miracles."

Derrick relished the melodious sound of her contralto voice. "I guess we both survived pretty damn well, considering."

She stopped laughing and smiled at him in an easy, natural way. Once again Derrick felt blown away at the beautiful, accomplished woman she'd become. Leaving her would be painful, but at least he knew she still had a good life.

"We sure did. Okay, we've covered the heavy stuff." Talia stood and held out her hand. "Come on. I'm going to take you to some of the funkiest music places in town."

He stood and took it. "My dance moves are rusty."

"I don't believe you," she joked. "You may be an upright citizen these days, but I'll bet you can still jam."

For the next four hours they had a good time, with no more talk of the past. They seemed to have turned a final page of their shared history. Derrick was able to push away pangs of what might have been as they danced. When he drove her home later, he vowed that no one else would reopen that book. He pulled to the curb in front of her apartment building.

"Take care of yourself," Derrick said softly. He curled a thick tendril of her silky hair around one finger.

"See ya next time, Big D," she murmured. Her bottom lip trembled. "I've never said good-bye to you in my heart."

Talia melted into his arms, and he welcomed her. Derrick put a forefinger under her chin and lifted her face. He kissed her hard, unable to leave without one last taste of her full lips. She moaned deep in her throat as she dug her fingers into the fabric of his cotton shirt. Then she let go and got out of the car. Talia waved to him once before she disappeared into the building.

"Good-bye, baby girl," he whispered, and put the rental car in gear. No matter what happened, he'd make sure she didn't have to hurt again.

The next week was a busy one. Talia welcomed the long hours. Hard work helped her cope with the memories of strong arms and a scorching kiss. She arrived back at the office after a long day of meetings and research at the library. Jasmine met her in the foyer.

"Hi, Stephanie." Talia smiled at the office secretary. "Make sure Pete gets these reports."

"Sure," Stephanie replied.

"Hey, Jas." Talia juggled her shoulder purse and leather briefcase until she dropped a stack of reports into a basket.

"Talia, your brother Karl called. He didn't have your cell phone number." Jasmine wore a somber expression.

Talia froze. "What's happened? Just tell me."

Jasmine twisted her hands together. "They found Miss Rose passed out on the floor in her bedroom. They're not sure if she had a stroke, a heart attack, or—"

"When?" Talia called out as she raced to her office with Jasmine on her heels.

"This morning."

"Damn!" Talia tossed her purse and briefcase onto a sofa in her office. She went to her phone.

"Here. He's probably still at the hospital." Jasmine handed her a message slip with the phone number.

Talia gripped the receiver hard as she dialed. "Karl, how is she?" She listened for a few minutes. "Is she able to talk? Yeah, I'm coming. Bye."

"I'm so sorry, honey." Jasmine put an arm around Talia's shoulder.

"She was fine a few days ago," Talia said as she hung up the phone. She rubbed her forehead with a shaky hand. "Listen, I've got to leave right away."

"Sure. Don't even think about work." Jasmine swept a hand out. "I'll take care of it."

Peter came in. "Jasmine told me, Talia. Just go. You've got everything organized. Eileen and Bill have already pulled a lot of info from our database."

Talia blinked back tears and stood straight. "Thanks, guys. I'll call you."

Jasmine handed her a printed itinerary from an online travel site. "I found this flight leaving tomorrow morning at six. I already booked it for you."

"We couldn't find one that left tonight," Bill added.

She hugged them both. "You're the best."

"Just tell Miss Rose we love her," Jasmine said with a sniff.

Stephanie appeared at the door. "Pete, the deputy secretary at Health and Human Services is on the line for you."

"Right. Talia, I'll be thinking about you." Pete pecked her cheek before he rushed off.

"Guess I'd better go home and pack. I'm not sure how long I'll be gone." Talia shivered as she picked up her purse.

Jasmine walked beside her with an arm around Talia's waist. "Take care of things at home and don't worry."

"Yeah, sure. Home," Talia repeated. "You know I haven't spent more than a week in Rougon since I left ten years ago."

"Guess it will feel strange after all this time," Jasmine said. "Like I said, don't worry about what's going on around this place."

Talia arrived at her apartment without remembering the drive home. She went straight to the extra bedroom in her apartment and pulled out her large suitcase. For an hour she carefully packed. While she went through the motions of pulling clothes out of her closet, Talia thought about what she would face. In a few hours she would be in Rougon. Their roles must now reverse. Mama Rose would need Talia to be strong for her. She had to put aside her fears, even with Monette stirring the pot again.

"God, I know this is short notice, and I don't call often, but please, *please*, let her be okay," Talia whispered.

She found Derrick's business card tucked inside a pocket of her purse. Talia sat down on the edge of her bed and stared at it for a long time. Maybe the final chapter of that part of her life had not been written.

* * *

Tired as she was, Talia couldn't sleep on the plane the next morning. She put the seat back, closed her eyes, and tried to at least let the tension go from her tired muscles. Monette kept popping up in her head, which didn't help at all.

Her mother had been blessed with a pretty face, a knockout figure, and a love for the fast lane. No matter where she landed, Monette always managed to find some man to take care of her, at least for a while. Indeed, Monette had a captivating way of charming most people. Unfortunately, charm usually turned into a con game. When she added cocaine to the mix, the result was predictable. Partying became more important than anything else, including being a mother. Talia went into foster care the first time when she was six years old. The system put a priority on keeping children with their biological parents, so Monette had chance after chance. Talia went through three foster homes before being placed with Mama Rose the first time when she was eleven. Their relationship lasted after Talia went back to Monette a year later.

Mama Rose became her surrogate mother even when the state wasn't paying her to do the job. She'd taken in fourteen-year-old Talia that terrible night without hesitation. Talia said yet another prayer that she would be all right. Even more, she hoped the past that included Monette and Earl would remain closed.

Chapter 4

"Stop racing around, Talia. You're making me tired just looking at you." Mama Rose shifted with a slight frown, trying to get comfortable in the hospital bed. "You'd think this place would have better pillows."

Talia arranged the plants, sent by family and friends, on a dresser in the room. "You're not going home, so don't start. St. Francis is an excellent rehab center. This suite looks almost like a cozy apartment."

"I don't like apartments, and this is a nursing home. They can dress it up with a fancy name, but that's all it is."

Mama Rose gave the sheet an aggressive jerk to straighten it. Her plump cocoa brown face screwed up with distaste. She was only five feet four inches tall. Yet Rose Travis was a force to be reckoned with when displeased.

"It is not," Talia said. She unpacked underwear and neatly placed it in a drawer. Then she went into the bathroom to put away toiletries.

"Oh, yes it is," Mama Rose said loudly.

Talia came back into the room. She put one suitcase

away in a large closet, then started unpacking a second smaller one. "No, it's not."

"It is." Mama Rose stared out the window with a sullen expression.

Talia held up a pretty pink sweat suit. "Bet you look cute in this. Who knows? You might meet a handsome gentleman friend." She smiled at her.

"Right, just what I need, a sickly old guy wearing a diaper."

Talia laughed out loud as she hung the suit in the closet beside more clothes. "You're too much."

When she turned around to tease Mama Rose some more the smile faded from her face. A single tear slid down her foster mother's cheek. The proud woman's hands were tightly clasped together in her lap. Talia sat beside her on the bed and placed an arm around her shoulders.

"You're talking to me the same way my friend Alice's daughter talked to her. Alice never went home. She died in one of these places." Her voice was a strained whisper.

Talia rested her head against Mama Rose's. "Miss Alice was in the last stages of terminal cancer. That was totally different, cher."

"Maybe you and that doctor haven't told me everything." Mama Rose reached into the pocket of her bed jacket and pulled out a tissue.

"Look at me, Mama," Talia said. "We've always been honest with each other. I wouldn't lie to you about this."

"You're sure he didn't say anything more about those tests? I can take it, Talia." Mama Rose stared back at her intently.

Talia felt the strength in her yet saw fear in her hazel eyes. "I'm sure. He didn't see any new scarring on your heart to indicate a second attack. But he's concerned at the way your blood pressure dropped so low. Dr. Jeansonne wants nurses checking your vital signs every four hours the first week at least, just as a precaution."

"I can get nursing care at home."

"And he wants you near the medical equipment here," Talia added firmly. "Otherwise, I would have been just as stubborn about taking you home. This makes sense."

Mama Rose plucked at the floral top sheet. "I'm not staying one minute longer than necessary."

Talia smiled. "You always told me when things got tough to use my brain. We both know the doctor is doing what's medically best for you."

As though unwilling to go that far, Mama Rose merely waved a hand. "And what are you going to do in that house all alone? Maybe Derrick can—"

"I'll be fine," Talia cut in with a cheery tone. She patted Mama Rose's cheek and stood. "I'm going to make sure your dinner is ordered. Where did I put that menu?"

"It's right here." Mama Rose pointed to the oak table on rollers. It could be raised to different heights so she could eat in bed.

"Right. Hey, baked fish with garlic-roasted potatoes, green beans, and pears for dessert. Maybe I'll stick around." Talia grinned at her. "Move over, and I'll spend a few days."

"You like it so much, you stay, and I'll go home," Mama Rose said in a dry tone.

"At least you've still got that sense of humor. Now settle down while I finish fixing this place up. My goodness, did every kid you ever taught send plants?"

Talia shook her head when she looked into the small living room to find more plants had arrived. She set about making the room look as homelike as possible.

Mama Rose gave directions from the bedroom despite Talia's instructions that she should rest. Soon Talia heard the muted sound of the television. There was a strong knock on the door left ajar. Her brother Karl stood in the door with a vase of small sunflowers.

"Whassup, sis? Just came by to see how Miz Rose is doin'."

At least six feet tall with a wide handsome face the color of caramel, he was thinner than she remembered. He also had a touch of gray in his hair. Though only thirty-five, he looked older. Talia did not smile back at him. She crossed her arms. Still, he kissed her on the cheek lightly.

"She's doing just fine, and I plan to keep it that way," Talia said, gazing at him through narrowed eyes.

"Peace. I didn't come to upset her or you." Karl's familiar charming smile flashed.

"Okay." Talia turned away and continued arranging family photos on a mantel over the fake fireplace. "So why did you come?"

"Aw c'mon. I care about Miz Rose. She was my foster mama, too." Karl's smile faltered. "Don't be like that."

"Uh-huh. Except you—"

"Who is that?" Mama Rose came in using the walker. "Karl! Baby, I'm so glad to see you." She smiled with genuine pleasure.

"Had to come see my best girl," Karl said. He hugged her gently. "You got no business movin' around. Come over here and sit."

"No, she should be in bed. That's why it's called 'bed rest.' " Talia pursed her lips.

"Nonsense, I can rest just as well sitting in this chair." Mama Rose lifted her nose.

"You know Talia is right. Don't be hardheaded. Tell

you what, I'll sit with you and tell you the latest gossip," Karl said.

"Oh, you are such a scamp." Mama Rose laughed as Karl led her back into the bedroom. He kept up a steady stream of banter all the while.

Talia ground her teeth at the sound of their laughter. If the tough lady had one soft spot, it was Karl. Though she never hesitated to condemn his actions, Mama Rose never gave up on him. Karl had been more than a handful the brief time he'd been in Mama Rose's care. Even though he'd been removed and placed in a group home, she continued to visit him.

Fifteen minutes later Talia heard a mild debate through the open bedroom door.

"I'm not tired," Mama Rose said.

"Then relax before you get all worn-out," Karl replied. "I'll come back on my day off and make sure you're behavin'."

Mama Rose laughed. "That's what I used to tell you."

"Yeah, and remember what else you'd say? 'Mind these folks and follow the rules.' Bye, darlin'. I'll see you soon."

Talia was in the compact kitchen when he came out and shut the door quietly. She looked at him as he walked toward her. He wore a frown.

"She's lookin' weak. I ain't never seen her look that way before." Karl rubbed his chin with one large hand.

"Mama Rose is sixty-nine years old with a heart condition. She's worked hard all her life raising other people's wild kids and teaching school, too." Talia folded a white dish towel with a large pineapple print and hung it on a metal rack.

"She's a special woman alright. She stood by me

when a lot of people walked away." Karl sat on one of two barstools at the breakfast counter.

"Like me." Talia felt no guilt in the admission.

"I can't blame ya, little sister. I was a mess. But I've got a real life now—a job, wife, and kids."

Talia stared at him with a blank expression. "Sounds good."

Karl laughed softly. "Yeah, you've heard it before. This August it'll be three years I been clean. And it feels good. Look." He took out his wallet and showed her a picture of two smiling boys and an infant girl.

"Beautiful children, Karl. Take care of them." Talia's heart turned over at the sight of nephews and a niece she'd never seen.

"You gotta meet LaTrice and the boys. Come on over for Sunday dinner after church."

"Yeah sure. Maybe if I have time."

Karl wore a proud expression. "I'm a deacon at the Sunrise Baptist Church."

"I know and I'm real glad you finally got it all together."

"I realized I couldn't fill up the emptiness with drugs, liquor, women, or nothin' else I tried." Karl wore an earnest expression. "You welcome to come worship with us."

"Thanks," she murmured, unsure of what else to say.

"I'm sorry for not being there to protect you while you was little. Even though I wasn't that much older, once I got to be grown, I shoulda done somethin'."

"Don't be silly. You had to deal with Monette and our dad. But let's not rake up the past." Talia realized too late that she shouldn't have mentioned Karl's father.

"It's okay. I made peace with the man." Karl nodded

with a wise, thoughtful expression. He studied Talia for a few seconds. "And I'm finally talkin' to Mama."

Talia tensed. "Would you like something to drink? I think we have some diet cola in here." She started to rise when he put a hand on her arm.

"No, thanks. Have you been to see her yet?"

"I've got other priorities. Mama Rose needs me." Talia walked back into the kitchen and put away pot holders. "I might try to cook something. Mama Rose will probably get tired of institutional cooking."

"Talia, Monette been askin' 'bout you. Now that Miz Rose is all settled and taken care of, you could maybe go see her," Karl said.

She faced him sharply. "No. I'm not going to let Monette pull me into her latest plot."

"I ain't sayin' you got to make like she's some angel or nuthin'. I'm tellin' you from experience that anything could happen."

"Monette is healthy and still playing her games," Talia said with scorn.

"Sure, she's still young at forty-nine, but tomorrow ain't promised. If somethin' happened to her, that unfinished business would eat you up." Karl rested both elbows on the laminated counter as he gazed at her.

"Everybody is so worried about my mental state when it comes to Monette. Well, let me ease your mind." Talia crossed her arms. "My business with Monette is finished, Karl. I let go years ago. I don't intend to let her yank my chain."

Karl gazed at her several moments, then sighed. "I know it hurts. But—"

"Mama Rose, you, and Derrick don't get it. It doesn't hurt anymore. I survived and moved on." Talia's voice rose as she waved her arms.

"Okay, okay. I didn't come here to get you all upset,

little sister." Karl walked to her and gave Talia a brotherly hug. "I ain't gonna harp on that."

"Good." Talia accepted a peck on the cheek. She felt awkward, not used to having affection expressed within her family, and definitely not from her brother.

"So you an' Derrick hooked up again. I always liked him. He didn't let circumstances drag him low." Karl went back and sat down again. "He's a good man."

"Derrick and I haven't 'hooked up.' I saw him a few times when he was in D.C." Talia cleared her throat.

"He's a good friend is all I meant." Karl's bushy eyebrows went up.

"I haven't had time to socialize with schoolmates and old acquaintances." Talia busied herself arranging an already neat line of canisters.

"Yeah." Karl's mouth lifted at one corner. "Good as this place is run, you gonna have time on your hands. Have some fun."

"Once I'm sure Mama Rose is stable again, I'll be going home."

"Louisiana is home, Talia. Where you start will always be part of you." Karl wore the look of a sad wiseman for an instant, before the bright smile came back. "I better get goin', or my wife will have my backside. Don't forget, baby sister, Sunday dinner."

"Thanks, Karl." Talia smiled back at him. "I'm really happy for you."

"Bye now." Karl gave her another quick hug and left.

"He's right on both counts." Mama Rose stood in the door without the walker. She wore a blue floral housecoat and powder blue slippers to match.

"Just what do you think you're doing? I'm going to get that walker and march you right back to bed." Talia put her fists on her hips.

"Don't take that tone with me, Talia. My doctor says

I shouldn't lie around like an invalid, and I should walk without that thing if I can. I'm not sleepy."

"Fine. Sit and watch television. I'll call the kitchen and order your dinner. What do you want?"

"There is nothing on television I want to see. I'll order my own dinner, thank you very much." Mama Rose sat down on one of two large easy chairs.

"You are so rebellious! What did Karl just say?" Talia glared at her.

Mama Rose waved a hand, dismissing her disapproval. "I wiped his bottom and yours. I'm a long way from taking orders from two babies."

Talia shook her head. "You're driving me up the wall."

"Now back to Derrick. He's a good boy, even if he still is kind of wild." Mama Rose fluffed a throw pillow and positioned it behind her back.

"What do you mean?" Talia forgot to be irritated with her. She sat on the sofa across from her.

"He's been in the papers at least three times. Everybody knows he's the reason the district attorney got reelected." Mama Rose scowled. "A few brainless Black folks say he sold out."

"Because he helps gather the evidence to convict people." Talia tucked her legs under her.

Mama Rose nodded. "Exactly. Course they don't like to dwell on the havoc those no-good criminals cause. You wouldn't believe it, but we've had drive-by shootings in little old Rougon!" She sighed. "Times have changed for the worse, sugar."

"Let's not talk about that kind of thing. You'll get all worked up and want to go back to your volunteer work at the community center."

"My doctor says I should keep active. I'm in charge of the summer reading program for the children.

And—" Mama Rose stopped at the look Talia gave her and smiled impishly. "You busted me."

"That's right. Forget it." Talia rose and went to the phone. "I'm going to order dinner for you before I leave."

"Okay, I give up. For now," Mama Rose added quietly.

"I heard that," Talia shot back.

"Will you see Derrick tonight? The house is all fixed up. That nursing service sent an aide over."

"I'll be back. The social worker here said I can spend a couple of nights with you. Just until you feel comfortable," Talia said.

"Nonsense, go home and have dinner with Derrick." Mama Rose gazed at her.

"Stop with the Derrick stuff. Nothing is going to happen between us." Talia spoke through clenched teeth.

"Interesting. I never said anything was going to happen. Which tells me it already has," Mama Rose murmured.

Talia pretended she hadn't heard her. "Yes, this is for Mrs. Travis in suite 344-B." She ordered the dishes Mama Rose had checked on the menu list. "You're all set."

"Good. Don't let me keep you, sweetie. The six o'clock news is coming on." Mama Rose waved at the door. "Now go."

"The way you're rushing me out maybe you've got a hot date," Talia said with a grin.

Mama Rose turned on an icy glare. "Out!"

"Uh-huh, you can give it, but you can't take it." Talia darted out the front door just in time to avoid what was surely a razor-sharp reply.

Talia drove toward Mama Rose's house thinking of

her older brother. Seeing him again hadn't been at all what she had expected. Karl had always been as much of an embarrassment to her as Monette. As a child she'd endured taunts first about Monette and then Karl. Still, they were her family, and she'd gotten into fights when other kids called them names. Then Monette would take off with yet another boyfriend, and Karl would get arrested again. More and more she'd given up trying to defend them.

As impossible as it seemed, Karl had turned his life around. Could Monette be trying as well? Talia tried to imagine Monette living a conventional life. All she knew was the flamboyant, unreliable woman who'd left her alone to face a scary world. And from what little Derrick told her, Monette hadn't changed at all.

"Just let me help Mama get straight and out of this state before she lets the dogs out," Talia muttered as she turned into Mama Rose's driveway.

A week later Talia talked into the headset of her cell phone while making notes. She walked around the temporary office she'd created in one of the five bedrooms of Mama Rose's house. Pete gave her a rundown on what was going on at the office in Washington. Talia had insisted over objections from her colleagues, assuring them that things were going very well with Mama Rose. Although she wouldn't admit it, Mama Rose actually made friends and enjoyed the recreational activities at St. Francis. Still, she never missed a chance to say that she fully intended to return to her home of forty-five years.

"Yes, Pete. I'll meet with Larry Perrilloux next week on Wednesday." The phone on a desk rang just as the doorbell sounded. "Geez! The other phone is driving me crazy and someone's at the door. Let me call you later. Right."

She let the answering machine take care of Mama Rose's phone while she jogged to the door. Mrs. Lanier, one of her foster mother's longtime friends, chirped that she would visit and bring a casserole later. The woman had three eligible nephews and thought all of them were perfect for Talia. Talia had spent the last week dodging her attempts at matchmaking. Then she'd had to deal with leaking faucets, the tree-cutting service for the acres around the house, and a host of other domestic duties.

"This was supposed to be a relaxing visit once Mama got settled. What the hell happened?" Talia muttered.

She opened the door prepared to deal with yet another late repairman. Instead, Derrick stood on the front porch. "Tall" and "gorgeous" were the first words that popped into her head as she gazed at him. His muscular biceps bulged from the white short-sleeved knit shirt tucked into olive green slacks. He still held his car keys in one hand.

"I hope you don't mind." Derrick's dark brows drew together over the rim of his sunglasses. "I could come back another time if you're busy." He gestured to the headset.

Talia blinked at him, still dazed by his appearance. "What? Oh, I just hung up anyway." She took off the headset.

"How are things going?" Derrick fidgeted with the car keys. "Mama Rose is doing very well from what I hear."

"Yeah, and loving every minute of being difficult." Talia shook her head. "Payback for all the trouble I gave her as a teenager I guess."

Derrick grinned. "You weren't that bad. But she looks great."

"Oh?" Talia looked at him.

"I went to see her the other day. You'd just left." Derrick cleared his throat.

"I see." Talia stepped back and opened the door wider. "I'm losing my mind. Come in out of the heat."

"I just stopped to say hi is all. I don't want to interrupt your day or anything."

"It's okay. Come on in and have some peppermint lemonade." Talia beckoned him inside. "Whoa! I sound like a Southern country lady."

Derrick laughed as he came in. "In another three weeks you'll be wearing Miss Rose's favorite yellow apron with the ruffles and baking a cake."

"When pigs fly!" Talia retorted. She led him down the hallway past the living room. "Come on into the kitchen and don't say a word."

"What do you mean?"

Talia opened the refrigerator and took out a glass pitcher with large lemon slices floating in it. On the counter was a plate of tea cakes. "Not one word," she repeated. "I only made this because of all the folks trooping in and out of here."

Derrick pressed his lips together for a moment before he spoke. "Miss Rose's special peppermint lemonade recipe. Confess, Talia. You wore the apron." He took off his sunglasses and placed them on the countertop.

"No, I did not!" Talia fought the urge to grin back at him.

"Alright, if you say so." Derrick shrugged. "Next thing you'll be making little lace doilies."

"You want to drink this lemonade or wear it? I'm not into domestic chores."

"Right. You're a high-powered, big-city consultant, a twenty-first-century career woman." Derrick nodded. "But I'll bet you look darn cute in that apron."

"Very funny!"

Talia started to toss a plastic straw at his head, but he caught her by the wrist. Heat shot up her arm and went straight to her head. The feel of his smooth skin against hers set off an erotic tingle. His grip was loose, more like a caress. She stared at him in a trance as he pulled her against his chest. Her heart beat faster with each breath. Closer and closer his face came toward hers, until their lips were only an inch apart. Derrick's gaze drifted up to her hair. He touched the curls against her forehead with such tenderness she gasped. Then he traced a line down her cheek and along her jaw with the tip of his forefinger.

They stood that way for several minutes, with only the ticking sound from the wall clock breaking the silence. Talia fought off the sexual hunger that was slowly building into a roaring storm. Derrick leaned down just as she moved away. She escaped to the other side of the kitchen.

"You want a tea cake with your lemonade?" She turned her back to him and took two glasses from the cabinet.

"I want whatever you have to give."

When he spoke right over her shoulder she dropped them. Derrick's hands shot out with lightning speed, and he caught both before they hit the floor. He put them on the counter without taking his gaze from her face. Talia swallowed hard at the double message in his response.

"I don't know how much I have to give," she said quietly.

Derrick wore a wise and patient smile. "You're going to be here at least another month, maybe two. Even though the time will rush by, I won't rush you."

"I'm going back to D.C. There's no doubt about that," Talia said.

"I know. But I can't pretend you're not here and that I don't want to see you," Derrick replied.

Talia gazed at the hard chest outlined by the soft knit cotton of his shirt. She imagined rubbing her hands over the skin, savoring the texture of soft curly hair on it beneath her fingertips. As if he could read her mind, Derrick leaned forward, placing his palms flat on the counter on either side of her. He was making it hard to resist temptation. Every ounce of common sense she had screamed at her to back away from this man. He was too much of what she had left behind. Still, she struggled to remember exactly why being with him was dangerous. She tried hard to conjure up the fear and pain that had driven her from Rougon years before.

"You don't have to run from me. I'll let you go."

He was offering her heaven even if it was fleeting. Talia closed her eyes, dizzy, as her mind argued with her body over what to do next. Reason said she should tell him to get out. The woman inside her said, "Take him, girlfriend!" She opened her eyes again to gaze at him. As though sensing she was overwhelmed, Derrick backed away.

Talia crossed her arms in a posture of emotional defense. "No, you won't *let* me go. I make my own decisions."

He picked up his car keys. "Maybe I'd better leave."

Talia wanted to lighten the moment and make some kind of peace with the strange electricity between them. She would leave Rougon. There was no doubt in her mind about that. Still, she wanted to be with him for the few weeks she'd be in town.

"Without tasting my version of Mama's lemonade and tea cakes? Chicken." Talia hoped her smile worked.

"Okay, I'll hang out with you. Just don't give me the 'We'll always be friends' speech." Derrick smiled back, his head tilted to one side.

Talia felt a flush of sexual energy at the simple gesture. He made it hard for her to give that speech with his sensual magnetism. She forced her gaze away from the full, smooth lips that called to her.

"Agreed. One tea cake or two?"

"One is fine."

Derrick sat down at the square-shaped kitchen table and watched her pour lemonade in the glasses. Talia placed the plate of tea cakes between them and sat across from him.

"So what's up?" Talia took a sip of the cool liquid.

"What do you—" Derrick stopped at the look she gave him over the rim of her glass. "Monette called me from the prison. She knows you're in Louisiana."

"Don't tell me. She wants to see me for a touching mother-daughter reunion," Talia added with a grunt. "Who told her I was here?" She raised an eyebrow at him.

"Your brother had already called Monette. I just confirmed you were in Rougon." Derrick picked up a tea cake. "It won't hurt to see her once."

"With Monette once is too much." Talia shook her head. "I separated from her a long time ago just to survive."

"I know she took you through it and back." Derrick started to reach for her hand, then stopped. He picked up his glass instead. "At least think about it."

"Can we talk about something else?" Talia pushed away thoughts of her biological mother.

"Sure. Dinner is a good subject. We could go to Satterfield's tonight." Derrick wore an innocent expression.

Talia squinted at him. "I'm not sure."

He held up both hands. "No hidden agenda, I swear. I'll treat you to a good meal, and we'll talk about the weather. Don't tell me you're going to eat your own cooking."

"Hey!" Talia swatted his arm. "Just for that I'm going to cook you a great meal."

"Uh, I appreciate the offer, baby girl. But you've been working hard all day. Let's go out."

She stood. "I get the hint. Before I leave you will eat my cooking."

His expression softened. "That sounds great."

The temperature of the air around Talia suddenly shot up. Without thinking, she'd stepped closer to the edge. "Ahem, right. Come back to get me around six-thirty. I need to check on Mama Rose and finish a few projects first."

Derrick drank the rest of his lemonade and grabbed another tea cake. "Will do, ma'am. I'm looking forward to it."

Talia felt a spike of anticipation and apprehension when she looked into his dark eyes. "See you then."

She walked ahead of him down the hall. She was conscious every step of the way of his gaze on her body. By the time they reached the front door, all her nerve endings seemed to tingle. When she turned around to say good-bye one last time, the desire in his eyes shook her to the core.

"I'll see you in a little bit." Derrick leaned down and brushed her forehead lightly with his lips.

Damn, he's not playing fair! Talia suspected from his expression that he knew exactly what effect he had on her. She squared her shoulders, determined not to give in. "Good deal, pal."

Instead of a frown, Derrick gave her an affectionate pat on the cheek and a smile. "Right."

She watched him walk away, admiring the way his broad back narrowed at the waist and the great butt. As his black Toyota 4Runner drove away she took a deep breath. At least she had hours to fortify herself against another shot of Derrick Guillory's potent charisma. Why hadn't she just said, "No, I have plans"? Talia got busy with work to avoid thinking about the answer.

Chapter 5

∞

Talia took another turn around the Louisiana State Capitol building. Located in Baton Rouge, it towered over the compact yet busy downtown area. The historic building had beautiful marble floors that reflected images like glass. The regular legislative session had ended in June. She glanced at the large round watch face on her left wrist. Ten minutes until her appointment with Senator Jackson. She took the stairs down to the legislative offices instead of the elevator. Plush carpet the color of golden sand stretched down the hallway. Having scouted out the territory twice before coming, she knew the way to the offices of the chairmen of the three judiciary committees. Senator Jackson chaired Committee C, which handled the issue of sentencing laws. His legislative assistant, Marti Campo, was talking to a secretary when Talia walked through the door. Marti stood tall in three-inch heels and a form-fitting navy skirt. Her blond hair was neatly cut short and framed her heart-shaped face perfectly.

"I've got a few changes on this summary for the governor's people, Layla." Marti shuffled a thick sheaf of papers as she found her notations.

The secretary, a young woman of about twenty-five,

pursed her lips as the older woman talked. "Looks like more than a few changes."

Marti's frosty blue-gray eyes sparkled with anger. "That's why we call this 'work,' right?

"Yeah."

"I'll need a perfect copy no later than noon," Marti said in a clipped tone. She turned to Talia. "I hope you're Ms. Marchand. I've got to stay on schedule."

Talia stood and extended her hand. "You will be."

"Thank God! This has been a day, and it's not even ten o'clock." Marti glanced at her wristwatch. "This way. Senator Jackson had another meeting called at the last minute. Layla, do we have fresh coffee?" she called over her shoulder as she marched ahead of Talia down a short hall.

"I guess," came the bland reply. "With all this work I don't have time to check."

"Damn temp workers," Marti said to Talia, then opened a door whose top half was frosted glass. "She's pissed because I keep interrupting her social life on the phone. Have a seat. I'll get us some coffee."

Talia looked around the roomy office. Located in the basement, the office suites of legislative leaders had undergone a massive renovation. Marti had beautiful framed prints of Louisiana flowers and swamp scenes to substitute for windows. Talia sat down in one of several plush chairs that matched the golden-hued carpet. Talia had not missed a name that rang a disturbing bell in Marti's rush of words earlier. Marti came back with a steel coffee carafe on a tray with four mugs, sugar bowl, and nondairy creamer in small packets.

Talia accepted a cup of black coffee from her. "I'm glad you could meet with me so soon. I'll only be here a few weeks."

"You'd think with the session over I could take a breath. But no!" Marti sat in a chair on the opposite side of the brightly polished cherrywood table. "Enough of my problems. Mandatory sentencing." She looked at Talia and took a sip of coffee.

"I've read Senator Jackson's proposed bill. He's had a tough time convincing his colleagues." Talia put down the cup and took a notepad from her briefcase.

"Tough? We got our tails kicked." Marti shrugged. "Not that we were surprised. The public sees crowds of thieves and worse getting out of prison. Not a sight to encourage the average citizen terrified of crime."

"So the legislators who voted to kill it in committee are 'tough on crime' types?"

"It's election time. Two high-profile violent crimes took place during the session." Marti frowned.

"Senator Jackson decided to back off until next year?" Talia looked at her.

"Yeah, but there's a lot we can do before then. I guess that's where you and your outfit come in." Marti gave Talia an appraising glance.

Show time. Talia knew this tough lady wanted to know if she had a clue. "I have a rundown on the history of other states' efforts to tackle mandatory sentencing. California is the best known. They were one of the first states to enact the so-called 'three strikes' law."

"Right. I—" Marti stopped when a dark-haired man wearing gold wire-rimmed eyeglasses tapped on the door. "About time, Jim."

"Morning. Sorry I'm a few minutes late." The tall, lanky man smiled an apology. He held a gray suit jacket on one arm and carried a black satchel in the opposite hand.

"Talia, I'm assuming I can call you that," Marti said with a grin.

"Sure," Talia replied.

"This is James Rand. Jim, Talia Marchand of Pete

Gallagher and Associates in Washington, D.C." Marti smiled.

"Nice to meet you." James Rand held out a long-fingered hand as he studied Talia closely. Monette's new lawyer smiled at her.

Talia tensed. "Hi."

He glanced at the carafe on the side table. "Bless you, Marti." Jim put down his jacket and briefcase, then poured himself a cup.

"Jim is the director of the Tulane Law Center. He has a national reputation on this issue and a lot of others pertaining to sentencing patterns, including the death sentence."

"So I've heard." Talia took a deep breath.

Jim sat next to Talia. He drank deeply and sighed. "So what have I missed so far?"

"Talia has been doing her homework on other states." Marti nodded with an expression of approval.

"I've read several of your articles on the subject, Professor Rand."

"Even the most cursory examination shows the obvious; poor people end up in jail more often and with longer sentences." Jim set his mug down with a thump.

"Which doesn't mean they're not guilty," Talia said. "Something the critics are quick to point out."

"We're not trying to help people get away with crimes. If one segment of the population committing similar offenses gets the benefit of probation, shouldn't everyone?" He leaned forward.

"Okay, granted. But people should be held accountable for breaking the law." Talia lifted a shoulder.

"I thought she was here to help us." Jim wore a crooked grin as he drank more coffee.

"I see her point, Jim. We have to answer the opponents," Marti replied.

"Exactly, especially since they have valid arguments," Talia said. "There is no such thing as a victimless crime when you get right down to it."

"Not everyone sent to prison is guilty. Even those who did the crime shouldn't do the time longer because they're poor or Black," Jim countered.

"Liberals use those arguments. They're not in control at the moment."

"Don't I know it." Jim looked at Talia hard again. "I hear your firm usually comes down on the right of most issues."

"True, but my boss doesn't follow strict party lines. Pete likes to make his own decisions on individual issues." Talia took another folder from her briefcase.

"What about you?" Jim's bushy eyebrows arched over his dark eyes.

Talia decided honesty was the best route to take. "I'll admit to mixed feelings on the issue."

"Have you been the victim of a crime?" he asked.

"We all pay one way or another," Talia said smoothly.

"Well, I've been a victim. Some little creeps broke into my condo six years ago. I'd like to get my hands on 'em, too!" Marti wore a fierce expression.

"There you go. A typical gut reaction to crime." Talia nodded at Marti. "You've got to do a lot better than trying to get the public to feel sorry for convicted felons." She wanted to steer them away from the personal.

"Which is why I'm interested in your thoughts." Marti got up and poured more coffee into her mug.

"The wording in Senator Jackson's bill should change. Take the bite out of your opponent's best argument." Talia glanced from Marti to Jim Rand. "Emphasize getting tough on crime."

"What?" Jim wore a puzzled frown. He took off his glasses.

"You're joking." Marti blinked at her.

Talia sat forward. "Listen, I've seen the polls from his district. The biggest fear after job security is crime. Some of the poorest neighborhoods are held hostage by drug dealers."

"Yes, but they also have suffered the highest rate of incarceration. They see the ugly side of the law when it jails their kids," Jim said, pointing at her with his glasses in one hand.

"Most of those people, Professor Rand, are the victims of these so-called kids. While mama is trying to get her little darlin' out of prison, her neighbors are inside dancing for joy." Talia met his gaze head-on. "I grew up in the same kind of place."

"I'm not disputing the impact of crime, but—"

"You can't ignore it either," Talia broke in. She turned to Marti. "The opening of the bill starts out talking about how long sentences don't change crime rates. Then it goes on about the need for social services. I say begin with the need to concentrate limited law enforcement dollars on the most heinous offenders."

"I don't know. Senator Jackson has always been a vocal advocate for rehabilitation and crime prevention." Marti's neatly arched eyebrows drew together in concentration. "His base of support is mixed, but more liberal on the issue."

"Not when specific questions are asked." Talia pulled another report from her briefcase. "His constituency is 37 percent African-American. They're conservative on several issues, rising crime is one."

"He recently met with a coalition of Black leaders who are concerned about racial profiling." Marti shook her head. "I'm not sure he'll go for it."

"Show him the numbers," Talia said, and tapped the report with a forefinger. "He can still address community programs to prevent crime. As you said, it's election time."

"You seem pretty conservative on this issue, Talia." Jim Rand eyed her with interest.

Talia's heart thumped. "I'm not that different from the people Senator Jackson represents."

"Let's talk specifics. Give me bullet points to cover with him," Marti said.

"Sure."

Talia hadn't worked on the Hill without learning the value of distilling complex information down to basics. Most lawmakers depended on their staff to help them navigate complicated issues. For an hour and a half, they went over all twelve of the short paragraphs she'd written. Jim argued that race and economics as factors should be included. Talia stood her ground despite the glances he gave her from time to time. At the end of the meeting he followed her out. They went through a side exit door toward the parking lot. Bright September sunshine bounced heat waves up from the concrete surface.

"Good-bye, Professor Rand."

"Good-bye, Ms. Marchand. We've met before I think." He gazed at her with one finger on his bottom lip. "I was in D.C. last year for a symposium on prison reform."

"We've never been involved in prison reform." Talia put on her sunglasses as a shield.

"I see." Jim studied her for a moment longer then smiled. "Well, we've had an eye-opening discussion. I suppose you think I'm a typical white liberal from the ivory tower of academia."

Talia smiled slightly. "It helps to see all sides of a question."

"As long as we don't become the enemy. I don't want Kelvin to draft a bill that adds to the problem," he replied.

"The problem is getting people to take responsibility for their families and themselves." Talia extended a hand. "Nice to have met you." She hoped it would be the last time.

"Same here." He shook her hand and walked away.

"Lord, just let me get Mama Rose taken care of and out of this state," Talia muttered. She pressed the remote on her key ring, which opened her rented red Pontiac Grand Prix.

Derrick stared at her. "What's on your mind? It sure isn't what's left in the bottom of your cup."

They were seated in CC's Coffee Shop in downtown Baton Rouge. They'd been to a jazz performance at M's Fine and Mellow Café earlier. Now they sat at an outside table enjoying a breeze from the water. The riverfront was alive with strolling couples and families. CC's was in a renovated parking garage, with a view of the Mississippi River. The large bridge linking East and West Baton Rouge Parishes was strung with white lights. Traffic across it was barely visible. The cars and trucks looked like toys in the distance. Talia couldn't help but smile at him.

"You've got more answers than Miss Cleo," she teased, referring to the colorful psychic.

"Ah, darlin', I see what's goin' ahn," Derrick said, imitating Miss Cleo's Caribbean accent.

Talia laughed. "What do the cards tell you?"

"That you've been working too hard for one thing. Slow down."

She sighed and sat back in her chair. "I'd like nothing better. I've got as much to do here as I had back in Washington."

"You take on a lot because you enjoy the fast pace."

"You and your boss got me into this whole sentencing issue," Talia replied with a raised eyebrow.

"If I'm the reason you're back home, then I won't complain." His deep voice issued a sultry invitation.

Talia breathed hard as they stared into each other's eyes. The gray cotton sweater she wore seemed too hot suddenly. She squirmed in her chair as a tickle of lust surged up the insides of her thighs.

"I'll be gone in about three weeks." She looked out at the levee.

"So you keep reminding me. We have dinner, and you mention it. We go see a play, and you mention it." Derrick heaved a deep sigh. "I think I've got it, Talia."

"Sorry." She felt a stab of guilt at the sadness in his tone. "I didn't mean to beat a dead horse."

"Maybe you're trying to convince yourself?"

Talia toyed with a paper napkin. "I don't understand why you got hooked up in crime fighting after all we've been through," she said quietly.

"You mean avoid the kinds of people and places we grew up with, right?" Derrick shrugged. "I want to make a difference."

"Don't you get sick of the criminals, the lies, the sordid stories? We lived it." Talia grimaced at the memories.

"I'm not sure I can explain it." Derrick shook his head slowly. "I think we need to be involved in the criminal justice system. I guess because it had such a big impact on my life."

"C'mon, there are thousands of careers." Talia gazed at him.

"I'm not a desk job guy. I like being on the move and in the thick of things." Derrick smiled. "That paralegal course while I was at the community college got me hooked."

"You could have been a lawyer. With your brains you'd make a truckload of money." Talia leaned toward him. "My friend Jarrod—"

"I don't want to wear a suit and do lunch. I'm not into being upwardly mobile."

"There is nothing wrong with the good life," Talia shot back.

"You want a guy who can give you a luxury town house and theater trips to New York. I got ya." Derrick sat back in his chair and gazed past her to the river.

"So I'm superficial, is that it?" Talia ground her back teeth together. "Well, excuse me. I had my fill of living in the 'hood."

"I want to work to make sure that when the bad guys go to jail, it sticks," Derrick said, lowering his voice.

Talia looked at him through narrowed eyes. "You've just sublimated your addiction to adrenaline into fighting crime. I knew you when, Derrick. Well, who died and appointed you Batman?"

"I can't believe this!" Derrick waved a hand in the air.

"Mama Rose told me all about how you helped catch some dangerous thugs. Your mother must worry herself sick." Talia pushed the ceramic mug aside.

"Mama understands my work."

"Of course that's what she's going to tell you." Talia rubbed her forehead. "It's so inconsiderate. Who the hell wants to sit up nights wondering if you're dead?"

He reached out and took her hand down from her

face. "I'm not in that much danger. You wouldn't have to worry."

"Run around jumping in front of bullets if you want. I'll take my nice boring office job and my nice boring life, thank you very much." Talia tried not to answer the silent call into a tender moment from his touch. She avoided meeting his gaze.

"Nothing is going to happen to me. I promise," Derrick whispered.

"You don't know the future, so why take chances?" Talia tried to pull her hand away, but he held on tight. "And then there's my dear jailbird mother. God, I wish Mama Rose would come live with me!"

Derrick sat straight. "Something's up. Tell me what happened."

Talia shook her head. "I went to a meeting with Representative Jackson's assistant, and Professor Rand was there."

"He knows you're Monette's daughter?"

"No. Maybe he's seen pictures of me when I was a kid. Monette has some, I know. He kept trying to figure out why I looked familiar."

"Monette is real serious about protecting you. I don't see her showing pictures of you even as a little girl." Derrick frowned. "I have a feeling whatever she's holding back is heavy."

"You should know not to listen to Monette. If I had a dime for every lie she's told, I'd be set for life." Talia gave a bitter laugh.

"He just saw the resemblance. You look a lot like her." Derrick squeezed her hand as he tilted his head to one side. "But your eyes are a lighter shade of brown. Like walnut. Your hair is darker and shiny, like rich mocha coffee."

"I missed you so much," she said in a strangled

voice. Talia couldn't have stopped the admission if she'd tried.

"I know, I know," Derrick murmured.

Talia closed her eyes and pressed his hand against her breasts. Derrick whispered her name twice, then kissed her. He nibbled her lips as though savoring a sweet taste. She sighed at the tender attention he gave to exploring the inside of her mouth. His response to her seemed instinctive, as if he knew exactly how she needed to be kissed. When they finally parted, Talia had no doubts. She was in danger of falling in love with the man with the same intensity she'd loved the boy. Still, she didn't move away when he rested his forehead against hers. She didn't have the strength to resist right now. She felt safe with him.

"Derrick—"

"I know, you're going back to D.C.," he said, and took a deep breath.

"I was going to suggest we leave now." Talia looked into his eyes.

"My house is too far away. It will take us a good forty minutes to get there." His eyes gleamed with desire. Derrick lived fifteen miles from Rougon, in the larger town of New Roads.

"There's a nice new Sheraton Hotel five minutes from here." Talia nodded toward the tall building that was part of the nearby Argosy Casino complex.

Derrick kissed her hands and took a slow, deep breath. "I can't believe I'm saying this, but we should wait. I want us both to be sure."

"You're not?"

"It was hell letting you go the first time. I don't know if I can take it again." Derrick released his hold on her.

"I'm sorry. All I seem to do is think about myself."

Talia felt stinging regret at the hurt she had caused him.

"I know you need to leave." Derrick tapped his temple with a forefinger. "My brain knows that it's best for you. But my emotions get so caught up."

"So we're stuck? I don't think so." Talia shook her head. "We can have right now, and let tomorrow take care of itself."

"Live for today." Derrick seemed to turn over the words in his mind.

"We need to get to know each other all over again. I say we take the next few weeks to explore."

Talia tingled with anticipation. She felt like a wily seductress. Yet the look in his eyes told her how much he wanted to be seduced. They were poised for a long free fall into passion. Maybe the pleasure would be worth the pain.

"That means we need to spend time together. You like to work long hours," Derrick said. His brown eyes held a teasing glint.

"So do you from what I hear," she replied.

"Yeah, but work was really all I had until now," he said softly.

"I'm sure you've had girlfriends." Talia didn't really want to know, but couldn't help asking.

"I always held back a big part of myself."

Talia trembled at the expression of longing in his eyes. She burned to kiss away the sadness in his dark eyes. Without thinking, she touched her fingertips to the smooth-shaved skin of his face. A loud clatter of silver dropped by a passing waiter brought her back to reality. Talia started to lower her hand, but Derrick caught it in one quick move. She stared in fascination at the way his long, brown fingers laced through hers.

"We're both ignoring the warning signals. You just said—"

He nodded slowly. "I know. I don't have all the answers, but I can't stay away," he whispered hoarsely, and planted whisper-light kisses on her fingers.

"So what now?"

Derrick planted one last kiss, then lowered their entwined hands to the table. "We go fishing."

Talia's eyes popped open wide. "S'cuse me?"

He wore a mischievous smile. "Old River Landing was our place, remember? It's still there, and I've got my own boat. *Creole Lady Marmalade* is a beauty."

"This is a joke." Talia blinked at him. "I'm now a city girl."

"Don't give me that urban cool act. She's a fifteen-foot beauty with an eighty-horsepower engine, comfortable cushioned seats."

"I've got work, Mama Rose to look after, and—" Talia shook her head hard enough to make her thick hair bounce.

"Mama Rose is doing great; you just said so. Are you afraid of being on the river or of me?" Derrick arched one dark neat eyebrow as he gazed at her.

"Scared, ha! I've never been scared of fishing. And you're the least scary creature out in the swamp," she retorted with a wave of her one free hand.

"You sure, baby girl?" Derrick's deep voice hummed with an erotic challenge.

Talia surprised herself when she blushed. She didn't think it possible after her experiences in life. To cover her confusion, she pulled her hand free.

"I'm sure." She lifted her chin defiantly as she lied. Her heart thumped hard at the thought of them alone. They'd first made love surrounded by trees and flowers. Something about the countryside would always make her think of his body against hers.

Derrick's voice went deeper as he laughed at her acceptance of the challenge. He seemed to know she was putting on an act. "I'm looking forward to a long, lazy afternoon in the sun. Just you and me."

"You and me," she said quietly, and stared in a trance as he leaned forward to kiss her lips.

Chapter 6

∞

Derrick sifted through a pile of paperwork on his small desk in the district attorney's office. He wanted to pick up the entire mess and toss it in the trash can. The office manager looked straight at him when he glanced up. Kelsey Palmer, short, plump with red hair, pursed her lips and adjusted her reading glasses. The fifty-year-old grandmother ran a tight ship.

"Don't even think about it," she called out. Kelsey knew only too well his hatred of filling out forms.

"Yeah, yeah. I've got the expense forms right here and the voucher for witness expenses." Derrick waved two sets of triplicate forms at her.

"You're not leaving this office until I get back those files you pulled. And where is that report you were supposed to dictate?" Kelsey crossed her arms as though fully prepared to block the door.

"Hey, you know I stay up on my interview reports. Cheryl has the tape. Right, Cher?"

A pretty woman with ebony skin seated three desks away waved a cassette tape over her head. "He's always on time with the tapes. Now the other stuff, that's a different story." Cheryl brushed back her heavy woven braids over one shoulder.

"All I asked you about was the tapes," Derrick tossed back with a sour face.

"Okay, let me see." Kelsey walked to his desk with her hand out.

"Aw, geez! You're worse than my old grade school principal." Derrick eyed her.

"I'm sure she had just as much trouble out of you, poor woman. Now give it up." Kelsey's green eyes narrowed as she read. "Um-hum. Good, good."

"Thanks, Mrs. Palmer." Derrick mimicked the tone of a student talking to his teacher.

She lowered the papers and stared at him over the rims of her glasses. "Don't make me go there, Derrick. The boss will hound *me* if we don't keep good records, especially on the money you guys spend."

"Yes, ma'am!" Derrick saluted her. "I'm in full compliance as of today." He handed her another stack of folders.

She read a few labels. "Humph! Cheryl, I just solved the missing files mystery for three weeks. They were over here in Devil's Swamp," Kelsey called over her shoulder.

"I needed those for the Jenkins case. I've got a new lead on the kid that shot those grocery clerks." Derrick smoothed down his tie and faced two sets of disapproving eyes. "Crime fighting can't always follow bureaucratic office rules."

Kelsey made a sputtering sound as she spun around and marched off. "Give me a break!"

"Sign them out. That's what the log is for, ya know," Cheryl chimed in.

"Do you want neat logs or those punks in prison?" Derrick muttered.

"We want both, and with a little cooperation we can have it all," Cheryl said. She grinned at him. "Hey, we fight crime in our own way."

Derrick laughed. "You're absolutely right.

Larry Perrilloux came down the hallway. "Derrick, come into my office." He spun around and marched off.

Cheryl made a clicking sound with her tongue. "Somethin's up."

Derrick lifted a shoulder, then followed the DA into his office and closed the door behind him. "Yeah, Larry."

Larry went around the wide heavy oak desk but didn't sit down. Instead he folded his arms and sat on the window ledge. "I got a call from Winn Barron about this sentencing thing."

"Okay." Derrick sat down in a dark red leather chair facing Larry's desk and waited.

"He heard about our trip to D.C." Larry turned his back to Derrick and stared out the window. The manicured lawn stretched down to a pond with a fountain. "He made some good points."

The previous DA in Pointe Coupee Parish, Barron had helped Larry get elected. Barron left office to run for state attorney general and won. From a wealthy old Louisiana family, Barron had increased their political power in the two years since his election. Winn had made it quite clear that he was opposed to changing mandatory sentencing. Derrick knew Larry felt uneasy going against his mentor.

"What's bothering you, Larry?" Derrick said, after letting a few moments of silence pass.

Larry turned around. "I'm not sure."

"Barron is a 'lock 'em up' kinda old-school prosecutor. He carried that with him to the state capital."

"Yeah, right." Larry's frown deepened. "Anyway, I guess we'll have to agree to disagree."

"I don't get it. He knows the reality of prison overcrowding." Larry brushed back a lock of dark hair from his brow and sat down. "Anyway, we've got a perfect example of the problem right here." He picked up a folder.

Derrick didn't need to ask what case he was talking about. "Talon Jackson is going to rat out everybody to get a deal."

"And his fall guy, a seventeen-year-old, could get consecutive twenty-five-year sentences. Damn it!" Larry slapped the folder down hard. He gazed at Derrick. "I've got to stop this drug ring."

"Joe Claycut won't let it go though."

The president of the Citizen's Action Coalition, Claycut accused the local police and Larry of selective enforcement. An old-line civil rights activist, Claycut spoke loudly and often about what he saw as the new brand of racism.

"Maybe if you talked to him?" Larry leaned forward.

"Don't get your hopes up. Joe won't listen to me. He says I'm 'misguided.'" Derrick smiled. He had a deep respect for the older man. Joe regularly sought to put him on the right path.

"I'm between a rock and a hard place." Larry sighed.

Derrick knew he was thinking of the election in two more years. "Talia is right about one thing. African-American communities are sick and tired of being war zones."

"Speaking of her, I'm eager to get her first report." Larry stared at Derrick. "Have you gotten any kind of feel for what she's learned so far?"

"She'll make her report to you and the DAs' Association, Larry." Derrick kept his voice and expression bland.

Larry nodded with a slight smile. He seemed to accept the deft sidestep of his subtle probe into Derrick's personal life. Then his expression grew serious again. "I hope it's soon. Winn will be at our state conference next week."

"Will he push this as a make-or-break issue?" Derrick wondered if Barron would punish Larry for opposing him.

"No, no, nothing like that." Still, Larry's tone did not seem confident. He put aside the Talon Jackson file and opened another folder. "Winn asked for information on some old cases. I'm not sure why, but I think he's going to use them to argue against changing the sentencing laws."

"That's strange. He's been out of this office a long time."

"Kelsey pulled these archived records for me." Larry pushed six folders across the desk. "I don't remember any of these. Do you?"

"We were both in high school," Derrick joked. His grin faded when he saw Monette's name on a file label. "Why did he say he wants these?"

Larry continued to read through another file. "The parole board meets in a month. He said something about filling me in on questions from the media. Give me a quick-and-dirty summary on the cases."

"What does he care if these folks have done a big chunk of their time?"

"Families of victims don't forget. Maybe they want help in persuading the board not to grant paroles." Larry flipped another page. "We get calls like that every once in a while."

"Yeah, if it's murder, but usually not in a drug case. I don't get it." Derrick frowned at the folders in his hand.

"Some involved young kids being sold drugs. Or maybe there was violence involved." Larry shook his head. "One more thing to butt heads with him about."

"What do you mean?"

"Unless those convictions involved egregious circumstances, I won't oppose parole." Larry rocked back in his chair. "I came down on the side of helping to relieve prison crowding. I really don't think keeping people locked up forever is the answer."

As Larry went on talking about his dilemma, Derrick paid token attention. His thoughts were on Monette and her efforts to be released. If the attorney general took a personal interest, media attention was a foregone conclusion. Derrick stood abruptly.

"I'll get right on it," he said, cutting Larry off.

"You don't need to put aside stuff we're working on right this minute." Larry gazed at him in curiosity. "Recognize one of these names?"

"You know I find old cases interesting." Derrick forced a half smile.

"Yeah, well on second thought read them in the next couple of days if you can. Winn might call back soon." Larry scowled at the files as though they were a source of trouble for him. They well might be.

"No problem." Derrick held the folders as though they were just another assignment.

Once back at his desk, he opened Monette's old case file and started reading. He made notes on other files and cross-referenced them. All the while he considered when and how to tell Talia about this latest development.

Derrick and Talia stood on the banks of Old River enjoying the view. He'd backed his 4Runner down to the edge, and his boat was ready to be launched. Sunlight bounced off waves kicked up by a passing jet ski. A young couple laughed as they shot by, waving to friends on a nearby party barge. The balmy September weather was perfect for a boat ride down the river.

"Ready?" Derrick rubbed his hands together.

"Yeah, I guess." Talia frowned slightly behind her dark sunglasses.

"Aw, c'mon now. Don't go getting wimpy on me like some prissy city girl." He reached out to tickle her side, and she danced away.

"Cut it out." She slapped at his hand.

Derrick laughed, then walked down to the bank and unhitched the boat from the trailer. After making sure it was securely tied so it wouldn't float off, he moved the 4Runner to a parking space. He walked back to her and enjoyed the view. Talia looked lovely in denim shorts, a pink cotton shirt tied at the waist, and a denim-and-pink cap on her head. She wore blue socks and white athletic shoes. Derrick loved to watch the smooth movement of her silky brown legs as she walked.

"Here we go." Derrick hopped into the boat first. He held out a hand and helped her climb aboard. "See? You've still got the moves."

"The smallest boat I got on in D.C. was a yacht owned by a big chemical company. You do have caviar and white wine, right?" Talia flashed a dazzling smile at him.

His pulse rate jumped at the beauty before him. "Anything you want today, my lady. Anything."

Talia squeezed his hand. "Don't promise what you can't deliver, bad boy."

He laughed. "Okay, how about corn chips and Barq's Red Creme soda?"

"You didn't!" Talia squealed with delight. "I haven't had Barq's in ages."

"That's just for snacking. I tossed in a few pieces of my mama's fried chicken, her world famous potato salad, and some French bread." He held up the insulated wicker basket he'd bought a few days before.

Talia sighed and sank down onto one of the vinyl seats. "I'm in heaven."

Derrick flushed with pleasure that he was the source

of her happiness. He started the boat and steered them out toward the open water. They rode along at a leisurely pace. Wind pushed against them as they moved along the river. Swamp oak and maple trees lined the banks on either side. Snowy white egrets floated above or swooped down to land in the lush tall grass on shore. The graceful birds dotted the green landscape like decorative statues standing very still, beaks held high with dignity. Twenty minutes later he cut the motor.

"This is a good spot for perch and catfish. Maybe we'll get lucky." Still seated next to her, Derrick took fishing rods from the racks on the sides of the boat. "Speckled trout."

"I love baked speckled trout." Talia watched him.

"Well, now is your chance to work for your supper." He handed her a rod and reel. "I hope you remember how to use one of these."

"I'll see what I can do." With a smug expression, she grasped the rod and executed a cast with one fluid motion.

Derrick let out a low whistle. "I don't think it all came back that fast, girl."

"I've been on a few fishing junkets. You know, schmoozing courtesy of the big boys." Talia laughed.

"Rubbing elbows with mad power brokers." Derrick shook his head with a mock frown.

"Being from the bayou country had some advantages. I help the wheels of government run smoothly." Talia reeled in her line slowly.

"You enjoy the fast pace of making things happen." Derrick tugged on his line. The colorful metal floats of both their lines glittered in the sun.

"You betcha. I enjoy knowing all the inside dirt on how things get done." Talia cast again. She glanced around briefly before focusing on her line again. "But I'd forgotten just how peaceful being out here can be."

"Yeah," Derrick said in a quiet voice. He gazed at the tall grass swaying in a slight breeze.

They fished in silence for an hour. Derrick caught the first fish, a big perch as wide as his hand. Talia pretended to be angry that he'd beaten her. Moments later she gasped when her line went taut. She reeled in a fat catfish weighing at least three pounds. Over the next hour they landed six more fish. Derrick put them in a wire basket that hung over the side of the boat in the water. He'd brought an extra cooler of ice to store them on the ride home.

"I'm getting hungry," Talia announced. "It's almost eleven. I say we eat."

"Okay. I know a good spot for a picnic."

They put the rods away, and Derrick started up the motor. Ten minutes to the west of them was a bend in the river. He guided the boat to a small natural harbor and dropped anchor. They jumped onto the soft grassy bank, and Derrick pulled the boat up closer. He got the picnic basket and a large blanket from a storage bin in the boat.

"My, my. We came prepared." Talia grabbed the cooler with soft drinks.

"I didn't want my city pal to suffer too much." He grinned at her. "Guess what else? Biodegradable wet wipes."

"My prince!" Talia said, then burst into laughter.

"I'm going to make sure you're comfy and well fed. This way." He led her to a clearing.

Talia spread the blanket on the grass. Then they sat down and unpacked their lunch. They teased and laughed as they ate. Derrick felt as though they'd slipped back in time, yet it was so much better. Now they were adults having a relaxing day out, not kids escaping from bleak daily lives. Still, even on this sunny, early-fall day, dark clouds waited in the distance. He thought of Monette's case file in the locked drawer of his desk back at the office. Something in his expression must have changed. Talia wiped her hands after finishing a piece of chicken and tapped his knee.

"You've got something on your mind, Mr. D," she said. "Pass me a bottle of Barq's and talk it out."

He debated for ten seconds before deciding not to spoil the day. "I'm glad you're home."

"It's not all bad," Talia admitted. She drew her knees up and hugged them. "It's like . . . I built up an image of home as full of misery. I didn't remember the beauty of this place, the bayous and swamps."

"Especially when you're with someone special," he said. He moved over and put his arms around her.

"I never really thanked you, Derrick." Talia molded against his body with ease.

"For what?" Derrick tingled at the feel of her soft hair against his cheek. She smelled like fresh lavender and soap.

"I hurt you when I left to attend prep school and then college. I'm sorry."

"I could see what being in Rougon was doing to you, baby girl. I understood." Still, Derrick would not lie and say he was happy that she'd left.

She sighed. "And here I am."

"Safe." Derrick hugged her closer. He would do whatever it took to keep it that way.

Talia looked into his eyes. "I want to believe you, Derrick."

"I'm going to make sure you're safe, baby girl."

Hunger and fire ate at him until he felt dazed. He could only see her face and hear the whisper-soft sound of her breathing. Talia was the most beautiful woman in the world to him. In that moment she was the only woman in the world. Thick eyelashes framed her lovely brown eyes. Her full sensuous lips parted, inviting him to taste, and he accepted. Derrick moaned when she allowed his tongue to taste hers. She said his name softly, and all restraint was blown away.

Derrick caressed her breasts, enjoying the full round shape of them through the cotton fabric. They kissed each other harder and with urgency. Slowly they eased down onto the blanket until he was on top of her. With one hand he unbuttoned her blouse. The other hand rubbed the silky, warm skin on her thighs. She tilted her head back as she managed to pull the top off her shoulders. Derrick moaned again and kissed the exposed smooth mounds above the pink lace bra. Talia opened the front hook. In seconds she was topless.

He ached all over to be inside her. But he didn't want them to regret making love later. That would be more painful than not satisfying the overwhelming need that gripped him. With every bit of strength he could muster, he held back before touching her.

"I'm sure, Talia. Are you?"

She stroked his face with one hand. "Yes," she murmured.

For a long time he held her, overcome with joy. He wanted to melt into her velvety brown skin. Derrick closed his eyes and buried his face against her breast. Cuddling was soon not enough. The hunger pushed him on. Slowly he licked each firm chocolate peak. In a fever they managed to undress each other. He didn't remember how and didn't care. All that mattered was that she lay naked beneath him.

Talia gently closed one hand around his erection. She kissed his face and neck. Her fingers teased the taut skin until Derrick cried out in pleasure.

"Let me inside you now!" he pleaded.

She let out a low throaty laugh. "I want to play with you a little longer."

"You're trying to kill me, woman," he groaned when her fingers tightened then eased, tightened then eased.

"Not a big strong man like you, baby."

Talia nibbled his earlobe. Then she traced a line of fire down his chest with her tongue. Derrick gasped when she licked his nipples and squeezed his buttocks with her free hand. Derrick tenderly pried her legs apart and entered her slowly. Penetrating her felt like sinking into a tight, hot, satin glove. He lay still, shuddering at the powerful shock to his body and soul. Both arms wrapped around him, Talia rocked her hips slowly while whispering to him.

He answered, though his words didn't make sense. All he knew was that he needed to feel her more if that was possible. His rhythm matched hers as they moved against each other. Though he tried, he couldn't speak. All he could do was cry out again and again as he dug his fingers into her thighs. After only a few more seconds of the delicious torture, Derrick thrust inside her again and again. Out of control. He couldn't stop. From a far-off place he heard his own voice shouting her name and a stream of words that were disconnected. With one sharp plunge he came. Seconds later Talia screamed as she ground her pelvis against him. Impossibly his pleasure spiked higher. They moaned together, moved slower, until they lay in each other's arms, breathless. A breeze brushed their sweaty bodies.

"We must have lost our minds. Some fishermen might have walked right up on us." She kissed his shoulders as she spoke.

"Too bad." Derrick pressed his face against her breast. "I couldn't have stopped if they'd set the grass on fire."

"I think we did." Talia let out a husky laugh.

He raised his head to glance around them. They were indeed alone, blissfully isolated in their own world. Derrick rested his head against her body again with a sigh of happiness. "Yeah, we sure did. Let's do it again soon."

Talia laughed and hugged him tightly. They lay together for a few moments more before she spoke. "Derrick?"

"Yes, baby." He snuggled against her.

"I'm hungry again," she murmured in a sexy voice.

"What? You ate half a chicken," Derrick teased. "Ow!" he yelled, when she slapped his bottom.

"Get up and feed me, man!"

Derrick raised himself on one elbow. "Look here, woman—"

He broke off when he gazed at her lying next to him. Her lovely honey almond skin shimmered in the rich fall sunlight.

"Well?" Talia stretched like a sleek cat. A sly smile tugged at her mouth.

The little devil knew exactly what effect she had on him! "Your wish is my command."

They dressed and washed up, using the moist towelettes. Derrick discovered he was even hungrier than Talia. As they finished the last of the chicken and French loaf, he wiped his mouth with a paper napkin.

"It doesn't get much better than this." Derrick shook his head. "Yes, indeed."

Talia laughed out loud. "You found a way to combine all your favorite sports in one afternoon."

"I like to multitask just like you fast-lane city folk." He grinned at her.

"Cut the simple country boy act, Derrick Guillory. You're no hick." Talia poked a finger into his chest as she spoke.

"Thank you, ma'am."

She smiled then sat silent for a few seconds. "What next?"

"I don't know, Talia," he admitted. "Having you back in my life is all that matters at this moment. I can't see into the next few weeks if you decide to leave."

"Derrick, I have decided," she said. Talia looked away from his gaze.

"Then I want to make the most of what we have right now. I won't ask for more than you're willing to give."

"I don't think it's fair to you," she replied quietly.

Derrick reached out and touched a stray tendril of her thick hair. "I know what's coming, and I'm willing to deal with it."

She put her arms around his waist and rested her head on his shoulder. "I'm loving what we have right now, too."

They pushed aside thoughts of "what if" by silent mutual agreement. Nonetheless, the file on his desk stayed at the back of his mind.

Chapter 7

∞

Monette walked into the visiting room of the prison. She wore a pair of faded blue jeans and a white T-shirt with the letters LCIW stenciled on it in black. She sat down and smiled at him. James Rand clasped his hands together on top of the table between them. He waited until the female security guard closed the door on her way out.

"What haven't you told me, Monette?" he said before she could speak.

Monette didn't lose the easy, charming smile. She tilted her head to one side and brushed back her hair, the gesture of a woman who knew men found her attractive. Despite her age and being in prison, she was still pretty. Her black hair, peppered with strands of gray, was pulled back into a single thick ponytail. Only a few lines were etched at the corners of expressive eyes the color of black coffee. Yet the smooth pecan brown skin showed signs of a hard life. She paid particular attention to her appearance for a male visitor. This morning had been no different. A friendly male guard had allowed her to put on makeup. So she'd assessed her flaws and assets the way she'd done for years. It was survival.

"What are you talkin' about, Professor?" Monette put on her best guileless expression.

"The visitors' log is public information. If you're talking to the press, I should know."

"It's normal for reporters to show up here around parole board time. You know, sniffing out those 'Whatever happened to' stories. Nothing but filler for a slow news week." Monette lounged back in her chair.

"You're good. That's what got you in here," Jim said, his tone sharp as a needle.

Monette's large brown eyes narrowed. "Now look, just because you're helping me out is no reason to come in here insulting me. I—"

"No, you look." Jim leaned forward. "Now is not the time to pull a fast one. Not with me."

Monette smoothly switched gears. With a soft sigh, her tough cynical expression melted away. "I'm sorry, Jim. Being locked up in here gets to me."

"I can do the best job for you if we're honest with each other. Two-way street, Monette." Jim stared at her. "I've told you we've got a big job getting you released."

"Yeah, I figured as much." Her pink-polished fingertips clicked against the cheap laminated tabletop as she tapped it. "Every damn body in here is whinin' they didn't do it. Well, some of us ain't lyin', Jim."

"I know, Monette." Jim softened his tone. "I understand your frustration."

"You're a nice guy, Jim. I ain't attackin' you or nothin'. But you got no idea what it's like." Monette clenched one hand into a fist. They sat in silence, and after five minutes she relaxed it.

"Being convicted for smuggling cocaine when you didn't do it is a nightmare." Jim placed his hand over hers.

Monette cleared her throat and lifted her chin. "You

didn't come to listen to a lot of cryin' the blues. Let's talk about my case."

"It's okay if you need to get it out," Jim said quietly.

Monette gazed at him with affection. She'd seen that look before and used it more than once. Part of her had reformed. She didn't want to hurt one more good man trying to help her. The other part of her was very practical. Jim needed to concentrate on her case. He was falling and didn't even know it.

"I've got a social worker poking around my brain for that. You should hear the sob stories in those group therapy sessions." Monette withdrew her hand from his. "Lotta poor-ass excuses for doin' what we wanted to at the time is what I say." She lounged back in her chair again.

He gave one curt nod as if he understood. "Okay, then tell me about this reporter from the *Times-Picayune*."

"AnnaLise Theroux? She's a real smart young woman." Monette blinked hard as a hitch caught her heart unexpectedly. "Reminds me of . . ." Her voice trailed off.

"Who?"

Monette wore a slight smile and pushed away a memory. "Myself if I hadn't gone down the wrong road."

"I know about AnnaLise Theroux. She's an award-winning investigative reporter. What I don't understand is why she's interested in your case." Jim raised a dark eyebrow at Monette. "She usually goes after political corruption stories."

"The DA's Office messed up on my case like I told you. She asked questions about that. Especially since the attorney general was the prosecutor back then." Monette kept close to the truth. She didn't want Jim to know too much. He might be scared off.

"Winn Barron is sure to take an interest in being called incompetent or worse." Jim rubbed his chin.

"Interest hell," Monette retorted. "He's gonna be pissed."

"Which is why we need to have all the facts in this thing. Barron has political aspirations."

"He wants to run for governor," Monette murmured.

Jim glanced at her sharply. "Yes, he does. How did you know that?"

Monette lifted a shoulder. "Hey, I've got nothing but time. I read the papers, and I can read between the lines. The guy is always schmoozing with party leaders and spouting off about state government."

He nodded with a smile. "Very astute. I shouldn't forget that you don't miss much."

"Damn right. Especially when it affects me getting out of this place." Monette swept one hand around at the drab walls.

"But don't give Theroux another interview without checking with me first, okay?" Jim peered at her. "Promise me, Monette. You don't want to mess up your chance of getting paroled."

"Yes, sir. I promise on my honor as a Girl Scout." Monette grinned as she crossed her heart.

"You were never a Girl Scout," Jim quipped, and opened his leather briefcase.

"I wanted to be, just as good," she tossed back.

"Let's get down to business. I've reviewed the file on those witnesses. There were all kinds of holes in their testimony."

"Sure, three drug dealers tryin' to stay out of prison. They cut a deal." Monette gave a snort of contempt. "Some days I think I got what I deserved for hangin' out with scum. But then I was scum, too."

"Stop that kind of talk," Jim said tersely. "You've

done a lot of hard work to change in the last sixteen years."

"I have," she agreed. "But I can't lie to myself or you, Jim. I probably would have done the same thing to get a hit."

"Which is how you're different. Those folks never changed. You have insight." Jim sorted through the papers in an expanding folder.

"Yeah. So, did you find my old buddies?"

Jim frowned. "It's hard, Monette. Addicts don't exactly lead stable lives."

"They could all be dead by now. Overdose, AIDS, or . . . murdered," she said, almost whispering the last word.

"I've got a few leads. One has been in and out of treatment programs. Maybe she's just back in one. Her family has pretty much cut her loose, so they haven't been helpful."

"Who is that?" Monette sat straight.

"Vicki Thompson. I've been able to track her movements using arrest records for the last seven years at least." Jim held up one sheet of notes scribbled on yellow legal paper.

Monette's expression darkened with disappointment. "Vicki won't know too much. That poor white girl was mostly wasted out of her mind. No, we've got to find Andre or I'Eisha. They know the real deal."

"Don't get discouraged. We're making progress. Just think of how far we've come in the last six months."

"Yeah, you're right." Monette smiled sadly then she brightened. "Hey, Vicki was crazy about Andre. She might know where he is. I think she even had his baby."

"Excellent lead." Jim wrote on another sheet of his pad. "The state may have gone after him for child support." He glanced up. "We're on our way, Monette. Just don't keep things from me," he said.

"Got ya, Professor."

Monette gazed at the dark hair as he bent his head. He talked and made notes at the same time. She had to make hard decisions to protect people she cared about. Still he'd have to know about Winn Barron eventually. Good timing was the key, she mused.

Mama Rose looked fit and happy. Her iron gray hair was brushed back neatly, with short curls framing her cocoa brown face. She wore a pink sweater over a white short-sleeved shell and a floral skirt. When Talia hugged her neck and kissed her forehead she caught the scent of gardenia perfume.

"Well, you seem to have blossomed in this, and I quote, 'Godforsaken rathole.' " Talia grinned at her.

"So maybe I was a bit melodramatic. Who wouldn't be? I was kidnapped out of my home—"

"Excuse me, you were rescued by emergency technicians after you foolishly failed to follow medical advice," Talia corrected.

"Practically locked away—" Mama Rose pressed on.

"You couldn't move because you were so sick. And by the way, pickled pork cooked in your mustard greens isn't on your diet."

"Karl must have squealed," Mama Rose said with a scowl. "He didn't complain when he had his size thirteens parked under my dinner table.

"You know better." Talia sat down and crossed her legs.

Mama Rose made a sharp hissing sound before she went on. "The point is, once I got over the initial shock I accepted my situation."

"Boy, did you ever. Tai chi classes on Tuesday mornings, quilting club on Thursday afternoons, and lunch with the girls on Fridays." Talia ticked off the activities on her fingers. "I haven't tried to keep up with the weekend."

"Don't exaggerate. I go to church on Sunday as usual." Mama Rose smoothed down the front of her sweater.

"Yes. I hear a certain gentleman from the assisted-living duplex has been your guest." Talia pressed her lips together when Mama Rose's eyes widened.

"My Lord! You've got spies watching my every move!" You've got some nerve, missy. I'll bet it was my neighbor Ernestine."

"I think it's cute," Talia said.

"Cute my eye. Talking to me like I'm in my second childhood," she grumbled.

"Okay, I'll stop teasing you."

"You just love saying 'I told you so.' "

"No, I'm thrilled that you're getting better every day and enjoying life again. That's the truth." Talia felt tears forming in her eyes. "I love you, Mama."

Mama Rose's petulant expression melted to a gentle maternal smile. "I love you, too, baby. I'm sorry for being such a grumpy old lady at first."

"You were scared, and so was I." Talia sniffed to keep from crying. "I need you to take good care of yourself," she said quietly.

"Don't worry, sugar. I'm going to hang around until you give me that first grandbaby. Speaking of which, how is Derrick?"

Talia blushed. "I'm not having any crying little tyrants, thank you. And what does Derrick have to do with it anyway?"

Mama Rose looked smug. "I have my sources.

Ernestine tells me how often he's been at the house. 'All hours' is the phrase I recall." She arched an eyebrow at Talia.

"I can't believe her," Talia burst out. "That cute little face under snow-white hair hides a sneak."

"Ernestine is an equal opportunity gossip." Mama Rose laughed. "Now tell me about this love affair."

"Mama!"

"Oh please, Talia. Don't look so shocked. I know where babies come from, you know." She threw back her head and laughed harder when Talia squirmed.

"We were talking about you," Talia mumbled.

Mama Rose's laughter trailed off, and she dabbed at her eyes with a tissue. She took a deep breath.

"It's not a crime to be happy. You were always too intense. I'm glad you let loose."

"I'm not planning on anything permanent. No picket fence, no dog, no SUV, and definitely no kids." Talia twisted a corner of her blue tunic blouse.

"Why not?" Mama Rose put her head to one side and studied her.

"Because for one thing I don't believe in fairy-tale domestic life. Second, I'm not mommy material." Talia brushed back her hair. "I like working hard and being free to travel."

"I see."

"Derrick knows how I feel. In fact, he feels the same way," Talia said. She heard the defensive note in her own voice.

"Does he?" Mama Rose pursed her lips.

"Don't give me the look," Talia snapped.

"What look?"

"You know what look." Talia lifted her nose in the air. "You happen to be wrong. I'm not running from the truth."

"I didn't say—"

"You didn't have to," Talia broke in.

"Oh, the *look* said it all?" Mama Rose wore the shadow of a wise smile.

"Okay, we care about each other. A lot," Talia added, when Mama Rose didn't respond. "But we've got an understanding."

"An understanding. I see."

"Yes. I'm going back to D.C." Talia avoided her gaze. "We can still see each other. Derrick travels there on business."

"A few times a year will be enough?" Mama Rose lifted a shoulder. "Hmmm."

"I've got my career to consider. Besides, I can't live in Rougon." Talia jumped up and went to the window.

"I don't see why you'd have to live in Rougon. Louisiana is a big state."

Talia fingered the lacy curtain that framed the window. She stared at the manicured lawn of the courtyard. Patio tables with wide umbrellas were scattered around the grass. More were on a covered paved terrace. Residents sat outside enjoying the day. The peaceful scene reminded her of what she wanted. Her life in Washington was hectic, but orderly. The only drama she had to deal with was on the Hill. That's the way she liked it. Talia wanted a simple, even dull, personal life. Dull was a welcome change from her childhood. Even her breakup with Jarrod had lacked drama. He'd simply accepted the distance between them and backed away.

"Derrick lives this crazy cops and robbers thing working for the DA. I don't know why he wants to get involved in all the mess people make of their lives," she said.

"His career is truth and justice," Mama Rose said, her voice firm. "And just as important to him as yours is to you."

"I know. I shouldn't criticize his choice. He's trying to do what he thinks is right."

"Derrick is a good man. He's done a lot for our young people. He works with a youth program to keep kids out of gangs."

Talia crossed her arms. She no longer saw the blue skies or sunshine. "The bottom line is there won't be a storybook ending. But then there never is."

"You're not Monette, Talia. Just because she made mistakes as a mother doesn't mean you will," Mama Rose said.

"So did her mother. Her sisters haven't been nominated for parenting awards either. Anyway, let's drop it." She came back and sat down again.

"Baby, I hate to see you pushing away happiness. Even Monette would tell you the same thing. You haven't repeated her life, not at all. She wants the best for you."

"I'm glad she's reformed." Talia crossed her legs. "Instant Mother of the Year. Just add hot water and stir."

"Stop it. She is still your mother. You have unfinished business, young lady." Mama Rose's tone deepened.

"No, I don't." Talia returned her gaze. "I don't hate Monette, Mama Rose, but I don't want her in my life again."

"Coming to terms with your mother means you need to talk to her." Mama Rose raised a hand to forestall Talia's protest. "Listen to me. I've lived a few more years than you, so I do know a little something."

"Yes, but—"

"I said listen," Mama Rose cut in sternly. When Talia clamped her mouth shut, she continued. "I know she's done a lot of terrible things, but you have to forgive her. You can't move on emotionally until you do."

"Monette is the queen of getting people to let her off the hook," Talia said sharply. "She's got all of you feeling sorry for her."

"Forgiving her doesn't mean you forget what she's done. It's not a magic formula that will make the pain she caused go away. Sure, let Monette know she's accountable for the life she led. I'm not even saying you have to keeping seeing her if you don't want to." Mama Rose watched Talia closely as silence stretched between them.

"I wouldn't know what to say if I went to see her." Talia pulled on a tassel at the end of the small throw pillow.

"What is it you're scared of, Talia?"

"I'm not scared." Talia shook her head hard. "I just don't want one more dramatic scene."

"You don't want to be let down one more time," Mama Rose said quietly. "She's hurt you too many times before."

"Lies. I'm so sick of her lying to me that everything will be alright," Talia blurted out. "Well, everything didn't turn out right. In fact, life always got worse."

Talia thought back to her tenth birthday, the turning point, when she started to realize Monette wouldn't change. She'd waited for hours in the visiting room at the bleak child welfare agency office. Dressed in her best dress, she'd looked forward to seeing Monette for weeks. They were supposed to have their own party at the local McDonald's. Her then foster mother, a stern woman named Hattie Gray, had worn an "I told you so" expression. Talia hadn't cared about presents or even ice cream and cake. She'd needed to see her mother. The ride back to Miss Hattie's house had been agonizing.

"You're not a little girl now. She's not in control of your life. You can walk away, go back to D.C." Mama Rose leaned forward. "The difference is you can feel good that you forgave her. Even if she hasn't changed, you have."

"No, I haven't!" Talia said. Her throat felt tight with emotion. "Deep down I'm still the little girl that wants her mama to be there for her."

"The woman in you will have to accept Monette for who she is." Mama Rose sat back again. "Lord knows I have. You know what a hard case I can be."

"Yes indeed, Mrs. Travis." Talia wore a half smile.

"I got to know a lot about Monette from her letters." Mama Rose cleared her throat. "And the times I visited her at the prison."

"What did you just say?"

"That's right, I went to the prison."

"I'm stunned, speechless." Talia blinked at her in surprised. "You never criticized her in front of me, but I know how you felt about the drugs and the men."

"If I'm going to spout off about Christian love, then I need to practice what I preach. Monette had a hard life."

"I know, but that's not an excuse." Talia frowned.

"She doesn't use it as one. Did you know she was raped when she was seven years old?"

Talia's stomach tightened and she felt ill. "Did Monette tell you that? She's been known to play people."

"Her oldest sister told me. Monette only made some vague reference to being mistreated as a kid." Mama Rose sighed. "I suspected as much. I had a lot of training in that area as a foster parent. She had all the signs. The stealing, wild behavior with men, and using drugs."

"All the more reason she should have protected us,"

Talia argued. Still she felt a sharp stab of sympathy for the seven-year-old Monette.

"Like I said, she has to own up to her mistakes. Still, there's a lot you need to know about her," Mama Rose said. "Her life didn't just begin when you were born."

"You're saying I should get to know her past to deal with my own." Talia glanced at Mama Rose.

"I think knowing more about your mother will help you understand." Mama Rose stood.

"Maybe so," Talia said. She stared ahead at the wall, but her thoughts were miles away, at the women's prison.

"I'll make us some lemonade to go with those cheese curls I baked. Then we can look at the movie." She patted Talia's shoulder as she walked past her to the small kitchen.

Talia grabbed her hand. "You're one special lady, Mama. Now about you coming to live with me . . ." She looked up at her.

"Forget that," Mama Rose said promptly. "I'm a warm weather creature. It snows where you live. Besides, I've got my land. Of course you could stay here in my house."

"If you really need me to stay with you, I will." Talia held on to her hand.

"I've been thinking I don't need that big house. But it's perfect for a growing family." Mama Rose's dark eyes twinkled.

"You cut that out!" Talia let go of her hand.

"I'm just saying—" Mama Rose wore an innocent expression.

"Yeah, yeah. Go get the lemonade." Talia got up and turned on the television. She put a tape in the VCR. "I'm not even going there again with you."

"What is wrong with Rougon? I know it's a little

town, but you're near Baton Rouge. You could do consulting with all kinds of companies."

Talia stood very still, with her back to Mama Rose. "I can't live with the memories here," she said.

"Derrick could smooth all those bad memories away. He'd move the world to make you happy." Mama Rose came back into the living room. "And I'll tell you something else—"

She spun around, wearing a forced smile that made her cheeks ache. "Mama, you've given me enough to think about with Monette. Harass me about my love life later, okay?"

Mama Rose opened her mouth, then closed it for a few seconds before she spoke. "You're right, baby. I'm throwing out my opinions like cheap Mardi Gras beads at a parade. You've got enough on your hands for now. I'm making things worse."

"You're just making me feel loved. Like you've done for the last twenty years." Talia crossed to Mama Rose and pecked her cheek. "You're precious."

Mama Rose blushed with pleasure. "Fresh-squeezed lemonade and cheese curls coming up. I can't wait to see that suspense movie."

"Me too. Just like old times, huh?" Talia felt a flood of warmth at the memory of feeling safe and nurtured as a wounded little girl.

"Just like old times, baby." Mama Rose hummed a tune as she walked to the kitchen.

Unfinished business, Mama Rose had said. Her foster mother had no idea what she was asking Talia to dredge up. Still, Monette at least owed her some answers. Maybe it was time she faced her fears and her mother. Talia stared at the telephone. She had the phone number to the prison memorized even though she'd never used it.

"Get to know the real Monette," Talia whispered.

* * *

Layers of smoky dark blue, orange, and pink made the horizon look like a beautiful oil painting. Talia and Derrick were on the porch of his small house on False River. They sat on a cypress swing suspended from the ceiling. Neither had spoken for a long time, content to hear only the soft creaking as the swing moved back and forth. A few boats passed by with their motors buzzing like distant giant insects. The evening air smelled of wet earth, a slight scent of fish and grass. An aroma of spices floated from the open door.

"Your specialty smells wonderful." Talia snuggled into the crook of his arm.

Derrick rubbed his cheek against the top of her head. "I hope the taste lives up to the buildup."

"I haven't had homemade jambalaya in a long time." Talia looked up at him with trusting eyes. "Thanks, babe."

"Wait until you taste it," Derrick teased.

"I meant for making me feel safe here. You even kept me from stressing over Monette. I know what's going on with you, mister."

He tensed. "I don't understand."

"You don't mention my mother or the past. I can concentrate on Mama Rose. And us." Talia kissed his chin.

His conscience pricked at him for several minutes before he spoke. He'd put off talking to her about the parole hearing far too long.

"I'm going to spoil the hero image."

Talia laughed. "I don't see how."

"You will in a few seconds." Derrick gazed at her when she moved away from him.

Talia wore a serious expression. "So tell me what's up."

"The parole board meets in about a month. Monette

will be one of the cases they consider." Derrick rubbed his face hard. "Our office is involved."

Talia moved farther away. "You're going to help them present evidence that she should stay in prison?"

"Let me explain first," Derrick said quickly. "We—"

"Don't worry," she cut in. "I think Monette got what she deserved."

Chapter 8

∞

"You can't mean what you just said." Derrick stared at her in dismay.

"Exactly when do they meet?" Talia said.

"October 21, four weeks to the day."

"I see." Talia took both his hands in hers. "I'll be gone by then. But I'm not running from you. We can still be together. There are so many opportunities for you in D.C."

"One thing at a time, baby girl. First your mother," Derrick said.

"I've heard more than enough about the power of forgiveness. Don't bother." Talia stood and walked to the edge of the porch.

"You're running away from Monette. Baby, it's time to stop running—period."

"I've never told anybody just how bad things were at times," Talia said in a hushed voice.

Derrick went to Talia and put his arms around her waist. They both watched a bass boat chug along, leaving a wake of white waves behind. Neither spoke for a time.

"You didn't have to tell me. I was there. I saw," he said finally.

Talia rested against his chest. "That law professor Jim Rand is going to put on an aggressive defense."

Derrick tightened his embrace. "Winn Barron is planning to get involved, Talia."

"Why is the attorney general interested?"

"He was the DA who got the conviction. Monette and three others went on trial at the same time."

She turned to face him without leaving the circle of his arms. "So you've got access to her file."

He nodded slowly. "Yes."

"You've read it?"

"I just started reviewing the first sections. It's pretty extensive. I didn't realize the investigation had gone on for over seven months before her arrest. Monette was hanging with rough characters. Andre Louis and Demetrius Nance were pretty big dealers back then. They were partying, taking trips to Florida, and the Caribbean. No doubt making drug connections."

"I don't want to know," Talia said quickly.

"Talia, I really think you should at least listen to—"

"No." She shook her head until her soft long hair bounced.

"Monette could be innocent. She was arm candy for the dealers, and they probably provided her with cocaine, but I just don't see any evidence she was smuggling drugs or even helping them. What if she's been in prison all these years for a crime she didn't commit?"

"She was on drugs at the time. Everyone knew it. The other guys they caught were her buddies." Talia frowned. "I remember one of them hanging around the house."

"Okay, she was on drugs. But she wasn't into drug smuggling," Derrick insisted. "We both know Monette wasn't selling coke."

"She was in the car with those guys. They came

back from Florida with cocaine hidden in a cooler stuffed in raw meat." Talia let out a bitter laugh. "Not exactly the smartest plan."

"Monette says they picked her up at a nightclub. The Crystal Palace, remember it?" Derrick frowned. "She used to hang out there all the time."

"Of course I remember that dump. I went there looking for her often enough."

"Right, so her story makes sense. She didn't know anything about the coke that night. She was just looking to party. They told her they could hook her up after they settled a little business."

Talia let out a harsh hiss. "She told a lot of versions about how she ended up in the car. Monette wasn't going to admit she knew about the coke."

"I don't think she did it, Talia. I really don't." Derrick brushed her hair.

"Wait a minute." Talia frowned at him. "Damn it, you can't afford to let her pull you into this," she said low.

"Talia—"

"I don't want you to get involved. She's got this big-time law professor working on it." Talia gripped both his arms. "Stay out of this whole thing with Monette, Derrick."

He could see fear in her brown eyes. "Larry wants me to prepare a summary for Winn Barron."

"I don't understand why the attorney general should care." Talia stared into his eyes. "Just how big was this drug operation?"

"I'm not sure yet, but Barron has political ambitions."

"I don't give a damn about him. Promise me you'll just give them a summary and nothing else." Talia tugged on his arms for emphasis. "Please!"

"I want to know the truth, too, Talia."

"We know the truth where Monette is concerned,"

Talia snapped. "You're safe as long as she's in prison," she said.

"Oh, baby." Derrick pulled her into his arms. "Is that what you think?"

"If they dig enough, you don't know what they'll find," Talia whispered.

His heart turned over at the tremor in her voice. "I've told you not to worry about me. What happened is gone."

"Unsolved cases are reopened all the time." Talia gazed at him steadily. "How can you be sure?"

"Earl's disappearance was connected to a drug deal gone bad. He stole money and drugs from a big-time distributor."

"Tell me you didn't tamper with an investigation." Talia searched his face anxiously.

"I won't tell you any details, but it's okay." Derrick tried to sound as reassuring as he could.

Talia shook free of his embrace. "You should have told the police. She did it, not you."

"I couldn't do that back then any more than I can do it now." Derrick reached for her.

She dodged his attempt to close the gap between them. "You're into drama just as much as she is!" Talia tossed out the words like an accusation. "Look at what you're doing. A quiet life isn't enough for you, is it?"

"Larry would have known something was strange if I'd refused to read Monette's file. I've prepared reports on old cases over a dozen times since I took the job." Derrick did not get angry.

"Yes, that job. You could have been a lawyer, anything else. You're smart." Talia paced. "Instead, you're up to your neck in criminals all day long."

"I'm not in danger."

Derrick could smell the fear radiating from her.

Talia wanted to be far away from the kind of street life Monette had inflicted on her.

Talia stopped in front of him. "I can't live like that anymore, Derrick. I *won't* live like that."

"Come here," Derrick said quietly. He held out his arms. "Talia, please."

She went to him slowly, as if afraid of him. Derrick put his arms around her again, but loosely. He wanted her to know he would not force her into anything. Talia let go of a ragged sigh and rested her head on his shoulder. Dusk had fallen, and the sound of insects in the night seemed oddly comforting to him. He rocked her and softly hummed a Creole tune, his lips close to her ear. It was a song of love they'd often danced to years ago.

"I feel like a terrible monster is waiting behind every tree, every bush," Talia whispered.

"We can love it away."

Derrick kissed her forehead, her cheeks, and her lips as if to prove his words. Talia squeezed her arms around his waist as if begging to be convinced. He took her hand and led her inside to his bedroom.

"The food will burn. We'd better—" Talia started for the kitchen.

"The slow cooker will keep dinner for us."

Derrick sank onto the queen-size bed. Talia looked into his eyes as she lifted her long, full denim skirt. She straddled his lap. Derrick rubbed his face against the red sweater she wore, relishing the full breasts beneath the fabric. His hands eased under it to caress the smooth skin of her midsection. They kissed long and hard.

"Touch me here," she whispered as she guided his hand.

Derrick cupped her breast, his thumb rubbing the

hard nub. Talia whimpered sweet and low in the back of her throat until he could feel the vibration in her body. He found the front hook of her red bra and pushed it aside. She lifted her arms so he could pull the sweater over her head. His tongue circled each nipple.

Their lovemaking started slowly, building like a fire that had smoldered for hours. Talia kissed his neck and shoulders until Derrick thought he would explode. They undressed each other in stages. Wearing only silk bikini panties, Talia rubbed against his erection.

"Baby, baby, baby." She sighed.

Derrick pushed aside the filmy fabric. She lifted her hips and lowered herself onto him. He lay back on the bed, both palms flat against her breasts. Now that they were joined, the slow rhythm gave way to urgent need. Talia rolled and rocked him until Derrick lost touch with every other sensation. Nothing else mattered except holding on to her forever. His head filled with words that he wanted to say but couldn't. A slow, all-consuming heat pounded through him. Warm, pulsating flesh lifted him up to heaven until his entire body stiffened. Talia came and pulled Derrick over the edge into a powerful orgasm moments later. They thrashed against each other, frantic to grab every ounce of pleasure they could. Both groaned as they came to rest finally.

Talia went limp across his body. "Derrick," she whispered.

"I know, baby. I know."

Each time they touched, his responsibility tripled to make all his words of reassurance come true.

"Good to see the old place, Larry."

Winn Barron strode forward with his hand out. Derrick took a good look at the man he'd only seen in newspaper photos. Just over six feet tall, his brawny body had turned soft around the middle. His brown hair was styled and combed back. He still had the polished good looks that had carried him through two election campaigns.

"Made a few changes, Winn." Larry grinned and shook his hand firmly. "We got the budget to redecorate and upgrade our technology."

"You were the right man to take this office into the twenty-first century." Winn glanced around. "I see you've got new staff. Put my old standbys like Jerry Hines out to pasture, eh?"

"Mrs. Jenkins retired six months after you did. I don't think she was very impressed with me." Larry laughed. "Come on in, buddy." He slapped Winn on the shoulder and ushered him into his office.

"Humph! Thank goodness that old hen retired. I didn't think I'd ever get promoted," Kelsey said once the door closed.

"Before my time," Derrick murmured. He stared at the closed door.

"Be grateful. We used to call her a few choice names at least once a day." Kelsey gave a wicked laugh. "There's a darn good reason I'm the only staff left from those days."

"Really?" Cheryl forgot about typing and turned from her computer.

"I started the same year Larry first got elected. Mrs. Jenkins was seventy-two, and the others weren't that much younger." Kelsey shook her head. "They squealed like stuck pigs when Larry mentioned computers."

"I heard most of them were relatives of Barron's pals," Cheryl said in a low voice.

"Half the time they didn't know what the heck they were doing." Kelsey rolled her eyes.

"You're a mess, Kelsey." Cheryl chuckled as she turned back to her work.

"Hey, I tell it like it is, sugar."

The women continued to share gossip about the office under Winn Barron. Derrick paid close attention while he reviewed notes of two interviews he'd conducted the day before. Using one finger, he tapped the keyboard of the computer on his desk, adding comments. His ability to catch details while doing another task served him well once more. Winn Barron had a fondness for flirting and liked to milk the old boy network. Kelsey joked that he could keep one hand on the telephone and the other on his secretary's rear end.

"Sounds like this was a more colorful place to work back in those days," Derrick said casually. He pressed the key to print pages.

"Colorful is right. I—" Kelsey broke off when Larry's door opened again.

"Derrick, step in here a minute," Larry called out.

"Sure," he said.

Winn Barron sat in one of the large leather chairs. He looked in charge even though the office was no longer his. Up close, Derrick, noticed the unhealthy flush to his wide face. Barron had the red skin and large pores of a heavy drinker. His breathing was audible. Derrick smelled the faint odor of cigar tobacco when they shook hands.

"The best investigator we've ever had, Winn. Derrick Guillory," Larry said. He sat down at his desk and rocked his chair.

"Hello, sir." Derrick stood to the right of Larry's desk near the window.

"You must be good. Larry is damn hard to please." Winn gave a curt nod. "You from around here?"

"My family moved from Lakeland to Rougon when I was seven."

"Sit down, son." Winn slapped the arm of the chair next to him. "You're tall, and I'm going to get tired looking up. Played basketball I'll bet."

Derrick pushed down his gut reaction of irritation. "Yes."

"Got a scholarship, too. Right?" Winn wore a faint smile.

"I did."

"What did you do after your eligibility ended?" Winn glanced at him.

"Got my degree and left," Derrick replied in bland voice.

"Derrick wasn't just another jock. He actually studied," Larry put in.

"Humph, that's the exception for those kids." Winn looked at him with a bit more interest before he turned back to Larry.

Derrick knew what he meant. *Typical,* Derrick thought as he watched him. Here was a member of the Southern gentry used to getting what he wanted.

"How are things in Baton Rouge?" Larry said. He tilted his chair.

"That damn woman!" Winn's thick eyebrows formed a straight line above his watery brown eyes.

"Remember your blood pressure." Larry pursed his lips in amusement. "She's doing her job as chairwoman of the Judiciary Committee C."

"Like hell! Eloise Bertrand just likes pushing my buttons," Winn thundered. "Senator Jackson has hired some smart-assed consultant out of Washington. I can't believe you buy into their crap."

"Mandatory sentencing, like most worthy ideas, started out good. But now we know the unintended negative effects." Larry kept his tone reasonable despite Barron's fearsome expression.

"Hell I say!" Winn sat forward suddenly. His eyes

narrowed. "Like that crew going before the parole board next month. Look me in the eye and tell me they deserve to get out."

"So they weren't model citizens." Larry lifted his hands. "But we've got to use our resources wisely."

"You've been hanging around liberals too damn long." He glanced at Derrick, then back at Larry. "I'll tell you one thing, the people agree with me."

"I'm not the only conservative who has reexamined this issue. Why spend all our time reeling in small fry while the sharks swim away?" Larry sat up straight and looked his mentor in the eye. "It's a matter of working smarter, not harder, when it comes to catching the bad guys. I'd rather use tax dollars to lock up major distributors."

"You get the big fish using the small ones as bait," Winn said, jabbing his forefinger in the air at Larry.

"Maybe, but often as not the big fish just let them take the fall and keep swimming," Larry countered.

"Or scare them into taking the fall," Derrick put in. "The last couple of years we've had a tough time getting them to take deals. A lot of these guys and women wind up dead. Even in jail."

"Look at the Vincent case. We sent him to prison for life and shut down the biggest drug network in Avoyelles Parish." Winn talked to Larry as though Derrick hadn't spoken. "A coordinated effort between the state police and sheriff departments in three parishes."

"True," Derrick said before Larry replied. "But Lloyd Vincent operated for six years before we got him. His conviction was the result of a change of focus, the same change that led us to realize mandatory sentencing doesn't help."

Barron turned to Derrick after a few moments of silence. "You seem to know a lot about the big picture for a part-time investigator."

"Derrick has a degree in criminal justice. He's gone to special Justice Department training seminars since I hired him." Larry nodded to Derrick. "And it's paid off for this office. He's looked over the files on those prisoners you called me about."

"I see." Barron studied Derrick with a less-than-happy expression. "And what do you think, son?"

Derrick maintained a cool pose despite Winn's intense stare. "The three men have long records, two have previous convictions for assault."

"Not exactly candidates for leniency," Larry said with a scowl.

"The other guy had multiple theft convictions, mostly petty stuff." Derrick looked back at Barron. "I think he was sacrificed by the big guys."

"He's scum," Barron shot back.

"The woman had a history of drug offenses, some were dismissed for lack of evidence," Derrick went on smoothly without mentioning Monette's name. "I understand she's hired Jim Rand to help her."

"The governor will take care of those law school social engineers," Barron said with a grim smile of satisfaction. "They blocked the opening of a huge Japanese plastics plant in St. James Parish. He's pissed, and I don't blame him. Rand and his crew cost this state much-needed jobs."

"So far his efforts to punish Tulane Law Center have backfired," Larry replied.

"Now these people are working to get drug dealers out of prison. Disgusting!" Barron's cheeks puffed up in outrage.

"Rand doesn't take on lost causes. He has reviewed the case and trial transcripts extensively." Derrick kept his casual pose. "There are a few points in her favor."

Barron's beady eyes narrowed to slits. "Such as."

"Her codefendants testified against her, but their accounts conflicted. Plus they had closer ties with the cocaine distributors." Derrick lifted a shoulder. "Just from what I've read she looks like the classic sacrificial lamb."

"The deals we made with those bums sickened my stomach, but they'll stand up to scrutiny," Barron said with an edge to his tone.

"All through the trial she repeatedly denied knowing the details of their operation. From her record she was always a user, not a player on the distribution end," Derrick went on in an even voice.

Larry rubbed his chin. "One of the guys went back to prison last year. He was on parole when the state police in St. Charles Parish stopped him. They found an automatic weapon in his Jeep Grand Cherokee."

"He's serving time," Derrick added. "Andre Louis hit another dealer who tried to stiff him. Because he took weapons and money, they sent him up for robbery."

"What does it matter? The point is she knew about his operation," Barron said.

"Knowing about it and being an integral part of the business are two very different things," Derrick said. His words caused Barron's cheeks to turn red.

"Listen to me, young man." Barron leaned forward and stabbed a thick forefinger at Derrick. "You've got one helluva nerve suggesting that I put together a sloppy prosecution!"

"Hey, Winn, cool off here." Larry shot from his chair and came around his desk. "Derrick isn't suggesting any such thing."

"Damn right he is!" Barron spat. "I was reciting criminal procedure while you were still in diapers."

"No one is questioning the fine work you did as district attorney. Right, Derrick? Certainly no one in this office." Larry glanced at Derrick with a frown.

"I'm identifying the likely points I think Rand will make." Derrick wondered at the man's fiery reaction.

"I assigned Derrick to review the files after you called," Larry said in an even voice. "That's what you wanted. We have to know what our opponent will do to counter his claims."

Barron huffed in silence for a few moments before he spoke. "My political enemies would like nothing better than to attack my record, Larry. You know that."

"Then we'll fight back with your excellent conviction rate. Derrick, tell us about the evidence against her." Larry raised one dark eyebrow as a subtle signal to smooth things over.

Derrick cleared his throat. "Ms. Victor was a known associate of the men involved. She traveled with them to Florida several times, and Jamaica."

"See?" Barron said loudly. "We tracked her running with Landry and another guy, can't remember his name. Doesn't matter he took off."

"I didn't see any other guy mentioned except the three that testified against her and Devon Landry." Derrick's gut tightened. Could he be talking about Earl?

"Some lowlife street dealer. These people are transients." Barron waved a hand. "I'm surprised we didn't get him. He hung out with the rest."

"The point is we think Rand has an uphill battle." Larry nodded to Derrick to go on.

"It won't be easy for sure. She's been denied every year because of her record," Derrick said.

"Of course," Winn said with grim satisfaction. "Once we gave them the facts they had to."

"This isn't the first time you've contacted the parole board about this case? I thought you needed to refresh your memory on the facts." Larry wore a puzzled expression.

"It's been years, man. Of course I don't remember every detail of every case." Winn stood and slapped Larry on the shoulder. "Good seeing you. You're doing a fine job."

"Thanks, Winn. You and Barbara should join Marilyn and me for dinner at the Ox Bow Friday night."

"Let me take a rain check on that one. I'll be down at my camp this weekend. I'll give you a call." Barron smiled at him.

"Sure thing," Larry said.

"You'll get me a report in say another week? Not that I'm rushing. I just like to be prepared."

"No problem, Winn," Larry replied.

"Good man. Look, Larry, there are no small cases to me." Barron stood tall and closed the one button of his dark brown suit jacket. "Even though I'm dealing with larger issues, public safety is still my number one concern."

"Which is why you would make an excellent governor or United States Attorney, whichever comes first." Larry faced him with a wide smile. "I know you're ready to move on. Being appointed U.S. Attorney would be a nice stepping-stone to national office."

"We'll see, we'll see." Barron flashed a smile back at him, then became serious again. "Right now I'm working hard as attorney general of this great state," he boomed as though giving a fund-raising speech.

"And you've done an outstanding job, too," Larry replied. "Good seeing you. Now you call me real soon."

Barron started to walk out ahead of him but stopped. He turned to Derrick. "Anybody who believes a word Monette Victor says is either incredibly stupid or naive. She's a pathological liar."

Larry and Barron went out together, exchanging small talk. Derrick sat deep in thought, going over his observations of the man. Winn Barron held no surprises. He was the pompous, quick-tempered autocrat he appeared to be from a distance. Although he respected Larry, Derrick found he had a distinct dislike for Barron. Another curious thing was his reaction to the mention of Monette's name. His animosity seemed to border on being personal. Larry's voice broke into his thoughts.

"Winn hasn't changed one bit. Same old bulldog." Larry walked around his desk and sat down in the leather captain's chair.

"Yeah, bad-tempered bulldog," Derrick said evenly.

"Don't take it personally," Larry said with a wave of one hand. "Winn is a little touchy. He's taken a lot of heat for years."

"Like his family position got him where he is?" Derrick looked at his boss.

Larry nodded. "His opponents always bring that up. Winn didn't get this far just because of family connections."

Derrick bit back a rejoinder about how his family's money *and* connections helped him. "Right."

"Let's talk about this Terrio rape case." Larry flipped open a folder on his desk.

While he talked Derrick continued to turn over his view of Barron and Monette's case in his mind.

Hours later he was at his mother's small garden home. Derrick rang the doorbell twice, then opened the door with his key. Ruthann Guillory sat in a wheelchair in a small living room staring at a color television set. Her expression was flat, as though her thoughts were miles away. Derrick sighed, then put on a cheerful face.

"Hello, my favorite woman in the world." Derrick leaned down and kissed her forehead.

"Hi, baby." She patted his face with a bony hand. A light came on in her eyes when she smiled at him.

"Stop watching that trash. Look at those fools." Derrick waved at the television screen. A couple engaged in hand-to-hand combat while a stocky man tried to break it up.

"What? Oh yeah, she just confessed she had an affair with a nephew or uncle, maybe both." Ruthann laughed. "These things are educational, son."

"Yeah," Derrick said with a grunt. "You look gorgeous." He sat down in the chair that matched her small floral sofa.

"Oh stop, you." She waved a hand at him. "I'll show you my latest trick." She grabbed a metal cane with a rubber tip on its three-pronged end.

"Hey, don't do that!" Derrick started to get up.

"Sit down. My physical therapist is like a drill sergeant. I've got to walk at least three times a day now. She'll know if I'm not doing it, too."

With great effort, Ruthann rose from the wheelchair by balancing her weight on the cane. Once she was up, she straightened with a soft gasp. Derrick had to restrain himself from rushing to her.

"Mama, that's fantastic. Now you rest." He watched her with a wary expression.

"You want a glass of sweet tea? I made a pitcher at lunch." She walked slowly toward the small kitchen adjacent to her living room.

"I'll get it." Derrick jumped up. "You rest."

"Stop babying me, son. I've done this twice today already." Ruthann spoke as she made slow but steady progress.

Derrick walked beside her, feeling like a bundle of nerves. "That's wonderful, babe. But really I don't need a glass of tea."

"Nobody *needs* sweet tea, sugar. It's a treat. My next goal is to bake one of my pound cakes."

"Now don't do too much." Derrick couldn't resist. He went to the refrigerator. He found the yellow plastic pitcher, then took two tumblers from a cabinet.

Ruthann got a tray and placed it on the countertop. "Put them on here. My new home health aide brought me some of her special muffins. Low in sugar and fat. Ah, here they are!" She found napkins and placed several on the tray.

"Mama, you sit at the table and let me get those." Derrick put down the tray.

"Nonsense, I feel better when I move around. Might as well since I'm stuck in here all day." She took two muffins out of a plastic container with daisies all over it.

"You need your rest." Derrick tried to keep the insistent edge from his voice.

"Let's go back in the living room, have our treat, and talk." Ruthann put the muffins on the tray and walked ahead of him.

Derrick followed her. He put the tray on a cocktail table in front of the sofa. Ruthann sat next to him. She sighed as she got settled against a large pillow.

"See? You've tired yourself out." Derrick poured tea in the two glasses and handed her one.

"Quit fretting over me."

"I just don't want you to do too much," Derrick said. He smiled as he patted her hand.

"The Lord will take care of me, sugar. Plus I've got a nurse and that nice Keitha coming over."

"I know."

"I had a surprise visitor the other day. Your father dropped by," she said.

Derrick froze in the act of taking another sip from his glass. "What did he want?"

"He's changed, sugar."

"If I had a dime for every time you said that." Derrick clenched a fist.

"Yes, I stayed with him much longer than I should have. It hurt you, and I take the blame for it."

"You did the best you could. I sure don't blame you."

"Forgive him, Derrick. I have. It's time." Ruthann spoke in a gentle voice, the same way she'd coaxed him to take cough medicine as a child.

"I have. But he should stay away from you."

"I don't want you calling him up and telling him not to visit me." Ruthann wore a stern expression. "I'm grown. This is my house and I say who can come see me."

"But Mama—"

"Don't 'but Mama' me, son!" Her frown melted away. "Baby, you can't rush around fixing everything. I know you had to be strong as a boy. But just like this thing with Monette, you gotta be careful."

He glanced at her sharply. "How do you know about that?"

"I still read the papers. She's up for parole, and they mentioned something about the District Attorney's Office. Miss Rose tells me Talia is back in town. I may be weak in the body, but ain't a thing wrong with my mind." Ruthann tapped her temple.

"I don't want you worrying about that kind of stuff."

"I'm worried about how you take so much on your shoulders. You feel like you gotta right every wrong." Nell closed her gnarled hand around his. "You can't. Besides, you take some crazy risks."

Derrick glanced away. Talia had given him the same lecture. "I'm just doing my job."

"I'm proud of you, baby. Don't get me wrong. But you can't do it all yourself," Nell said.

"I'm always careful, sweetheart. You sure were right, this is good sweet tea!" Derrick chattered on about relatives to distract her and himself from worrisome thoughts.

Chapter 9

∞

Talia sat on the floor of Mama Rose's living room with the large pink photo album in her lap. She'd come across it while cleaning out a hall closet. Her hand shook as she opened it. Tears welled up in her eyes at the first photo. A small, grim child gripped a black baby doll with a frown at the camera.

The Life Book had been put together for her by foster care social workers. Pictures of her as a toddler with captions saying how old she was filled the first few pages. Like all foster mothers, Mama Rose had maintained the Life Book and added to it so that Talia would have some sense of a past. Often kids bounced around the system didn't have the simple mementos of baby pictures or school pictures. What seemed a normal part of growing up for most kids had to be a special project for children in foster care. Years had passed since she'd looked at the album. Determined never to cry again, Talia had refused to even touch it once she turned twelve. Just as determined, Mama Rose had snapped away with her little camera. The result was a history of her childhood right up until she graduated from college.

Talia smiled through tears at her fifth-grade picture.

She remembered that plaid jumper. It had been her favorite. Monette and her second foster mother had fought with her not to wear it to school every day. Then her chest grew tight with emotion at the photo two pages later. A young, lovely Monette dressed to kill stood proudly next to Talia dressed in a little cap and gown. The caption said "Sixth Grade Grad, Straight A Student! A proud day for us all!" in Mama Rose's handwriting. This was the mother she'd longed for, prayed for at Mama Rose's urging. Yet Monette had slid back into a sordid, dangerous world only a few days later. Gone for two months, she showed up one day dirty and looking years older. Talia leaned her head back against the sofa cushion and let the tears fall.

Evening shadows lengthened across the carpeted floor until the room was dark. The only light came from a single small lamp near the window. Talia started at the musical sound of the doorbell.

"Baby? Are you okay?" Derrick called out, worry making his voice deeper. His tall frame appeared in the window next to the front door. He peered through the sheer curtain.

"I'm fine. Just a minute."

Talia hastily wiped her face with the back of one hand. She stood and tossed the album on the sofa. In quick order she turned on the large floor lamp, smoothed down her oversize sweatshirt, and wiped her eyes once more. Derrick stared at her hard when she opened the door to let him in.

"You look—"

"I fell asleep. Now you know how puffy my eyes get. I'm a fright in the morning when I first wake up. Let me fix my face or you'll think I'm wearing a Halloween mask," she joked, the words coming out fast as she strained to sound buoyant.

"Okay," he said. His tone indicated he wasn't quite convinced.

"Be right back."

Talia headed for the bathroom in her bedroom. She splashed cool water on her face then put on more face powder and freshened her lip gloss. With three deep breaths, she smiled at her reflection in the mirror.

"God, you still look awful," she muttered. It was the best she could do.

Derrick stood holding the open Life Book in his large hands. "You were a beautiful little girl," he said quietly. "I remember the first time I saw you at Lanier Elementary. You had those two thick braids hanging down to your shoulders on either side. I stopped dead in my tracks."

"Good old Lanier. Or as I liked to call it the Halls of Hell," Talia wisecracked. "Some girl told everybody I was a 'welfare kid' and my mama was a jailbird."

"The next time we met was in the principal's office."

"She deserved a good shove and more. Besides, she pushed me first. Even my teacher said so." Talia smiled wickedly. "She hit that floor right on her butt."

"Such a bad girl."

Talia crossed her arms and eyed him. "And just what were you doing in the principal's office? Hmmm, I seem to recall something about setting ten white mice loose, one of which climbed up the math teacher's skirt."

"They never proved a thing. I was railroaded," Derrick said with a mock look of outrage.

"Sure you were."

"Circumstantial evidence."

"Mr. Browning didn't care about legal technicalities as I recall." Talia wore a slight smile. "He burned us both."

"You stood right up to him and said Marla was lucky she still had her teeth." Derrick chuckled. "You were one tough character."

"Yeah, I handled my business." Talia sat next to him on the sofa.

Derrick's expression grew serious. "That hard shell protected a soft heart. Such beautiful deep eyes." He looked at the album again.

Talia snatched it from his hands. "I should burn the damn thing. I don't need these memories."

He took it back. "It won't work, Talia. Besides, these are Mama Rose's memories, too. Look at the love she put into making it special."

Her throat closed as she fought not to cry again, not with him here at least. Derrick turned the pages slowly. Mama Rose had put pretty decals of flowers and baby animals to decorate the pages. Photos of her as a teen included some of Talia's favorite poems printed beside them. Even though she'd refused to work on the book, Mama Rose had gone on without her.

"She used to say everyone deserves sweet childhood memories," Talia said in a quiet voice. "She became a foster mother to make that happen for at least a few kids."

"Hard to believe you could smile, but you did." Derrick held it out so that she could see another photo. In this one Talia squinted in sunshine with a wide grin, a softball in one hand.

"Mama Rose did her best. One day Monette came over with this toy set of little people and a town. I was eleven I think. I remember we were laughing at some corny joke I'd told. Then Monette just started bawling like a baby."

"She was hurting, too."

"She kept saying 'I'm sorry, Talia, baby. I'm so

sorry.' " Talia stared at a high school photo of Monette. She looked fresh and hopeful. "God, what happened to you?"

"Ask her," Derrick said softly. His hand closed over one of hers. "I think she needs to tell you as much as you need to hear it."

"No matter what she went through, it doesn't excuse everything she's done."

"Has she ever tried to make excuses?" Derrick rested his head against Talia's.

She frowned. "Lies and elaborate stories to explain why she would just disappear, yes."

"I found out a lot of things about my father's upbringing that helped me understand. I don't excuse the way he treated us though." Derrick rubbed her arm. "At some point after you become an adult you make choices, you know?"

"Exactly," Talia said firmly.

"I even understood why my mother stayed with him. I think she always saw the hurt little boy inside him." Derrick's voice dropped. "And she loved him as a man."

"But she got over him."

"I suppose." Derrick sat back and gazed at Talia. "Back to you and Monette. No matter what has happened she's your mother. I don't think you can make peace with your childhood until you try to understand her."

"Have you?"

Derrick's jaw clenched before he spoke again. "I'm still working on it."

"Monette hasn't changed one bit either. All I'll get is more heartache." Talia stared straight ahead with a determined expression. "No thanks."

"Maybe Monette is the same. But you'll never know

unless you go see her." Derrick brushed a lock of her hair from where it had fallen across her forehead.

Talia took a deep breath and let it out. She'd thought her most pressing problem would be making sure Mama Rose had the best of care. Mama Rose seemed to be blooming. So were complications for Talia. Her plan to get in and out quick had been a fantasy. Her past, as thick as swamp mud, pulled her in inch by inch each day.

"Coming home just couldn't be simple, could it?" Talia pressed against Derrick for warmth. His solid body offered a measure of reassurance.

Chapter 10

Derrick watched her bustle around Mama Rose's kitchen. She seemed a bit nervous in a domestic role, yet had insisted she wanted to prepare him at least one meal. He stretched his legs out beneath the table. The cozy feeling of a simple dinner at home felt so good. Talia wasn't the homemaker type, and he didn't want her to be. Yet he had a brief fantasy of coming home to her each night.

"Honey, your shrimp Creole was delicious." Derrick traced a furrow in the cotton tablecloth with his fingers.

"Not enough red pepper." Talia's shapely eyebrows drew together. "And the French bread was too brown around the edges."

"Everything was fine. Guess you'll be in good practice by the time you get back to D.C." Derrick stared at the dainty yellow flowers as he continued to draw invisible lines on the table.

"Mama Rose will have a fit when she sees how I've rearranged things." Talia put the last dish into the dishwasher. "I just can't keep up with her system."

"Hmm. Yeah, I suppose the kitchen stuff in your apartment is pretty simple. You'll be glad to get back to it, huh?"

Talia hung the yellow dish towel on a white enamel rack over the sink. "Okay, come out with it." She sat down at the table next to him.

"What?" Derrick didn't look at her.

She put her hand on his and rubbed the back of it. "You're wondering when I'm leaving."

His heart thumped. For the last week he'd imagined the torture of watching her get on an airplane. Mama Rose would come home soon. Talia had prepared her report on the mandatory-sentencing bill and appeared at the legislature. There was no reason for her to stay. A month ago he'd lied to himself and to her. He hadn't come close just to living in the moment. Derrick kept thinking about a sweet future in her arms every night, of being beside her when she woke up each morning.

"I know you'll be gone soon," he said, forcing the words out.

"Well, I don't know." Talia chewed her bottom lip.

A tickle of hope traveled up his arm from her touch. "What do you mean?"

"For one thing she's got a gentleman friend, and I don't think she wants to leave him just yet." Talia wore a slight smile.

"She loves this house. I don't see Mama Rose giving it up." Derrick shook his head.

"I don't know. She's been saying it's real lonesome out here and getting harder for her to keep up the place." Talia pointed to the scenery outside. "Takes a lot to manage those pecan groves and the timber."

"She's lived here a long time since her husband died."

"Papa George was the only man I trusted and felt close to," Talia said, her voice pitched deep with affection. "Besides you."

"Thanks, baby." Derrick pressed his lips to her hand.

"Anyway, Mama Rose even mentioned building another house close to Shadow Road. That's almost three miles from here." Talia pursed her lips.

"Makes sense though. She'd be closer to stores, the post office, and her church."

"I guess." She looked around. "She put a lot of love into this house."

"She put a lot of love into raising you and the other kids. You stayed with her the longest, so I'm not surprised she'd want you to have it."

"I went back and forth. Monette convinced the social workers she'd changed at least five times." Talia did not look angry despite her words. "At least I had Mama Rose to count on."

"She's worth gold," Derrick agreed.

"Her doctor says Mama's attitude has really helped. This man has helped," Talia said.

"Have you met him?"

"She's been keeping him undercover." Talia laughed. "But he was visiting when I went over last week. Nice-looking distinguished guy with silver hair. Looks like the kind of man she'd find attractive."

"Okay, so what have you found out about him?" Derrick grinned when she hesitated. "Come on, you've got the story on the dude."

She laughed again. "You know me so well."

He leaned toward her and put his arms around her waist. "Yes," he said close to her ear. "Now tell me what you've dug up."

"I didn't 'dig up' anything. You make it sound like I went through the man's trash or something," Talia protested.

"Quit stalling. You know you want to tell me."

"He's a retired postman. His wife of twenty-five years died three years ago. Get this, he's four years younger than Mama Rose."

"Go for it, Mama Rose. Younger men have more energy!" Derrick laughed hard when Talia's eyes widened with shock.

"Derrick! You don't think they . . ." Her voice trailed off.

"They're old, not dead." Derrick continued to laugh at her stunned expression. Then she grinned back at him.

"My, my." Talia shook her head slowly. "Anyway, who knows where this romance will lead."

"I think it's great. No one wants to be alone." He hugged her closer.

"Then there's Monette." Talia wore a thoughtful frown.

"Yes?" Derrick decided not to push. He sensed there was some change in her feeling toward Monette.

"She's stirring up a pot that could boil over and get her burned." Talia sat back and looked at him. "Winn Barron is always on the news."

"He was at our office last week."

"Barron keeps beating his chest about how he's protecting the public." Talia's eyes narrowed.

"I saw a newspaper article about the hearing." Derrick rubbed his jaw. "He's suddenly a very accessible state official, with the press I mean."

"Rumor has it he plans to run for governor." Talia sat forward with her elbows on the table.

Derrick nodded. "He's got a real shot at it, too. I just don't see why he's taken such an interest in this bill. There are other issues that grab headlines more."

"Sure, like the environment, education, and jobs," Talia replied. "But maybe his polls show crime is higher on the public's agenda."

"Maybe." Derrick wasn't convinced. "I'm going to read the trial transcripts. Monette and those folks she hung out with must have really been a problem."

"She sure seems to have made an impression on *him*." Talia glanced at Derrick. "I'd say with the attorney general fighting her parole, she's going to be in prison a long time."

"She's served fifteen years of a forty-year sentence." Derrick sat forward with his arms resting on the table, his shoulder against hers. "It's really a life sentence."

"Yeah," she said softly.

Neither spoke for several minutes. He could sense she was thinking about her mother. Talia leaned on him as though she needed support and physical reassurance. Her lovely brown eyes reflected the conflict within.

"Why don't we walk off that tasty dinner? The sunset will be great over the pond out back. We can watch it together like we used to." Derrick stood and held out a hand to her.

"Okay."

After Talia locked the back door, they crossed the wide back porch and headed across the backyard. A well-worn path stretched through thick brush and tall trees. With the temperature around seventy degrees, the low humidity made the evening pleasant. Reddish yellow leaves mixed with the still mostly deep green ones in surrounding trees. Cool breezes shook them until the woods seemed to whisper its secrets. Squirrels hopped from branch to branch, with acorns in their mouths. Derrick and Talia didn't talk. They strolled along with their arms around each other's waist. Fifteen minutes later they came to a small stream. They turned north and followed the stream to where it emptied into a small lake. Papa George had named it Lake Rose. He'd stocked it with perch and catfish. A cypress picnic table he had made sat twenty yards away under an old oak tree. Three cypress benches were spaced out around the water's edge, all with equally lovely views facing east, west, and south. Talia led the way to the closest one. Once they sat down, she sighed and gazed up at the deep blue sky. Fading light slanted across the water.

"Beautiful." She breathed in deeply.

"Yes." Derrick rested his chin on the soft cushion of her thick hair. "With the right person that is. I've said this a thousand times already, but I'm glad you're home."

"This is the first visit home I have actually enjoyed. Well, mostly."

He could tell she was thinking about Monette still. "What are you going to do?"

Talia snuggled into the crook of his arm. "Go see her. It's time."

"I think so, too."

"I don't like this Barron guy playing with Monette's life, just so he can score votes," Talia said in a steely tone.

"I don't much like the guy myself." Derrick stared at the water as a breeze kicked up small ripples across the surface.

"Winn Barron and your boss are close pals, Derrick." Talia shifted to look into his eyes. "Don't do anything crazy."

"What are you talking about?"

"Derrick, Monette has Jim Rand on her side. Senator Jackson has clout, and his bill could pass." Talia tugged on the rolled up sleeve of his cotton shirt. "You don't need to take risks to help us."

He took note of her use of the word "us." Talia had begun to see Monette's fight as hers, too. Derrick felt a swell of protectiveness. Barron would no doubt use the resources of the attorney general's office. No way would Derrick stand by and do nothing. Still the last thing Talia needed was to worry about him.

"Relax. I'm used to staying out of trouble these days." Derrick gave her an easy smile.

"I mean it. Promise me you won't do anything stupid." Talia poked him in the side with her elbow like she had when they were kids.

Derrick held up one palm out. "I hereby promise not to do anything stupid. Feel better?"

She stared at him hard. "You agreed too fast, which makes me suspicious."

"You've been in that cutthroat political town too long." Derrick kissed her forehead. "Have a little faith, baby girl."

Talia squinted at him. "I know *you*, Derrick Guillory."

"I'm hurt." He affected a pained expression. "I've always done as I was told."

"You? Pu-leeze!" Talia said with a glare. "Now I know you're up to something."

"No, seriously. I do promise." He returned her gaze, his smile gone.

"Okay. I'll be watching you." Talia pointed a finger at his nose.

"Good. Stay close and keep me out of trouble," he whispered.

Her stern frown dissolved. She arched to him when he placed both hands on her face. He wasn't playing fair, but it felt too good to stop. Talia's body, a combination of soft round curves and firm flesh, drove him crazy. Derrick wanted to forget politics and the rest of the world. What he wanted most of all was for Talia to wrap her velvet warmth around him. She pulled away.

"I'm staying a little longer than I thought," she said.

"Great, I—"

"Not for good," Talia added quickly.

"I hear you." Derrick's hopes soared despite her insistence that she would leave eventually. His head tried to make his heart listen to reason. Emotion won. *Longer could turn into forever.* Yet he knew their happiness rested on shaky ground.

"When are you going to visit Monette?"

"Thursday. Two days should give me enough time to prepare myself," Talia said. She grew quiet in his arms.

Derrick thought of Winn Barron and the files he'd read. Something about Monette's case and Barron's behavior bothered him. His instincts told him he'd only begun to peel back the layers.

"I'll be right here for you, baby."

Talia looked around the living room of Karl's house, a double-wide trailer in New Roads.

"You've got a great home and family, Karl. I'm happy for you," Talia said. She had to admit she'd been skeptical about his reform.

"Yeah, I've been given another chance not to throw my life down a sewer," he said with a wise nod.

His wife had cooked them a delicious down-home meal of chicken and gravy, rice, field peas, and hot, sweet corn bread. LaTrice had taken their three children to their bedrooms to play so Talia and Karl could talk. Kelly green curtains with ruffles matched the green in the floral print furniture. Sentimental pictures of cute puppies and flowers adorned the walls. LaTrice had decorated every inch of two bookcases with little discount store figurines. The entire house had a crowded, homey look. Not exactly Talia's taste, but somehow it didn't seem tacky. Maybe because of the love that filled in what little space was left, she mused.

"LaTrice done all this herself," he said proudly.

"Nice," Talia said sincerely. She sank against the sofa. Just then Karl's youngest, four-year-old Rashida shot into the room and bounced onto Talia's lap.

"Girl, you better get back in here." LaTrice scurried

down the hall. "I'm sorry, Talia. This girl is faster than lightning."

Talia enjoyed the feel of Rashida's plump little body snuggling against her. Talia tickled her round cheek. Her reward was a cascade of little giggles.

"It's okay, LaTrice." Talia laughed when Rashida tugged at her face with glee.

"She took a real likin' to her aunt Talia. That's my baby girl." Karl beamed at them.

"Sure did. Even Karl, Jr., said a few words, and that boy is so shy. Good in school though." LaTrice scooped the child from Talia's lap. "But you two need to talk. I'm gonna settle these kids down and finish in the kitchen."

Karl watched her walk out, swinging the child until she squealed with delight. He let out a long breath. "I just started living a few years ago, Talia."

"You're a lucky guy." Talia wondered for the first time about her solitary life and high-powered days.

"So, you're gonna go see Monette." Karl crossed one long leg over another.

"Yes."

Talia stared outside. The glass storm door was closed, but allowed light in. An occasional car zipped past on the blacktop road outside. Karl seemed content to let her gather her thoughts.

"What do you want to know?" Karl said at last. "Bet you got a lot of questions."

"Not really." Talia rested her head on the sofa cushion.

"Sure you do. Don't think you got all the answers about who Monette is, Talia." Karl clasped his large hands together against his stomach.

"I don't know what I'm going to say to her. That's the truth." Talia picked up a small stuffed bird Rashida had left behind.

"Been a long time," Karl said in a quiet voice.

"Real long." Talia turned to her older brother. "Just when I think I got that woman all figured out, she pulls something new."

"That's Monette up and down." Karl wore a faint smile.

"Most of the time it's an unpleasant surprise, too," Talia retorted.

"She's got her way, that's no lie." Karl chuckled.

"Remember that time they caught her with phony checks? I went to court with her. She sweet-talked her way into paying restitution." Talia shook her head with a laugh. "Hollywood actresses can't match Monette when she's in her game."

Karl laughed with her. "Our mama can charm the robes off a judge on her worst day."

"Why are we laughing? Monette is trouble with a big 'T.' " Yet she couldn't stop laughing.

Karl wiped his eyes. His expression serious again, he studied Talia. "Now really, what are you gonna say? Might be a good idea to think about it some."

"Once we get past the small talk of 'How are you?' and 'I'm fine, and you?,' the visit might be over," she replied.

"You ain't foolin' nobody but yourself," Karl tossed back.

"Right." Talia sighed. Her throat tightened. "I want to know why she couldn't pull her act together and be our mama."

"I know," he said simply.

They sat in silence for a long time. Childish voices floated down the hallway. LaTrice clanged together pots and silverware in the kitchen. Karl got up and turned on the table lamps. He sat back down again.

"She's coming up for parole. Winn Barron is planning to fight it," Talia said.

"The attorney general?" Karl scratched his jaw. "I follow the news pretty close these days. He's from around here I believe."

"He was the district attorney who got her convicted." Talia crossed her arms.

"Oh." Karl pursed his lips for a few seconds. "I was in a group home back then. They took me to the prison to visit her a few times."

Talia realized there was so much they didn't know about each other's lives. For once, though, Talia didn't feel anger at the thought of Monette's lifestyle then.

"Even though I was mad as hell at her, I hated seeing her shackled," Talia said softly. A long-suppressed memory popped back into her head. "The district attorney convinced the court she was an escape risk. They had her in leg irons and a leather waist restraint with handcuffs attached."

Karl nodded. "I remember one visit, I think it was the last one I went to, she had on this orange prison jumpsuit. I had an attitude. I was mad at her and the world."

Talia listened as LaTrice called to Karl Jr. to take out the garbage. Outside crickets set up a chorus of chirping. Talia and Karl were quiet, wrapped in thoughts of sad days gone by. Sounds of the present served as a background noise to memories. Karl cleared his throat. When Talia looked at him, his expression was less troubled. He seemed to have pushed the past back again.

"Monette has been a lot of things, but she wasn't no drug-smugglin' queen," Karl said in a firm voice. "What's this guy got against her?"

"Barron wants to run for governor in the next election. Her parole hearing is next month, and he wants to prove he's tough on crime." Talia grimaced at that argument. Somehow it didn't add up.

"He sent lots of folks to prison that did worse. Murderers for instance." Karl hit on Talia's thoughts exactly. "Why Monette and why now? The election is two years off."

"Derrick said something about him being U.S. Attorney in the meantime. I don't know." Talia shrugged. "He's a politician."

"Right." Karl nodded slowly. "They start thinkin' ahead long before the election. Buildin' up stuff he can brag on during the campaign."

"Yeah," Talia agreed with a sour expression. "Anyway, he's going to use Monette as an example of why mandatory sentencing is a good thing."

"It's great you helpin' fight that law," Karl said. "Mama Rose told me what you're doin'."

Talia blushed. "I didn't volunteer. And I wasn't thinking of Monette either."

"You could have said no." Karl made his simple pronouncement and gazed at her steadily.

"Well, he's my boss," Talia stammered, and looked away.

"Uh-huh." Karl continued to study her. "The point is you're back home workin' on somethin' that's gonna help Monette. You knew that goin' in."

"I came because Mama Rose got sick." Talia plucked at the throw pillow.

"Uh-huh."

"Will you stop grunting like that?" Talia slapped at the long black tassel on the pillow, causing it to bounce.

Karl held up one palm. "Okay, okay. So Monette is going up for parole, and this guy is fightin' it."

"Yes."

"And you don't like that."

"You'd think he's got better things to do. Like you said, Monette wasn't some big-time gangster." Talia looked at her older brother.

"She's got that Tulane law professor on her side. They got some other people out of prison," Karl said. "I been readin' 'bout them."

"Maybe that will help." Talia doubted it, given Barron's influence in the state.

"Kinda like in the Bible, David and Goliath. Don't seem right." Karl raised his thick eyebrows.

"I wouldn't exactly compare Monette to an innocent shepherd boy in the Bible, Karl. I mean she *was* with those men."

"Yeah," Karl rubbed his chin. "Maybe more like the woman surrounded by accusers about to be stoned to death. She'd done wrong but didn't deserve the punishment."

Talia smiled at her brother, the old-fashioned church deacon. "Sure, something like that."

"I'm real happy you're goin' to see her. She's gonna need our support."

"I don't know how I feel," Talia admitted.

"A lot of bad between y'all." Karl turned in his easy chair to face Talia. "But you got to heal that wound, Talia."

"What did you talk to her about?" Talia tucked her legs under her.

"It wasn't easy. First I went off on her. She didn't say nothin', just listened. Then 'fore I knew it we was both cryin'." His voice shook, and he stopped talking for several minutes.

"Y'all want some ice cream?" LaTrice stood in the door that led from the hallway.

Karl wiped a hand over his face. When he looked at his wife, he was smiling. "Yeah, baby. You know what I like."

"Vanilla fudge." She grinned back at him. "What about you, sugar?"

"That vanilla fudge sounds good to me, too." Talia smiled at her.

"Comin' up." LaTrice bounded off with energy. "Me, I'm havin' strawberry."

"The good life, Talia. Supper with my family and ice cream for dessert," Karl murmured. "I'm grateful every day."

"You've got reason to be proud of yourself," Talia replied.

"I didn't have one reason to be proud for years." Karl let out a sigh of satisfaction. He looked at Talia again. "You're successful, got a good life up there in D.C. I'm thinkin' you can afford to forgive Monette now."

"Here we go." LaTrice came in with two bowls on a tray. She handed one to Karl and the other to Talia.

"Thanks," Talia said. She spooned up a tiny scoop and ate it. "Hmm, good stuff."

"Blue Bell, best ice cream around." LaTrice glanced over her shoulder when a childish shout came down the hall. "Let me go get these wild children." She strode off, calling ahead that they'd better behave.

Karl swallowed a generous helping of the frozen treat before he spoke. "You goin' to see her soon?"

"Thursday." Talia felt a flicker of apprehension at how quickly that day was approaching.

"Monette used to talk to me a lot about them days," Karl said. "It was like she was wakin' up from a dream. She told me all kinds of stuff."

"Excuses I'll bet," Talia said.

"No, just tellin' me like it was. Our daddy got her on drugs. Well, he offered it, and she took some. Made all her troubles go away. At least that's what it seemed like."

She glanced at him sharply. "She told you about our

daddy? I never heard much about him. What I did hear was bad."

"He's up in Detroit. Monette said he did us a favor runnin' off." Karl smiled sadly. "Actually I found him once. He's got a family and ain't into street life no more. But he didn't want reminders of his past.

"We got a real pair of winners in the parent department, didn't we?" Talia said with disgust. "They made us and then went on about their business."

"God made us, Talia. He put them in charge of takin' care of us on this earth. Now they didn't do right, but if he can forgive 'em, so can we."

She looked at Karl for a long moment. Coming from anyone else she'd have found those words sanctimonious and naive. But Karl had suffered a lot of pain because of their parents.

"I was seriously thinking of not seeing Monette. It's too hard." Talia clenched her teeth to deal with the pain.

He sat forward suddenly. "Look, I ain't tellin' you what to do. But I believe Monette got set up by folks still around here." Karl spoke in a lower tone.

His shift in mood gave Talia the shivers. "Cut it out, Karl. You act like Dracula is about to show up." Talia tried to laugh, but his deepened frown cut it short.

"She ain't just pullin' some scam this time. Monette told me there was some funny business goin' down in the DA's Office. But she wouldn't say anything else. You know I was on the street back in the day." Karl clasped his rough hands together.

"Right." Talia lowered her voice in response to the change of atmosphere. "You were on drugs, running with a gang."

"Yeah. Well, before I got sent off to the juvenile center and then the group home, I heard stuff." Karl twisted his hands together. "I was even stupid enough to brag Monette was my mama."

"What kind of stuff?" Talia hugged herself as if to warm away a chill.

"Monette was runnin' with this real bad dude named . . ." Karl blinked rapidly for a few moments. "Can't remember his name, but you might. They was livin' together. You was with her then, right?"

Talia swallowed hard. "In and out of foster care mostly. Besides, Monette went through men like a hot knife through butter."

Karl nodded once. "You right about that. I'll think of it probably. He was always gettin' arrested. The word was him and Monette had a hookup with the sheriff's office or somethin' like that. All of a sudden he wasn't gettin' arrested no more."

"And?" Talia's fear was now overcome with intense interest.

"Monette was livin' real high, like she wasn't afraid of nothin' either." Karl sat back. "I remember her ridin' around in a fancy Buick Regal for a while. Long about that time this dude takes off. Nobody hears from him again."

"Those guys came and went fast. They lived like that. You know about that lifestyle." Talia's heart raced even though she kept an even tone.

"Sure. But it's funny how *nobody* knew where he went. Usually your partners on the street know somethin'." Karl gazed at her with a wide-eyed expression.

"So what were the theories on the street?" Talia asked.

"Lots of 'em. But only two made sense. Dudes was sayin' he got on the wrong side of this bad cop and had to run." Karl spoke barely above a whisper now. "I also heard maybe he went into that witness protection program."

Talia felt a finger of fear jab her ribs. She cleared her tight throat so she could speak. "What do you think?"

"This guy disappears, and next thing ya know Monette goin' to prison for a long time. Some coincidence if you ask me." Karl sat back with a grim expression.

"You think he rolled on her, and they gave him a new identity."

"I'll bet somethin' he did or said helped put Monette in prison. I think he's dead," he said bluntly.

"Let's change the subject." Her chest rose and fell as she tried to catch her breath.

Karl got up and sat next to her on the sofa. "I'm sorry, little sis. You had your bad times with Monette, but you wasn't exposed to that kinda dangerous thug life like me. I gotta learn to watch my mouth."

"I'm okay, I'm okay." Talia fought to bring her panic under control.

"Of course this ain't nothin' but street gossip."

"He's probably in some other town causing trouble."

"I got a feelin' Monette 'bout to uncover somethin' real bad, Talia."

LaTrice walked in. "I got more ice cream with y'all names on it." Her smile faded when she looked at them. "Karl?"

Karl stood. "Ain't nothin' wrong, baby. You got me spoiled, and now you spoilin' Talia."

Talia caught the message in his eyes and took his lead. "If getting more ice cream means being spoiled, then bring it on."

They both put on a cheerful face for LaTrice and the children. Karl was soon laughing with true warmth, surrounded by giggling children and a loving wife. LaTrice and Karl made her feel part of their family. The children called her Aunt Talia as though they'd known her all their young lives. After another hour she left and started the drive home. Other cars passed her on the lonely highway. Yet the night surrounded her car like a black blanket. Her thoughts went back to Monette, and Earl. Talia gripped the steering wheel and decided to take charge of her fear for once. She would find the truth before anyone else did.

"Yeah, Miss Brave. Then what?" she muttered.

Chapter 11

"I'm out of my mind," Talia whispered for the tenth time that morning.

A female guard dumped out the contents of her black leather tote-style purse. Talia had been asked to take her pager and cell phone back to the car. Now she was being checked once again.

"Rules, ma'am," the stone-faced guard clipped. A picture ID tag clipped to her shirt had the name Helen Batiste on it.

"I understand." Talia winced when the guard dropped her small cosmetic bag onto the metal table.

"What's this?" Officer Batiste held up a plastic bag

"Pictures of her grandkids," Talia said. "I just left them in the bag from Walmart where I bought the album."

"Uh-huh." Officer Batiste was already examining the contents.

You were going to look anyway, so why ask? Talia pressed her lips together to keep from tossing out a smart remark. This was not the time, or the place, and Officer Batiste was definitely not someone she wanted to annoy.

"Okay." Officer Batiste handed her the bag and her

purse. She nodded crisply and pointed to another female guard. "Officer Landers is taking everybody back. Have a good one."

Talia felt the urge to salute but had sense enough not to. She followed the line. Officer Landers, a short plump redhead with freckles, wore a sunny smile. She chatted with several visitors as she led them to a large room with tables and chairs.

"Y'all know the rules; no giving gifts we haven't checked up front. You can share food, but the ladies can't keep leftovers. No sitting on laps, no long passionate kisses. This is a *family* situation. I'll remind you if you forget." Officer Landers eyed several men in low-slung pants and baggy shirts. Despite her smile, she seemed just as capable of enforcing the rules as Officer Batiste. "Enjoy."

Officer Landers waved one hand to signal two officers at a door across the room. There was a rush of babbling voices and footsteps as women dressed in denim shirts and jeans came in. Most wore wide smiles. Others looked taciturn. Talia gripped the purse to her midsection. She wanted to bolt but stood firm as she scanned the faces. It suddenly struck her how long it had been. They might not recognize each other.

"You all right, miss?" Officer Landers spoke over her shoulder causing Talia to jump. "Must be your first time."

"I've been here before. It's been a while though." Talia felt guilt wash over her.

"Seeing somebody you love locked up is no day at the beach." Officer Landers touched her elbow lightly. "Who are you here to see?"

Talia felt like a little girl lost at the mall. She collected herself and squared her shoulders. "Monette Victor."

"Oh? She didn't have visitors for years. Now she's

gotten two in the last six months." Officer Landers looked at her with open curiosity. "Anyway, here comes another group. Let me know if you need anything."

"Thanks."

Talia found an empty seat at a round white table attached to the concrete floor. When Officer Landers waved at her from across the room, Talia gave her a shaky smile. Then an odd sensation washed over her. She looked around the room, and her heart thumped hard. A statuesque woman the color of nutmeg stood just inside the door staring at Talia. Her thick black hair, streaked with a few strands of silver, was pulled back into a ponytail. Her round face was still pretty, though it had more lines now. Other prisoners went around her to get into the room. Monette smiled at her tentatively as though not sure if she should. Talia inhaled deeply and let out a slow breath as she stood.

"Hey, you blockin' everybody else. Either go in or go out." A caramel-colored prisoner with her hair in cornrows grimaced as she brushed against Monette.

"Shut up, Candy," Monette replied without taking her eyes off Talia.

"You want some of this?" Candy bumped her shoulder into Monette's. The rough-talking woman raised an eyebrow.

Talia blinked hard at the glimpse into real prison life. How could she have ever wished this on her own mother? "Leave her alone," she blurted out before she knew it.

Candy paused in the act of scanning the visiting area and looked at Talia. "That's your kid. Gotta be with her bold mouth." The woman barked a gruff laugh and slapped Monette on the back.

"Shut up." Monette seemed to exchange a silent signal with her. Candy nodded and left.

Monette strolled across the floor. Even in prison

clothes she walked with self-possession. Several men noticed her hip-swinging stride as she passed them. Candy called out another joke, but Talia didn't hear it. All she could see was her mother, graceful in the midst of a harsh environment. Images from her childhood rushed back. Her mother must have sensed the effect she was having on Talia. Her steps slowed, as though she was giving Talia time to adjust.

"How ya doin'?" Monette's alto voice was husky with emotion. More men glanced around at the sensual timbre.

"Fine," Talia managed to say despite the lump in her throat.

"Sit back down," Monette said, with a gesture to the seat.

"That woman—" Talia nodded to Candy who sat alone at a table staring at them.

"What?" Monette looked over her shoulder. She waved at Candy. "Oh, don't mind that fool. We like messin' with each other."

"Oh." Talia felt only a little tension ease from her shoulders. She sat down on the small bench and put her purse on the table.

Monette sat across from her. She gazed at Talia from head to toe. "I'm glad to see ya."

"Good to see you, too." Talia's response was automatic. Her thoughts whirled as she stared back at her mother with equal intensity.

Monette seemed to read her mind. "Yeah, I've changed. Had a lot of work done on my teeth for one." She grinned revealing even, white teeth. "One thing about being locked up, you get pretty damn good dental benefits."

Talia nodded and continued to stare at her. "I see."

"Ain't many other benefits, but I been makin' the most of my stay. Got my high school certificate." Monette shrugged. "Couldn't sit still when I was a teenager. That ain't a problem here."

"Right."

"It could be worse. We got a library. I work on the newsletter, too." Monette's smile faltered. "Say somethin'."

Talia snapped out of the fog of memories and emotions.. She took the photos from the bag. "Karl sent these. Karl, Jr. plays pee-wee football. The baby, Rashida, just started kindergarten. She's the cutest thing. Looks just like my baby pictures."

Though she knew she was babbling, Talia couldn't stop. She dredged up every anecdote Karl had told her about the kids. Monette stared at the photos, nodding and smiling. She laughed at Talia's account of their exploits.

"They sure are some beautiful babies. And you right, Rashida looks just like you did at that age. Got that same spunky spark in her eyes, too." Monette looked at each picture at least three times. She pushed them back to Talia.

"Those are yours to keep. I got you this to put them in." Talia held up the small dark blue album with the words SWEET MEMORIES embossed in silver on the leather cover.

Monette touched the book's surface with her fingertips. She looked into Talia's eyes. Tears filled her own until one spilled down her cheek. "For me."

"Yes." Talia swallowed hard and looked away. "I mean you need something to keep them in. I didn't think they'd let you have frames. The glass and metal might . . ." Her voice faded.

"Thanks." Monette grasped Talia's right hand tightly, then let go after a few seconds.

"You're welcome," Talia whispered, and choked back her own tears.

Monette sat straight and took a tissue from her shirt pocket. "Came prepared," she joked through tears as she dabbed at her eyes.

Talia bit her lower lip and glanced around as though interested in the walls. Monette sniffed a few more times, then tapped her hand. When Talia looked at her again, the old cocky smile she knew was back.

"So tell me all about your hotshot career and big-city life. Miz Rose swears you got the town by the tail." Monette laughed. "You're using the family gift of fast talk honestly. 'Bout time one of us did."

"Mama Rose tends to exaggerate." Still Talia blushed. "I'm a political consultant on the Hill. I help organizations negotiate all the complications of dealing with the federal bureaucracy."

"A lobbyist?" Monette crossed her arms. "Good for you. Lotta money and influence."

"Well, I do some of what a lobbyists does, but more. I help educate congressmen on issues, give organizations information on federal policies and procedures, things like that."

"Oh, yeah." Monette nodded. "You use information and know lots of stuff."

"Definitely. We maintain our own database and use good professional research web sites."

"Gotcha. So you've got inside tips that folks need to get heard, like who to talk to and how to talk to 'em." Monette sat forward. "Sounds like a good spot to be in."

"I like knowing the ins and outs of all those complicated rules and regs, sure." Talia smiled.

"Bet you're good at it, too. Didn't need Miz Rose to tell me that. You always had a sharp brain." Monette gazed at her with pride.

"I work hard." Talia felt deep pleasure at the simple compliment. She'd always wanted Monette's approval.

"Sure, but you also got talent and spunk. I'm glad you didn't throw it away, like I did. Course, I was never smart in books like you."

"You're no dummy. When I was real small you had all kinds of books on history, psychology, and sociology." Talia didn't mention that her mother sold them over time.

"Yeah, tryin' to make up for wastin' my school years."

"You have a curious mind, that's a sign of an educated person. Not from a college, but from an interest in the world." Talia smiled slightly. "I remember you could argue politics with the best of them."

"Always was shootin' off my big mouth. Everybody knew my opinion." Monette laughed at herself.

"One time you were working at Rudy's Diner. Remember? Your boss got mad because you knew more than he did about managing the place."

"Rudy." Monette rolled her eyes. "His own kin was stealin' him blind. A fool coulda done better."

"He fired you for taking meat from the restaurant. Later on he found out it was his bum of a nephew." Talia looked down at her hands. "It wasn't fair."

Monette had made efforts to live a straight life, especially after ultimatums from child welfare workers. Talia remembered other jobs lost through layoff, relatives who stole their last money for rent, and friends who betrayed Monette's trust.

"I made a lot of downright stupid choices." Monette shook her head slowly. "One thing my Narcotics Anonymous group did was strip away the excuses. Life is hard no matter what. You can either face it clean or face it on drugs. Either way it ain't easy for nobody."

"You couldn't help the family you were born into or what adults did to you. You were just a kid. They were supposed to protect you." Talia bit off the last words.

Monette frowned. She rubbed a hand over her face. "I didn't want you to hear that crap. I ain't lookin' for an alibi, Talia."

"I know that, but—"

"Let me finish. Shoulda told you this a long time ago." Monette sighed deeply.

"I pretty much shut you out after the conviction. You tried talking to me," Talia said.

"You cut me off after years of me makin' your life miserable." Monette held up a palm to forestall Talia's response. "We was both there, so don't try to fix it up."

"I wasn't going to."

They sat in silence for a time. Talia wouldn't waste time arguing. As her mother pointed out, they both knew the truth. The difference now was Monette seemed to have faced the ugliness. Gone was the sugar-coated explanations or evasions.

"The past can't be changed. All you can do is learn from it and move on." Talia glanced into her mother's eyes, then looked away.

"I did my best, which wasn't all that good. But I also did my worst to you. I'm more sorry than you could ever know. I couldn't blame you for not speakin' to me again, for denyin' I'm even kin to you, much less your mama," Monette said with intensity.

"Don't, Monette." Talia gripped her hands together. Monette had summarized exactly how she'd felt for years.

"I'm not beatin' myself up. Just sayin' that if I was you, I'd have a hard time believin' these words. I let you down too many times." Monette looked past the crowd, through the windows covered with metal grilles.

"Maybe we can get to know each other on a different basis," Talia said in a faint voice.

Monette glanced at her. "I'd like that. I can't change the things I've done, but at least I can make you proud of me now."

"Yes." Talia didn't know what else to say. Part of her still held back. As her mother had said, there had been so many broken promises.

"I can't swear I'm some church lady these days. It's easy to say all you gonna do when you locked up." Monette swept a hand around. "Fact is a lot of inmates feel safe here with all the rules. What scares them is outside."

"Really?" Talia gazed back at her. "You mean people want to stay here?"

"Some of 'em, yeah. Oh, not all of 'em know it. But they do stuff that messes up their release."

"Your study of human psychology," Talia said with a slight smile.

Monette smiled back at her and shrugged. "I guess. A lot of these women got less than nothin' outside. Got a husband that beats the daylights out of 'em, family on drugs or into thug life, livin' in shacks. Hell, why leave?"

"And you?" Talia gazed at her. "What do you have?"

She could list the reasons Monette would want to stay. Except for Karl, her children wanted nothing to do with her. The two youngest kids had good lives. They didn't want to be reminded of their mother or the things she'd done. Monette's sisters and brothers were either addicted or in prison themselves. Her mother was in a nursing home suffering from alcohol-induced dementia. Monette wore an impassive expression for a few moments. Then she seemed to transform before Talia's eyes. A hard, cunning smile spread across her face.

"Long as I'm suckin' air, I got me!" Monette slapped a palm against her chest. "Unlike most of my classmates up in here, I *really didn't do it*."

She knew this Monette only too well. "Yeah," Talia said shortly.

Monette grunted. "You think I'm lyin' again. Whatever. I been on my own all my life with nobody watchin' my back."

"You were with those guys, and they had three kilos of cocaine. They were your party pals." Talia ticked off her points on the fingers of one hand. "You had been arrested before on a drug charge. And your 'friends' gave you up."

Talia stared at her hard. She expected Monette to get angry. Instead, Monette waved a hand as though brushing away a small pesky insect.

"First of all, running drugs is dangerous." Monette looked around, then lowered her voice. "Them dudes don't play. One speck of their stuff comes up missin' and so do you."

"Then why—"

"Let me finish Miss Know-it-damn-all," she snapped. Monette took a deep breath and let it out slowly. "Sorry. It's this place."

"What did you expect?" Talia said heatedly. "I'm supposed to just throw my arms around you and believe every word you say? I don't think so."

"Okay, okay. I got that comin'." Monette drummed her fingers on the table as silence stretched between them.

Candy walked over. "Here ya go, Monette. Got y'all some snacks." She put two soft drinks, a bag of Fritos, and a bag of oatmeal cookies between Talia and Monette.

"Thanks," Monette said in a subdued tone.

"Yeah, your favorites. Y'all been talkin', so I figured time might be up and you'd miss the goodies." Candy gazed at Monette with a question in her green eyes.

"It's cool, Can." Monette nodded at her to leave.

"Okay." Candy glanced at Talia, then strolled off.

Monette looked at Talia for a few seconds more, then gave a sharp laugh. "You somethin' else. I like you, girl. Mama Rose done a good job raisin' you."

"She did a fantastic job," Talia tossed back.

"Considerin' she had to deal with how I messed you up." Monette bit her lower lip. "You're right."

Talia sighed. "I didn't come here to fight with you."

"Yes you did. I got it comin', too." Monette shook her head with a grin. "Not like your little sister. That child so sweet, I wonder if there wasn't some mix-up at the hospital."

"Alyssa has had a great life. She's a kind, forgiving kid." Talia really had grown to love her sister.

"I'm glad you get to keep in touch. Best thing I did was not to fight her adoption."

Talia marveled at her selective memory. Monette implied she'd given Alyssa up for her own good. Still, she decided to let that one pass. "So, what about this evidence that impressed Jim Rand."

Her mother smiled at her with fondness. "Now you ain't like your baby sister. Uh-uh, you like them red and yellow hot peppers my tante Pauline used to grow in her backyard. They look all pretty 'til you bite down on 'em. Then they bite your ass right back!"

"Monette, the case you're building to get out of here?"

"I can't tell you too much. But I got the goods on some big people, and I'm gettin' outta here," she whispered.

"You mean Barron?" Talia whispered back.

"What do you know, Talia?" Monette's brown eyes widened in alarm. "Somebody botherin' you?"

Talia's eyes narrowed. "Why would you think someone is bothering me, Monette? He doesn't know I'm your daughter."

"And I intend to keep it that way," Monette said. "I don't want you involved. Period."

"Monette, I'm not just looking after Mama Rose. My firm is helping Senator Jackson with his effort to change Louisiana's mandatory-sentencing laws. Since I had to come down here, I'm on the assignment."

"Act like you don't know me." Monette wore an intense expression. "Got it? You don't know me."

"At least tell me *something*."

"Look, it shouldn't be hard. You been ashamed of me all you life, with good reason," she added quickly to cut off Talia's reply. "Just pretend we ain't kin."

"But I want to know—"

"Good thing you got your daddy's last name. You the only one was with me back then," she mumbled to herself as though alone.

"Hey!" Talia waved a hand in front of Monette's face to get her attention. "I've got a bad feeling you're in over your head."

"Just do what I tell ya." Monette touched Talia's cheek briefly, then drew her hand back. "I've done enough to you for one lifetime."

"I'm tough like you, remember? Besides, I'm going to find out anyway." Talia squinted at her.

Monette shook her head. "Not this you won't. This ain't the time to be all in my business, Talia," Monette said with a fierce expression. "Things gonna get hot and heavy one of these days."

"I should have known. You've got some con game working. This is another one of your dramatic productions, a ploy to grab attention and put the parole board on the spot." Talia scowled at her mother, hoping to bait her into revealing more.

Monette glared at her as the minutes ticked by and neither spoke. The rumble of dozens of voices talking at once filled the space between them. A male guard walked by slowly. He eyed them as they stared each other down, but kept going.

"Well?" Talia said finally.

"I'm not tellin' you anything. The less you know, the better I'll sleep at night." Monette's tone made it clear she wouldn't budge.

"You're scaring me, Monette," Talia whispered. Indeed, the hairs on the back of her neck stood at attention. "If you're into something so dangerous, you need help."

Monette grabbed both Talia's hands. "My bold girl. Hell, you're a woman now."

"That's right, and I know about swimming with sharks. One thing you did teach me was survival in a hard world." Talia's voice shook unexpectedly.

"Humph, yeah and in the worst way. But not anymore," Monette mumbled. Then her glum expression brightened. "I'm gonna be all right, sugar."

"I want to know if someone is threatening you," Talia persisted. "You hung out with some dangerous people."

"I don't have to worry 'bout them. Half of 'em dead, the other half in prison."

"Monette—"

"I want you far away when the you-know-what hits the fan." Monette smiled. "That's all."

"Really?" Talia let skepticism drip from her tone as she raised both eyebrows.

"Really. And you know me. It will hit the fan and hard."

"Yeah, I know you very well." Talia tilted her head to one side, eyebrows still raised in suspicion.

"Then you know I land on my feet." Monette leaned across the table with an intense expression. "You've got a beautiful life. The last thing I want is to drag you down again. I can't undo all the hurt. But I can damn sure keep from hurtin' you now."

"So you won't tell me. You're going to keep secrets from me." Talia frowned at her.

"Just knowing you *want* to help is more than enough, baby." Monette picked up the bag of chips and tore it open. "Want some?"

Talia knew it was no use. She threw up both hands. "Fine. You've got a good point."

"Oh yeah." Monette wore a skeptical expression. "Just like that?"

"I've tried sentimentality, guilt, and getting pissed off." Talia wore a crooked smile. "I can't play a player."

"Don't you try nothin', Talia René." Monette pointed a forefinger at her.

"I spent the last sixteen years putting distance between us. You're right. I'm going to leave well enough alone." Talia smoothed down the pearl gray sweater she'd worn over black jeans. She brushed back her hair.

Monette smiled. "There ya go. Don't risk nothin' you don't have to. I'll take care of myself like I said." She popped a corn chip in her mouth.

"Ten minutes left. Start packin' up and wrappin' up. Thank y'all for comin'," Officer Landers announced over a loudspeaker.

Monette and Talia stood at the same time. They looked at each other, both awkward about how to end this first visit in years. Then Monette took one of Talia's hands.

"Damn, it was good to see you." Monette's eyes glittered with tears. She blinked and lifted her chin. "Don't come back."

"Okay." Talia took a deep breath to fight off her own emotions. "Good-bye, Monette."

"Bye, sugar." Monette touched the tips of her fingers to Talia's hair. "Be good. And let Derrick take care of you."

"I don't need anyone to take care of me." Talia picked up her purse.

Monette smiled wisely. "I know you don't. But it ain't about *need*."

"What does that mean?"

"You real smart. Think about it." Monette winked at her. She strolled off and was joined by Candy and two other inmates. They lined up at the door leading back to the cellblocks.

Talia followed the other visitors toward the exit. She glanced over her shoulder to see Monette looking at her intently. She waved, but Monette didn't wave back. Monette had her game, but this time so did Talia. She had every intention of finding out exactly what had Monette so paranoid. Despite the still-potent anger from her childhood, Talia found she cared what happened to her mother. Her research on the consequences of mandatory sentencing had helped her understand the problems. Now the issue hit close to home for her. Derrick's question bounced around her head. What if Monette *was* innocent?

Chapter 12

∞

Talia stared at the screen of the microfilm reader in the small New Roads library branch. The old newspaper accounts of Monette's trial were a piece of her life as well. She scanned the headlines and pressed a button to print out a copy. Somewhere in these articles might be clues to help her understand.

"Hey," Derrick said over her shoulder. "This is a strange lunch date." He kissed her forehead and sat in the empty chair next to her.

"We can eat at Po-Boy Heaven in a few minutes." Talia continued to stare at grainy black-and-white pictures.

"I had something different in mind. Maybe we could get a table at Morel's with a view of False River."

"No way. I've got to get back to work." Talia shook her head. "And so do you."

"Right." Derrick gave an exaggerated sigh. "So I can forget about a little lunchtime delight."

Talia looked at him from the corner of her eye. "I didn't say that. I figure we'll save time eating at a fast-food place."

"Why eat at all?" Derrick whispered close to her ear.

Talia shivered. "This is the last article." She punched

the button. A soft buzzing sound came as the printer worked.

Derrick helped her gather up the papers. In minutes they left the library in his SUV. Bright autumn sunshine painted the scenery around them. They passed antiques shops on the small town's main street.

"So what have you found out?" Derrick glanced at her, then looked back at the road.

"I'm not sure." Talia opened the folder and shuffled through the sheets until she found an article. "Maybe nothing. Monette and her pals didn't make for sympathetic defendants I'll tell you that much."

"Yeah, their lawyers tried the 'bad childhood' defense for all of them," Derrick replied. "Most of the time that strategy doesn't fly."

"I thought jurors would feel sorry for them, you know, think 'There but for the grace of God.' "

"You kidding? Black folks are the toughest jurors." Derrick steered the 4Runner down the drive through a lane of Po-Boy Heaven.

"Interesting." Talia glanced up with a slight frown. "Wonder why?"

"Jurors are mostly working-class, some have even grown up in poverty. To them being poor isn't a license to steal or sell drugs."

"Makes sense." Talia started when a male voice jumped from the speaker.

"Welcome to Po-Boy Heaven. How can I help ya?"

Talia ordered a turkey sandwich and Derrick got a roast beef po-boy with fries and a large chocolate shake. He merely shrugged when Talia clucked with disapproval.

"Do you have any idea how much fat you're about to ingest?" Talia said.

"Sure do. Hmmm, can't beat fat when it comes to good taste!" Derrick laughed when she made a face.

"All that heavy food will slow you down for *hours*," Talia peered at him over the rim of her sunglasses.

Derrick glanced at her with his brows drawn together for a couple of beats. "Make that two turkey sandwiches and two diet lemon-lime sodas."

"Smart move. I'd prefer not to have you burping beef aroma during a special moment," Talia teased.

"Very funny." Derrick pretended to frown at her, yet a smile tugged at his full lips.

They drove to Mama Rose's house. Talia suggested they eat in the backyard to take advantage of the pretty weather. After getting napkins and a tablecloth from the house, she led the way to a redwood picnic table with attached benches. Two tall elm trees swayed in a cooling breeze. Their branches stretched out over the table in a leafy canopy. Seated side by side, they ate in silence for ten minutes. Both were lost in their own thoughts. Finally, Derrick spoke after wiping his mouth with a napkin.

"I'll tell you what I think about Monette's claim."

"Claim is right." Talia put in. "Monette is a smooth operator."

"Agreed, but I don't like what I'm seeing. The main evidence against her was the circumstantial and self-serving testimony of her co-defendants." Derrick finished his sandwich in two more large bites and looked at his wristwatch. "I'm gonna be hungry in thirty minutes."

"You'll be distracted in thirty minutes, trust me." Talia winked at him saucily, then slid away when he reached for her. "I'm eating. Now back to Monette's case."

Derrick smiled, but continued. "She happened to be with these guys, which implied she must have known about the drugs."

"Based on her history, believing she didn't know

about the coke would have been hard. I mean, dealers partied at her house."

"For sure. But it's still circumstantial. So she helped them find the house once they got to town. Doesn't mean she knew."

"Monette has never been that clueless, Derrick." Talia wore a sardonic expression.

"She was high. And we both know she was just as addicted to risky behavior." Derrick used the damp paper towel Talia provided to wipe his hands.

"True, and she's still in love with drama." Talia took a swig of soda. "I've got the feeling she's got a major production in the works."

"Life is never boring with Monette on the scene." Derrick wore a half grin.

"One day she's going to use up all her lucky chances." Talia felt a chill. "Monette is about to push the wrong buttons. I can feel it."

Derrick's grin turned now into a frown. "Yeah," he said.

Talia glanced at him. "You know something."

"Nothing more than I've told you already." He stared ahead at the woods, with one large fist on his right thigh.

"But you've got a theory." Talia put down the half of her sandwich she hadn't eaten yet.

"Not exactly. It's more like a feeling reading the case file. Why is Winn Barron taking her parole hearing so personally?" He glanced at her.

"Because he convicted her, and he wants to impress the voters," Talia said.

She had seen enough political posturing to recognize the moves. Still, Derrick's use of the word "personal" struck a chord. She studied the frown on his handsome face.

"Well, describe this feeling," Talia prompted, when he didn't respond.

"Barron could have just made some speeches using her as an example. I don't understand why he's making a trip to testify. He could have sent a letter to the parole board."

"Not as effective. Besides, you can't get the same attention from the media." Talia gave a cynical laugh. "I'll bet he makes sure television cameras capture the moment."

"Maybe. Or maybe he's trying to cover himself." Derrick looked at her. "I may be stretching now, but if Monette is telling the truth then . . ."

Talia picked up his line of reasoning in seconds. "Then his sterling record could lose its shine."

"I'm no lawyer, but he missed holes in the witness testimonies." Derrick crossed his muscular arms. "What if he knew they were lying? He could get her off the streets. It's not like anyone would care."

Talia felt a mixture of anger and shame. She'd turned her back on Monette then. Monette's family had made noisy protests, but their voices didn't count. Just as many family and friends washed their hands of the whole business. With their own legal problems, the last thing they wanted was to be visible. The police and DA might turn their attention on them. The family members who didn't have trouble with the police were disgusted with Monette's lifestyle. The result was she'd pretty much gone through it all alone.

"Like me," she said.

Derrick took her hand. "You were just a kid, and you were hurting."

"I was fifteen," she said quietly. Still she had a sour taste in her mouth. "She was still my mother."

"Don't beat yourself up over Monette's mistakes," Derrick said.

Talia closed her eyes and took a deep breath. "With all she's done, my mother deserves justice."

"Look, I'm not saying Barron did anything wrong on purpose. The man's full of it, but Larry swears by him."

"And you trust Larry." Talia looked at Derrick hard. She had her doubts given how closely he seemed tied to Barron.

"Absolutely," Derrick said with a nod. "I've worked with the guy for six years. They may be hunting pals, but they're not alike in some important ways.

"I don't know, Derrick." Talia drank the last of her soda. "Larry sure jumped to help him prepare for this parole hearing."

"It's not unusual for a prosecutor to testify." Derrick rubbed his chin. "But I don't know. His vibe was funny about it. Like he had some reason he wants Monette to stay in prison, and it's not just to protect the public."

"So he doesn't want his political future to crash and burn. How far would he go?" Talia's brow furrowed. "Monette tried to hide it, but she's jittery."

Derrick looked at her with a frown. "She mentioned Barron?"

"No, and I tried to pry it out of her." Talia ground her teeth in frustration. "She drives me up the wall!"

"That mother-daughter thing, huh?" Derrick's voice held a note of sympathy.

"Complicated by a lot of crap." Talia waved a hand. "But enough of that. I'm going to talk to her lawyer. Monette will throw a fit, but I'll help if I can."

"So will I."

"No!" Talia snapped.

"What about you?" Derrick wore a calm expression. "I thought you wanted to put miles between your old life and the new one."

"Trust me, I'm not doing this with a song in my

heart," she retorted. "But I can't leave Louisiana without doing something."

"I see." Derrick let go of her hand.

"My favorite answer to the question 'What's up?' is being able to say 'Nothing much.' I don't want the roller-coaster soap opera kind of life anymore."

"What's that got to do with me?" Derrick's jaw muscle tightened.

Talia chewed her bottom lip. She had to be honest with him. "You're a wonderful man. I care a lot about you. But chasing down crooks and creeps reminds me of living with Monette."

"C'mon, Talia!" he said angrily. "This isn't some ghetto lifestyle! This is my career."

"You crave the thrill, the excitement. The only fight I want is over the check with a client." Talia shook her head slowly. "I've had my fill of wondering if someone I love will come home alive."

"My job isn't dangerous." Derrick turned to her with a stiff expression. "You care about me, but not enough."

"That's not true at all." Talia put her arms around his neck, but he remained rigid in her embrace.

"Am I just keeping you warm until you get back to Jarrod?" Derrick carefully took her hands in his and took her arms off his neck.

"I can't believe you!" Talia stared at him in shock.

"Then what's your game? I thought you felt something real for me." Derrick's full mouth twisted into a bitter smile. "I'm feeling used right now."

Talia saw the hurt in his brown eyes. "Rougon isn't my home anymore. Being away has helped me to heal."

"Okay." Derrick stood up. He stuffed the empty wrappers and paper cups into the bag, then crumpled it between his large hands. "I've gotta get back to the office."

"Derrick, don't be angry with me." Talia stood, grabbed his arm to keep him from walking away.

"You made yourself clear for the hundredth time." Derrick handed her the bag, then put on his sunglasses. "Throw this away. I'm not coming inside."

"Yes, you are." Talia tightened her grip on his arm. "I'm not going to let go."

"You already have, Talia. Too bad it isn't so easy for me," he said in a strangled voice.

"It was hard for me to leave," Talia said. "I wanted to come back, but you know why I couldn't."

Talia inched toward him, afraid he would bolt if she moved too fast. When he didn't, she put her arms around his waist. They stood together for a long time. She could feel the warmth of his body through the light blue cotton dress shirt he wore. His hard muscles made her feel safe. After a while his chest rose as he inhaled deeply, then exhaled. Derrick relaxed in her arms.

"I know, baby. Guess I'm more of a dreamer than I ever thought I was." Derrick kissed the top of her head.

Talia trembled with regret at the despair in his tone. She hated being the source of his unhappiness. Yet something deep down felt a panic at staying in Rougon. She'd come close to kidding herself she could. Monette's dramatic behavior brought back all the reasons she'd stayed away. She would do what she could to help her mother, but at a distance.

"I truly want to help her, Derrick. I'm going to do a bit of digging on my own."

"I've got access to files and can—"

She glanced up at him. "Your whole career would be screwed."

"Then I'll give you what I find out," he insisted.

"Perrilloux and Barron will know." Talia put a hand

on his cheek. "Honey, please. Keep away from Monette."

"Most of what I tell you will be public record. The rest, well, any good reporter could get it with a little luck and inside sources." Derrick kissed her forehead. "Face it, we're in this together already."

Talia let go of him and walked around the table to stand in the shade of an oak tree. "See, this is what I didn't want. We have to think of all kinds of ins and outs."

"Life is always complicated," Derrick said.

She turned to face him. "Not everyone's life is about prisons and sensational scandals."

Derrick gave a short laugh. "Talia, you work in Washington, D.C., the capital of scandal and double-dealing."

"But not in *my personal life*!" Talia spread her arms out. "Most of the people who live there just work, play, and spend time with their families."

"And that's what you want," Derrick said.

"Yes." Talia rubbed her eyes.

"You think I'm threatening your dream? Tell the truth, Talia." Derrick walked closer to her.

"I didn't say any of what's happening is your fault." Talia let her hands fall to her sides. "Just stay out of it, okay? Jim Rand will have access to the same files you're reading. If there's anything funny, he'll spot it."

Derrick put a hand in his pocket. "Okay."

"You agreed to that mighty fast and easy, Derrick." Talia's eyes narrowed. "What are you up to?"

"Nothing. You want me out of it, I'm out of it."

"Good." She continued to eye him with suspicion.

"Wonderful. Look, I gotta go." Derrick's expression behind the dark glasses was hard to read.

"I just want you to be safe, that's all," Talia said, making sure to soften her tone.

"So you keep telling me. And I keep telling you I'm more than able to look after myself." Derrick joined her in the shade and took off his sunglasses. His eyes were intense. "Stop pushing me away."

"Talia, geez! When you said this place was in the sticks, you didn't lie." Jarrod strode down a path from the front yard, his suit coat over one arm. His expression tightened visibly when he glanced at Derrick. "Hello, I think we met in D.C." He stuck out a hand once he got close.

"Yeah." Derrick clasped it tightly for a second, then let go. They stood gazing at each other in silence.

Talia cleared her throat. She shot a warning look at Derrick, who seemed to be coming to a slow boil. "Hi, Jarrod. What in the world are you doing here?"

"I came to support you in any way I can. Jasmine told me you were staying longer. I got worried." He ignored Derrick and walked close to her. "Are you holding up okay?"

"Of course I am. You didn't have to come all this way to ask me that. There's e-mail and the telephone." Talia tried not to let too much of the irritation she felt come through.

"There's a mini-conference in New Orleans this week on a national gun-tracking system. We're training top cops on the department's updated computerized system." Jarrod flashed a charming smile. "I saw a chance to see you and grabbed it."

"Oh." Talia looked at Derrick. She recognized that blank expression. "So you've got to get back I guess."

"I've got plenty of time." Jarrod assumed a relaxed pose, as though he didn't intend to move for days.

"Like I said, I've got to go. I'll call you later." Derrick started off.

"Wait!" Talia called out louder than she intended.

She shot a tight smile at Jarrod, then followed him. "What's the rush?"

"Is this a coincidence?" Derrick gave a slight nod back toward Jarrod.

"I didn't know he was coming if that's what you mean. And I sure as hell didn't invite him," she said in a harsh whisper, then looked at Jarrod over her shoulder.

"He must have had a reason to think he'd be welcome. Bye, Talia." Derrick looked away. "I can't compete with a hot lawyer making three times my salary."

"This isn't a competition with me as the prize," she hissed. "Don't go all 'You my woman' on me, Derrick Guillory."

"I like the way you say my name with that dangerous edge to your voice." Derrick lifted one dark eyebrow, his full lips parted in a provocative expression.

Talia gasped at the shock of pleasure through her hips. "Don't patronize me."

Amusement faded from his expression. "D.C. keeps calling you, babe. He's part of that life. Maybe you're right, you belong far away from here."

She heard the unspoken words loud and clear. "Not from you."

"I really do have to go. I've got two witnesses to track down." Derrick leaned down and kissed her lips gently. His wore a devilish grin when he stood straight again. "Let him stew over that one."

"You, you . . ." Talia huffed, as he backed away and waved good-bye.

"See ya, babe," he called out. "Nice seeing you, man."

"Yeah, right," Jarrod replied in a dry tone.

Talia spun around and glared at Jarrod. Unable to vent at Derrick for his behavior, she turned her anger on Jarrod. She marched back to him and put both hands on her hips.

"You just happened to be in Louisiana. Then you drive over an hour way out here 'in the sticks' as you put it." She glared at the tall attorney.

He sat on the edge of the picnic table. "You got it. Looks like I came at the right time, too."

"Meaning?" Talia crossed her arms.

"I don't know all the details, Talia. But I listened when you were talking about home." Jarrod gazed at her. "You don't want to stay here."

"You've got me all figured out, huh?" Talia retorted.

Jarrod seemed unaffected by her anger. "Something bad went down. Something you'd rather not be reminded of. This guy is trying to convince you everything is okay now."

"Okay, Sherlock. I can't fool you." His words shook her. Talia tried to remember exactly what she'd said to him during all their long talks.

"Don't worry, you didn't give me details. I'm just good at reading between the lines." Jarrod stood. "I can help."

"No, you can't. I appreciate your concern, but I'll be okay." Talia smiled at him.

"I thought we were closer than this, Talia."

She shook her head slowly. "I don't know what you want me to say."

"Then I'll tell you." Jarrod walked within inches of her. "Say you want me to stay. Trust me enough to let your guard down finally."

"I can't. What's happening doesn't just involve me." Talia took his hand. "I appreciate the offer, really I do."

Jarrod pulled free from her grasp. "So I'll read it in the newspapers I guess. Was I Derrick's stand-in?"

"Okay, I've been understanding. Don't push it!" Talia tossed back angrily. "I'm not your possession, and I'm not Derrick's either."

"What did you expect me to think? I come all the way here to be with you and find him hanging out." Jarrod combed long fingers through his hair.

"Stop with the jealous boyfriend act. We agreed to be friends." Talia looked away when his hazel eyes clouded with hurt.

"I took what I could get. Let me in," he said softly.

"No, Jarrod." Talia sighed. "You'll be grateful I didn't get you mixed up with my troubles. Trust me on that one."

"No I won't," he said, his voice husky with disappointment. "I'd walk through fire for you, Talia."

"The last thing I need is one more person to worry about. Be sensible," Talia said with a frown.

"Come back to D.C. with me. We can wrap up anything we need to here." Jarrod brushed her hair with one hand. "Remember our favorite Friday night date?"

"Yeah, Chinese takeout and comedy videos." Talia smiled.

"Except it's my turn. Lebanese takeout and one of those vintage Eddie Murphy stand-up routines." Jarrod smiled back at her. "Then we could head over to see the latest art exhibits or take in a jazz performance. Or maybe go to our favorite Japanese restaurant."

Talia nodded slowly. She kept up a fast pace during the week, but she did occasionally slow down on the weekends. Washington, D.C., was the most exciting place she'd ever lived. And it was far from Rougon. Two major attractions.

"Listen, Jarrod." Talia placed a hand on his shoulder. "I'm going to make sure Mama Rose gets back to her normal routine of Women's Auxiliary meetings, church twice a week, and sticking her nose in my personal business. Then I'm outta here."

He studied her expression for several seconds. A relaxed smile spread across his face. "Good. Are you sure I can't—"

"Positively, absolutely sure! Now go back to that conference before your boss finds out you're goofing off." Talia turned him around and pushed him ahead of her.

"Hey, I don't even get to take you out to dinner?" he said over his shoulder.

"You can't hang around all day waiting for me. I have work to do."

"I'm going to the department's office in Baton Rouge. I'll be back by six." Jarrod whirled around to face her. "What do you say?"

"You're such a hardheaded guy. Fine. I'll treat you to dinner at the Ox Bow. Satisfied?" Talia shook her head.

"Totally." Jarrod gave her a quick kiss before she could dodge him. "I know, just pals." He waved and strolled off whistling.

Talia followed him to his rental car, a steel blue Chevy Lumina. Jarrod flashed another smile, then backed out of the driveway.

"Bye," she murmured.

Jarrod had arrived in time as a reminder of why she stayed in D.C. She'd fought hard to leave her childhood behind. Time and distance helped. None of that history had followed her, except for painful memories, and Talia had pushed those into a locked mental closet. Yet just as she'd feared, being back in Louisiana had changed the past into the present.

Talia promised herself she would return to the career and city she'd grown to treasure. An image of Derrick's smoky gaze popped into her head. The memory of his hard, warm body was almost too much to bear. Talia hurried inside the house. For five excruciating hours she distracted herself by studying every word that had been written on Monette's case.

Chapter 13

∞

Monette studied the man seated across from her. "I ain't seen you in years, Jerry. Kinda surprised to see you now."

"I've been neglectful of an old buddy. I came to say I'm sorry." Jerome Hines's attempt to look repentant only succeeded in making him look more suspect.

Jerome Hines had been Winn Barron's investigator when he was the district attorney. The bony man rubbed a scar on his right jawline. His long, cocoa brown face split into an edgy grin. His expression reminded her of the hyenas she'd seen on nature films. He enjoyed scaring people, especially women. Jerry had relished throwing his weight around back then. Monette wouldn't let him see the dread that had taken root in her belly the moment he walked in.

"Uh-huh." Monette leaned back in her chair and stretched one leg out. "We was never buddies."

"I hate to hear you say that, Monette. I'm here to help you out."

Jerry spread his hands out as he spoke. Gold rings, a heavy gold bracelet on his right wrist and a Rolex on his left wrist flashed at the movement. He wore a forest green Ralph Lauren polo shirt and dark khaki slacks.

Monette guessed his dark red leather loafers were designer and very expensive as well.

"Those fancy clothes and all that jewelry almost makes you look human." Monette let contempt drip from her voice like acid. She stared at him from head to toe. "Second thought, you ain't even close."

The smile on his narrow face froze into something terrible. "I got some advice. Silence is golden."

Monette felt a stab of fear but gave him an equally frigid smile. "Can't spend it though."

"Okay, so much for old-school shit." His eyes glittered with malevolence. "Let me put it to you in my words. You talk too damn much."

She knew this game. He only took orders. Monette decided to make a move that could make things better or worse. She leaned toward him and lowered her voice.

"Listen, baby, tell Winn I've got somebody on my side for once."

The cocky smile on Jerry's face slipped, and he glanced around him. "Keep your damn voice down, okay?"

"He didn't send you, did he? In fact, he doesn't know you came on this little visit." Monette laughed when he rubbed his face nervously.

"Look, don't be stupid. Maybe I can help you out. But we have too much on the line for you to get things all stirred up. You know what I'm talking about." Jerry's harsh whisper cracked with the sound of desperation.

"Earl was still breathing when you took him outta my house," Monette snapped. "What happened after that is on *you*."

"Who will they believe, me or you? I didn't pull the trigger." Jerry leaned so close their faces were only an inch apart. "We're in this together!"

"I know damn well you didn't keep the gun after all these years. You're too smart for such a dumb move." Monette shrugged. "You handled it, too. Jerry, you can't afford for anybody to start askin' questions about how y'all got those convictions. Earl can't talk, but I can."

Jerry let out a noisy breath and rubbed his face. "It wasn't my idea, you coming to prison. You know how he was about you. I've never seen a guy go that crazy over a woman. When he found out about you and Earl, he had me bring the dude in. Earl made the mistake of catching an attitude. Said we were his bitches, with all he knew on us."

Monette studied him for several minutes. She arranged players, events, and facts in a neat pattern. "You were going to do Earl anyway, weren't you?" she said, her voice barely above a whisper.

"I'm just trying to explain why you shouldn't use the wrong strategy to try and get paroled, alright?" Jerry's expression turned cold.

"Whatever went down between you, Earl, and Winn doesn't concern me. But I'm gettin' outta here by whatever means necessary."

"I don't have a choice. Can't you see that? Barron is even more powerful now than he was back then." Jerry shook his head.

"I'm not feelin' real sorry for you, Jerry. I'm sittin' in a cell, and you're living it up with your fat wife and big fancy house," Monette hissed.

"I know people that can help, talk to the parole board members. This social worker I know has a program for women released from prison. She can get you a job and—"

"Right. I'll be livin' in some dump halfway house in the 'hood and slingin' burgers for minimum wage. No thank you."

Jerry stood and buttoned the dark gray suit jacket. "Okay, I tried. I can't do anything for you, girl."

"Like I believe you got my interest at heart. You're tryin' to save your own ass." Monette pointed a finger at him. "He's got to pay for what he did to me."

He leaned forward with both palms flat on the table. "You have no idea what he's capable of. The man has too much to lose. So do you."

Monette stood to face him. "For over fifteen years I been fightin' off crazy women who wanna kill you for less than nothin' and livin' in a box with a toilet in the corner. What do I have to lose?"

Jerry clenched and unclenched his fists. "Damn, Barron wouldn't listen," he muttered low, and looked over his shoulder. "I tried to get you out of this mess."

"You didn't try hard enough. Bye." Monette turned and walked away.

Only when he disappeared from view did Monette let her shoulders drop. Her muscles ached from the tension of maintaining her gutsy facade. Candy kissed her visitor, an elderly man, good-bye. Then she joined Monette.

"You okay?" Candy nodded toward the door. "That guy looks meaner than a hungry junkyard dog."

"I been fightin' a long time, Candy. I'm tired." Monette inhaled deeply and let out a ragged breath.

Candy put an arm around her shoulder. "Hold on, girlfriend. You can make it. Let's pray."

"Yeah. God didn't save my low-down butt for nuthin'." She wore a poignant smile.

"I love it!" Mama Rose did a turn and walked back like a runway model. She wore a royal blue satin pantsuit. A lovely paisley silk scarf draped one shoulder.

"That's your color." Talia laughed. Seeing Mama

Rose back to her old form was a true delight. "You can wear that to the first Women's Auxiliary soiree. Your gentleman friend is going to have you dressed just right to go home."

Mama Rose smoothed down the long tunic. "I'll be right back." She went to her bedroom.

Talia turned on the television and flipped through channels while she waited for her to return. Not finding anything interesting, she glanced around the room. The family photos and Mama Rose's favorite Black figurine collectibles gave the apartment a cozy feel. Mama Rose came back in wearing a dark green pullover sweater and a long denim skirt.

"Well, tell me what's happening in your life," she said. She sat down in her favorite rocking chair, which Karl had brought from her house.

"Not much. Working on this project while I'm here. I don't feel so disconnected from the office." Talia put her feet up on a small ottoman.

"Good. Have you been back to visit Monette?" Mama Rose patted a few throw pillows.

Her casual tone didn't fool Talia. She cleared her throat. "Not yet."

"She's trying to get out I understand." Mama Rose glanced at Talia briefly. She reached into a wicker basket and took out a cross-stitch project.

"Hey, I didn't know you liked that kind of thing." Talia stared at her. "You're not the sit-at-home-knitting type."

Mama Rose lifted a shoulder. "It's not so bad. After I got over being mad about being here I finally went to the craft room. I'm learning how to make ceramics, too."

"You are?" Talia blinked at her in astonishment.

"There are art classes as well. I'm not that good at

drawing, but Harold does lovely watercolors." Mama Rose pulled the needle through the fabric.

"Harold? What happened to Mr. Franklin?" Talia's mouth dropped open even wider.

"Too clingy. I needed space," she said. "We're still friends though."

"My, my. You've got a whole new life here." Talia couldn't believe her ears.

"The ladies and I have fun. I wouldn't have believed it six weeks ago. Me having a good time in an old folks home." Mama Rose's coffee brown eyes twinkled behind her bifocals.

"Assisted-living residence," Talia corrected.

"Right, let's be politically correct." Mama Rose chuckled. "But seriously, I had the stereotype of a nursing home from the old days. This place is nothing like that."

"So it will be tougher than you thought going home?" Talia smiled at her.

Mama Rose stopped sewing and put her project down. "The doctor talked to me yesterday."

Talia felt a prickle of apprehension. "What did he say?"

"Don't be alarmed, sugar. I'm doing fine. My recovery is going well, and this medication has me shipshape."

"You're telling me everything, right?" Talia replied with a touch of suspicion in her voice. "Don't try to protect me."

"Of course I'm telling you everything." Mama Rose's expression was one of maternal affection. "You were always such a tough little girl on the outside. But inside you were a sensitive child."

Talia picked up a throw pillow. She smoothed the fabric with one hand, then realized she was more like

Mama Rose than Monette. Maybe she'd be making pottery and embroidering cute kittens on fabric one day. *Scary thought*, she mused, and put the pillow down.

"I just don't like surprises," Talia said.

"That hard shell has helped you through bad times." Mama Rose rocked as she gazed at Talia. "It's time to take it off."

"We were talking about you, Missy," Talia said. "What did the doctor say?"

Mama Rose nodded as though she understood some unspoken message. "He doesn't think I should live alone. My nearest neighbor is almost two miles down the road. Though you wouldn't think it the way Olivia knows all my business."

"I'll stay as long as you need me," Talia said.

"Karl told me Monette has some plan to get out of prison. Something about being set up."

"You concentrate on getting well. Besides, you've known Monette long enough to know how she is. More of the same drama." Talia stood. "Want something to drink? I'm thirsty."

"No, thanks. There are soft drinks in the fridge."

Talia came back with a can of lemon-lime soda. She popped the top and took a sip. "I think maybe she has a chance. But you don't need to get involved," she added pointedly.

"I'd be glad to testify to her character. She's made real changes, Talia. For one thing, she's gone back to the church."

"Monette will try anything if it means getting her rear end out of a tight spot."

"She's sincere this time. I can feel it," Mama Rose said with a frown. "Shame on you for being so cynical about your mama."

"Maybe you're right," Talia said after a few moments of thought.

Mama Rose sighed with contentment. "All in all things will work out. Thank you, baby, for coming home. You just don't know how much you helped."

"Nothing could have kept me away, Mama. You stuck with me when a lot of foster parents would have given up. Thank *you*," she said softly.

Mama Rose held out both arms. Talia put down her soda and crossed to her. They hugged, and Talia rested her head on Mama Rose's shoulder.

"You're my baby girl no matter what. We always did have a connection, didn't we?" Mama Rose murmured.

Talia breathed in the sweet scent of Cashmere Bouquet soap and cinnamon that always reminded her of Mama Rose's love. "I love you, Mama Rose. Which is why I want to make sure this new boyfriend is straight," she added teasingly.

"Speaking of affairs of the heart, let Derrick in. He's the one, Talia."

"I can't stay here, Mama." That was all Talia dared tell her.

"So stubborn. And what about Monette? Karl tells me you're going to help her."

"Karl talks way too much," Talia retorted.

"I know how to pry information out of him. What is all this about you going up against the attorney general?"

"I'm helping Senator Jackson get mandatory-sentencing laws eased, and Barron's against it. Monette's case could be used as an example of good intentions leading to bad consequences." Talia gave her the short version of the issue.

Sharp as ever, Mama Rose nodded her understanding. "I know. Much too harsh a response in 99 percent of the cases."

"Right. Monette is no church lady; well, she wasn't

until now," Talia added with a smile. "But forty years is excessive."

"You and Derrick will help her." Mama Rose pinched her cheek. "That kind of bond will spark a fire between you."

"Mama Rose," Talia scolded. "No matchmaking maneuvers."

"Hmmm." Mama Rose hummed a tune and went back to working on her cross-stitch.

"You're a rascal, you know that?" Talia laughed and kissed her cheek. "I'd better go get some work done. Obviously, you don't need me hanging around when Harold might show up." She stood.

"Very amusing." Mama Rose gave her a playful swat on the hip. "Don't forget lunch tomorrow."

"No way. I gotta check this dude out." Talia waved good-bye and let herself out.

Talia headed for home. She had several reports she planned to send back to the office via e-mail attachment. The sight of Derrick's SUV surprised her. He got out as she pulled into the driveway.

"Hi," he said. His expression was serious behind the dark sunglasses. "I wanted to talk to you."

"Sure." Talia didn't look forward to it. Still she managed to smile at him. "How are you?"

"Okay," he said shortly and followed her inside.

"Nice weather. I love this time of year." Talia walked across the front porch and unlocked the front door.

"So much for small talk." He drew her into his arms and kissed her.

Talia attempted to push him away at first. Yet the taste of him, hot and strong, flowed down her throat like fine Creole hot sauce. His hands roamed up and down her sides until they finally rested on her hips. Derrick pulled her tight against him as though to emphasize his need. She moaned low in her throat at the hardness through the fabric of his slacks.

"I want you now," Derrick mumbled, his mouth still on hers.

"Hmmm," Talia replied.

She could only babble when his hands roamed again, finding their way to her buttocks. In minutes they were undressing each other in a fever. They found their way to her bedroom. Without a word, she sank onto the bed and brought him down with her. They made love fast and furiously on the soft rose-colored comforter. Talia thrilled at the way the soft cover cushioned her as Derrick penetrated. Their thrusts were hard, quick, and pushed them both into trance, screaming for more. Nothing else mattered, only satisfying the wild hunger that dominated them. Derrick came first, with Talia tumbling into a powerful climax seconds later. The intense pleasure lasted forever, yet ended much too soon. His movements slowed until Derrick gasped and laid his head on her neck. Talia shuddered with one last jab of pleasure. She rubbed her lips on his forehead as she stroked his hair lovingly.

"What was all that about?" she whispered.

"I need you, Talia," he replied simply.

His voice, full of emotion, shook her more than a long impassioned speech ever could. Her growing realization of how much she needed him terrified her. Need led to excruciating heartache, a hard lesson she'd learned early in life.

Talia stopped stroking his hair. "You know how much you mean to me."

Derrick lay very still for ten seconds then lifted his head and stared into her eyes. "Do I? What do you want from me?"

His question wasn't a demand. Rather, it seemed a plea to explain. Talia blinked back tears because she didn't know the answer. Derrick sighed and rolled away. He lay with one arm across his eyes as he spoke.

"There's no way to fix this, is there?" Derrick said.

"I don't see how." Talia bit her lip. "Maybe we could have a commuter love thing. Fly to each other on alternate weekends." She tried for humor in the situation.

"You want the best of both worlds."

Derrick stood and strode into her bathroom. Moments later she heard the shower. Talia got out of bed. She placed a clean fluffy towel inside on the vanity counter. Then went into the kitchen. Twenty minutes later Derrick came in fully dressed.

"I'm going back to the office." He waved away her offer of a glass of lemonade.

"You're mad at me again." Talia sighed.

"I want more than you do. House, kids, toys all over my SUV, the works." Derrick smoothed down his silk tie."

"Honey, please—"

"I'm cool. I figured it out."

His words went into her heart like a filet knife. "This place . . ." Her voice faded at the hard expression on his face.

"Don't even try it, Talia. Settling down with a trophy husband is safer for you." Derrick did not raise his voice as he spoke.

"So, you took Psychology 101, and you know it all," she snapped.

"I know you, baby." Derrick took a deep breath and let it out as he pulled a hand over his face. "Just forget it."

"Jarrod and I aren't picking out china patterns." Talia laid her palm against his chest. "We only had dinner."

"Yeah, and one day you'll realize you can have that D.C. life with him," he said.

"What do you want me to say, damn it?" Talia let her hand fall.

"We could face anything together. But you don't trust me to take care of you."

"I don't need you to take care of me. Just be here."

"Oh right, on your terms. Well, maybe that's not enough." Derrick's voice was weary. "I can't lie and pretend I'll walk away from you, Talia. I'm stuck."

"You're stuck!" she repeated. "Makes me seem like quicksand." Talia clenched her fists.

"To be honest, sometimes I feel like I'm sinking." Derrick shook his head with his eyes closed.

Talia pressed the heel of one hand against her forehead. "I'm trying to handle so much right now."

"Don't tell me to give you more time!" Derrick looked at her, his dark eyes flashing. "I've given you fifteen years."

"We've had beautiful days and nights together," she countered.

"So, it's not Jarrod?" He looked at her searchingly.

"I told him straight up how I felt months ago."

"But it's not me either," Derrick said in a flat voice.

"Let me handle Mama Rose and Monette. Then we can—"

"Yeah, never the right time or place. I gotta go." Derrick walked away.

Talia followed him. "This is hard for me, too."

He stopped, and Talia held her breath. Derrick didn't turn around immediately. She expected him to blast her with accusations and anger. Instead, when he faced Talia his expression was sad.

"You don't want to try, Talia. No, don't give me all the usual excuses.

"That's not fair. This isn't just about me," she insisted.

"Uh-huh. Like I said, I'm going back to work. I'll

let you know what I find out about Monette's case." Derrick unlocked the front door and left.

"Derrick, don't do anything—" She stopped when he kept walking.

He put on his sunglasses. Strikingly handsome, his brown face bore an indomitable expression. She wanted to tell him once more not to take chances, but he wouldn't listen. Derrick was hell-bent on doing what he thought needed to be done. She slammed the door hard enough to rattle the door facing. If Derrick didn't have sense enough to keep himself safe, she'd have to do it.

Chapter 14

∞

Larry tapped Derrick's shoulder. "Let's talk," he said, and headed for his office.

"Sure." Derrick exchanged a glance with Kelsey.

The administrative assistant raised her arched reddish brown eyebrows over wire reading glasses. "Barron called here three times today."

The lanky man was seated at his desk. He waited until Derrick closed the door. "How much have you found out about Monette Victor?"

"She had one arrest before this big conviction, served a short sentence for possession. Got probation several times as a teenager. She hung out with some nasty dudes, mostly small-time thugs who—"

"I meant what do we know about her personal life." Larry rocked back and forth in the chair.

"She went through rehab two, three times, drug of choice cocaine. Had three kids by the time she was twenty-seven. All of them ended up in foster care."

Derrick felt a twist in his stomach at the memory of one of those children in particular. He remembered big brown eyes that mirrored longing and a need to be cared for. Larry's next question yanked his attention back with force.

"What about boyfriends?" Larry sat motionless suddenly.

"Not really." Derrick maintained his matter-of-fact pose, but his invisible feelers were vibrating like crazy. "Is it important?"

"Just asking," Larry said quickly. He cleared his throat and rocked his chair again. "What else?"

Derrick knew Larry well enough to know he didn't just ask questions for no reason. His process seemed random, then suddenly a pattern would emerge. At times Derrick would see it before his boss did.

"Got pregnant when she'd just turned fourteen years old. She was in foster care herself at the time. She liked to party, which is what got her into the drug scene when she was just a kid. She had a string of men run through her life from what I can tell." Derrick was careful not to make his knowledge sound firsthand.

"What my grandmamma used to call a fast woman on her way to nowhere," Larry said in a pensive tone.

"In this case right to prison unfortunately. Men sure like her." Derrick sorted through his own thoughts. Pieces began to click in place, and a picture emerged.

"Yes." Larry flipped open a file. "She looks like she'd be a pretty woman, even on this mug shot."

Derrick followed his gaze. "Obviously she finally hooked up with the wrong men. A forty-year sentence is a high price for flirting." He stared at Larry.

"Derrick, I'm always amazed at how *foolish* smart people can be." Larry swung his chair around and gazed out of the window.

"Anything wrong?"

"I don't like cleaning up after other people, Derrick. Winn was a zealous and ambitious DA. Using informants can backfire." He continued to stare out the window, but he wouldn't say more.

"What are you saying?"

Larry spun the chair around. "You're too bright not to figure it out."

They gazed at each other for a time. The district attorney wore a grim expression. Derrick recognized a man between a rock and a hard place.

"You only suspect something is rotten. Just a whiff, but smelly enough to stay in your nose a long time," Derrick said carefully.

"I don't like mandatory sentencing," Larry replied. "It's bad law, period."

"Yeah." Derrick waited for him to go on.

Instead he sighed and sat straight. He smoothed down the front of his expensive cotton-and-linen-blend white dress shirt. "I'm going to send a report to the parole board and a copy to Winn. That will be the end of my involvement."

"Okay." Derrick stood.

He knew his boss well enough to read his signals. The subject was closed, for now anyway. Somehow, he knew they'd talk again. Larry would need someone to confide in soon. Derrick went back to his small office. He sat staring at another case file without seeing it. Kelsey appeared in his open door, hand on one hip.

"What's up?" She nodded toward Larry's office.

"Tension between politics and getting the job done," he replied as he tapped his pen against the stack of papers.

"In other words SOS—same old you-know-what." Kelsey grunted. "Barron is at the bottom of whatever is going on. He and that investigator he used, Jerome Hines, were a little too slick if you ask me."

"Hmm," Derrick said.

Kelsey continued talking and listed the many reasons she didn't like Winn Barron. Derrick heard her voice as background to his own thoughts. Possibilities bounced around his mind like balls on a pool table. Larry's comments had set them in motion. He sat back in his chair and waited for them to settle into a position that would tell him which one to tap.

"I just hope Larry doesn't let that windbag pull him down." Kelsey put a typed report in a file basket on his desk. "Here, check it for typos and give it back to me."

"Uh-huh."

She frowned at him. "You okay? I'm here talking to myself."

Derrick snapped out of his reverie and picked up the report. "Sorry. What did you say?"

"Never mind. I'm going to lunch. Want anything?"

"I'll eat later," Derrick mumbled.

When she left he picked up the telephone receiver. Derrick had checked out the bad guys involved in Monette's case until he knew them inside out. Now he decided to check on the good guys.

Talia took a deep breath and knocked on Jim Rand's office door. She was startled when he swung the door open immediately.

"Hello, Dr. Rand," she said, and cleared her dry throat.

"Hello, Ms. Marchand. Come in. I'll be right with you." He smiled boyishly, very different from the intense expert she'd met in Senator Jackson's office. She walked into the room. The walls were lined with bookcases. Papers and file folders were stacked on chairs, a round table across from his desk, and the floor.

"I know it looks a mess, but I can find everything like that." He snapped his fingers.

"I'll bet you can." Talia stared around her.

"Let me finish up one thing. Sorry to be so rude, but this can't wait." He looked at her expectantly, an apologetic expression on his face.

"No problem." She read the spines of books. "Are these real?" She pointed to a row of old books.

"Got those at an estate sale in the Garden District." Jim's eyes sparkled with enthusiasm. "Bound copies of the city's laws handwritten in French, circa 1799. Please, sit while I finish up."

"Sure." Talia continued to read.

"You're welcome to take one down. This isn't a museum. I read them all the time."

He waved permission to her as he went to the large desk. Seconds later he stood while making furious notes on a legal pad. A law student came in, and Jim issued succinct instructions. The pretty young Asian woman wrote down his instructions, then left. His phone rang twice. After answering it both times, he set his answering machine to pick up.

"So we won't be disturbed." Satisfied his task was done, he sat back in his chair. His dark eyes mirrored a keen interest. "Now how can I help you?"

"I'm from Louisiana. I came down on a personal matter." When his eyebrows went up, Talia continued. "The woman who raised me is ill, and I came home to take care of her."

"I hope she's doing better."

"Actually she is. In fact she's close to running circles around me." Talia smiled briefly.

"Having you here probably made all the difference." He wore a kind expression.

"Thanks. I've done research on this mandatory sentencing." Talia realized she was floundering for a reasonable explanation for this meeting.

"Marti told me." Jim seemed willing to be patient.

"Right. In fact, I've read a few of the articles you've written on the subject. They've really been a big help."

"Glad to hear it."

"Right, right. You're considered one of the foremost

experts in several criminal law areas." Talia cast around for a way to go on.

"So this is part of your research?" Jim asked.

"I'm just wondering about the Monette Victor case. What made you decide to accept it?"

"The amount of attention paid to putting her in prison versus the circumstances of her alleged crime," Jim said promptly. "Frankly, that's what caught my student's attention."

"Really?" Talia forgot her unease.

"That was she who came in a moment ago. Lucy is one of five students on my poverty law team. Sharp young minds that don't miss much."

"So if any of them smell a rat, you listen."

"I make them present a solid case. And I'm tough." His boyish smile flashed back, as if to belie the notion he could be tough at anything.

Talia returned his smile. "I'll bet you've been mistaken for a pushover more than once in your career. You even got the governor angry about your successes."

"My students did a lot of good, hard work. I guide them," he said sincerely without a trace of false modesty in his tone. "As for the governor, he's entitled to his opinion."

She decided she liked Jim Rand. "You took him on and the state supreme court backed you up."

"Eventually. Politics has a long reach, but the rule of law does prevail occasionally." Jim wore a tight expression.

The governor had put pressure on the chief justice to rein in the law school's poverty law program. The chief justice ordered the team only to help the poorest of the poor. After several setbacks, Jim Rand and his lawyer had won. The chief justice had backed down in the face of protests from the state and national bar associations.

Jim Rand was nobody's fool or doormat. Talia liked him very much indeed.

"Power to the people." She quoted the seventies slogan with a grin.

"Amen." Jim's frown relaxed into a smile once more. "Now tell me about your interest in Monette's case, Ms. Marchand."

Nobody's fool for sure, Talia thought. "The attorney general seems to be making hers a test case so to speak. And I wondered why, aside from the fact that he prosecuted her."

Jim rocked his chair gently without answering immediately, as though mulling over her explanation. "It's not all that unusual if a prosecutor feels strongly about one of his convictions."

"Except he's not the DA anymore. What makes her so special? There was no violence, and no police officer was hurt. Why all the attention for a few grams of cocaine sixteen years ago? Seems odd to me." Talia shook her head.

"He's running for office. The public feels strongly about drug dealers, and he has found a way to make headlines," Jim offered.

"Doesn't add up. The election is two years away. The public and the media both have short memories. Monette isn't even a big fish," Talia countered.

Jim's gaze sharpened as he focused on her. He became the seasoned litigator in an instant. "You'd make a fine law student, Ms. Marchand. You fell right into arguing your points just the way we train them."

"Thanks."

"Very good points, exactly the line of thought we've been following." Jim nodded slowly. "Keep going."

Talia leaned forward in her chair. "He's spending a

lot of time having Larry Perrilloux pull the records and report to him."

"I know. There is nothing in the case that explains his level of indignation. No, that's not the right word." Jim rocked his chair again.

"He seems determined to make sure she stays in prison, like he's on some kind of vendetta. And I don't think he wants headlines. I mean the press is preoccupied with events overseas and the budget crisis. I didn't even see a small mention of this issue." Talia looked at him.

"Monette's trial didn't get that much press." Jim rubbed his chin.

"Exactly. So why is he pulling out all the stops?"

"He's a politician pushing a hot button. I wouldn't characterize his actions as 'pulling out the stops.' "

"Okay, call it an intense interest in Monette's case." Talia tried to grab an elusive thread but missed. She tapped a fist on the arm of her chair.

"Unfortunately, my client is keeping secrets from me." Jim's frown returned, only more intense.

"Bad move." Talia pushed down a rise of anger. Count on Monette to make the situation worse.

"I tried talking sense to Monette, but she's slippery. Too slippery for her own good I'm afraid."

Talia nodded. "Jailhouse jive. Always working an angle."

"She's trying to survive the best way she knows how." Jim's stern expression eased. "For some reason I think she's trying to protect me and someone else."

Talia blinked rapidly and forced her hands to relax. "Why would she do that?"

"I wish I knew."

"Her defense wasn't all that vigorous, and she didn't make for a credible defendant protesting her innocence."

"Happens a lot, I'm afraid," Jim said.

Talia sat back in her seat. "Did you interview the people who worked for Barron?"

"Yes. One investigator, Jerome Hines, pretty much recited everything already on record. We hit a brick wall."

"Barron is pulling strings in the background. I've seen it enough in D.C. to recognize the signs." Talia tilted her head to one side. "This is personal for him, I'd swear it."

Jim fixed a penetrating gaze on her. "I get the same feeling about *your* interest."

Talia gazed at him in silence, gathering her thoughts. The antique wall clock ticked away. "You could say it's very personal. Monette Victor is my mother."

He stopped the rocking motion of his chair and sat very still. "Why didn't you tell me before now?"

"The truth?"

"Please."

"I grew up in foster care. We're not what you would call close." Talia looked away.

"You don't want people to know she's your mother," Jim said in a quiet tone.

"Having an addict for a mother isn't something I put on my résumé," she snapped.

"I'm not passing judgment," he replied.

"What do you know about it? I had to live with her." Talia pulled back from the explosion that was building inside. She took a deep breath and let it out. "That's in the past."

"I've gotten to know Monette in the last ten months. She's acutely aware of her mistakes."

Jim Rand was another man intrigued by her lovely mother. Maybe it was the bad-girl persona that appealed to this Ivy League–educated man. Jim wore no wedding band. He was an attractive man in a starched kind of way. Just the kind that might be excited by Monette's brand of spicy wit and charm. Talia did not want him to become another casualty.

"Monette can sound sincere and truthful. At her best, she's the smoothest operator you'll ever meet," Talia said.

Jim smiled. "I'm not naive, Ms. Marchand. I've got a highly developed sensor for bull."

"You said yourself she's lying to you."

"I said she's not telling me everything. There's a difference," Jim said stubbornly.

"No there isn't."

He glanced away. "I expect to find out what she's holding back anyway."

She sighed. He'd have to fend for himself and find out the hard way. "Fine. I'm telling you Barron figures in this some way."

"Sure he does. He wants to use her parole hearing as an opportunity to look good. My guess is he'll have others point out he got her and the dealers she ran with off the streets."

"If Barron's office did mess up or engaged in misconduct, her chances of being paroled shoot way up." Talia leaned forward. "And I smell something rotten in this whole thing."

Jim said nothing for a long time. Talia watched him closely. She could almost see him arranging facts in his head.

"You're a smart lady. I don't think you're just being emotional about your mother," he said finally.

Talia let out a dry laugh empty of real humor. "Trust me, sentimentality went out the window years ago."

"How sad," he said with compassion.

Talia stood abruptly and tugged at her jacket. "I suggest you talk to Jerome Hines again. I'm going to talk to Monette. Maybe I can convince her to tell the truth for a change."

"Okay." Jim stood. "By the way, Monette is trying to protect you. Most inmates trying to get out play the 'suffering mama' card early in the game."

"I've known her a lot longer than you." Talia looped the long strap of her purse over her shoulder. "She must have another game, or she would have. I'll let you know anything I find out, but I'll be going back to D.C. soon."

"I see." Jim looked at her steadily. "But you plan to visit your mother before you go."

"Once more, yes," she said shortly. "Good-bye."

"Good-bye, Ms. Marchand." He held out a hand with long fingers. "I'm glad to know you."

She shook his hand firmly for a moment and let go. Talia left without looking back. Still, she could feel his perceptive gaze on her back like a laser beam. She had no intention of being Monette's pawn. She would help him find out the truth. Monette deserved that at least. Outside in the October sunshine she put on her sunglasses and felt better, protected somehow. Then Derrick stepped around the corner of the building and beckoned to her. His tall, broad-shouldered profile startled and delighted her at the same time. Talia fought off the familiar tingle that crept up her spine. Then she frowned with irritation at the sudden thought that he had followed her.

"What are you doing here?" she said tersely. "I don't need an escort or a shadow."

"Let's go somewhere and talk," he replied in a clipped tone and guided her toward his SUV with one strong hand on her elbow.

* * *

"I hope you have a damn good reason for this stunt," Talia hissed.

Derrick steered the 4Runner expertly out of the parking space he'd managed to find off St. Charles Avenue. He could feel the waves of anger from her honey brown skin. They passed Tulane University.

"And by the way, my car is still back there," she continued in a controlled voice. "What is this about, Derrick?"

"I've been reading Monette's case."

"You followed me to New Orleans to tell me something I already know?" Talia glanced at him sideways.

"Let me finish before you start with the smart remarks," Derrick snapped. Then he took a deep breath to calm down. "I think I've found something."

"Good. Write it down, and I'll give it to Jim Rand. Then get back to your regularly scheduled program."

"I don't think so." Derrick said. He parked in front of a small Italian deli. "Let's get a soft drink."

Derrick purposely ignored her stormy expression and got out before she could react. He crossed in front of the 4Runner and opened the passenger door. Talia glared at him as she swung her shapely legs around.

"I don't find this side of you terribly attractive," she said.

"What side of me, darlin'?"

"We definitely need to talk," she said sharply, mocking him.

Talia marched ahead of him to a sidewalk table. They were the only customers outside the small eatery. A waiter came out and took their orders for iced tea, then left. Derrick watched the traffic for several minutes. An olive green trolley car clattered by, loaded with tourists and city dwellers. Bright sunshine painted the scene. Everything suggested this should be a relaxed, romantic interlude in an enchanting setting, the Garden District. Instead his temper threatened to boil over, and so did hers.

"Well?" Talia crossed her arms and gave him an "I want an explanation, Mister!" look.

"Did you know Jarrod was in Louisiana?"

"No," she said curtly. "And I won't beg you to believe me."

"Don't be silly." Derrick continued to stare into the distance without seeing the lovely scenery.

"Right, no need in both of us acting like children."

Derrick glanced at her. Talia pursed her lips in annoyance as she gazed back at him. He sighed and shook his head slowly. "I don't have any right to hold on to you. I know that."

"Will you stop?" Talia said fiercely. "We both know it's a hell of a lot more complicated than that." She broke off when the waiter appeared.

"Sure you don't want something else? Our shrimp cocktails are the perfect afternoon snack." The waiter flashed a professional smile.

"No thanks," Talia said.

Derrick paid him, and he left. Talia opened her mouth to speak but didn't. They sat in silence for a long time, sipping through the straws in their glasses. The worst part of it was Derrick understood only too well why she didn't want to be with him. In fact, what he was about to tell her would confirm her desire to leave Louisiana for good. No sense in putting it off.

"So, what is the big news flash that brought you all the way to New Orleans?" She tapped a foot impatiently.

"Earl was a police informant," he said in a low voice. "He was paid out of the DA's Office."

Talia stared at him in shock as the words sank in. Then she slapped a palm on the table. "Damn! Monette must have known."

Chapter 15

"What exactly do you want from me?" The tall dark-skinned Black man stood in front of Barron, twisting his hands together.

"Sit down, Jerry." Barron nodded to a chair.

"I don't plan to be here long. Just spit it out." Jerome Hines wore a tense frown.

"Jerry, what is this hostility about?" Barron lifted his hands as he spoke. He sighed when Hines didn't answer him.

A large ornate clock in a cherrywood frame ticked loudly on the wall, its large round pendulum swinging east to west. Barron went to the wet bar across his spacious office. Outside the window lights from downtown Baton Rouge twinkled in the twilight. The Mississippi River and the bridge leading to West Baton Rouge Parish were visible from his fifteenth-story window. Barron poured a glass of wine, then walked to the window. He sipped slowly.

"I love the view," he said in a quiet tone. He turned to Hines. "You know what I mean?"

Jerry's left eyebrow twitched. "Yeah, I know what you mean."

"Money makes the world go round, sure. But I like

being able to effect change." Barron turned his back to Hines again.

"You mean power."

Barron nodded. "I think of it as a way to make things right." He drained the wineglass and set it on the desk. "Enough philosophy."

"So why did you summon me? I don't work for you now."

"You came because of everything we've been through together." Barron gazed at him with a solemn expression.

"Yeah, right," Hines said with a grimace. He looked away.

"You visited the Victor woman in prison. That wasn't a very prudent thing to do." Barron smoothed down his silk tie and sat on the edge of his desk.

"I've been doing some investigative work for a private law firm. One of their clients—"

"Don't bother lying," Barron broke in. His deep voice was even, like a school principal chastising a truant. "Why?"

"Like I said, I was there on business and happened to see her. We just talked for a few minutes." Hines met his gaze without blinking.

His eyes narrowed. "She's going before the parole board in a few weeks. Rand agreed to take her case and months later you visit her. I don't believe in coincidences."

"You got a question, ask it." Hines did not look away, but a fine sheen of sweat coated his upper lip.

"I don't need to ask you anything. As I said, we've been through a lot together. I appreciate all you did for me." Barron nodded slowly.

Hines eyed him warily. "Thanks."

"You performed the duties as lead investigator for my

office very well. In fact I nominated you for the award you got back in 1987. Remember?" Barron smiled.

"Sure I remember." Hines shifted from one foot to the other.

"Nice big brass plaque with your name on it as I recall. For outstanding contributions to law enforcement," Barron murmured. "Those were glory days, Jerry. We put away a lot of bad people."

"Uh-huh. Look, my wife is expecting me for dinner." Hines squared his shoulders. "Nice talking about old times, but . . ." Still the tall man didn't move.

"Yes, a lot of water under the bridge so to speak. Remember the Broussard brothers? Disgusting white trash. You helped put them away." Barron pointed a thick forefinger at him.

"Right, right." Hines wiped a trickle of perspiration from his temple.

"And the Collins boy. We were so sure he killed that little girl, but we just couldn't get him to talk." Barron smiled. "Until you stepped up to the plate."

"He didn't kill that girl." His voice cracked. "I didn't do anything but my job. I can't help it if he got stabbed to death in prison."

"Don't be modest. Besides, he'd molested a child three years before and got probation. What kind of justice was that?" Barron held out his palms again. "I could name at least ten more cases where you made the difference."

"What do you want?" Hines whispered hoarsely.

"Nothing, Jerry." Barron walked to him and clapped a hand on his back. "I won't keep you from your dear wife. How is Delores these days?"

"Fine."

"Those fine twin boys of yours out of college?" Barron kept his hand on Hines's shoulder.

"One more year," Hines replied.

"Of course. Brian plans to go to law school and Brendon will work on getting his MBA. Expensive to educate kids these days." Barron smiled at him. "Wonderful how you've provided for them."

"I did what I had to."

"I'll never forget all you did, Jerry." Barron squeezed his shoulder with one large hand, then let go.

Hines stepped away from him. "I won't forget you either."

"We worked well together. But you were quite independent back then. I didn't look over your shoulder at every move you made."

"Oh, so that's how it is. You'll bury me." Hines wore a cold smile despite the fear in his black eyes. "Don't threaten me."

"Jerry, we've always been on the same side." Barron nodded. "Trust me."

"Yeah, right," Hines said.

"I'm just giving you advice." Barron's expression hardened until his face looked like cut stone.

"Which is?"

"I worked very hard to clean up Pointe Coupee Parish. Monette is exactly where she should be. Don't exercise poor judgment." Barron's eyes glittered.

Hines blinked rapidly as though he'd been slapped hard across the face. They stared at each other for several seconds until Hines looked away. He rubbed his forehead.

"I gotta go."

"Sure, sure. Thanks for stopping by." Barron patted his shoulder once more. "And be sure and tell Delores I said hello."

Barron's smile remained until Hines disappeared

through the outer door past his secretary's desk. Once he heard the elevator bell Barron stopped smiling.

Talia ached to feel Derrick's arms around her. But life wasn't so simple. She'd never been able just to reach out and receive love easily. There was always a price to pay. Derrick wore a stiff expression. They hadn't talked for four days since he'd met her in New Orleans. Correction, since he'd followed her to New Orleans. And what was up with that? He was investigating her now. Still, she'd accepted his invitation to dinner. Bad idea. Now they were at his house. Tense silence was broken only by awkward small talk. Soft blues from a Baton Rouge station did little to ease the taut atmosphere.

"Your favorite." Derrick handed her a glass of merlot.

"Thanks." Talia moved over to give him more room next to her on the butter soft leather sofa.

"So." Derrick held his wineglass in both hands.

"So," Talia repeated, and took a long sip.

"We've talked and said very little. Definitely not like us." Derrick cleared his throat.

"Maybe we don't want to say too much," Talia replied.

"How is Miz Rose?" Derrick did not look at her.

Talia gave him a sideways glance. His jaw muscle seemed stretched tight. "She's doing great. In fact, she's got a new man."

"At least somebody will live happily ever after," Derrick said with a thin smile that vanished quickly.

"Yeah." Talia squirmed.

"And what about you?" Derrick put the glass down on the coffee table.

"I told Rand what you found out. He's got a great

team of students. He'll do his best for Monette." She paused. "I plan to leave in a week, maybe two."

"Everything all neat and tidy. At least it is for you." Derrick glanced at her then away.

"It's not like that, Derrick."

"Don't worry, I'm not going to pick a fight." He stood and crossed to the bar in a corner of his living room.

Talia finished the rest of her wine and held out the glass. "More please."

Derrick walked over and placed his hand over hers without taking the glass. They stared at each other for a long time. A sensual blues song flowed from the compact disc player. He guided her hand down, and she put the glass on the table. Talia rose at the same time Derrick gently tugged her arm. She went into his strong embrace, eager to feel his heat. His mouth brushed hers as if he wanted an appetizer first.

"I'm trying to be mad at you, but . . ." His tongue eased between her parted lips. A groan came from deep in his throat.

Their kiss lasted a long time, through the scant few minutes it took him to take off her blouse and bra. Talia removed his shirt. She placed both palms flat against his chest. The curly hair felt wonderful on her skin. Derrick held each of her breasts in his hands. His thumbs rubbed the nipples until she felt weak.

"You're so beautiful. What will I do when you're gone, baby?" he said, his words muffled by her flesh.

"Don't talk, please," she whispered.

Derrick answered by pulling her down on top of him on the sofa. Without remembering doing so, Talia managed to take off her black jeans and panties. She helped him push down his pants and bikini briefs. They stared into each other's eyes as she lowered herself onto him. Derrick caressed her hips as she rocked gently at first.

"I missed you so much. So much," Derrick said.

Talia gripped his shoulders. She let out a moan that was half sob as he continued to whisper to her. Derrick shifted and rolled her onto the sofa so that he was on top. He lifted her legs to his shoulders and thrust deep inside her. She cried out as the powerful orgasm took control of every muscle in her body.

She stroked his hair as he came with sharp, deep thrusts. His soft moans lifted her up until she felt a second climax. They held each other tightly, the sweat from their bodies mixed together. For a long time they lay unmoving. Finally, Derrick lifted her from the sofa. Without speaking, he carried her into his bedroom. The comforter and sheets had been turned back neatly. He placed her in his bed and lay beside her. The only light came from a small lamp.

"You have to leave me," he said as he tangled his fingers in her long hair.

"I'm not leaving you."

"Yes, you are," he said firmly. "You can't handle dealing with Monette or the past. I'm tied to both."

"Please, please don't get mixed up with Monette's case."

"I can't even promise if I wanted to. I have a bad feeling about this thing, Talia. Larry is going to need my help as much as Monette." Derrick propped himself up on one elbow.

"Like hell!" Talia clutched his strong bicep. "When push comes to shove, he and Barron will protect each other, and you'll be out in the cold."

"I can't stand by and do nothing," Derrick insisted. "This is who I am. Do you love me for who I am, or do you want to change me?"

"Do you love me enough to make a change?" she countered. "I had enough of living on the edge to last three lifetimes."

"You're trying to invent this world that doesn't exist."

"That's the point, Derrick. It *does* exist for other people." Talia pushed herself up and sat back on the fluffy pillows. "I don't want to know about drug dealers, addicts, prostitutes. I've been there, done that, and got all the souvenirs I need."

"We're back to the same place." Derrick sat up and swung his muscular legs down to the floor.

Talia rose and started to get dressed. "You want to hold on to the past, and I want to let it go."

Derrick pulled on a pair of dusty blue sweatpants. He faced her. "No, *you're* holding on to the past, not me. You're carrying around all this baggage, and you know what? I think you like it."

"Don't play therapist with me!" Talia snapped. She hopped from the bed.

"You're not a foster kid anymore. There isn't any danger to you or me."

"Now who's living in a fantasy world? I'm sick of having this argument."

"Me too. I guess we've both been unrealistic." Derrick walked out of the room.

"I never made promises," she called after him angrily.

Muttering to herself, she went into his spacious master bathroom and took a quick shower. Fifteen minutes later she was dressed. She found Derrick seated at the breakfast counter in his kitchen, drinking a cup of hot orange tea. The aroma filled the air.

"Want some?" he said, without looking at her.

"No, thanks." Talia leaned against the far end of the counter.

"No sense in dragging it out." Derrick stared into the cup as though seeking answers from tea leaves.

"Yeah." She didn't trust herself to say more.

Talia felt like they were light-years apart. He stood straight and crossed his arms. His white cotton T-shirt molded to the outline of his chest. Talia stared at the powerful brown arms that had held her moments before. She missed him already.

"Like I said, I'm going to help Monette." Derrick lifted his square chin to gaze down at her.

"I figured that out." Talia walked out toward the living room. She heard his padded footsteps behind her as he followed.

"By the way, I haven't seen anything that suggests she knew Earl was an informant."

"Oh please! She knew."

"Probably. Winn Barron is somehow in the mix," Derrick said with a frown.

"All the more reason for you to stay out of it. But I won't repeat myself." Talia held up a palm toward him. "Your mind is made up."

"I wish you had more faith in me," he said quietly.

"That isn't the issue here."

"It is for me," he said.

Talia spun to face him. "Get it through your head. You can't fix everything. Bad people get away with stuff, justice doesn't always prevail, and the weak get eaten up by the strong."

"So you're going to escape again."

"Damn right!" Talia rubbed her eyes. "Take me home, please."

"I'll get my keys."

Derrick strode out and came back in minutes. He opened the front door, and Talia walked out ahead of him to the driveway. They drove through the dark to Mama Rose's house without speaking. He turned on the radio. When a love song came on, Derrick quickly changed the station. Talia's heart grew heavy when he turned into the driveway. Derrick turned off the engine. Both stared straight ahead through the windshield.

"Good night," Talia murmured.

"Bye," he said shortly. "I'll contact Jim Rand if I find out anything else."

"Thanks." Talia didn't move. "There's no reason we have to avoid each other."

"Yes, there is." Derrick gripped the steering wheel.

"I see." Talia twisted the thin strap of her small purse. "Derrick, I'm sorry."

"Right."

Talia opened the door but looked at him. Derrick continued to stare ahead. She got out of the 4Runner and walked to the front porch. He sat in the driveway until she was inside, then the engine roared to life. She watched the red taillights fading into the distance. With a sigh, she closed the door and locked it. The ringing phone made her jump.

"Hello," she said.

"You the one working with that senator, Jackson is his name," a muffled male voice said. "Y'all are trying to get the mandatory-sentencing law changed. I read about it in the news."

"Right. Are you a reporter?" Talia looked around for her notes. She had every intention of letting Senator Jackson get all the media attention. "Call his aide at—"

"I've got information that might help. Winn Barron is using one case in particular to show why the law shouldn't change. Monette Victor. He's got his own reasons for wanting her to stay in prison."

"What? Who is this?" Talia shivered. The eerie voice gave her chills.

"I'll tell you what happened, but not right now. Meet me at the public library in Lafayette. Wednesday at ten o'clock."

Talia got control of her fear. "Don't be ridiculous. If you know something, you should talk to the police, and—"

"Look, little girl, it took a lot for me to make this call. You want your mama out of prison or not?"

Talia had another thought suddenly. "How did you know about me?"

"You want answers, then meet me Wednesday."

"Wait a minute," Talia began.

There was a click and a dial tone. She started to call Derrick but stopped. Instead she looked up the street address of the Lafayette library in a phone book on Mama Rose's bookshelf.

Determined to find out the truth, Derrick set up a meeting the next day with Jerome Hines. Derrick tapped the eraser end of a pencil on his desk in frustration. Hines stared at him from hooded eyes. The man had a cunning way of saying a lot without answering any questions. They were alone in the office at seven in the evening. The rest of the staff was gone.

"Monette Victor had been picked up before by the police numerous times. You questioned her twice at least before this drug distribution conviction on unrelated cases."

"I interviewed beaucoup people back then. You know how many poor Black kids jumped into coke back in the eighties? A lot, man." Jerome shrugged.

"This town isn't all that big, Mr. Hines. You must remember her. She made a pretty big impression." Derrick held up a photo of Monette wearing a form-fitting red dress.

"Those kinda women blend together after a while," Hines said without looking at the picture.

"Okay." Derrick dropped it back into the folder and closed it. "Nobody else is here. We can talk."

"That's what we've been doing for . . ." Hines broke off and looked at his wristwatch. "Almost an hour."

"No, we've been dancing around for almost an hour. Pardon me, but you're not my type." Derrick gazed back at him with a stony expression.

"Son, I played this game while you were still sucking a pacifier. We're on the same team, okay?" Hines leaned back in his chair and propped an ankle across one knee. "Everything you want to know is right there." He pointed to the stack of folders on Derrick's desk.

"Uh-uh, 'cause I want to know what *really* happened," Derrick tossed back curtly. "Monette Victor was no big-time drug dealer. I can't find anything but a stitched-together case on her."

"Yeah, well she was long overdue." Hines let out a gruff laugh.

"Winn Barron seems intent on keeping her locked up more than the others. I keep asking myself why."

"What are you talking about?" Hines seemed calm.

Derrick watched him closely. "He keeps calling my boss, had us pull the case to send him a report, and he's been asking about her visitors."

"He's a politician. Some people might think it's a nasty way to get votes, but then politics is a nasty business." Hines shrugged.

"I get a feeling this means a lot more to him than votes."

"She was with those bums, they had a large amount of coke, and under the law they were *all* guilty."

"So he wanted to clean up Pointe Coupee Parish and Monette Victor was a major source of dirt? Hardly." Derrick held up one volume of the file, then let it drop with a slap.

"Every little bit helps," Hines said, his expression

impassive. "Now if that's all, I'll be on my way." He started to get up but stopped when Derrick spoke.

"For someone who is on my team, you sure don't seem to be forthcoming with information."

"It's all in the files." Hines leaned forward and squinted at Derrick. "Besides, I'm not real sure why I'm here. You gave your report to Barron. What's it to you?"

Derrick decided to take a gamble. "Monette Victor says she was set up."

He didn't know that for sure, but he had a hunch. Monette was acting as though she had some secret weapon. She was being very cagey with her own lawyer. Derrick guessed that meant she was going after a real big dog. Barron was the biggest dog connected to the case. Hines sat up straight—a small sign, but enough to let Derrick know he'd struck a nerve.

"She'll say anything to get off. Look, son, I hear you're good. You must know better than to believe a woman like Monette."

"She's got a credibility problem, I'll admit," Derrick said with a lift of one shoulder.

"What an understatement." Hines stood. "You're doing a damn good job covering all the bases. But don't worry. Her conviction was solid, and the parole board will see through her act."

"I guess my boss doesn't want any unpleasant surprises. I mean, between you and me, all this attention from Barron has him wondering," Derrick said casually.

Hines was about to turn away, but stopped. "What?"

"Don't get me wrong now. He hasn't come out and said so, but . . . Look, we both know how it is. They take care of each other." Derrick raised his eyebrows.

"Uh-huh." Hines watched him.

"Larry is going to help Barron out if there are any—let's say—minor bumps in the case."

"And you're going to back your boss," Hines replied.

"Larry is a good guy. Besides, he signs my paycheck." Derrick put on a crooked smile.

"I heard he's pretty straight and narrow." Hines rubbed his jaw and stared at the floor.

"He sure is. Hey, you're right. I don't see anything to support what this Victor woman is saying." Derrick waved a hand as though dismissing her.

"Yeah, yeah." Hines stuck out a hand. "Nice to see you're on your job." He grinned.

Derrick shook his hand. "Thanks."

"I don't miss it though. The late hours and dealing with thugs got old after fifteen years." Hines looked around the office.

"I understand you came here after retiring from the army at a fairly young age. Nice." Derrick nodded.

"Joined right out of high school. Put in my twenty years, got all the schooling I could, and took retirement," Hines replied.

"And I hear you're a damn good investigator. Served as a lieutenant in the military police."

Hines studied him for a few moments. "You've done your homework. Like any good investigator would before he talks to a potential witness."

"You've had an interesting career."

"So have you. You were a cop for two years before Perrilloux recruited you for this job. Since then you've taken a lot of criminal law courses." Hines's mouth lifted in a slight smile.

"Like I said, you're a good investigator, too." Derrick smiled back at him.

"Keep at it, son. You'll do fine." Hines turned to leave.

"One more thing. Was Monette an informer for you guys? One of her boyfriends was from what I can tell."

Derrick picked up a file and pretended to read a passage. "His name was Earl Glasper. He was just a petty crook that ran off."

Hines faced him with a scowl. "I don't remember every two-bit low-down piece of garbage we swept up. It's late, and I'm hungry."

"Whoa, I just asked a question." Derrick affected a puzzled frown. "Is there something you need to tell me?"

He strode up to Derrick until their faces were inches apart. "Listen, kid, don't screw with me! You and your boss got suspicions, then say so."

"Okay." Derrick sat down on the edge of his desk. "Monette was definitely no Sunday school teacher. But as the old folks used to say, something ain't clean in the milk." He tapped one section of the thick file with a forefinger.

"We had a chance to get them off the street, and we did." Hines put both hands on his waist.

"Monette was a nuisance, not one of America's Most Wanted."

"I'm not gonna stand here playing tag team detective. We got the goods on her, and she went down. Case closed." Hines took his car keys out of his pocket.

"Not yet," Derrick replied. "Monette is about to open it up again. I mean wide-open."

"Then whatever happens happens. See ya." Hines walked off. His heavy footsteps thumped down the hall.

"Yeah, we'll definitely be seeing each other. Sooner than you think, pal." Derrick crossed his arms and stared at the closed door for a long time.

Chapter 16

∞

Mama Rose folded up the last blouse and placed it in the large suitcase. She glanced around the room. Talia watched her out of the corner of her eye. Instead of dancing for joy that she was leaving the rehabilitation center, Mama Rose seemed nostalgic.

"Where do you want this, Mama?" Talia held up a ceramic clown. "The boxes are packed tight. We talked about maybe leaving some stuff behind."

"No!" Mama Rose scurried over to a box. "Here, give me that." She almost snatched it from Talia's hand.

Talia watched as she lovingly wrapped it in newspaper until it was well cushioned. "You hate that kind of hokey knickknack. Sure will look strange beside your porcelain bird collection."

"This was a gift. And it's not hokey." Mama Rose frowned at her. "I didn't raise you to be snooty, young lady."

"Well excuse me!" Talia pressed her lips together to keep from laughing. "I think I know who made that for you."

"Hush and keep packing." Mama Rose turned away.

"Mama, if you don't want to leave, there are plenty of spacious apartments here."

"No, indeed! I miss my house. I know you're eager to leave." Mama Rose continued packing.

"My boss has been wonderful. Besides, I'm working on a project here."

"Then there's Derrick." Mama Rose sat down on her bed and gazed at Talia.

"Don't meddle," Talia said in a light tone. "Like you always say, young folks do things differently these days."

"Talia René Marchand, we need to talk." Mama Rose patted the bedspread. "Come sit."

"We've got too much to do. We can talk later." Talia pretended she was engrossed in her task.

"I need to take a break. I'm not as young as you," Mama Rose said. Her voice sounded quite strong despite her words.

Talia raised an eyebrow at her. "You look pretty fresh to me."

"Don't argue, sit."

Talia reluctantly put down a stack of paperback books. "Okay. Short break and a *short* discussion."

"I know you have horrible memories of growing up in Rougon. But, baby, that's not enough to keep you from the man you love."

"You don't understand, Mama Rose." Talia looked out of the bedroom window.

"Then tell me so I can help." Mama Rose took Talia's hand.

"Derrick wants a picket fence around a cottage, a dog, and kids. I don't even like dogs that much."

"I know what you're saying, and it's not about a dog either," Mama Rose said.

"Do you?" Talia rested her head on Mama Rose's shoulder.

"Yes. Let me tell you about yourself. You're afraid you can't be a good mother. Monette, your grandmother, and your aunts weren't exactly good role models."

"There's some kind of flaw in the maternal instinct genes. I've never daydreamed about having a baby to love." Talia sighed. "Most of the girls I met in foster care wanted it so bad."

"They all have three kids or more by now," Mama Rose added.

"Right!" Talia sat straight and looked at her. "What's wrong with me? I never once said, look how beautiful. You remember my best friend Shaunice?"

"Sure. You were like sisters."

"She's got four kids now. Four! We saw each other over a year ago, and we just didn't have much to talk about." Talia looked down at their entwined hands.

"Your lives are so different. Nothing wrong with that, baby."

"My point is I didn't feel an ache looking at her kids. I'd probably feel tied down by a child and run the streets just like Monette. Except I'd have my career instead of drugs and partying."

"You would be a wonderful mother. You get that from me."

"You did a beautiful job of raising this wild child." Talia smiled at her with affection. "I gave you fits, but you stood by me."

"We were a team. I never tried to be your mother."

"You're my second mama." Talia paused and stroked her cheek.

"We couldn't be more bonded if I'd given birth to you." Mama Rose kissed her on the cheek.

"But I'm still Monette's daughter. I've got those wild genes." Talia wiped a stray tear away before it slid down her face. "Not to mention that Marchand guy. I wouldn't even call him a father. Promised to marry her, so she put his last name on my birth certificate."

"You're not like Monette or your daddy. Look at your performance in school, and your career."

"I achieved to escape," Talia murmured.

"You're still doing both, baby," Mama Rose said gently. "I think it's time to have a fantastic career *and* a fulfilling personal life."

Talia kissed Mama Rose's forehead then stood. "Enough talk. We have work to do."

"Fine. I have just one last thing to say."

"Mama," Talia warned.

"You'll never be complete without Derrick. I never saw two people more bonded, even as kids. There, I said it, and I'm not sorry." Mama Rose marched from the room with her head high.

"Oh God." Talia sank onto the bed again. Her body and soul knew Mama Rose was right.

Talia threw her car keys onto the coffee table and swore. She'd waited for three hours at the library, and the guy hadn't shown up. Her mysterious connection must have gotten cold feet. The phone rang. She snatched up the receiver.

"Yeah," she barked into the phone. "I waited for you all morning and—"

" 'Scuse me?" Jasmine said.

"Oh, it's you." Talia kicked off her pumps and dropped into a wing-backed chair at a small desk in the living room.

"I've missed you terribly, too," Jasmine wisecracked.

"Sorry. It's been one of those weeks. How are you?" Talia yawned. Sleep had eluded her for the past two nights.

"Okay. Hmm, not getting much sleep I see. You're better than okay with that fine private eye to keep you warm. How is Derrick?"

"I've been busy working, and so has he," Talia said quickly.

After a pause, Jasmine made a clicking sound. "Oh-oh, the Love Train jumped the wrong tracks so soon?"

"Change of subject," Talia clipped.

"We're friends, Talia. What's up?" Jasmine replied.

"The same argument, the same conflicting world-view." Talia suppressed a sigh. "I really don't want to talk about it."

"I'll let it go for now. We will talk," Jasmine said in a resolute tone.

"Yeah, yeah. Later. What's the hottest news around town?" Talia forced a cheer into her voice that she didn't feel.

"The gun control issue is about to be revisited as the politicians like to say. Don't worry I'm on it. Your clients won't be neglected."

Talia put the receiver down and turned on the speaker. "I'm pulling up my files now," she said as she turned on her notebook.

"You downloaded the notes to me last week, remember?" Jasmine asked.

"Oh, right." Talia blinked her dry scratchy eyes. "I've been a little distracted."

"By the same subject we won't talk about I'll bet." Jasmine made another rapid clicking noise with her tongue.

"You sound like a hyperactive cricket," Talia retorted. "The mandatory-sentencing project is intense."

"Yeah, right." Jasmine's tone implied she wasn't convinced. "Anyway, you should be getting some material over your fax machine right now."

Seconds later she heard the screech of the fax machine's modem. "What is it?" Talia said. She accessed her database and tapped at the keyboard.

"A coalition of powerful folks down your way has been making the rounds. Smart money, too. They had heavy-hitting legal guns visiting the Justice Department. Didn't Jarrod tell you?"

"No." Talia pulled up the notes section to add information from Jasmine.

"He was down there with you. Hey, wait a minute. I just figured it out." Jasmine let out a low whistle. "Two men, double trouble."

"About the lawyers," Talia said sharply.

"Darn, you're not going to tell me," Jasmine whined.

"If you don't get on with the business at hand—" Talia said through clenched teeth.

Jasmine let out a dramatic sigh. "Geez. They're making sure conservatives fight any changes to mandatory-sentencing laws at the federal level."

"Interesting," Talia muttered. She immediately thought of Winn Barron. "You know whom they represent?"

"A coalition of law-and-order advocates, victims' rights activists, and law enforcement officials. These lawyers are based in Louisiana, but the coalition has members from several states." Jasmine read off a summary of the states.

"No problem. We knew the opponents would work hard. Give me what they've done so far," Talia said.

Jasmine gave her a concise account of the contacts they'd made and the issues they raised. Talia typed bullet points into her database as Jasmine spoke.

"Here's what isn't generally known. The attorney general in Louisiana is making personal phone calls to key policy makers and congressmen."

"He's really interested in this thing." Talia stopped typing. "But why so top secret?"

"Apparently he wants it that way. Strange, huh? He's got political plans for a national run I hear. You'd think he'd want to use this issue."

Talia stared at the computer screen without seeing the words on it. "I've got a funny feeling about this guy."

"I've got a funny feeling about the whole thing, T. What the heck is going on down there?" Jasmine said.

"When I find out, I'll let you know," Talia answered.

Jasmine gave her more information once Talia retrieved the pages from the fax machine. They spent thirty minutes going over other projects just to update Talia. Once she said good-bye to Jasmine, Talia signed on to the Internet. She wanted to find out more about the coalition. More importantly, she planned to do intense research on Winn Barron. Pete had an account with two database services that could provide detailed information on any subject and anybody. She muttered a curse word when the phone rang only minutes later and kicked her off the Internet.

"Yeah," Talia said impatiently.

"Talia, Monette's been hurt bad," Karl said. "They took her to the hospital in Baton Rouge. The prison infirmary can't handle it."

"What happened?" Talia's stomach churned as she stood.

"The social worker that called said she'd been in a fight with some other inmate." Karl was breathless. "I'm leavin' work now."

"I'll meet you there." Talia crossed the room and put on her shoes as she spoke.

"I don't think you oughta. I'll call you once I get there."

"I'm going, Karl."

"Look, Monette has always said she'd just as soon everybody thinks Miz Rose is your mama. You got a good life," Karl spoke low into the phone.

"We don't have time to discuss this now. Which hospital?"

"Earl K. Long Memorial, the charity hospital on Airline Highway. See you in a little bit."

Mama Rose came out of her bedroom. "I didn't mean to nap the day away." Her smile faded when she looked at Talia. "What's wrong?"

"That was Karl. Monette's been hurt in a fight at the prison. I'm going to the hospital." Talia picked up her purse and car keys.

"Lord, have mercy! Is she going to be alright?"

"I don't know yet." Talia stopped and took a deep breath.

"I'm coming with you. Just give me ten minutes to get dressed." Mama Rose started out of the room.

"No way," Talia said loudly. "The home health nurse will be here at six o'clock. There's food in the refrigerator. All you have to do is heat it in the microwave. Don't forget to take your pills at four o'clock."

"I'm fine. You get going, and don't worry about me."

Talia gave her a hug, mostly for her own comfort. "Okay."

Mama Rose held on to Talia tightly for a few moments then let go. "I'm going to be praying for her."

"Where are my keys?" Talia turned around in a circle.

"They're in your hand, sweetie. Drive carefully because you're upset right now. And call me soon as you can."

Talia waved once, then got in her rental car. She made the drive to Baton Rouge in twenty minutes, half the time it usually took. The parking lot of the charity hospital was crowded. After a frustrating five minutes, she found an empty space. Large signs pointed the way to the emergency room. Karl had already arrived and was pacing near the wide glass doors. His bleak expression told her the news would be bad.

"How is she?" Talia blurted out before she was close to him.

"She's in surgery. They say she might be bleeding inside, especially if the knife cut her liver or spleen."

"Tell me what happened." Talia tried to calm her hammering heart.

"Let's go in here." Karl led her to a small waiting room for families. "I don't know any details. Just somebody jumped her while she was in the prison laundry."

"That's outrageous! We should have more information. I'm going to call the warden's office right now." Talia took out her cell phone.

"Talia, slow down." Karl placed a hand on her arm. "Let's deal with Monette and whether she pulls through."

"What do you mean? Of course she's going to pull through. She's tough." Talia heard her own voice rising in hysteria yet couldn't stop. "Nothing gets Monette down. She's got a plan for anything!"

Talia paced back and forth in the tiny room. Karl watched her for a few minutes. Suddenly he walked over to her and put his arms around Talia. For the first time in their lives they held each other like family. Both of them started to cry.

"So many years of pain and bein' separated," Karl whispered. "I just can't stand the thought of her dyin' in prison without us bein' a real family."

"No." Talia cleared her throat. She found a tissue in her purse and wiped her eyes. She offered him one and he took it. "I care what happens to Monette, but we'll never be a family like other people."

"Thanksgiving is comin' up. I was hopin' she'd get out and we could have dinner at my house." Karl sniffed. He dabbed at his eyes.

"Her parole is a long shot no matter what Jim Rand says. Besides, Monette isn't the type to sit around a table and be maternal." Talia wore a melancholy expression as she sat down heavily.

"People change," Karl insisted.

"People have to want to change," Talia replied. "Sure, Monette is talking the talk now. But look how many chances she had before."

"Bet you said the same thing about me." Karl smiled at her with affection. "Did you think I'd ever be anything but a thug?"

Talia blushed. "Karl, I—"

"Uh-huh. You don't have to say it." He patted her shoulder. "Can't say I could have blamed ya either. At one time I didn't believe it myself."

At the moment a man wearing green scrubs walked in followed by a woman. "I'm Dr. Morrison. You're Ms. Victor's family?"

"I'm her son," Karl said before Talia could answer.

"Okay." He glanced over his shoulder at the woman.

"The social worker at LCIW confirmed it. I'm Shelly Peak with social services here at the hospital," she said to Talia and Karl.

"Hello. How is Monette?" Talia said.

"The blade nicked a kidney. Then they stabbed her again hard enough to chip a rib and puncture a lung." Dr. Morrison shook his head.

"Will she be alright?" Talia asked.

"The next twelve to twenty-four hours are critical. If she doesn't start bleeding internally or if her lung doesn't collapse, she'll do pretty well. But she'll have a long recovery."

"Lord, please stand by her," Karl murmured with his head down.

Talia put an arm around his shoulders. "I hear Earl K. Long has the best treatment around, even for an understaffed, underfunded charity hospital."

"We work hard and have some fine doctors, ma'am." Dr. Morrison nodded. "Nice meeting y'all. If you have any questions, here's the number of our unit.

If I'm not in, another resident or chief resident can answer your questions." He glanced at Shelly Peak, then left.

"Your mother will be in intensive care. Visiting hours are very restricted. Only one family member can be present at a time for fifteen minutes," the social worker said.

Talia looked at him. "You two have gotten close. Monette will feel better if she sees you."

"Ms. Victor is still in recovery. She can't have visitors until at least eight o'clock tonight."

Talia looked at her wristwatch. "Quarter to six. I'll wait."

"Me too. I'll go call LaTrice to tell her what's goin' on."

"Why don't you both get something to eat and try to unwind?" Ms. Peak looked Talia, then Karl.

"I'm not hungry." Talia was sure anything she ate would sour in her stomach. "I need to let Mama Rose know how Monette is doing, then I can make some phone calls." She looked at Karl.

"Come on. At least have some soup. Somethin' light." Karl put a hand under her elbow. "You can't help Monette by hangin' 'round here makin' yourself sick."

Derrick walked in at that moment. Before she realized it, Talia rushed into his arms. He held her close and whispered soothing words in her ear. Ms. Peak made a discreet exit. Karl patted Derrick's shoulder.

"Thanks for comin', man." He gave him a fraternal nod of approval before he left them alone.

Talia shuddered in his arms. "Monette could die."

"The doctor didn't say that, did he?"

"No, but she could get worse in the next day."

"Or she could get better," Derrick said soothingly.

Talia squeezed her eyes shut. "I've been so mean to her. No matter what she's done, she is my mother."

"You won't help Monette with this guilt trip. She needs you to be strong."

"You're right. There will be plenty of time for self-pity later."

"I'm getting funny vibes, and it seems to lead right to Winn Barron." Derrick wore an intense expression. "I talked to his former investigator Jerome Hines. He's got something to hide. I don't think the attack on Monette was just another prison fight."

Talia wiped her eyes and sat down. A wave of exhaustion washed over her suddenly. "I hate this drama."

"I'm going to look into the fight at the prison." Derrick took out a Palm Pilot from the back pocket of his gray chinos.

"As soon as she's able to talk, I'm going to tell Monette to back off. Whatever game she's playing has to end."

"As much as I hate to say it, I think someone is running scared. This attack may mean we're closing in on the truth. I should stay on Hines." Derrick made notes. "I'd like to talk to her when she's up to it, too."

"Why?" Talia felt a growing ball of rage take root in her chest.

"She'll know the real deal behind this 'fight.' I might smoke something out." Derrick's dark eyes gleamed, as if he couldn't wait to start the chase.

"Let me see if I've got this straight." Talia stood, legs apart and both hands on her hips. "My mother is on death's door, and you see it as a good sign that you're making progress?"

"I'll go back over my contacts and the leads Rand gave me," he murmured to himself.

Talia could barely contain herself. "You'll keep digging even now that Monette is in intensive care."

"Monette wanted my help." Derrick glanced up at her. He grimaced. "Are you blaming me for what happened?"

"Well, let's examine the facts. You just said Monette's attack means you've struck a nerve somewhere." Monette stood toe-to-toe with him. "You figure it out!"

Derrick stared at her with a horrified expression. "Monette was going to make a splash no matter what I did. If I thought for one minute anything I was doing would put her in danger—I was trying to protect her!"

"Oh really? Guess you miscalculated somewhere along the way, sport!" Talia was shouting at him.

"Honey, you're upset. Anyone would be." Derrick tried to embrace her again.

She slapped his arms away. "Don't patronize me."

"Is there a problem?" Shelly Peak stood in the door of the waiting area.

Talia and Derrick stared at each other as though she hadn't spoken. All three stood frozen until Derrick put his Palm Pilot away.

Derrick turned to the social worker. "We'll be fine."

"If you need anything, to talk or ask questions, have the ER nurse page me. I'll be in my office." With one last glance, the short, blond woman left.

"I can't believe you!" Talia said, her voice lower so as not to attract more attention.

"I was thinking the same thing. I'm trying to help your mama," Derrick said in a calm voice as though trying to reason with a child.

"She's got a legal team working on her parole. Jim Rand is the best around."

"They don't have funds for a good private investigator," Derrick countered.

"Isn't that a conflict with you working for the DA? So you ignore my wishes, put Monette's neck in a noose, and throw away your career. You don't go halfway, do you?"

Derrick pointed a forefinger at her nose. "From the moment you hit town you've been complaining about not making waves. Monette deserves justice even if it upsets your neat little bourgeois world."

Talia's red-hot anger crystallized. "I'd like to give you some credit and chalk this up to blundering knight syndrome."

"What are you talking about?" Derrick clenched his square jaws.

"I'd prefer to think you really were trying to help. But somehow I have a nasty suspicion you like the excitement." Talia tucked her Coach purse beneath one arm.

"You went through hard times, and you've still got issues. But don't push it." Derrick's handsome eyes darkened like storm clouds. Lightning seemed to flash deep in them.

"Good-bye, Derrick." Talia turned her back on him.

He closed his huge hand around her right arm and forced her to face him. "I won't crawl back to beg for attention. Do you understand what I'm saying?"

"What part of good-bye didn't you get?" Talia glanced down at his hand on her arm.

"I'm through." Derrick let go of her and walked out.

Talia watched him leave. She forced herself not to follow him out despite her anger. After a few seconds she sat down heavily and covered her face with both hands.

"Excuse me. I'm looking for Ms. Victor's son." Shelly Peak said softly.

Talia sat straight and looked up at the social worker. "Karl will be back soon."

"Dr. Morrison says he can spend a few minutes

with her. Are you a relative?" She wore a concerned expression.

"Yes." Talia rose quickly.

She followed the social worker down through a maze of hallways and into a room. Monette lay sedated on a gurney, her eyes closed. Her caramel complexion looked washed-out and pale. Talia took her hand and held on tightly, willing her to survive.

"Studies show that they respond to a familiar voice even when they're in a deep sleep," the social worker said over Talia's shoulder. She nodded encouragement, then quietly left them alone.

"I'm not sure what to say." Talia gazed at Monette's thin outline beneath the white sheet. "I'm sorry, Mama," she whispered, and started to cry.

Chapter 17

∞

Derrick drove along the highway with a grim expression. He didn't have to look at his reflection to know it. His facial muscles felt tired from the permanent scowl he'd worn for the last sixteen waking hours. His final scene with Talia had kept him up until two o'clock in the morning. Nothing he did had helped him relax or feel good. Derrick chided himself for being a fool. More than miles and the past stood between them. She wanted him to become a clone in a suit, like that Jarrod character. Well, she could forget it. Not to mention her irrational accusation that he'd put Monette in danger. An unpleasant twinge grabbed his stomach. He pushed away the sickening thought.

He turned up the radio hoping the driving zydeco beat would blast away troubling thoughts. Flashing blue lights appeared in his rearview mirror. He looked down at the speedometer and saw he was going eighty-five miles an hour. He eased his foot off the gas pedal too late.

"Damn it!" he muttered angrily as he pulled onto the narrow gravel shoulder of Highway 1.

"Step out of your vehicle please." The state trooper's voice sounded hollow through the loudspeaker mounted on his car.

He retrieved his registration card and got out. A tall man the color of milk chocolate with gray hair walked toward him. The trooper's trained gaze swept the scene. Derrick waited calmly.

"Do you know why I stopped you, sir?"

"I was going too fast." Derrick could have kicked himself.

"Way too fast. Let me see your license and registration, please." The trooper stood with his legs apart.

"I'm with the Pointe Coupee District Attorney's Office." Derrick took out his identification card.

The trooper took it, glanced at Derrick, then walked back to his car. He called in the information, all the time keeping an eye on Derrick. Ten minutes later he walked back.

"I thought you looked familiar. I'm Brandon Myles. I testified in that drug bust we took down on Highway 190, remember?"

Derrick squinted at him. "Yeah, too bad they got off so easy."

"Defense lawyers make me sick," Trooper Myles retorted. "What's the rush? You don't want to end up spread all over the road."

"I got distracted. I'm on my way to interview someone." Derrick slipped his wallet back into his pants pocket. "How long have you been with the state police?"

"Twenty-four years and two months. I'll retire in ten months." Trooper Myles grinned. "Not that I'm counting."

"Right." Derrick smiled back at him. "You worked these parishes, including Pointe Coupee the whole time?"

"Just about." Trooper Myles relaxed his vigilant pose a bit. "I spent maybe four or five years in Troop A first."

"You know Jerome Hines? He was an investigator with the Pointe Coupee DA's Office years ago."

"Sure, I know him. Jerry was Barron's right hand back in the day." Trooper Myles nodded.

"I'm on my way to interview him about an old case. I hear he was good."

"I guess he got the job done." Trooper Myles crossed his arms. "So what's up?"

"Something strange about how it went down. One of the principals is trying to get paroled," Derrick said.

"Oh yeah?"

"She's suggesting there was some wrongdoing with the whole deal." Derrick watched the older man's expression change.

"Yeah, well . . ." Trooper Myles rubbed his jaw. "Like I said, he got the job done. Whatever it took, if you know what I mean."

"He bent the rules every now and then," Derrick said carefully.

"All I'll say is this—if I ever testified for those two, I made sure my butt was covered." Trooper Myles leaned against the 4Runner with one large hand on the vehicle. "I'm all for putting away crooks, but not at any cost. I've seen too many of 'em walk because some smart lawyer busted a funny investigation."

"I got ya," Derrick replied with a nod.

"Don't get me wrong, Jerry's a likable enough guy. He just pushed the limits a few times. His place is kinda tricky to find. I'll lead you there."

"Thanks a lot."

"No problem. I'm going on my dinner break anyway. There's a little café out here that serves the best fried shrimp po-boys in the world." Trooper Myles gave him a friendly wave, then got into his car.

Derrick followed him down Highway 1. The white

patrol car turned onto Highway 978, then took a sharp turn down another smaller road. Thick shrubs and tall trees crowded right up to the blacktop pavement. Late-afternoon sunlight made the red and gold maple leaves look brilliant. Yet Derrick didn't notice the autumn beauty. Talia's angry words kept replaying inside his head. He knew only the passage of time would turn off that awful recording, a very long time. Yet his sense of justice and right drove him on. No way could he simply ignore the loose threads he'd uncovered. Maybe someday Talia would understand.

Trooper Myles turned onto a gravel driveway that was almost hidden by thick vegetation. Even in mid-October wildflowers bloomed. They rode only a few yards when a wide expanse of green lawn appeared. A large brick wall with the words BAYOU TRACE in bold white letters announced the name of the neighborhood. Upscale homes were scattered about. Myles drove toward a white-and-redbrick two-story house. A long driveway circled in front of the house. Another paved pathway led to a three-car garage on the south side of the house. Derrick parked behind Trooper Myles and got out.

"Man! I never would have guessed Hines lived here." Derrick let out a low whistle as he took in the scene.

"You telling me you don't make this kinda money working for parish?" Trooper Myles said in droll tone.

"If Hines financed this lifestyle on his salary, then I'm gonna have a serious talk with my boss," Derrick quipped.

"We should all be so lucky." Trooper Myles wore a tight smile. "But luck had nothing to do with it."

"Yeah," Derrick said.

He went to the wide double entry doors and pressed the doorbell button. Musical chimes sounded a second later. They waited, but no one came.

"Nobody in the house I guess." Trooper Myles walked to his left to a set of windows and peered in. "He's got an office around back. Maybe he's there."

"Nice place." Derrick let out a low whistle as they approached a swimming pool with a waterfall in one corner.

"Jerry Hines lives good, huh?" Myles said over his shoulder. "Here we go." He pointed to a guest cottage.

"A car is coming. Maybe they're coming back from a shopping trip." Derrick turned around and back toward the garage with Myles following.

The automatic garage door hummed open just as they emerged. A heavyset woman the color of mahogany drove up in a black BMW. She looked alarmed when she saw them. Dressed in a tan silk pantsuit, she sprang from the car almost before the engine shut off.

"What's wrong? Where's Jerome?" She left the passenger door open.

"Calm down, ma'am. We came out to talk to your husband. Mr. Hines isn't here," Trooper Myles said, taking the lead.

"Of course he's here. This is his car. I left him catching up on work." Mrs. Hines pointed to a pearly white Lexus, then scurried off. "It's this way."

"Jerome," Mrs. Hines called out as she pushed through the door of the guesthouse. She screamed moments later.

Hines lay on the floor with his legs at a crooked angle. Dark red stains dotted the light green carpet around him. Mrs. Hines fell to her knees and shook him.

"Jerome, wake up!" She flailed her arms.

"Does your husband suffer from heart problems, asthma?" Myles knelt beside her and scanned the prone man from head to toe.

"No, he's healthy for a man his age. Do something!" she wailed. Still, she didn't move aside enough to allow Myles much room.

"Ma'am, c'mon. Officer Myles knows emergency first aid." Derrick pulled her back.

Myles was down on his knees gingerly touching the man's body. He leaned down and placed his cheek near Hines's mouth and nose. Then he paced two fingers against his neck.

All the while Derrick struggled to calm Mrs. Hines. She finally collapsed against him sobbing.

"Faint pulse, breathing is shallow," Myles said. He took out his cell phone.

Derrick managed to tug Mrs. Hines along with him toward the open door. "Let's go get some first-aid supplies we might need. That way Trooper Myles won't have to leave your husband."

Mrs. Hines nodded eagerly. "I've got a kit in the laundry room.

Derrick glanced over his shoulder and heard Myles say foul play was suspected. He started talking to keep Mrs. Hines from hearing more. She'd have to face the hard truth soon enough.

"Great. A first-aid kit will be a big help until the paramedics get here."

"Jerome believes in being prepared. We've got two first-aid kits in the house, one downstairs and one upstairs. One in each car, and we had one on our boat." She chattered on from nerves.

"Good, good," Derrick replied vaguely. While she talked he scanned their surroundings. "I'll get the one upstairs in case we need more supplies."

"Look in the second guest bathroom on the top shelf of the closet." Mrs. Hines went to a wide cabinet near a washer and dryer.

"I'll be right back."

Derrick searched the first floor before he went upstairs to make sure no one was in the house. He did the same thing upstairs and found nothing out of place. Tall windows gave all of the second-floor rooms a lovely view of the neighborhood. Going from room to room, he saw nothing suspicious outside. He found the first-aid kit and went back downstairs.

"Let's go back, please. I've got to help Jerome." Mrs. Hines rushed off ahead of him.

Myles was still talking into his cell phone when they arrived. "Yeah, he's barely hanging on," he said.

"Oh my God!" Mrs. Hines pushed Myles aside and fell to her knees next to her husband.

"Don't move him, ma'am. We don't know what kind of injuries he has." Trooper Myles managed to scoop the plump woman up into his arms. "The ambulance is about ten minutes away. I've done as much as I can for him. He's holding on."

"Mr. Hines is a tough guy from what I know of him." Derrick nodded at Myles over her head. Myles handed her off to him.

"What will I do without him?" Mrs. Hines went down on her knees next to her husband and sobbed.

"Try to be strong," Derrick said, and patted her back.

"Looks like he did a good job of defending himself. He's got bruises on the knuckles of both hands," Myles said quietly to Derrick.

"Yeah, this room shows it, too." Derrick glanced around. Two chairs, a table, and a small bookshelf were turned over.

The high whining sound of sirens sliced through the air coming closer. Minutes later the small guesthouse was swarming with people. The emergency medical technicians treated Hines while talking into radios to get instructions from a doctor. Then they put him on a gurney. Mrs. Hines, once again wailing in distress, followed them.

"Please, let me go with him in the ambulance," she said.

"No problem. A familiar voice will be a comfort to him," one of the emergency technicians said.

Mrs. Hines stopped crying and looked at Derrick hard. "Make sure my house is locked up tight. I don't want some thief stealing me blind."

"Yes, ma'am," Derrick replied.

"Give me your card so I can get in touch with you later," she commanded. She looked at Trooper Myles. "I want your card, too. Y'all better not tear up my house either."

"We'll do our best." Trooper Myles handed her one of his cards.

"You'll pay for anything you break. I don't have no cheap stuff," she clipped. Then she turned on the tears again.

"Man!" Myles muttered.

"She's probably already calculating her widow's benefits," Derrick quipped.

"I'd hate to wake up in a hospital bed with her bending over me." Myles shook his head and joined two sheriff's deputies.

Derrick watched from the sidelines. He knew better than to get underfoot. The state police had sent a crime scene unit out. Two men took their time making a list of everything in the room. One drew a diagram while the other called out the location of furniture and other items. Nothing found was considered trivial or irrelevant. The shorter man then took photos at different angles.

"You Guillory?" a sheriff's deputy asked.

"Yeah." Derrick glanced at the tall redheaded woman.

"Your boss wants you back at the office."

"What?"

"I'm just deliverin' a message."

"Thanks." Derrick took out his cell phone and called the office.

Talia rubbed her back when she stood. The padded blue hospital chair was old and not very comfortable. Within forty-eight hours of her surgery Monette's condition had stabilized. She'd been moved from intensive care to a room two days earlier. Since that time she'd slowly gained more and more strength. Talia walked over to the bed and stared down at her mother. Monette seemed to be sleeping peacefully.

Talia stretched, then went to the fourth-floor window. She pushed aside faded curtains to stare out. The view was as disheartening as the dingy pale green walls around her. Traffic moved sluggishly along the four-lane highway below. Brown tuffs of grass dotted the few places it grew. She watched birds sail through the bright blue autumn sky. *Signs of hope,* she mused, without feeling any inside.

"Hey, you," Monette said in a low scratchy voice.

Talia whirled around and went to the bed. "You took a long nap."

"Yeah," Monette croaked. She gazed at the room, moving only her eyes. "Lousy interior design. State?"

"The charity hospital in Baton Rouge." Talia smoothed down the sheets around her.

Monette winced when she tried to shift in the bed. "Damn! That bitch tapped me good."

"Be still," Talia replied.

"Shoulda told me that before," Monette wisecracked. "Glad you're here." She winced in pain again, but still lifted her hand.

Talia held onto the hand gently. "Had a close call, Monette," she said quietly.

"Tell me about it," she said hoarsely and rubbed her neck. "My throat feels like I've been eatin' sand."

Talia poured water into a plastic cup and held the straw while Monette sipped slowly.

"That's better."

"The warden is looking into the fight," Talia said as she refilled the cup. She put it on the table close by, so Monette could reach it easily.

"Lotta good that's gone do. Nobody will talk." Monette shifted again. This time she was successful in moving a bit to her right. "Better."

"You amaze me. I'd be screaming for action."

Monette shook her head slowly. "Survival, honey. You learn to deal with a lot when you're locked up." Monette closed her eyes for a moment then they snapped back open. "What else is happening?"

"In the world, state, or Rougon? You've been out of it almost six days now. Better turn on the news." Talia reached for the television remote.

"No. I mean what else happened that's connected to me. Derrick say anything about Jerome Hines?" Monette's eyes sparkled with intensity.

"I haven't talked to Derrick, and I don't intend to. Between your theatrics and his playing detective, you were almost killed." Talia's anger flooded back.

"Blamin' him don't make a bit of sense, girl. I was gonna take my chances whether he helped me or not."

"As usual the quiet approach isn't your style." Talia crossed her arms and grimaced at her.

"Ain't no other way. If you knew everything, you'd understand." Monette touched her fingertips to her hair gingerly. "I must need a perm real bad. Any reporters been around?"

"This isn't a game," Talia snarled. "All my life you—" She clenched her back teeth until her jaws ached.

"Go on let it out."

"Forget it." Talia went back to the window.

"I was on my own with nobody who gave a damn," Monette said.

"Right," Talia retorted. Neither spoke for several minutes.

"Talia? Come on and look at me." Monette sniffed when Talia turned to her. "Can we get past the anger for a while? Seems like I never had much more between me and my kids." A tear slid down her cheek.

Talia swallowed a lump in her throat. Her mother sounded like a sad little girl. When Monette stretched out her arms, Talia went to her, and they embraced for the first time in many years. Feeling awkward, they let go after a few seconds.

"I know we got a ways to go. I hope we can at least be friends," Monette said softly. "I know Miz Rose is your true mama in a lotta ways."

"I won't lie to you, Monette. You're right about Mama Rose." Talia took a deep breath and let it out slowly. "But I never stopped loving you. I just didn't like you very much." She handed her several tissues from a box on the bedside table.

"Baby, I've been trying real hard. I still ain't got wings, but I'm not what I used to be." Monette smiled through sniffles. She dabbed at her eyes and nose. "You're smart and strong like your mama. Once I handle my business the world will know me."

"I thought you were going to change."

"I'm a work in progress." Monette grinned at her.

Talia laughed. "You could talk the devil into installing air-conditioning in hell."

"With all the stuff I've done, I may get the chance," Monette joked.

Talia grew serious again. "Now about that meeting with your lawyer."

"What do you—" Monette stopped when Talia faced her with a frown. "Okay. Better talk to Jim soon I guess."

"Stop lying to him. You should have told him everything from the beginning." Talia squeezed her eyes shut, then opened them again. She swallowed her anger. "Just talk to him."

"Sure. Give him a call for me, will ya? Don't tell the nurses, or they'll put a stop to it. Y'all just come like it's a regular visit." Monette smoothed her sheets around her.

Her comment brought Talia up short. "Maybe we should wait."

"We got to move now. Before they do somethin' else."

Talia shivered at her words. "Then let's meet tomorrow evening. That will give you another sixteen hours to sleep. I'll call Professor Rand."

"And Derrick." Monette eyed Talia with her brows drawn together.

She felt a stab of pain at the prospect of seeing him. "And Derrick," Talia agreed finally.

Chapter 18

Derrick walked into Monette's hospital room. Rand stood close to the bed talking to Monette in a low voice. Talia sat several feet away, legs crossed. Derrick's gaze drifted from her lovely round face down to the shapely limbs showcased by black hosiery and a short black skirt. The contrast with her businesslike crisp gray linen shirt with large cuffs only heightened the sensuous effect. His first thought was how long it had been since he'd held her. Talia wore an emotionless expression when she looked back at him.

"Good to see you," Rand spoke first. He crossed the room and shook hands with Derrick.

"Hello. Talia." Derrick nodded to her.

"Hello," she replied in a bland tone.

Monette glanced from Talia to Derrick. She smiled at him widely. "Come over here and give me a hug. Don't you get finer by the day," she exclaimed.

"I'm glad you're feeling better." Derrick hugged her gently.

"I'm like an old hen, tough," Monette joked. She looked at Talia. "Quit actin' like you don't know this man."

"Monette," Talia clipped, a warning note in her voice and eyes.

"Let's get down to business so we don't tire you out," Derrick said.

"Guess we gonna have to skip the chitchat this go-round," she quipped. Her sassy grin didn't fade when Talia squinted at her.

Jim cleared his throat. "The parole board meets in three weeks. I can't get a feel for the outcome. Of course it helps that we don't have victims lined up to speak."

"Yes, but we've got the Barron factor," Derrick said with a frown. "His office has issued press releases to the media about the illegal drug trade and the violence that goes with it."

"There was an article about the parole hearing in the *Baton Rouge Advocate,*" Jim added.

"Not only that, the reporter went into Monette's arrest history." Talia uncrossed her legs and sat forward. "A coincidence? I don't think so."

"Barron has a subtle campaign aimed at Monette," Derrick said with a frown. "At least that's what I think."

"Okay, let's say he does." Jim leaned against the headboard of Monette's bed with one hand. "Why? What's his special interest?"

"Good question," Talia said, her lovely eyebrows arched high. "We're here so Monette can fill us in."

Monette blinked rapidly when all three turned to her. "What?" Her big brown eyes widened.

"She's good. Girlfriend has broken every one of the Ten Commandments at least fifty times, and she can still look innocent as a baby," Talia said dryly.

"That ain't no way to talk to your mama." Monette pursed her lips.

"Cut the crap, Monette. I know the truth is unfamiliar territory, but give it a try." Talia's eyes narrowed.

"Miz Rose raised you better than to smartmouth your own mama." Monette waved a hand in the air when Talia opened her mouth. "Okay, okay. Don't show out."

"We can't protect you unless we know everything, Monette. I gotta know who to watch and who to go after," Derrick put in.

"Quit playing Batman, alright?" Talia turned on him. "If there's a threat to Monette, we'll call the police."

"The police won't care about me." Monette wore a bitter smile. "Just as soon see me in a box."

"Their job is to enforce the law no matter what," Talia replied heatedly. "They damn well better care, or I'll raise hell."

"There's a little thing called proof. And don't jump on me. I'm on your side." Derrick grimaced at the cold look in Talia's eyes.

"With friends like you we don't need enemies," Talia hissed.

"He gave us leads to follow up on that paid off," Jim said.

"One of his 'leads' attacked Monette." Talia glared at Derrick, her arms crossed. "I think a bit more caution is in order," she said acidly.

Derrick winced at her accusation. "I certainly didn't intend to put Monette in danger, Talia. But maybe I could have been more careful. Especially when I realized Barron was involved somehow."

"Hindsight is perfect vision," Talia retorted. Before he could respond, she turned her attention back to Monette. "Which brings us back to *you*, lady."

"Damn, she's on everybody's butt today," Monette muttered.

Jim glanced briefly at Talia, then at Monette. "Bad

mood or not, she's right. Start from the beginning, and don't leave out anything this time."

"Talk," Talia ordered. She sat down and fixed her mother with a stern stare.

Barron paced the floor in front of the wide window. He ignored the sparkling lights that lit up the French Quarter to the east and the riverfront to the west. The view from the fifteenth floor of New Orleans Marriott Hotel was dazzling but wasted at the moment. His brother watched him and sipped from a heavy tumbler filled with cognac.

"You've known Larry a long time. Our fathers have been friends since college. He's loyal to you," Thomas said.

"I don't want to test his loyalty, not with this." Winn wore an anxious frown as he rubbed his face.

"So you're not sure he's with us." Thomas gazed at his brother steadily. "I'm surprised."

"He goes by the book," Winn blurted out.

"Real smart," Thomas snapped. "You helped him get elected knowing you had skeletons in the closet."

"Don't start with me." Winn went to the minibar and poured himself a whiskey and soda.

"I'm always pulling your rear end out of a tight spot." Thomas rubbed his forehead with the tips of his fingers.

"Jerry won't talk. He's got too much on the line."

"Maybe, maybe not." Thomas had a thoughtful grimace on his narrow face. He unbuttoned his jacket and sat down.

"What do you think we should do next?" Winn asked. He gazed at his older brother expectantly.

"Pity you didn't ask me that question fifteen years ago!" Thomas's voice cracked like a whip.

"No one will believe her," Winn said weakly. Beads of perspiration popped out on his forehead.

"You'd better hope not. In the meantime you should cross your fingers Hines takes a turn for the worse."

"Maybe we'd better talk to him again." Winn wiped his mouth.

Thomas gazed at Winn, his eyes narrowed to icy blue slits. "Not '*we*.' I suggest you go visit him."

"You're joking of course." Winn's eyes widened in terror.

"No, I'm not. He was your faithful employee. It would look odd if you didn't go," Thomas replied in a dull voice.

"They could be waiting for me to show up, a trap," Winn spluttered.

"Don't be absurd!" Thomas turned a look of scorn on his younger brother.

"I—I just don't know." Winn gulped down the last bit of liquor and went to pour more.

"Talk to him alone, assure him that Ms. Victor's gangster co-defendants are still a threat. Tell him you'll protect him and make sure the state police work around the clock to solve the crime." Thomas nodded slowly as though pleased with his plan.

"He won't buy that line, Thomas! Jerry isn't a fool."

Thomas stood. He carefully smoothed the silk-and-wool-blend suit fabric, then tucked his tie neatly inside the jacket before buttoning it. "I suggest you give the performance of a lifetime, dear brother."

"Unbelievable," Talia whispered. She stared at her mother. "You've done some wild things in your life. But this . . ." She shook her head slowly.

Jim Rand stood with his back to them all and spoke

over his shoulder. "Just when were you going to let me in on this little bombshell, Monette?"

"I really thought it was safer if y'all didn't know, at least not until the very end." Monette balled up a section of the bedsheet in one fist. "Considerin' all that's happened, I still think so."

"No, it's better for us to know," Derrick said. He glanced at Talia. Her stunned expression worried him. "Are you okay?"

Talia seemed to shake herself in an attempt to recover. "I'm fine," she said without looking at him.

Derrick wanted to wrap her in a blanket of protection. He could feel her fear. This was what she'd most dreaded about coming home, being drawn back into the same cycle of being on the run.

"I don't want my daughter caught up in this stuff, Jim. Derrick, take her home," Monette said.

"No," Talia said loudly.

"Listen to me. You don't know these folks like I do." Monette beckoned to her. "Come here, please," she added when Talia didn't move.

Talia walked to the bed. "How long before everything you've done stops bouncing back on us?" she said in a strained voice.

"Please, Talia, I'm beggin' you. Listen to me this one last time. If Mama Rose is okay, go back to D.C.," she said with intensity, tugging on Talia's hand for emphasis.

Jim frowned. "You might best help the situation by being out of harm's way."

Talia extricated her hand from Monette's hold. "Some jerk called me and claimed he had information about your trial. I was supposed to meet him, but he didn't show."

"Who was it? When? And why didn't you tell me?" Derrick fired the questions at her in irritation.

"First, he didn't introduce himself. Second, it was a

week ago, and third, I didn't want you charging in making things worse," Talia fired back. "I was going to find out what he knew and tell Jim."

"You could have ended up in a hospital bed, too! Damn it, Talia." Derrick put his hands on his hips. "Being stubborn is one thing, but stupidity is not your style."

"No, stupid is your department." Talia stared back at him without flinching.

"Stop it right now!" Monette shouted, then gasped for breath.

Jim rushed to her bedside. "Take it easy." He turned to Derrick and Talia. "Fighting each other is only going to give them an edge."

"I'm okay." Monette put a hand on his arm and smiled when he covered it with hers.

"I'm sorry," Derrick said quickly. He raked his fingers through his hair in frustration. "Talia stopped talking to me, and now I find out she put herself in danger."

"I understand, baby. You care about her," Monette said gently. "You, young lady, oughta get a spankin' for what you did!"

Talia's mouth dropped open. "You're kidding."

"Derrick's too much of a gentleman to say so, but I will. Hell, you been mad at me for twenty years, so I figure I ain't got nothin' to lose." Monette sat up straighter. "Stop bein' so hardheaded and let him help you."

"Drop the indignant mama act, not after you kept us in the dark about the truth." Talia turned her ire toward Monette again.

"Don't upset your mother." Jim tightened his grip on Monette's hand protectively.

"Unbelievable! The whole world has gone insane!" Talia threw up both hands.

"Okay, everybody chill." Monette took a deep breath as Jim fluffed her pillow.

"We need to work together, kids. Put aside the feuding for now. Monette's life is at stake." Jim and Monette gazed at them intently, waiting for a reply.

Derrick cleared his throat. "Of course you're right. Sorry, Talia."

"Yeah," Talia replied with a sullen expression.

"Excuse me? 'Yeah' is all you got to say?" Monette said to Talia.

"Don't press my last nerve, Monette." Talia glanced at Derrick. "I made myself clear about his sticking his nose into your case."

"I couldn't ignore what I found out, Talia. Guess we'll have to agree to disagree."

Derrick gazed at her full lips set in an angry line. He wanted to feel the fire that burned in her lovely eyes, even if anger fueled it. Talia's unyielding pose didn't dampen his hunger to stroke her fine body.

"You got something right, we disagree."

"But since he's on the right track, then he needs to keep working it," Jim insisted as he gazed at Talia. "Well?"

"It's not like anybody is listening to me anyway." She strode back to the vinyl chair and sat down hard. "So let's hear the rest, Monette. I'm sure there's more."

"Start with you and Barron again," Derrick said. He saw Jim wince.

"I got one of those jobs through a welfare program down at the courthouse. Winn was the DA, and he noticed me. He liked to party, and so did I."

"Uh-huh." Talia raised an eyebrow at her.

Monette cleared her throat and went on. "Lots of so-called respectable people lead double lives. You'd be surprised at the lawyers, doctors, even politicians I used to hang with at nightclubs in New Orleans and Houston."

"No I wouldn't," Talia said in a sour tone.

"Talia, come on." Derrick shook his head at her.

"Then I had a little bit of trouble, nothing serious at first. Just a speeding ticket. Winn started keepin' up with me sorta." Monette glanced at Jim. "He, uh, helped me a coupla more times, and one thing led to another."

"You became lovers," Jim said. He pressed his lips together.

"He was good to me at first. I mean buyin' me stuff. Remember all those presents I got you one Christmas? You had a Black Barbie and her beach house," Monette said to Talia, who only nodded. "He owned a lot of rent houses, so I always had a place to stay."

"Those roach motels weren't exactly mansions. Seems like he could have given you a nice house," Talia retorted with a grimace.

"He did. I sold it and partied with the money." Monette sighed. "But he got it back for me. I think that little shack is still in my name. You know the one, Talia." She looked at Talia steadily.

"You mean . . ." Talia's voice faded.

Derrick knew without asking. He remembered the house all too vividly. An image of a lanky dark man lying on the cracked wood floor flashed in his head for a second. Somehow he'd assumed, no, hoped, it had been torn down years ago. He snapped out of his reverie and looked at Talia. She looked pale from what must have been terrifying memories rushing back. Derrick went to her and placed a hand on her shoulder.

"Don't worry, Talia," Monette said quietly. She wiped a hand over her face and went on. "Anyway, I started runnin' with somebody else behind his back. Real smart, right?"

"Earl?" Talia said.

"Damn," Derrick murmured, when Monette gave a sharp nod.

Monette nodded. "Drugs drain what little sense you got right outta your brain. About two weeks after Earl was gone, Winn told me he knew."

"I'm assuming he didn't take it very well." Jim frowned.

"He acted real cool like he didn't care. Winn smiled, and said, 'I'll see you're taken care of, sugar.' Six months later I got arrested. He wore that same smile the first day I saw him in court."

They all fell silent for a long time, each contemplating the implications of having a powerful man as an enemy. Monette had gone to prison. Derrick stood close to Talia, hoping she'd turn to him. She stiffened when he put his arm around her. Talia shrugged free of his embrace and stood.

"The fact is, Monette, you were with those guys, and they were carrying drugs," she said in a flat tone.

"It's true I was partyin' with them, but they got the coke *after* they dropped me off. They made a buy, then picked me up again. Winn offered each of them a deal, made it clear I was supposed to go down. Jerome knows."

"No wonder—" Derrick broke off when Jim gave a slight shake of his head.

Monette glanced at him then at Derrick. "What?"

Talia waved a hand at the two men. "They always kid themselves that they're protecting us. Jerome Hines was beaten up. The newspapers say it was a botched home invasion."

"Like hell," Monette retorted promptly.

Talia's eyebrows drew together. "I'd bet he was the guy that called me."

Monette wore a pensive expression for several minutes. "If he's turned on Winn, then he's tryin' to protect himself. Of course he might feel bad about me bein' in prison."

"Too bad I can't ask him." Derrick crossed his arms.

"Dead?" Monette asked and the others looked at Derrick sharply.

"No, but he's been slipping in and out of consciousness. The doctors won't even let the police detectives question him. Not that they'd get much," Derrick replied.

"So my best witness might not live another day, much less another three weeks," Jim said, his voice glum.

"We don't know he would have cooperated. He certainly wasn't too happy to answer questions when I talked to him," Derrick said.

"That's not all, Winn was always cuttin' shady deals. Jerome knows where the bodies are buried," Monette said.

Talia took a step back from them all. "Just leave it alone. Too many people have gotten hurt already. It's not like you can prove anything. Monette's kept her record clean in prison. That should be enough to influence the parole board."

"Winn got me convicted of a crime I didn't do. Every two years he wrote letters to the board arguin' against me bein' released," Monette said, and strained forward. "I ain't takin' this lyin' down."

"Relax, Monette." Jim gently guided her against the pillows.

"Well, maybe I'm gonna have to take it lyin' down for a while." She smiled weakly at Jim.

"I know how you feel. I take heat for working with the district attorney. But it's about the truth, not just locking people up," Derrick said heatedly. "I'm with you, ma'am. Sick or not, I'm going to talk to Hines. If he did call Talia, then he's willing to right this wrong. Either way I'm going to find out."

"Be careful. Your boss is close to Barron," Jim said.

"Larry won't stand by him if he knows about this," Derrick said. "But he's going to want hard evidence before he believes it."

"Who would? All they gotta do is look at my history and compare it to him. He's old money, from judges, congressmen, a lieutenant governor even." Monette closed her eyes. "Time for me to quit doin' things the hard way. I'm always stirrin' up trouble. I been so selfish all my life. Here I'm puttin' all of y'all in danger and for what? Talia's right."

"Monette—" Jim held her hand.

"No, the fact is I was hangin' with them dudes. I paid the price for makin' one more bad decision. Just present my record before the board and forget the rest." Monette's voice faded, and her eyelids fluttered closed.

She seemed drained of energy as her breathing became regular. Jim nodded toward the door, and they left quietly. Derrick led them down the hall to the elevator.

"I've never seen her give up like this." Jim glanced back over his shoulder.

"She's being realistic," Talia said. "I don't want her hurt again despite what's gone down between us. Just do what she asked. I'm going home to check on Mama Rose."

"Wait, let's talk." Derrick reached out and grabbed her arm. He hated the sight of her walking away.

"Monette made herself clear, and so have I. Let me go," she said coldly.

Derrick drew his hand back. "You're both making a mistake."

She didn't answer him. Instead, she got on the elevator when the doors opened. Talia did not look at either man as she punched the button. The doors whisked shut.

"Two very willful ladies," Jim said finally. "Now what?"

Derrick stared at the elevator wishing it would open and Talia would come back to him. He knew she wouldn't. "I'm going to do what I think is right," he said.

Chapter 19

Talia rubbed her forehead. The dull thud in her temples seemed to have taken up permanent residence. She stared at her laptop screen. Her last report to Pete was coming along, but slowly. At least she'd accomplished her goals on the sentencing project. Senator Jackson and Marti were pleased at the progress they'd made. With a sigh, Talia went to the kitchen to refill her cup with coffee. With any luck she could wrap up this report, make sure Mama Rose was settled, and get out of Rougon. She willed herself to leave the window.

"Get back to work. The sooner you finish, the sooner you can go home," she muttered.

A crunch of gravel and a car door slamming stopped her. Moments later Mama Rose and Karl came through the back door. Karl carried two large plastic bags and wore a big smile.

"Hey, little sister." He wore a relaxed expression. "I talked to Monette, and she's feeling better."

"Hi, baby." Mama Rose kissed Talia's cheek. "Whew! The Dollar General Store was packed, but I got a lot of bargains. Can't wait for the doctor to say I can drive. Then I won't have to worry you children."

Mama Rose put away napkins and other household supplies as she talked.

"It's no problem, Miz Rose. You know I don't mind." Karl went back to the car and returned with more bags.

"Looks like you're stocking up for the whole town," Talia said with a teasing grin. She shook her head at the packages of toilet tissue, aluminum foil, and other items.

"Habit, sugar. From the days when I never knew when the social workers would drop a buncha kids on my doorstep," Mama Rose said.

"And you loved it," Karl chimed in.

"That I did." Mama Rose laughed.

"Well, I'm on my way back to work. I'm working the late shift tonight. Hate it, but the money is good." Karl rubbed his hands together. "Call me if you need anything, ladies."

"Thank you, baby." Mama Rose patted his face with affection. "But you got your family to look after. We'll be just fine."

Karl nodded. "Yeah, anyway, you got Derrick lookin' out for y'all."

Mama Rose raised her eyebrows. "Uh, we don't mention that name these days. They had a little spat," she said in a stage whisper.

"He's a good guy, Talia. Hold on to him. I know how hard it is to find the right person, somebody that's always got your back." Karl launched into a big brother lecture with a serious expression. "See I—"

"Thanks, but I'll deal with my personal life on my own. Bye-bye." Talia pecked him on his cheek.

"In other words stay outta your business." Karl wore a good-natured grin. "Okay, but you know I'm right. Bye." He blew them both a kiss and made a quick getaway.

"That's not minding your own business." Talia stood

in the back door with one hand on her hip. He only laughed and waved good-bye as he got in his van.

"He's right." Mama Rose stacked cans of fruit in her pantry.

"What's for dinner?" Talia said with forced cheer.

"Fine. I'll drop it." Mama Rose stood back to look at her handiwork and sighed with satisfaction. "Think I'll bake some cakes for the brunch at church."

"Good for you. Don't tire yourself out though." Talia poured out the now-cold coffee from her cup. "I'm going to get this report finished so I can e-mail it to the office."

"Running away again." Mama Rose folded her arms and gazed at her.

"No, my work and home in D.C. mean a lot to me," Talia replied. She headed for the living room.

Mama Rose followed her. "Okay, sugar. I won't argue about it. You got a great job and a nice home up there."

"Yes, I do." Talia sat down at the desk and started to type.

"Of course you're weak in the romance department, but we know why." Mama Rose cleared her throat. "I'm going to make some chicken salad for lunch. Want some?"

"Yeah, get busy at something other than dropping hints at me."

"I don't know what you mean." Mama Rose strolled out.

"I bet you don't." Talia tapped the keys harder than necessary as she willed words onto the screen.

"Hi, Talia."

She started at the deep familiar voice and looked around. Derrick stood in the doorway of the living room as though reluctant to come farther. His tall lean body filled up the space, and his head almost brushed the top of the frame. He wore a dark olive short-sleeved cotton knit shirt that molded to his chest outlining his well-defined torso. Talia's gaze drifted from his stunning masculine form to the smooth brown skin of his muscled arms. She remembered very well what it felt like to press her breasts against his body, to feel those arms around her. The room became too hot and close.

"Hi." Talia went to a wall switch and turned on the ceiling fan. She needed cool air fast.

"Can we talk?"

"No." Talia turned from him. "Please don't make this any harder. We both know saying good-bye is better for you and me." *Harder for me,* she mused. All she could think of at the moment was peeling that shirt from his body.

"No problem. I'm here to talk about Monette and this investigation."

"Oh, well—" Talia turned to him. His composed expression combined with his words was like a cold dash of water on her face. "Nice to know you've moved on so quickly," she muttered softly.

"Isn't that what you wanted?" Before she could reply, Derrick held up a thick folder. "I've got three more stops to make, so let's get to this."

Talia clenched her teeth at his curt attitude but said nothing. After all, he was right. Instead of tossing out an acid reply, she folded her arms and assumed an all-business demeanor.

"Okay, what's up?" Talia leaned against the desk.

"Obviously the attack on Hines is related to the attack on Monette. Unless, of course, you believe in incredible coincidences." Derrick opened the folder on the desk next to her. He held up a cassette tape. "Here is a recording of an interview Hines did. Let's see if you recognize his voice."

She took it from him and looked at it. "The sound system is in the den."

Derrick followed her down the hall into a wide room with brown leather sofas, a big-screen television, and a compact stereo system. Talia put the cassette tape in and pushed the button. A man identified himself as a sheriff's deputy after stating the date and time. Then Hines introduced himself. As the two men talked with a male witness in another case, Talia frowned.

"Well?" Derrick looked at her expectantly.

"Sounds a lot like the voice on the phone, but it's hard to tell. The tape isn't that clear," Talia said, shaking her head and waving him to silence before he could speak again. She listened for five more minutes. "I'm pretty sure it was him. Sorta kinda."

"Close enough. I'm going to talk to him as if I'm sure he called you. When he's able to talk that is." Derrick hit the STOP button and removed the tape.

"He's bad off, huh?" Talia shivered. "My God, there are some cold-blooded people in this world."

"They beat him pretty bad, ruptured his spleen. But they were sending a message." Derrick slipped the tape in the folder again.

"Some message. They tried to kill him."

"No, if they'd wanted to kill him they would have put a bullet in his head." Derrick stared at the brown folder as if the answers were in it. "I think he's holding some kind of incriminating evidence."

"So they're trying to convince him that being loyal is more healthy than being moral?" Talia threw up both hands. "I'm starting to talk like you. Now I know it's time to get out."

Derrick gazed at her with a glint in his dark eyes.

"As a matter of fact I think you'd make a good private investigator."

"Oh please! I've had my fill of sordid people, places, and things—thank you very much." Talia rolled her eyes.

"And you went to Washington, D.C., with wall-to-wall politicians to escape?" He wore a tight grin. "Yeah, right."

"Funny man." She shot him a severe look. "So what's next?"

"Like I said, I'm going to talk to Hines. But first I'm going to see if his wife knows anything. She might be able to give me leads on a wall safe in the house, a safety-deposit box, anywhere he might have stashed away a security blanket."

"Brave man to keep the goods on Winn Barron," Talia said.

"No, a scared man. He must have foreseen the need to cover his behind should it ever hit the fan." Derrick slapped the folder against the palm of his left hand.

"If he knew Monette well enough, he must have known it would most definitely hit the fan—big-time—one day." Talia put her hands on both hips.

"Yeah, she's one of a kind," Derrick said.

"Thank the Lord."

"Gotta give her an A+ for making things happen." Derrick grinned. "She finally got the Tulane Law School project on her side."

"Oh, she always passed that test with flying colors." Talia heaved a deep sigh. "Before she went down so low on the drugs, she had style. I used to watch her every move. She dressed with class even from the thrift shops."

"Remember the time she threw a party, and the cops showed up because there was too much noise?" Derrick perched on the wide arm of one of the two large sofas.

Talia nodded. "We lived in a pretty good neighborhood. Monette had straightened up and gotten me out of foster care again." They'd moved around the area, but never left the parish.

"The churchgoing ladies next door did not approve of your mama I'm afraid." Derrick laughed again.

"Maybe it was the way she made their husbands' heads spin and their tongues hang out. Skin tight jeans and tank tops will do that to a guy," Talia said and laughed with him. "Not to mention teeny-tiny skirts up to your ying-yang."

"The cops showed up, and she charmed 'em."

"Monette always had a way with men." Talia's smile faded. "She also had a habit of choosing guys with a mean streak. Of all people, she had an affair with the district attorney."

"Amazing." Derrick shook his head slowly. "But very practical."

"Wait a minute." Talia closed the door to the den. "Monette is still keeping something from us. You didn't ask her if she knew Earl was an informant."

"The other day was the first time I'd talked to her since she was stabbed. I don't know that it matters though." Derrick shrugged. "Sounds like Barron set her up out of revenge because she dumped him."

"Maybe."

Talia sat down on the other end of the sofa. Neither spoke for several minutes. She tried to sort through all the twists and turns of the facts. Monette had lived a complicated life on the edge. Good memories of being with Monette were tainted by the bad ones and far outnumbered by them. For all her charm, Monette had a hard core formed by a tough childhood and adolescence. Monette seldom took any action that wasn't calculated to get something she wanted. Everything she did had layers upon layers of motives. A chilling thought took root in Talia's head.

"Monette knew Earl was informing on her and her pals. When did he start getting payments from the DA?"

"Nineteen eighty-six I'm pretty sure. I still haven't seen anything that suggests Monette knew." Derrick looked at her with interest. "What are you thinking?"

"Let's say she knew or found out. He's making money while she gets tossed in the parish lockup." Talia did not like the picture forming in her head.

"I don't see it, Talia," Derrick said.

"She started the affair with Barron around April or May in 1986 off and on, right? I was out of foster care and back with her in August of 1986, but Barron isn't somebody she would have brought home."

"You kidding? He'd have stuck out like crazy in our neighborhood. Monette said they mostly went out of town to see each other."

"She started sneaking around with Earl about the time I got out of foster care. She shoots him two months later and he's out of the picture." Talia looked at Derrick. "In the meantime Barron knows about them, for how long we're not sure."

Derrick continued to flip through pages. "Monette was arrested in April 1987. But I still don't see why it matters."

"I can come up with lots of motives for murder among the three of us. Barron could very well start thinking about Earl's disappearance and Monette." Talia leaned forward and pointed a forefinger at him. "Let it alone, Derrick."

"I doubt he even remembers Earl. We can't just pretend Monette wasn't attacked. They could go after her again. She's a threat as long as she's breathing." Derrick stared back at her with a determined frown.

"You're being totally unreasonable!" Talia stood.

"No, I'm using my head. You're letting fear blind you to what we need to do."

"You want to fight crime, then do it without me. I'm going to do what Monette wants."

"Because it's easier for you." Derrick slapped the folder shut and stood. "Just like it's easier to walk away from me and blame it on the past."

Talia blinked hard. His words cut like sharp rocks being thrown in her face. "You think this is easy for me? I've never had anything easy."

"But now that's all you want." Derrick let out a gruff laugh.

"Yes. I don't want surprises, police interviews, courtroom drama, or looking over my shoulder." Talia waved her arms. "Excitement is another name for chaos."

"So you'll settle for a bland life and a predictable guy." Derrick looked at her hard.

"What you call bland, I call normal." Talia met his gaze without flinching.

His clenched his jaw until the muscles jumped. "Well, I'm not able to give you either one. And I'll be damned if I'm going to try."

Before she could react, Derrick tossed the folder down and kissed her. His kiss wasn't hard or demanding, but a searching tender caress. His hands rubbed her back, then slid down to cup her buttocks. She gasped and stood on her tiptoes, wanting to taste more of the spicy sweetness he offered. Taking her cue, Derrick offered more by pressing his hips to hers. For a long tantalizing time they moved against each other.

Talia wanted him, but even more she needed him. All the tension and fear of a lifetime seemed to dissolve in the circle of his arms. A tingle moved through her body like an electric shock. Just as she craved removing the barrier of clothes between them, he broke contact. His kiss was a powerful closing argument to the case he'd presented. He said nothing as they looked at each other for a full five minutes. She stared at the folder. Pieces of her life were summed up on police reports and court documents.

"I wish we could make it be simple, but we can't. This isn't a fairy tale, where everything can be solved with a kiss." She had dreamed of just such an ending countless times.

Derrick picked up the file again. "I'm sorry."

"I'm not upset. We've both been through hell in the past few weeks."

"That wasn't an apology, Talia," he said as he went to the door. "Go on back to your so-called normal life and find a nice, 'normal' guy. You've worked hard to get both."

"I'm tired of fighting," she said.

He faced her with one hand on the doorknob. "So am I."

"Let's not say good-bye in anger." Talia started to reach for his arm, then drew her hand back. She couldn't trust herself to touch his warmth again.

"Looks like I can't give you anything you want today." Derrick's eyes narrowed. He opened the door, seemingly about to speak again. He walked out instead.

"Stay a while and have some of my lemon icebox pie." Mama Rose came down the hall with a smile.

"Sure wish I could, ma'am. But I've got to go. Take care of yourself." Derrick left after kissing Mama Rose on the cheek.

"What—" Mama Rose glanced at Talia, then followed him. She came back a few minutes later. "He wouldn't tell me anything."

"Nothing to tell. He wants one thing, and I want something else." Talia went past her to the living room. She sat at the desk and started typing.

Mama Rose joined her seconds later. "Are you ever going to tell me what happened that night years ago?" she said.

"You know what happened. Monette got high and wild just like she had a hundred times before," Talia said without looking at her. She tapped the keyboard a few more times, pretending to concentrate on the screen.

"I know part of it." Mama Rose sat down on a chair next to the desk. She folded her hands in her lap and waited.

"Don't start seeing conspiracies everywhere." Talia forced a light tone. "Derrick seems to have that effect on people with his cops-and-robbers lifestyle."

"I wasn't a foster mother for fifteen years and a teacher for thirty years for nothing. I know when I haven't gotten the whole story." Mama Rose lifted her chin. She gazed at Talia through her bifocals, every inch the suspicious grade school principal examining a deceitful student.

Talia called up some part of Monette in her genes. She turned on a winning smile as she looked at Mama Rose. "Darlin', you know more about me than I do. Now can I please finish this report that was due yesterday?"

Mama Rose studied her long and hard for two minutes. Then she stood. "Alright."

"I promise we'll have a heart-to-heart like the old days when I'm through. Hot cocoa and cookies would be great." Talia licked her lips as she had as a little girl.

"Sure, honey. I'm going to find out eventually, you know," she called over her shoulder.

"Lord help me," Talia muttered.

Two mothers equaled twice the aggravation. If she couldn't keep Monette safe, at least she could protect Mama Rose. The passage of time had not lessened the danger. Talia only wished she could make Derrick back off. She felt helpless. The one thing she still had was her work. With iron will, Talia focused. Yet her neck and back ached from the tension. After only ten minutes she gave up.

"I'm going out for a break," she yelled down the hall. Before Mama Rose could question her, she grabbed her keys and left.

Chapter 20

Derrick slowed his steps when he saw Winn Barron emerge from the hospital room. He started to step around a corner, but Barron looked straight at him. Barron's eyes widened in what Derrick thought was a guilty expression. Instead of turning back, Derrick strode forward.

"Hello, sir. How are you?" Derrick extended his hand.

Barron seemed to collect himself as he shook it. "Hello. I was just visiting Jerry. Ah, you know each other?"

"We've met." Derrick gazed at him. "I talked to him about that drug case. You know, the one you asked Larry to look into because of a parole hearing."

"I've followed up on so many of them it's hard to remember." Barron smoothed down his wool jacket and cleared his throat. "I have to go now."

"Sure. Say, you didn't happen to ask Mr. Hines about the Victor case? Before he got hurt I mean."

"I hadn't talked to Jerry in months before this. We don't keep in touch like we should." He spat out the words rapidly.

"Oh, I see. Maybe you could ask him. You might have had more luck jogging his memory than I did."

"Well, it was a long time ago." Barron wore an easy smile.

"He put in lots of overtime on that case." Derrick did not move when Barron walked around him.

"Why would you examine his time sheets?" Barron's eyes narrowed.

"You did ask us to be thorough," Derrick replied. "That a problem?"

"Listen, whatever your name is," Barron snapped.

"Derrick Guillory," he answered.

"Well, Mr. Guillory, your job is to protect the public from criminals. Remember that! Now if you'll excuse me, I have a meeting with the governor." Barron brushed past him.

"Nice seeing you, too." Derrick did not flinch at the hostile glance the powerful man gave him. He went into the hospital room.

Hines looked around sharply when the door opened. "You." His voice was scratchy. With a shaky hand, he picked up a plastic cup and sipped through the straw in it.

"Sorry about what happened. Man, crime is out of control these days. Feeing any better?" Derrick walked over to the bed.

"What do you think?" Hines turned his head away from him.

"Yeah, dumb question. But you look a whole lot better than the day we found you." Derrick took in the room. There were only two vases with flowers. "Sure nice of your old boss to come see you."

"He's a real sweetheart."

"You need anything? Guess the wife is taking care of most things." Derrick probed what he thought was another sensitive area.

"Like emptying my bank account, maxing out the credit cards, and planning my funeral," Hines said bitterly. "I'm tired. What do you want?"

Indeed, the man looked worn-out. His dark skin was ashen and seemed stretched thin on his bones. Derrick studied him. This man needed a friend, someone on his side. Yet he was no fool who would fall for any line. Derrick walked around the room to buy time. He'd tried to get information from Mrs. Hines with no luck. She was as hard as her husband.

"You still here?" Hines cast a glance at him, then away again.

"Monette Victor was stabbed. Supposedly she got into a fight. We both know it wasn't, any more than what happened to you was a botched burglary."

"Is that what the warden's investigation says?" Hines glanced at him.

"Supposedly this inmate named Wanda Odom accused Monette of stealing from her. Odom has a history of being violent."

Hines grunted. "Happens all the time in prison. So you've got nothing."

"Odom also has a history of carrying out attacks for hire," Derrick said.

"If the warden concluded it was a fight, then there's no evidence she was paid to stab Monette. Stop reaching. As for me, the sheriff's office called me the other day. They caught a little punk trying to pawn my DVD player." Hines shifted in the bed.

"You can identify him as your attacker?"

"Maybe."

Derrick went around the side of the bed and looked down at him with a frown. "So it's all just a coincidence. You don't believe that any more than I do."

"The world is a violent place. Look at the news." Hines met his gaze with an impassive expression.

"Uh-huh. Course when your own buddy turns on you . . ." Derrick lifted a shoulder. "Bet he still knows a lot of thugs from the old days, and he can call on them."

"Don't know what you're talking about." Hines turned his face to the wall.

"Barron isn't going to risk his career, much less his neck. You know better than I do that he uses street thugs when it suits him. I've read the files on the informants y'all used." Derrick sat down in the chair next to his bed. "It's the downside of relying on scum to make cases. And they lie."

"You should write novels. You got a wild imagination." Hines didn't look at him.

"How's this for a plot. You listening?" Derrick tapped the bed.

"Not really. But then, I don't have anyplace to go right now."

"I think it could make a great movie even. A small-town DA uses informants to help make his cases. Problem is he cuts corners, steps on the Constitution. Then maybe he figures out, or doesn't care, that these guys are lying to him about the crimes. Maybe they even committed crimes and tossed him sacrificial lambs." Derrick nodded when Hines glanced at him.

"You're really reaching." Hines looked away from Derrick's steady gaze.

"Wait, I haven't gotten to the best part. One of the informants, let's call him Earl, decides he's got the DA in a tight spot and makes threats. Earl disappears. The DA takes care of a certain lady who knows too much, a long prison sentence. Everything is all tidy and life goes pretty good for him. He becomes a top state official with political ambitions that might come true."

"I don't buy it, and neither would anybody else," Hines cut in.

"The big-mouthed lady gets some sharp lawyer to listen. The lawyer starts poking around places that make Mr. Big Stuff jumpy. So Mr. Big Stuff decides to use his power to make sure this lady stays in prison a long, long time. People might wonder how those crooks were able to prosper for so long."

"I never helped a gangster operate." Hines made small gasping noises as he breathed hard. "Never!"

"Y'all didn't question these guys too hard while they were helping you. I mean, about how they made a living." Derrick sat back. "It's not a new story. A DA with too much political ambition and too few scruples."

"Don't quit your day job." Hines lay very still.

Derrick had to admire him. Hines was scared but tough. "Look, I want to help you out."

Hines started to laugh, but the effort ended in a hacking cough. His face twisted in pain. After a few moments he lay back against the pillow. Derrick held the cup of water for him. Hines looked at him with suspicion in his dark eyes but drank all the same.

"Thanks," he said in a croaky voice. "If you want to help me, then get the hell outta my room so I can rest." He pulled the top sheet up to cover more of his chest. "Appreciate the visit though."

Tough guy for sure, Derrick thought. Yet he didn't move from the chair. Instead he sat watching the older man for several moments. "I understand. Why risk getting these guys more upset than they already are? Yeah, I definitely see where you might want to take your chances. But then again, with friends like Barron you better watch your back."

"Give it up, kid. I'm not impressed." Hines closed his eyes.

"Not only did you put an innocent woman in prison for fifteen years, but you put her in danger. Obviously you can live with murder."

Derrick clenched his fist. Hines wasn't going to give an inch. Which meant Monette would stay in prison. Worse, she'd be in peril every moment she was there. When Hines didn't look at him, speak, or move Derrick started to stand up. The gruff voice stopped him.

"I was the first Black man to work for the district attorney in Pointe Coupee," Hines said, his voice even and matter-of-fact. "Funny, huh? Things changed real slow out here, civil rights or not."

Derrick waited a few beats before he spoke. "You had it from both sides. I got the same thing at first."

"You got nothing compared to what I went through," he said with force. Hines looked at Derrick. "I was grateful Barron hired me."

"How grateful?"

Hines looked away again. "Should have known there was a price. Daddy always said ain't nothing free in this life."

"You have to choose which price you're going to pay." Derrick was thinking as much of himself as Hines.

Hines smiled and looked at Derrick. "I'll be sixty next month. Here I'm being lectured by a youngster. You weren't born back when I started training. I was in the military police, army. Did two tours in Vietnam."

Derrick pushed back his own bad memories for the time being. "I heard how you put away some bad dudes. Cleaned up the neighborhoods."

"Things started changing around '84 or '85. Crack hit the streets. Folks got less grateful when I helped round up their kids and grandkids." Hines wore a bitter expression. "I got sick of them getting in my face, calling me Barron's houseboy."

"But you stuck it out." Derrick sighed.

"Damn straight." Hines looked at him with a fierce

light in his eyes. "I could have quit. But watching thugs use kids to sell drugs to other kids turned my stomach."

"You did what you thought needed to be done. Things just got out of hand," Derrick said in a sympathetic tone.

Hines stared ahead at nothing through narrowed eyes. "Barron didn't care about little details like finding out the truth. He wanted convictions."

"No matter how he got them," Derrick prompted.

"I wanted those creeps off the street, too." Hines replied.

"Different motivations, same result. You bent the rules."

"I got tired of thieves and drug dealers getting off. Most of the time they didn't even spend a night in jail." Hines shook his head slowly. "Our neighborhoods just went downhill overnight."

"You blame Monette for street crime? Get real."

Hines didn't answer him immediately. "Monette was always a charmer. She honestly tried to turn her life around a couple of times. She became Barron's woman," he said in a low voice. "Very few people knew. He was real careful."

Derrick tensed. "She's still planning to tell that story, Jerome."

"Monette should leave well enough alone. I would have tried to help her." Hines looked somber.

"Sure, like you've helped her for the last fifteen years. Time is short. What are you going to do, be smart or stupid?" Derrick studied his expression.

"I missed my one chance to be smart fifteen years ago." Hines wore a sour smile. "Shoulda quit that damn job."

Derrick stood. "I thought you were a better man. I was wrong."

"Keep on living, son. You'll get tired of watching

crooks get away with murder. Besides, I learned nobody on this earth is innocent."

"Don't tell me you were on some righteous mission." He headed for the door. "Your old boss is probably already figuring out how to take care of you. You're unfinished business for him. Good-bye, Jerry, and good luck. You're going to need it."

"Wait a minute," Hines said, straining to speak loudly. He panted from the effort.

"Yeah?" Derrick turned to face him, one hand on the metal door handle.

"I want to help you write a real exciting ending to that novel we've been talking about. You might even get a movie deal." Hines raised a dark eyebrow. "Just make sure I get a bit part."

Derrick walked back into the room and sat down. "It's a deal," he said.

Talia read the last e-mail message from her office and sighed with satisfaction as she signed off the Internet. Catching up on work and the politics of D.C. felt good. Still, Talia felt a twinge of guilt on occasion. She'd been relieved when Monette insisted she stay away from her. Despite her words, there was no mistaking the pain in Monette's eyes when Talia agreed with little argument. The specter of her painful childhood had proven too strong.

Mama Rose hurried into the den and turned on the television. The screen lit up immediately. "You have to see this, Talia."

"No, I don't."

Talia jumped up from the sofa and scattered papers everywhere. She marched to the television and punched the power button, cutting off the blond anchorwoman on the five o'clock news.

"What is the matter with you? They—"

"I don't want to know."

"But, but—" Mama Rose pointed to the television, her mouth working.

"Forget it, Mama. I just want to concentrate on my work and my life." Talia picked up the sheets from the sage-colored carpet as she talked. "Monette has good legal representation and with her injuries she'll get the sympathy vote. Her words not mine."

"Will you listen to me?" Mama Rose put her fists on both hips.

"I know you're trying to help. But please understand. This is what Monette wants." Talia organized the draft of her report while crouched on the floor.

"What Monette wants," Mama Rose repeated.

"Yes." Talia didn't look up from the papers. "I'm really busy here."

Mama Rose sat down on one of two large matching chairs near the sofa. She watched Talia for a time in silence. Talia sat cross-legged on a huge accent throw pillow with her laptop on the coffee table. Determined to clear everything from her mind but the report, she tried to pretend Mama Rose's eyes weren't trained on her like hot laser beams. A rush of air amid the rustle of papers was her only warning. Mama Rose snatched the stack from the table.

"No work gets done until I have my say." Mama Rose raised her bottom and sat on the report.

"Real mature! Now hand it over." Talia held out her hand.

"Right after you hear me out." Mama Rose shook a forefinger at her nose.

Talia recognized the expression on Mama Rose's face. She'd never won a battle of wills with her. "Okay. Get it out of your system. It's the only way I'll get any work done."

"This isn't about what Monette wants. You've been

running away for most of your life. It's time to face reality."

"Reality? I knew more about the real world by the time I was six years old than most people. I educated you on new stuff, remember?"

Mama Rose nodded. "You taught me some new ways to cuss and street terms for drugs I'd never heard of before. I know what you went through, sugar." Mama Rose's tone softened along with her expression. Yet the determination remained. "Those days, as horrible as they were, are part of you. Let your experiences make you strong, not weak."

"I love you, Mama. But you don't have any idea what you're talking about. Just leave it alone." Talia folded her arms tight against her body to fight off a shiver.

"Not now. Your mother is doing the bravest thing she's ever done. She risked her life to tell the truth. Derrick's career is on the line as well."

"I warned him to mind his own business," Talia said with fervor. "I warned Monette not to grandstand. Neither of them listened."

"They would have if you'd been talking sense," Mama Rose said sharply. "Do you know what's going on out there?" She waved a hand toward the window as though the drama was on her front lawn.

"Yes. Monette made a big splash with her allegations about Winn Barron. I don't have to read about it or watch the news on TV to know the media are going wild." Talia met her gaze.

"He set her up as revenge because she ended their affair. The man should be horsewhipped." Mama Rose seemed to vibrate with outrage. "His pal, Larry Perrilloux, suspended Derrick."

"Just as I predicted if you recall. I'm not going join the soap opera." Talia looked away from her uncompromising gaze.

"Real nice. Something to be proud of for sure." Mama Rose made a hissing noise to emphasize her displeasure.

"They want me to stay out of it."

"So they're taking all the hits. Does that mean you should let them?"

Talia flinched. The words struck home like a steel-tipped arrow in her chest. For days she'd avoided glancing at headlines or watching the local news. Instead she'd focused on CNN and the Fox News Network. Still, with such a big story hitting the airwaves, Talia knew it would attract national attention soon. Winn Barron had retreated behind a barricade of attorneys. His only statements were to remind reporters of Monette's arrest record and family history.

"You can hide, Talia. But I don't think it's the best thing for you." Mama Rose broke into her thoughts.

Talia couldn't stop her hands from shaking. "Lord knows I've lived with this monster all my life."

"At least talk to Derrick. He deserves your support. I'm right here. You don't have to face this alone, baby."

The image of Earl's lifeless body flashed before her as if no time had passed. "Yes, I do."

"Alright, sugar. I won't say any more. Just think about it." Mama Rose hugged Talia and left.

"That's all I do is think about it," Talia whispered.

"You can have this job." Derrick dropped the office keys onto Larry's desk. "We don't have to waste time meeting."

Larry rocked forward in his chair. "Sit down."

"For what? I don't need a long explanation that comes down to the same thing."

"So you've got all the answers." Larry's jaw muscles worked as he clamped his mouth shut.

"Most of 'em, yeah," Derrick snapped.

"Just for my information then, 'cause maybe I'm dense, fill me in." Larry's dark eyes flashed with anger. He folded his hands tightly until his knuckles were white.

"Barron is calling the shots. He knows I helped pull his nasty skeletons out of the closet."

"I'm his puppet?" Larry's voice strained out the words.

"He's a powerful man." Derrick gazed at him with an impassive expression.

"That's the real deal as you call it."

"Yeah."

"Try this on for size." Larry held out one hand and ticked off points on his fingers. "One, you went off half-cocked without filling me in."

"I wasn't going to say 'Hey, Larry, your old school chum is a liar,' " Derrick cut in.

"Two, you interviewed witnesses without consulting me," Larry went on in a cold tone.

"Right, like you were going to build a case against Barron." Derrick gave a cynical snort.

"Three, your actions resulted in danger to two people. If you'd gone through proper channels, we could have offered them protection." Larry's voice got louder.

Derrick leaned on his desk with both palms flat. "Don't give me that bull, Larry! One, you know damn well you wouldn't have believed my suspicions about Barron. Two, you definitely wouldn't have believed Monette Victor's story. And three, there would have been no protection since Barron has influence in the sheriff's office and the prison system."

"I've defended you when others said you were reckless, a grandstand artist. Now I see their point." Larry glared at him across the desk.

"I defended your good name, too. Now I feel like a first-class fool. I told people you wouldn't operate like Barron, friend or not," Derrick shouted.

Larry's expression turned rock-hard. He took a folder from his desk and slapped it open. "Earl Glasper disappeared years ago. We're opening an investigation again because it relates to Monette Victor's sensational claim. You know anything about him?"

Ten seconds passed as they stared at each other. Then Derrick stood straight, careful to keep his expression blank. "Why should I?"

"Rule number one in an interview, if a question is answered with a question, the subject is either buying time or trying to find out how much you know." Larry squinted at him.

"So I'm a suspect? Barron really must be running scared. An old strategy, go after the people who can bury you."

Larry put on his reading glasses and looked at the open file. "You grew up in the Victor woman's neighborhood. You had a few minor brushes with the law as a juvenile. Did you know her?"

Derrick felt a rush of anxiety. Not for himself. He was thinking of Talia. Still, he reminded himself to stay in control. "Barron has been investigating me. I'm not really surprised. Or did you help him?"

"It doesn't matter at this point. I could excuse your going off on your own with an investigation. But this . . ." Larry tapped the stack of typed sheets. "When you were fifteen Monette Victor lived only a couple of streets from your house."

"A petty crook with a history of disappearing has been missing for sixteen years. You're questioning me about it?" Derrick laughed. "You and your partner gotta do better than that, Larry."

"Monette Victor was the last one to see him alive according to witnesses. Nothing was made of it at the time. Like you say, Glasper lived a transient lifestyle on the wrong side of the law. Winn has raised some legitimate questions." Larry looked at him hard.

Derrick returned his gaze without losing his relaxed stance, one hand in his pocket. "Real thin."

"Glasper had information about Monette Victor. He was an informant. I think you've found out more. Tell me the truth, and maybe I can help you."

"I'll tell you another rule in interviewing, Larry. Make the subject think you know more than you do, so he'll spill his guts." Derrick walked toward the door. "Shove it."

He went to his desk, picked up a cardboard box, and headed for the exit. Kelsey followed him to the parking lot. Derrick unlocked his 4Runner. She waited until several court employees passed before she spoke.

"What the heck is going down? The entire building is buzzing. I can't believe you and Larry are at each other's throats," Kelsey said in a breathless rush. "I've been dying to find out something."

"Stay clear of this one, Kelsey." Derrick slammed the back door shut.

"Tell me the rumors about you taking on Barron aren't true." Kelsey put a hand on his arm. "You don't want to mess with him."

"Thanks for your concern, but I can take care of myself." Derrick opened the door and got behind the wheel. "Nice working with ya, Kel."

"But—"

"Don't put your job on the line." He glanced back and saw Larry standing in the glass double doors watching them.

Kelsey followed his gaze. She turned back to him with a defiant scowl. "I'm a civil servant. They'd have to blast me outta that office."

He grinned at her. “Lord help them if they tangle with you.”

“Call if you need anything. I’m serious.”

“Don’t offer what you might have to take back,” Derrick warned. He put on his sunglasses.

“I never do.” Kelsey waved to him and went back inside.

“I might take you up on that offer,” Derrick said to himself.

He drove off thinking of Talia’s last words to him. Maybe she’d been right all along. His hot dog style might have made things worse. Earl Glasper wouldn’t stay dead somehow. Derrick’s palms sweated as he gripped the steering wheel. He’d have to dig up his own skeleton and deal with the consequences. *How* was the million-dollar question.

Chapter 21

∞

That old saying is true, Talia mused, with a grim sinking sensation. Though appalled, she couldn't look away. It was like staring at a bloody car accident. For the last three days she'd watched the television newscasts from Baton Rouge. She switched between the two major stations, one a CBS affiliate and the other ABC. Monette and Winn Barron were the stars on both.

"Talk about drama," Talia muttered. A redheaded news reporter rattled off a time line of the events, including a dour mug shot of Monette.

"Each day brings more shocking revelations," the redhead said, and looked down at her notes. "According to our sources an employee has been fired from the District Attorney's Office for uncovering this scandal involving the state attorney general, Winn Barron. Derrick Guillory helped find the smoking gun as it were . . ."

"What did I tell you?" Mama Rose marched in talking rapid fire. "I was watching on the television in my kitchen! This is outrageous. That boy does the right thing and—"

"Shush!" Talia waved at her frantically.

"So, Bob," the redhead spoke to the anchor at the studio. "Attorney General Barron is hitting back hard. We've also been told that Monette Victor, her attorney, and Guillory have received death threats. District Attorney Larry Perrilloux had this statement."

Video of Perrilloux came on. He refused to comment on confidential personnel matters. Questions about Barron flew at him like angry wasps from a group of reporters. Perrilloux deftly made a few remarks without saying much of substance.

"Look at him! He sure won't get my vote again." Mama Rose glared at the television screen.

The redhead came back on. "We're working on another interesting angle in all this, Bob. The investigation into the disappearance of a man involved with Monette Victor sixteen years ago will be reopened. This is Leslie Wheeler reporting."

Talia hit the MUTE button when a shampoo commercial came on. "Damn!" she whispered.

Mama Rose looked at Talia sharply. "You know who they're talking about, Talia?"

"Derrick had to go sticking his nose in." Talia sprang from her seat and paced.

"Answer me, Missy." Mama Rose grabbed her arm. "If you can help Derrick, you have to do something."

Talia pulled away from her. Fear crawled over her like tiny cold feet with sharp claws. "I'm leaving in four days."

"Baby, you look like ten goblins just walked in to get you. Tell Mama what's wrong."

"You've seen the news. Can't you guess?" Talia could hear the note of hysteria in her own voice. She closed her eyes and took a deep breath.

"Come over here and sit down next to me." Mama Rose herded her to the sofa. When they sat down, she put an arm around Talia's shoulder. "Now stop holding in this secret you've been keeping."

Talia shivered. "You don't want to know, believe me. I've been trying to forget for years."

"Obviously you can't. You're scared. Maybe this bogeyman won't be so big if we talk about him."

"Mama, I—"

"I thought you trusted me." Mama Rose looked at her hard.

"I can't drag you into my nightmare." Talia brushed away tears to keep them from falling.

"Child, I've faced down rowdy thirteen-year-olds in the classroom. Nothing scares me." Mama Rose smiled at her.

Talia was so tired of carrying around the burden alone. Mama Rose's solid presence helped steady her. Talia sighed and leaned against her. She started off slowly in a flat voice while Mama Rose listened. Talia told her everything.

"He didn't get up," Talia said. Her voice strained, as though the words were too big in her throat.

"My Lord!" Mama Rose made the sign of the cross. "What happened to the body."

"Derrick went back to help Monette move him. He said when he got there Monette had somehow managed to wrap it up in an old quilt. Derrick wouldn't tell me anything else. But I think they buried him in the woods."

"Around Creole Bayou," Mama Rose murmured. She took her arms from around Talia and seemed deep in thought.

"God! I wanted to tell the police. But Monette said to keep my mouth shut." Talia shook her head. "I haven't talked to her about it since."

Talia was afraid Mama Rose would finally withdraw

from her. Yet she wouldn't blame her. Mama Rose sat very still, twisting her hands together for a long time. Talia watched the television screen, feeling as though she'd lost everything.

"There won't be much left to find after all these years. Especially with the heat, insects, and humidity," Mama Rose said. "So that should help."

Talia blinked at her in shock. "Mama!"

"What? Oh, I learned that from watching the *Forensic Detectives* on the Discovery Channel," she said matter-of-factly.

"You don't think we should have told the truth and faced up to it." Talia looked at her with wide eyes.

"You and Derrick were just babies." Mama Rose gave a curt nod. "Monette should have called the police."

Talia nodded at the television. "Between Barron, Perrilloux, and those reporters, everything might be out soon."

"Monette sure is in deep." Mama Rose gasped. "Have mercy! To think I was trying to push you into getting involved even more. Thank God you're leaving on Friday. In fact, why don't you leave sooner?"

"Well, I—"

Mama Rose stood up. "Sure you can. I'll help you pack."

"Right now?"

Mama Rose yanked Talia to her feet. "Far away is exactly where you need to be. Those sharks don't know you're Monette's child. Let's keep it that way."

"I'll stick to the schedule," Talia said over her shoulder, as Mama Rose pushed her along down the hall.

"No sense in taking foolish chances. You start throwing stuff in your suitcases. I'll call the airline." Mama Rose gave Talia one final shove into her bedroom.

"You're freaking out. Calm down and be rational."

Talia spun around, but Mama Rose was gone. She strode into the kitchen to find her already on the phone.

"I hate these voice mail things." Mama Rose punched buttons on the phone, apparently following instructions.

"Give me that." Talia took the receiver from her.

"You're right. You should do it. Hey!" Mama Rose shouted when Talia hung up the phone. "Now you'll have to start all over with that stupid menu."

"No I won't. I'm not changing my flight time, okay? Chill."

"Talia, you don't leave for four long days. Plenty of time for Barron to drag your name through the dirt." Mama Rose reached for the phone again.

Talia jumped between Mama Rose and the phone. "I'm leaving Friday as planned. Trust me, I'm looking forward to getting back to a normal life."

Mama Rose let out a long sigh, like a balloon deflating. "I guess you're right. Poor baby, no wonder you hate coming home."

"I definitely prefer short, uneventful visits," Talia murmured with a half smile.

"I hear ya, sugar." Mama Rose sat down at the kitchen table. "Derrick sure is in a tight spot."

Talia frowned. "I warned him. Naturally, he jumped in with both feet."

"Trying to make things right as always. He's got guts." Mama Rose glanced at Talia.

"He's impulsive and hooked on his own adrenaline, always chasing after a fight," Talia replied.

Mama Rose shook her head slowly. "That boy is giving up a lot."

"And for what?" Talia threw up both hands. "He should have stayed out of the whole thing."

"He doesn't believe in playing it safe, that's the

truth." Mama Rose pursed her lips. "It's just sad Derrick is going to lose his career and maybe worse."

"I'm sorry Derrick is in trouble, too, but he has no one but himself to blame." Talia handed Mama Rose a glass of raspberry ice tea.

"You may be right. I'm glad you're leaving Louisiana." Mama Rose stood and patted Talia's shoulder.

"Yeah," Talia muttered as she watched her walk out.

The word "blame" kept bouncing in her head. Derrick had risked his neck more than once to rescue her and Monette. Well, she'd warned him repeatedly, hadn't she? Talia pushed the glass of tea aside. She had little appetite for anything these days. All she wanted was her carefully constructed life back. Would she have it by simply returning to Washington, D.C.?

Marti Campo, Senator Jackson's aide, beamed at Talia. "We couldn't have arranged this media frenzy better if we'd planned it! I love these headlines." She waved three major daily newspapers from around the state. More were stacked on her desk. "We're getting national coverage."

"Wonderful." Talia looked at the bold headlines that shouted Monette's name. "I just wanted to bring this last report before I leave Friday."

"Good, good." Marti paced in front of her desk. "I'm just sorry Derrick is catching hell."

Talia flinched at the stab of guilt that was now too familiar. "Call me at my office in D.C. if you need anything more."

"This Monette Victor scandal will put us over the top. Winn Barron is up to his neck in doo-doo. I love it!" Marti clapped her hands and giggled wickedly.

"Right. It was nice working with you and Senator

Jackson." Talia stuck her hand out. The last thing she wanted was to discuss her mother's former lover.

"Don't run off. Derrick and Jim should be here any minute." Marti grinned at her. "Stick around to find out how we move in for the kill. We get to attack that mandatory-sentencing statute and twist the knife in good old Winn."

Talia picked up her leather briefcase. She wanted to see Derrick even less than she wanted to discuss Barron. "I have to get going. Bye."

"Oh, okay." Marti crossed the space between them and shook her hand. "You've been such a help. Thanks for the great work."

"Thank you. Call on us anytime."

Talia left Marti's office. She turned the corner of the hallway in time to see Derrick and Jim get off the elevator. Derrick stopped in his tracks as their gazes locked.

"Hi, Talia," Jim said with a nod.

"Hello." Talia forced herself to look away from Derrick's intense dark eyes. She nodded back at Rand. "I'm on my way out."

"When are you leaving?" Derrick asked. His tone was even, almost lifeless.

"Friday. I, uh, have a lot of work waiting for me in D.C.," she added.

"Have a safe trip." Without another word, Jim headed down the hall.

Derrick didn't follow him. "Can we talk?"

"Don't you have an appointment?" Talia looked down the hallway where Jim had gone toward Marti's office.

"They can start without me. Let's go outside." Derrick nodded toward the glass door at the end of the hallway.

Talia owed him at least a little of her time before she

left. Still, the need to escape was strong. Derrick must have sensed her hesitation.

"Please," he said in a quiet voice.

She nodded and followed him out into the fall sunshine. A cold day had turned mild in typical subtropical Louisiana fashion. The sixty-degree temperature made for a comfortable day. They walked from the basement exit down the sidewalk and crossed the street behind. A paved path wound around Capitol Lake. Neither spoke for ten minutes.

"Nice day," she finally said. "It won't be this balmy in D.C." Might as well get it out on the table.

"No." Derrick stared ahead, his dark brows drawn down.

"Thank the Lord for computers, e-mail, and cell phones. Keeps me out of the snow and traffic." Talia glanced at him.

"Great," he replied.

He wasn't going to make it easy. Talia stopped. Derrick took a few more steps, then turned to face her. They gazed at each other in silence. He seemed to be searching more than her expression; his examination reached into her heart. Talia lost the staring match. She looked away out over the water.

"I don't blame you. We just have a different view of the world," Talia said.

"Maybe I do push the limit sometimes." Derrick took in a deep breath and let it out slowly. He walked a few feet to a bench and sat down. "I hate seeing people trampled, especially women. Guess we both have mother complexes." He wore a brief smile that winked out like a small lightbulb seconds later.

Talia followed and sat down on the other end of the bench. "Guess so. Rescuing underdogs and righting wrongs is a big part of who you are, whatever the reason."

"Living a quiet, upwardly mobile lifestyle is what you want." Derrick looked at his large hands clasped between his knees.

"I love waking up and feeling secure knowing exactly what my day will be like. Every minute of the first sixteen years of my life was the exact opposite. My stomach stayed in knots. I can't count the number of times I went straight from school to a new foster home." Talia's throat tightened. "Then after that night when Earl . . . you know."

"I'm sorry I brought it all back. Damn it!" Derrick sprang from the bench and walked a few feet away, his back to her.

"Monette did her part." Talia crossed her arms tightly until she hugged her body.

"When I was a kid, I used to get between my daddy and my mama when they were fighting. He'd beat her up, then sit down to eat like nothing had happened."

"God, how awful."

She'd known it was bad for him at home, too. In a small town people talked, and she'd heard the gossip. Yet this was the first time he'd spoken about it so openly.

"We finally got him out of our lives. Then I had to watch people mistreat her because she was poor, Black, and a woman. I hated it. My anger got me into trouble more than once. Anger at the world, 'the system,' didn't matter which one. I was pissed at all of them—the educational system, the welfare system, the legal system, you name it. I finally learned to use the system to fight back. Otherwise, I might be in prison with a lot of other brothers."

"You survived," Talia said.

He turned around. "We both did. I have my way of dealing, and you have yours."

"Yes." *We each learned to cope with the past in different ways,* she thought.

"I really want you to be happy and feel safe. I'm not selfish enough to hold you back because I—"

"Because you what?" Talia's heart pounded.

"I'm sorry, Talia."

Talia swallowed hard. What had she expected, a declaration of love that would magically make everything fine? "So am I," she murmured.

"I'll make sure you're out of it."

She shook her head gently. "There you go, putting yourself on the line to rescue someone else."

He waved a hand. "I'll be fine. Barron is desperate enough to try anything, including going after you to scare Monette. I won't let that happen."

Derrick's tone scared her. "Please don't do anything crazy," she said.

His expression relaxed in the ghost of a smile. "Who, me do something crazy? Never!" Derrick took her hand. "Good-bye, baby girl. I'm proud of everything you've done."

The word "good-bye" stuck in Talia's throat as she watched him stride off quickly.

Chapter 22

Talia sat in her brother Karl's living room with his family. They all stared at the television. His youngest climbed into her lap and insisted Talia look at her stuffed bunny.

"Not right now, honey bee." Talia kissed Rashida's soft woolly curls.

"Lord, what else can happen?" LaTrice, Karl's wife, said.

"A whole lot," Karl said with a grave frown. "You know anything about this Earl guy, Talia?" He looked at her. Anxiety made his brown face even longer.

"Not much. Monette did run with him back in the old days." Talia hugged Rashida, savoring the sweet innocence that radiated from her little body.

"You think she did him in?" Karl asked.

"C'mon, y'all," LaTrice said to the children playing on the carpeted floor. "Go back in the playroom with your toys." She shooed them out despite whining and protests.

Talia gave Rashida a final pinch on her velvety tan cheek before releasing her. "Karl, you shouldn't even ask me that question."

"Yeah, you're right. Our mama ain't no killer."

Talia glanced away from his gaze. She'd learned to dodge the truth from the best, Monette. Although she didn't like it, Talia told herself it was for his own good. The less Karl knew, the better for him.

"Hey, they doin' more on the story," Karl said.

Talia leaned forward and stared at the television again. "Now what?" she muttered.

A slim blond male reporter read from a sheet of paper in his hand. "So in a stunning reversal, Winn Barron seems to have struck a serious blow to Ms. Victor's allegations. We couldn't reach her attorney James Rand for a comment. However, sources close to the investigation tell us court records document that Earl Glasper was last seen with Ms. Victor before his disappearance. Hank Sherman reporting."

Karl shook his head. "I went to visit Monette up at the prison. First thing she wanted to know was if you was gone yet."

"She called and told me to get out of town." Talia no longer looked at the television screen.

"You leaving, right?" Karl said.

"Yes."

Karl let out a sigh of relief. "Great. You got something good up there in Washington, D.C."

"Right."

"Derrick is being questioned. They found out he knew Monette and been talking to her." Karl continued to stare at Talia. "Sure hope they don't drag him down just cause he was tryin' to help."

"Men like Barron destroy anyone in their path." Talia tapped her clenched fist on the sofa cushion. "So much for Perrilloux's integrity. He's helping Barron."

"Wish we could do something." Karl let out a grunt to show his frustration. He combed his long fingers through the thick hair on his head.

Talia didn't answer him. She shivered with fear at the thought of what might happen. Her worst nightmare was coming true. Karl and LaTrice talked on about the news reports and local rumors circulating. Everyone old enough to remember had a theory it seemed. After refusing to stay longer, Talia headed back to Mama Rose's house. Mama Rose was waiting for her when she pulled into the driveway.

"I've been watching the news. It's horrible." Mama Rose had started talking before Talia had gotten out of the car.

"Don't get upset. You know what the doctor said." Talia took her arm. "In fact, stop watching the news."

"Listen to me. They just said Derrick might be arrested for obstruction of justice and tampering with evidence."

"What!" Talia gripped her arm tightly. "Who said that?"

"I thought you were watching the news at Karl's! They broke in toward the end on Channel 7. That news reporter showed them leading Derrick into the sheriff's office."

"This is insane." Talia felt dazed. The whole world seemed to be spinning out of control.

"Just when I didn't think this whole situation could get any worse," Mama Rose said.

"I can't believe it. Derrick might go overboard, but . . ." Talia thought about his need to protect others. Derrick was bold, even reckless at times. "What have you done?" she whispered.

The phone rang, and they both rushed inside. Talia grabbed it first. "Derrick, what the hell is going on? I can't believe Perrilloux would stoop so low," Talia said in a rush. His deep voice cut her off. "Yes. Yes. I wish I could help in some way."

"Tell him my cousin's son is a top attorney in New Orleans. We won't let them railroad him!" Mama Rose shook a fist in the air.

Talia paced as she listened to him. "I understand. Good-bye."

"Don't hang up. I'm going to give him Wayne's office number. I've got his card in my desk, or somewhere."

Talia had already pushed the OFF button. "He's talked to a lawyer already."

"I'll find that card anyway." Mama Rose scurried out mumbling to herself. "I wouldn't trust the lawyers around here. All of them are too chummy with the Barrons and their crowd."

Talia sat down hard on the sofa. She dropped her purse without looking to see where it landed. Derrick was caught in a swirling undercurrent that threatened to suck him under, along with Monette's chances of freedom. He and Monette begged her to stay far away from them, something she'd done so easily for years. The terror twisting her insides told her to take their advice. Running away was exactly what she'd done before.

"Found it!" Mama Rose yelled. She hurried back into the den holding a business card over her head. "Give me Derrick's cell phone number."

"It's 567-3344," Talia said in a wooden voice. She rubbed her eyes.

"Humph, voice mail." Mama Rose left a message talking rapidly. "Now you be sure and call him. Bye, darlin'. You call me if you need anything! There." She heaved a deep sigh.

"Where did it start?" Talia said.

"Winn Barron is behind all this," Mama Rose hissed. "He's a no-good—"

"No, Mama Rose. What has happened in my life, in

Derrick's life, started before we were born. And I still don't know why. Why me? I used to cry so and ask myself that question over and over until I'd scream."

"I don't know the answer either, sugar." Mama Rose sat next to her.

"After a while I quit wondering. I accepted that for whatever reason my life was always going to be miserable."

Talia remembered being cold and alone when she was five years old. Not cold because of the temperature. The chill she felt was being surrounded by chaos with no one to help her feel safe. When Mama Rose squeezed her hand tightly, Talia blinked back to the present.

"Monette had so many problems," Mama Rose said in a gentle tone.

"Then I met you. I remember the first time they dropped me off here." Talia put her head on Mama Rose's strong shoulder.

"You were only a little bitty thing."

"You let me cry until I was exhausted. You didn't lie and tell me everything was okay like a dozen adults had done before. Remember what you did?" Talia moved closer until Mama Rose put her arms around her.

"Lord, baby, my memory isn't what it used to be." Mama Rose said, a smile in her voice.

"You just kept talking to me about that one raggedy little toy I brought with me. Once I stopped shaking you put me in that big bathtub full of bubbles and little boats floating in it. I remember feeling so warm and clean. Then you let me put on these cute yellow cotton coveralls. The cloth felt soft against my skin and smelled like flowers. Later on we had milk and gingerbread cake. I went to sleep without being afraid for the first time in my life." Talia drew in a shaky breath and let it out.

"When I started taking in children I'd get so discouraged. I'd wonder if I was making any difference."

"You did. Even when I went back to live with Monette, what you did for me and taught me gave me strength. I love you for it, Mama. I always will." Talia felt a tear slide down her cheek.

"I love you, too, baby." Mama Rose sniffed. She let go of Talia. "Now we'd better finish packing your bags. Thank the Lord you leave tomorrow. I'll feel a lot better knowing you're safe from this mess. I'm going to fold up those clothes I washed for you." She stood.

"Hmm." Talia stared ahead without seeing anything. Her thoughts were on Derrick.

"Come on now. With all the clothes and things you've got, we can't do it in the morning. Lord, child! How many shoes can one woman wear?" Mama Rose laughed.

"Yeah, right."

Her expression turned serious again. "I'm going to make sure my cousin's boy helps Derrick."

"I hear you." Talia felt a thudding pain around her eyes.

"Don't you even think of missing that plane!" Mama Rose put both hands on her hips. "Derrick and Monette—"

"I know, I know," Talia broke in

Mama Rose headed down the hall. "You coming?"

"In a minute."

Talia continued to stare into space. Every nerve in her body screamed that she should get out of town fast and not look back. The voice of reason told her she couldn't do anything to help them anyway. Still, she felt sick at the thought of leaving. Could she go back to carefully selecting which designer pumps to wear with her designer power suits? Sit sipping mocha latte while she swapped Beltway gossip with other buppies? Talia went into her bedroom and started emptying the large open pullman suitcase lying on the floor.

"Damn it," Talia muttered. "I must be out of my everlasting mind."

"I've got a plan," Talia announced the moment Jim Rand opened his office door.

"Monette won't be happy with me if I—"

"You scared of her or something?" Talia crossed her arms.

"Trying to bait me won't work," Jim said mildly. "I work for her, remember? And it so happens I agree with her reasoning. You shouldn't get involved."

Talia brushed past him and strode into his office. "I *am* involved, like it or not."

Jim sighed and closed the door. "I know you're upset about Derrick. I'm sure he'd say the same thing. Go back home, Ms. Marchand."

"Do I like having a mother in prison? No. Would I love to be far away from here? Yes. Am I scared? Dumb question considering we're talking murder. But I can't leave her and Derrick to face this without doing everything I can," Talia said with force.

"What you've done already is more than enough."

"Real nice, but I'm not leaving. I can put my plan in action with your help or without it." Talia stared at him steadily. "What's it going to be?"

"You're just like your mother. Hardheaded, impulsive, and unreasonable." Jim leaned against his desk and crossed his arms. "Alright, the plan."

Talia sat down in one of the chairs in his office. "My boss, Peter Gallagher, has friends in high places. These friends have friends in high places all over the country."

"Including Louisiana."

"Pretty quick for a college professor and lawyer," Talia quipped.

"Smart-mouthed like your mama, too." Jim squinted at her.

"I'll take that as a compliment." Talia wore a brief half smile before she got serious again. "Pete called around and found out something interesting. Larry Perrilloux isn't as thrilled with his old pal Winn as everyone thinks. In fact, this is just the latest crack in their crumbling friendship. Seems he's privately expressed to power brokers that Barron crossed the line on this one."

"Maybe, but they won't cut him loose until they do damage control. Which includes discrediting Monette. The result of which will be to keep her in prison." Jim's expression deepened into a deep frown.

"Not to mention ruining Derrick and linking them both to a possible murder." Talia felt a cold shiver of fear.

"The sheriff's office is searching the woods behind your old neighborhood with help from the state police. They've turned it over to their 'cold case' specialist."

"Cold case?"

"Cases that remained unsolved for years because they hit a dead end. When they get new information the case is reopened." Jim rubbed his jaw. "Barron provided that new information by linking Glasper's disappearance to Monette."

"Right." Talia turned that fact over in her mind. "So how did Barron know Monette was with him the night he disappeared?"

"He knew about her and Glasper. A logical connection." Jim shrugged.

"She and Earl could have broken up by then. In fact, they took turns dumping each other," Talia said. "They weren't quiet fights either. Trust me, I lived through it. The cops were called at least twice."

"Maybe Barron didn't care until his neck was in the noose?" Jim looked at her with interest in his dark eyes.

"Barron is known for being a real snake when he's crossed. He could have smoked her for murder and the cocaine then." Talia shook her head. "I think there's another reason."

"Such as?"

"I know my dear mama. Five dollars says Monette is still holding back." Talia raised an eyebrow at him.

Jim growled like an irritated pit bull. "She'd better not be. I've told her—"

"Yeah, which means exactly nothing to Monette. And then there's Jerome Hines. He knows more than he's saying, too." She tried arranging the pieces of the puzzle in some way that made sense.

"Derrick thought he might help, but he's getting jumpy now. Murder allegations tend to do that to people," Jim said in a morose tone.

"Bum!" Talia tapped a foot hard and thought some more.

"We'll discuss your theories with Derrick." Jim didn't wait for her response. He got up and went to the desk phone. "I'm sure you know his home number." He gazed at Talia.

"I don't know why you'd assume such a thing." Talia cleared her throat. "It's 337 555-0002."

Jim tapped the number pad on the phone. "I'm quick, remember?"

"Monette talks too much about some things and not enough about others," Talia muttered.

"Answering machine. What's his cell phone number?"

This time Talia didn't bother to offer a token denial.

She gave him Derrick's mobile number. "Same area code."

"Derrick, Jim Rand. Can we meet this afternoon at my office? Talia is here. Lunch is good. I'll order in. What do you like?"

Talia felt a rush at the prospect of seeing Derrick once more. Still, she would make sure this would be the last time. They both knew being together only made the inevitable parting more painful.

Jim hung up the phone. "So what is this plan?"

Derrick negotiated the busy New Orleans traffic with his mind already at Jim's office. He had resigned himself to not seeing her again. For the past three weeks he'd sweated her out of his system. Each morning he rose early, usually after a restless night. Fortunately, two old pals, both private detectives, gave him skip-tracing jobs. Every evening he exercised as though he was in training for a triathlon. Then he would sit in the hot tub at his health club. The pain was down to a manageable throbbing sensation in his chest. Not pleasant, but he could at least concentrate. His emotional shell would be tested much sooner than he'd expected.

He circled around a good fifteen minutes, searching for a parking spot. Finally, a car pulled out from a side street and he beat out a gray Lexus for the coveted space. Derrick walked the three blocks and used the extra time to shore up his defenses. When he entered the building that housed Jim's office he took a deep breath and let it out. He repeated the exercise once he was at the door. He knocked and braced himself.

Jim opened the door. "Hey, buddy. Come on in. The food should be here soon." He clapped a hand on Derrick's shoulder.

"Sounds good. How are you doing?" Derrick nodded to him.

"Okay. What about you?" Jim wore a concerned expression as he studied Derrick's face.

"I'll survive." Derrick flashed a grim smile that faded quickly.

"Hi, Derrick."

"Hello." He turned to face Talia. Might as well get a full dose right off the bat.

Talia wore a dark green and brown tweed jacket. Her chocolate brown jeans were tucked into brown riding boots. The outfit molded to her full curves. The colors made her honey brown skin seem even tastier. She lifted her chin to gaze up at him fully. Derrick forced himself not to stare into those beautiful eyes for more than a few seconds. At least not right away. More time, a small voice in his head echoed. *Sure, a couple of dozen lifetimes should do it.*

"You really okay?"

"Great," Derrick blurted out. He looked away.

"Glad you could make it," Jim said, and sat on the edge of his desk.

"Anything else on the charges against you?" Talia asked.

"Larry just says the investigation is continuing. Which means just what it says. I'll be okay." Derrick waved a hand. "They've got nothing."

"What about Earl and that night?" Talia said in a low voice.

"I'm not your lawyer, and I can't claim client privilege," Jim interrupted.

"Relax, I know. Talia, the charges have to do with divulging information not considered public record that might interfere with an open case."

"Which also covers the obstruction of justice charge," Jim said.

"They allege that I used my position to help Monette make a bogus claim and fed her information.

Then, knowing she was implicated in a possible murder, I kept her informed so she could fight it." Derrick shook his head. "The only reason it works is because they found out I knew Monette years ago."

"What made Hines change his mind about talking?" Jim asked.

"I'm not sure. One minute he wanted to give his former boss some payback, the next minute he had memory problems." Derrick tapped a fist on the tablecloth.

"What a sleazy character!" Talia grimaced. "I'll bet he got a nice fat deposit in his bank account."

"Try finding it. He and Barron are experts at hiding dead bodies." Jim saw Talia wince. "Poor choice of words. Sorry."

"It's okay. I'm over it. Mostly." Talia smiled weakly.

Derrick gazed at her silky skin. Her fragrance, a light citrus scent, drew him like a strong magnet. He wanted to wrap his arms around Talia in a protective shield. Instead, he clasped his hand together tightly. His reaction to her proved his emotional defenses were pitifully inadequate.

Jim rubbed his forehead. "Monette will age me fifty years before this thing is over. Geez!" He took a long drink of ice tea.

Derrick let out a short laugh, then grew serious again. "So what is this plan?"

"It's more like a few red flags that might suggest a plan." Talia squirmed in her seat when both men stared at her. "Well, don't give me those looks! I've got some ideas."

"God, you're like Monette," Jim muttered.

"Hush and listen," she snapped at him. She leaned across the table and lowered her voice. "Earl was an informer, and Barron used him. Earl was a known scumbag who drifted around spreading his dirt. Why would Barron focus on his disappearance after all these years?"

"He didn't care enough to spend time or money. But then he didn't lose much of an informant." Derrick lifted a shoulder.

Jim nodded. "Earl had served his purpose. He'd given Barron a few low-level thugs."

"Earl disappears, and maybe his gangsta buddies did him in. Barron didn't really care. But now he has a chance to really bury Monette. Maybe Barron has always suspected she at least knew what happened to him." Derrick sat down and stretched out his legs.

"So he broke the law," Talia said quickly.

"Not if he didn't have solid evidence against her," Jim replied.

"And I'm sure he didn't go looking for it. Suspicion isn't enough to launch an investigation," Derrick added. "He can easily offer that as an explanation."

"It will look fishy, but he's got a bigger worry. Barron is in the fight of his life." Jim leaned forward as he spoke quietly. "He's trying to stay out of jail."

Talia waved a hand in a gesture of impatience. "We all agree he's desperate. But here's the thing, I think he's always known more about what happened to Earl."

Derrick shook his head. "I don't see how."

Talia started to reply but stopped short when there was a knock on the door. They exchanged looks. Then Jim's shoulders relaxed, and he smiled.

"Talk about paranoid. I ordered lunch, remember?"

He went to the door. Derrick and he argued briefly over who would pay. Jim finally agreed to let him get half. They split the forty-dollar cost. The delicious aroma of hot, spicy Creole dishes came from the large bag. They spread the food on the round table next to a window. Yet none of them started eating. Instead they picked up where they'd left off.

"How do you figure Barron knows about Earl?" Jim

said. He took a sip of cola through the long straw.

"First, I want Derrick to tell me what happened that night. And don't get nervous, Jim. This is relevant to Monette's case." Talia looked at him.

"A hazy legal point, but I'll go with it." They both looked at Derrick.

"Are you sure you want me to talk about that night, Talia?"

Derrick worried about the effect on her. Talia had never been able to tolerate more than vague generalities. She nodded, a silent message in her lovely eyes. His heart turned over at the trust in them.

"I should have asked before now. It's not fair to let you carry the entire burden. Go on." Talia sat straight, her shoulders back.

She looked so brave. Still, Derrick knew how hard this was for her. Her courage made him love her more. He nodded. "When you leave town maybe the distance will help."

Talia glanced at the gold watch on her wrist. "My plane is taking off right about now without me."

"What?" Derrick gazed at her in shock.

"I'm not leaving, at least not for a while." She crossed her shapely legs. The fabric of her slacks molded to them. "So let's hear it."

"Honey, you shouldn't hang around." Derrick used the endearment without thinking. Her pecan brown eyes seemed to soften, though her tone remained neutral.

"I can take care of myself. Come on," Talia prompted. "What happened?"

Derrick glanced at Jim for support. The older man shrugged. "She knows what she's doing. Let me say this before you go on. As an officer of the court, I can't be a party to concealing a crime of any kind."

"Understood," Talia said. She looked at Derrick.

"Of course. But it's not what you're thinking. Either of you." Derrick rested against the cushioned chair back and returned to the past. "Earl was alive when I got back to the house."

Chapter 23

∞

"What?" Talia gripped the arms of her chair.

"Oh boy," Jim said, and dabbed perspiration from his forehead.

"When I got back Earl was moaning. He took a swing at Monette, and she hit him with a chair. On the way down he hit his head on that old table. He didn't move after that. Anyway, Monette said he wasn't breathing. Not that either of us tried CPR or dialed 911." Derrick glanced at Jim. "Sorry."

Talia felt as though a large rubber band was squeezing her chest. She worked hard to steady herself before she tried to speak. Derrick reached toward her but drew his hand back.

"I'm okay," she said.

"Go on." Jim sat forward. His dark brows pulled together as though the legal wheels in his head were already turning on a defense.

"She told me to leave. She said she'd call the police and say they'd both gotten high, Earl became abusive," Derrick said. He glanced at Talia.

Talia's fear turned to wrath. "I can't believe this! She didn't follow through, and you covered for her."

"I didn't know what else to do." Derrick combed his dark curls with his long fingers.

"I'm not blaming you," Talia said quickly. Her eyes narrowed to slits. "Monette lied."

"And actually that story wasn't far from the truth. It might have worked. Glasper had been charged with assault and battery more than once." Jim wore a thoughtful expression.

All three fell silent for several minutes. "So how did she get rid of the body? Monette couldn't have moved him by herself." Talia looked from Jim to Derrick.

"I never asked. Somehow I always assumed he'd ended up under the house." Derrick sat forward, both elbows on the table. "Remember it sat off the ground. All she had to do was pry the floor up and shove him through."

"So Monette disposed of the body alone?" Jim shook his head. "She's not that strong, and she'd been using only hours before."

"Somebody helped her. Now whom would she call? Someone she thought could get things done, someone with power." Talia looked at Derrick and Jim.

"Barron wouldn't get his hands dirty." Derrick shook his head.

"Hines? That might explain why he suddenly got amnesia." Talia took a sip from her cup.

"He realized his butt was at risk and decided to shut up," Jim offered.

"Barron had to have known Earl was dead. He didn't just wake up last week and say 'Come to think of it, what happened to Earl?' " Talia frowned as she teased out the puzzle.

"He knew Monette was with Earl when he died." Jim looked at them.

"Right. Now the question is, how much did he know?" Talia said.

"And when." Derrick stared ahead in concentration.

"Doesn't matter," Jim replied. "If we can uncover enough evidence to raise suspicions about Barron's behavior back then . . ."

"Which brings us back to my plan." Talia sat straight when both men glanced at her sharply.

"If this involves you being in danger, then forget it," Derrick said with a determined scowl.

"He's right. I'm sure Monette would agree." Jim eyed her with disapproval.

Talia glared at the two men. "Listen to me, I didn't cancel my flight, suspend my career, and lose three nights of sleep just to do nothing."

Derrick squinted at her. "Talia, I'm not going along with anything that puts you in—"

"Shut up and let me finish!" she shouted. The two men blinked in surprise. When neither spoke, Talia cleared her throat and continued in a normal tone. "We have theories and suspicions but no proof. So what do cops do when interviewing bad guys in that situation?"

"One technique is to make the suspect think they know more than they do and have evidence to back it up." Derrick crossed his arms. "So what?"

"So we can do the same thing. Maybe Monette kept records, items from Barron's office and other things as insurance." Talia lifted a shoulder.

"No, she didn't," Jim said with a dubious expression. Then his eyes bulged. "Did she?"

"I don't know, but I'm going to find out. I know you can't engage in deceitful practices as a lawyer, Jim." Talia wore a smile.

"A bluff won't work. Barron and Hines are too smart," Derrick said. "They know Monette would have used it before now."

"She's got a lot of old clothes and personal items stored at her sister's house in a shed. What if I went through the belongings she thought was just junk and found something? Or at least made them think so?"

"Then they'd come after you. No! End of discussion," Derrick said firmly.

"Same here," Jim added with a deep frown. "Forget it."

"I'd make sure the world knew it wasn't true." Derrick stared at her hard.

Talia struck the table hard enough to make their food containers bounce. "Then damn it, *you* come up with a plan!"

"I have a great one. You go back to D.C. and let us handle it," Derrick snapped.

"First you make me feel guilty about leaving Monette when things get tight, now you tell me to run. I think you're nuts."

"Yeah, crazy enough to care what happens to you. So insane that I'd rather not see you again than put you in danger," Derrick tossed back. "Don't try to ease a guilty conscience by doing something stupid."

"I'm going to help my mother with or without you," Talia said calmly.

"You might as well send Barron an invitation to put a gun to your head, Talia. Use common sense," Derrick said.

"We all want to help Monette. We're just not sure which is the best way." Jim used the measured tone of a diplomat on the front lines. "Now think this thing through clearly."

Talia sat down. She gave Derrick one last icy look before she turned away from him. "Fine," she said.

"Okay." Jim sat down again. "Talia, we need a Plan B for sure." A tense quiet stretched for ten minutes.

"There could be something in Monette's belongings." Derrick looked at Jim.

"Knowing Monette, she would have mentioned it by now." Jim waved away his suggestion.

"Monette traveled light, like most folks living the street life." Talia twisted her hands together in frustration. "Damn it, Barron is going to win!"

"I don't want you risking your license or jail." Derrick looked at Jim with a worried frown.

"The authorities already know most of what you've told me. They've linked Monette to the case. It's a fine line, but I'll consider it privileged because she told me the basic details first."

"Be careful. We're swimming with sharks," Derrick warned.

"Tell me something I don't know." Jim wore a grim smile. "My first order of business is a visit with Monette."

"I thought she'd changed." Talia stared at Jim. "She's been pulling crap like this for years, Jim. Join the club."

Jim's expression softened. "Talia, Monette has changed."

"Not enough," Talia replied in a tart voice. Then she sighed deeply and rubbed her eyes tiredly. "I've been through this kind of drama with Monette all my life."

"I know, I know." Jim put a hand on her arm briefly, then withdrew it.

"I wish Monette did have some box of junk we could go through. What she didn't sell usually got left behind when we'd move. But I was a pack rat. I always hoped we'd be a family. I'd hide little things to keep her from selling them or so they wouldn't get stolen by one of her drug buddies." Talia shook her head slowly and stood. "I'm sick of crawling around in the past."

"I think we've raised enough questions about Barron. Maybe some of it will help," Jim said.

"It's a long shot. Monette's track record on telling the truth is terrible, Hines won't talk, and now Barron's raking up this Earl thing." Talia picked up her purse. "I say we hit back with every piece of dirt we can find on Barron. If you two won't help, I'll do it myself."

"Attacking Barron will only make things worse. He's holding all the cards. We've got nothing more than guesses. Monette has more to lose," Derrick said.

"So does Derrick, Talia," Jim added with a sober expression.

"Barron is going to dig until he finds Earl, literally. We've got big trouble either way," Talia countered. "I say we go down fighting."

Derrick's irritated expression relaxed into a smile. "And you say I'm reckless. I appreciate the passion, but I can't let you do it, honey."

"You can't stop me. Calling me 'honey' isn't going to change my mind." Talia started for the door when Derrick grabbed her arm.

"Wait a minute!" Derrick tugged her back.

Jim blocked the door. "Talia, be rational."

Talia faced them both with her chin up. "Monette was never much of a mother, but she's *my* mother. I'm going to go after Barron, Perrilloux, or anybody else who tries to hurt her."

Derrick exchanged a glance with Jim, who lifted both hands. "Okay, at least talk strategy before you charge off." He paced for a few minutes.

"Maybe we've missed something." Jim pulled a hand over his face.

"Stalling me won't help." Talia crossed her arms. "I'm not going to stand by and let that high-class hoodlum— Oh!" She blinked rapidly.

"Now what?" Derrick stared at her with a dubious expression.

"All that stuff I dragged around with me as a kid!"

Talia laughed. "Those darn social workers, bless their hearts."

"What are you talking about?" Jim exchanged a worried glance with Derrick.

"I'm not cracking under the strain, guys. Listen up." Talia dropped her purse. "Even if home is a hellhole, having familiar items is a comfort to a kid in foster care. So, social workers would always allow me to carry my bag of junk when I moved. Like I said, I was a pack rat."

"Okay, you've still got your favorite stuffed bunny rabbit. How does that help?" Derrick sat on the edge of Jim's desk.

"Funny guy," Talia retorted. "I kept Monette's old address book and some other stuff."

"Another long shot, but it's better than nothing." Jim looked at Derrick. "I'll go talk to Monette. You and Talia search through her 'bag of junk.' Maybe we'll get lucky working both angles."

"Let's go." Talia started for the door. She stopped when Derrick didn't follow her. "Well?"

"I'll let you look through your things, Talia," he said quietly. "I'll follow up on a few other leads and get back to Jim."

"Oh." Talia cleared her throat. "Yeah, that might work better anyway."

"Right." Derrick turned away from her. "I'll call you if I find out anything, Jim."

Jim glanced at Talia, then back to Derrick. "Sure. Maybe you two could compare notes later on. I know Monette will feel better if you work together."

"I've got a few other private contracts to work. I'll be in touch though. Bye." He walked out before either of them could reply.

"I tried," Jim mumbled, and scratched his head. "I'm a pretty clumsy Cupid."

"You're a sweet guy for a lawyer," Talia said with a sad smile. "Our problems go a lot deeper than any Cupid could fix. I'm going to go home, change clothes, and root around a dusty attic."

Talia patted his shoulder and left the office. The drive back to Rougon was long and lonely. She turned the radio up until music was blasting. For the next fifty miles she didn't want to think.

"I don't know why you don't call him," Mama Rose said for the tenth time in the past hour. She sat in an old cane chair next to Talia in her attic.

Talia sneezed when dust flew everywhere as she pulled out another box. "You need to have a serious garage sale." She grunted with the effort of shoving aside an old trunk.

Mama Rose held up a huge ceramic rooster painted a strange shade of pink. She went to the small circular window and examined it in the light. "These are heirlooms."

"I'm sure the Smithsonian would beg for *that* thing. I'd like to point out that you've got these 'heirlooms' hidden in the attic." Talia sneezed again.

"Don't be a smart aleck. And you should call Derrick. Not that you listen to me these days. If you ask me, you both should get out of this state." Mama Rose wrapped the rooster in an old blanket and set it aside carefully.

Talia held a shoe box stuffed with papers on her lap. She sat on a short squat stool that had been owned by Mama Rose's great-aunt. The woven tapestry that covered the cushioned seat was still comfy, though faded and moth-eaten. Under different circumstances, Talia might have enjoyed searching through Mama Rose's collectibles.

"Derrick and I have talked, argued, made up, and

talked some more. Let it go." Talia put the shoe box aside and picked up another one. "We have."

"Bull! You're both hurting and too proud to reach out. Love is too hard to find in this world to just throw it away so easily." Mama Rose shook a forefinger at Talia.

"You've been watching those Lifetime movies again," Talia tossed back.

"You know I'm right." Mama Rose was not deterred by her sarcasm.

"Mama, I appreciate your love and concern. But Derrick and I are adults, who can handle our own issues," Talia said.

Mama Rose looked out of the window and smiled. "Of course, sugar. I'm sure you can."

"That was easy." Talia examined a stack of old letters.

"I'll get the front door." Mama Rose left, humming a tune.

"I didn't hear anything." Talia glanced up in time to see her disappear down the narrow stairs. Seconds later the door chimes sounded. "Now she's psychic and a relationship expert, too."

Talia brushed a thick layer of dirt from the top of a vintage hatbox. She removed the lid and found stacks of receipts from the sixties. Mumbling about Mama Rose's penchant for holding on to useless paper, she dropped it. A familiar object caught her eye. The leg of a stuffed toy the color of swamp mud stuck out of a cheap blue overnight case.

"Monkey Muggs!"

Talia climbed over boxes and shoved aside an old coat rack. Cracked blue vinyl flaked away in several places as she picked it up. She sat down on the trunk. The fragile old metal clasp popped apart and broke when she opened the case. Inside were bittersweet memories from her childhood. Here were things that had given her some small measure of comfort. Talia stared at the stuffed toy chimpanzee on top. Monkey Muggs, modeled after the puppet character on a Baton Rouge kiddie show, had been her favorite toy. With a sigh, she cradled him the way she'd done at age five.

"I see you found that stuffed bunny." Derrick stood in the doorway with both hands in the pockets of his black jeans.

Talia held up the toy. "Monkey Muggs. Mr. Muggs to you."

" 'Scuse me. Can I intrude on the moment?" His full lips curved up in the hint of a smile.

"Come on in. M and I have the rest of our lives together." Talia gave Monkey Muggs another squeeze, then perched him carefully on a broken chair next to her.

"Lucky monkey," Derrick said softly as he walked toward her.

Talia pretended not to hear. "So what are you doing here? I thought you intended to avoid me at all costs."

"I started to," he answered. He took a seat on the cane rocker.

She looked at him. "Honest answer."

Derrick nodded. "Something we've always had between us. The real deal, right?"

Talia looked away from him. She sorted through the open case without really seeing any of the items. "Right. So what changed your mind?"

"Two reasons. First, Mama Rose called and ordered me over here to help you."

"I'm going to have a serious talk with that lady!" Talia glanced at the stairs with a frown and back at him. "You said there were two reasons."

"I figured staying close would keep you out of trouble. You just might get the crazy idea to threaten Barron." Derrick tilted the chair back.

"I don't need a baby-sitter these days," Talia retorted.

"I'm not so sure." Derrick picked up Monkey Muggs and shook him until he seemed to dance.

"Funny guy. Don't worry about me." Talia coughed when a puff of stale air mixed with dust wafted up from the case.

"Can't do that. Worrying about you is a habit with me," Derrick said. He stood, cleared a pile of old curtains from a table, and held out a hand. "Let me help."

Talia gazed up into his eyes. She read her life in the coffee brown gaze. Derrick had held out his hand to her in the same way years before. He hadn't let her down since that day. She might question his method, but never his motive. Strong arms, a sincere heart, and deep passion wrapped up in his fine muscular frame made him one hell of a man. Her body felt as though warm honey had been poured down her back. She touched her fingertips to his palm. The tingle became an electric shock strong enough to curl her toes. He grasped her hand and gently pulled her up. Talia held her breath when he circled her in an embrace. Like a slow-motion romance scene from a movie, his sensuous lips parted as his face moved closer to hers.

"I love you more than I can say. I'd better show you, since I'm not so good with words," he whispered.

"Derrick," she whispered back.

"Yes?" He brushed his lips across hers once while staring into her eyes.

"I don't know if we . . . What I mean is . . ."

Talia lost her train of thought when he nuzzled her earlobe, nipping it tenderly. He proceeded to kiss the nape of her neck. Pushing her long hair back, his mouth grazed her skin, making a circle like a necklace of fire. Indeed she felt scorched all over when his large hands stroked her lower back. She gasped when he stopped short of touching her bottom.

"Sorry, you were trying to tell me something." His deep voice was muffled since he continued pressing his mouth against her throat.

Talia tipped her head back and closed her eyes. "We've talked about our . . . differences," she finished weakly.

"Umm-humm." Derrick kissed the hollow of her throat.

She moaned at the sensation, trembling when his hold on her started to tighten. Somehow, she summoned up the strength to push away from him. "No. We can't pretend."

He brushed his long fingers through her hair. With a sigh he let both arms fall to his sides. "You're right, of course."

"We've discussed this from all angles." Talia stepped back from him and cleared her throat. "Nothing's changed."

"Maybe not. But I have one last point to make." Derrick wore a solemn expression.

Talia gazed at his full mouth, the strong jaw, and the way the soft curls of hair on his head resembled fine lamb's wool. She took him in as though imprinting the vision on her brain. They might not see each other for a long time, if ever again. Was that a good-bye in his eyes? Talia steeled herself for the big blow.

"Go ahead."

"I don't want to be without you. I'll do whatever it takes to keep you with me." Derrick let out a long breath when she continued to stare at him. "I know what you're thinking."

"Do you?" Talia put a hand to her chest. Her heart hammered like a drum.

"I'm a rescuer, and I take stupid chances. Once we have a family, I'll be more careful." Derrick paced the floor as he spoke.

"Wait a minute. I missed the engagement and we're already out of the delivery room!" Talia's mouth hung open.

He seemed not to hear her. "I can't stand to see people kicked when they're already down, you know that. I can't promise to change overnight. You see what I'm saying?" Derrick stopped pacing for a moment then started again.

"Well, I guess. I mean . . . , well, yeah . . ." Talia's voice trailed off. She felt dazed.

"Okay, so I can't just stop being who I am. We both have to compromise, Talia." Derrick faced her. "Do you want to live without me?"

Talia blinked as though he'd given her a hard shake. He had. One simple yet profound question that led to others. Did she want to continue running from the past? If she stopped running, how would she handle the memories, the pain that went with them?

"We should deal with the past, our past, together. I'll be stronger with you by my side, and so will you. What do you say?" he asked.

"I'm not sure how to stop running, Derrick," she whispered.

"I don't have all the answers either, baby." He reached out to her.

She stood gazing at him for several seconds. "Let's not make any decisions right now. All I can think about is Barron and what he's trying to do to Monette."

He nodded slowly and lowered his arms. "Fair enough. Just don't run from me again. Will you promise?"

"Yes." Talia swallowed hard and fought for control.

"The best thing is to sort through everything and try to make sense out of it."

"Together," he said, a glint of hope in his dark gaze.

She could only nod in response. Talia wanted to feel hope, but she couldn't lie to him. Fear ruled instead. The light in his eyes dimmed, and he turned away. They sorted through more dusty boxes in silence.

Chapter 24

∞

"Nothing." Talia fell against the cushioned sofa back in surrender. "Dust, a few dead bugs, and a lot of frustration. Three hours of searching."

Mama Rose came into the den. "You look good together!" She beamed at them.

Derrick smiled back. He sat on the floor nearby, surrounded by old notebooks and papers. "Yeah, we do make a cute couple."

"I cooked a pot of gumbo just the way you like it, cher. Lots of shrimp and sausage. The hush puppies are coming right up." Mama Rose wiped her hands on the floral apron tied around her middle.

"Hmm, nothing better. Can I take some home to mama?" Derrick stretched his legs out with a small grunt, then stood.

"Sure you can. I haven't see her in months. You ought to bring her by." Mama Rose was in full swing to take care of the world.

"Sounds like a winner. She needs to get out more and—"

"Excuse me," Talia broke in. "May I remind you that we haven't taken care of business here."

"We've still got a lot of stuff to look through, baby." Derrick looked down at the floor. "A lot."

"Lord have mercy. I had no idea what was in that attic." Mama Rose threaded her way through four piles of items on the floor.

"Me either," Talia grumbled. "Look at it. A fire hazard and not much else."

"Don't be discouraged, sugar." Mama Rose sat down in a large chair. "Here, I'll help."

"Don't waste your time. We won't find anything." Talia stared at the ceiling with a morose expression. "Of course, there is another option."

"Don't start." Derrick's eyes narrowed when he looked at her.

Mama Rose glanced at Talia then at Derrick. "What is she talking about?"

"A real dumb idea that isn't worth repeating. If we don't find anything here or in Monette's old stuff—"

"We won't," Talia said.

Derrick continued in a level tone. "And if we don't, then Jim will go on with his defense."

"Just tell me this 'real dumb' idea anyway." Mama Rose sat back in an attentive pose.

"I—" Talia began.

"She was going to take a chance and have Barron go after her," Derrick said quickly. "Which doesn't make a lot of sense."

"Talia Marchand, you've got to be kidding! Do you want to get yourself killed? That does it, you're going back to Washington, D.C., on the next plane."

"I agree," Derrick chimed in.

"Alright, alright. Don't jump all over me. Geez!" Talia pursed her lips.

"I'm glad that's settled." Mama Rose gasped. "My

food! Lord, have mercy." She dumped the stack of old papers from her lap and hurried out.

Derrick continued searching through boxes. Talia sorted through an old accordion file Mama Rose had found. The only sound came from the kitchen. Pots clattered, and the radio in the kitchen played gospel music, with Mama Rose humming along. Talia stole sideways glances at Derrick. He wore a serious expression, like a man on a mission.

He sifted through documents methodically. Every few seconds he would pause, scan an item, and put it aside. Talia had never seen this side of him, the investigator. Derrick and Mama Rose would do everything in their power to make it easy for her. Monette joined in to relieve her of any major responsibility, too. All she had to do was make a minor contribution. Talia thought about the plane ticket confirmation she'd gotten via e-mail that morning. Her schedule change completed, she would leave in five days. She sighed and stared at the assortment of old memories in her hands. Just go back to a normal life, climbing her way up the career ladder, dining with equally ambitious pals twice a week, and taking trendy vacations. *Nice and neat.*

"You've done a lot to help Jim. Not to mention all the work on mandatory-sentencing laws." Derrick seemed to be on the same wavelength.

She looked up to find him gazing at her. "Yeah." Had she done enough?

Two days later, more searching, and they were no closer to finding answers. Talia watched the news with dread. Barron growled at a group of reporters.

"No one will find evidence to support her bizarre allegations because it doesn't exist. This is a fairy tale cooked up by a drug dealer and addict in a desperate attempt to avoid what she deserves, a long prison sentence." Barron barked out the words. "That's all I have to say," he snarled when reporters tossed more questions.

"Damn." Talia pushed the MUTE button on the remote when the female news anchor went to another story. Feeling stifled by the four walls, she decided to get out for a while. She found her sunglasses and went onto the front porch.

A chilly October breeze blew. Blue skies and bright sunshine did nothing to improve her mood. She doubted anything could. Talia went down the steps and started walking. Before she got to the path behind Mama Rose's house, Derrick drove up. He parked in the driveway and joined her.

"Hey. All packed and ready to go?" He fell in step with her when she started walking again.

"Yes." Talia breathed in deeply and exhaled. "Somebody's got a fire going. So familiar, the smell of burning wood, cut grass, fish, and muddy water all mixed up."

"Phew! No place stinks like home." Derrick grinned.

"Yeah, but where is home?" Talia said. "Sorry. I don't deserve to whine. I got what I wanted."

"No easy choices for us. We're doing the best we can."

They went on without speaking for several minutes. He grabbed a handful of plants as they went deeper into a small wooded area. Talia watched him. His long-legged stride was the same. He braided the long wild grass stalks the way he had as a boy. They might have been walking back in time.

"Still so vibrant," Talia said. She followed his gaze across still-green trees. "When I tell people how warm it stays right into January they shake their heads."

"I kind of like the snow myself. It sparkles in the

sunshine, like a blanket of magic. Anyway, there's lots of green where you live. Nice parks." Derrick waved his newly fashioned rope. "And D.C. is the center of action."

"Uh-huh."

They came to a small bayou. Three men sat on the far bank with fishing poles. The wind caused ripples on the water. One man reached into a cooler and passed cans to the other two. Their voices drifted over the water, muffled by distance.

"They won't catch much—too windy, and the water seems kinda high." Derrick stood with his legs apart slapping the grass against one thigh.

"Not the point though. They're enjoying the day." Talia walked to the water's edge. "Brothers sticking together. Doesn't matter if everything turns out perfect. Life isn't perfect."

"Maybe they're not brothers," Derrick said as he walked to her. They stood side by side without touching. "Could be three pals playing hooky from work."

"Brothers by blood or some other bond, it's the same." Talia stared at the men. "Being connected is important."

"Yes it is. We're so much alike, Talia. I always dreamed of having a stable, loving family."

They stared at each other. Talia longed to tell him their dreams could come true. She was tempted to take him in her arms. She wanted to feel his strong body, drink in every bit of consolation he offered so willingly. Derrick's expression was open and inviting. Only a step to him would ease her loneliness. Instead she turned away. The real world wasn't filled with happy, neat endings like an old romantic movie.

"I need to stand by Monette and stand up to Barron. Let me finish," Talia said when Derrick started to protest. "I don't expect to fix our relationship like in some made-for-television family movie. Fact is, I doubt we'll ever be close. But I have to admire her. She's got her own kind of courage. No. I guess I'm tired of running."

"You picked the wrong time to stop." Derrick dropped her hand.

"Will you listen before I get the full lecture?" Talia said.

"Okay. This I've gotta hear. Explain to me how doing something totally insane in an already surreal scenario makes sense."

"Thanks for keeping an open mind." Talia arched her eyebrows.

"You're welcome. Go on." Derrick crossed his arms.

"We both know Earl Glasper was scum. Not that being scum is a capital offense, but Monette was defending herself."

"So far we agree."

Talia sighed. "That night just summed up all the reasons I wanted to get away from her forever. But I was with her then, and I should be with her now."

"I doubt they'll find Earl's body. I can only guess what she did, but Monette found a way to hide him for good." Derrick pursed his lips.

"She was in a real tight spot. Whom would she call?" Talia squinted as though the action would help her see answers. "Monette had the district attorney panting after her like a dog in heat. He had the power to get things done in this parish. Barron had to have helped her, Derrick. Even if he did it through other people and kept his hands clean."

"All was forgiven in a few moments? Not him."

"A nice revenge though. He got her later," Talia said.

"Why not let her go down for murder right then? Doesn't add up." Derrick shook his head slowly.

"Maybe Earl was a problem he needed to just disappear. A murder investigation might uncover some inconvenient facts about their relationship." Talia spread her arms out. "Huh?"

"I looked at his old files for hours on end. I'd say some of Barron's cases smelled. Earl was the informant on more than half." Derrick stared at the countryside, but his thoughts were obviously not on the scenery.

"And he probably knew enough about the other half to make Barron and Jerome Hines pretty uncomfortable."

"Good reasoning." Derrick looked at her again. "But there's no proof."

"Maybe Jim could get the hearing delayed?"

"Not again. I asked. To make matters worse, Hines is going to be there. Kelsey says Larry insisted. His presence will really add credibility to Barron's account."

"Which brings me back to my earlier point. Barron and Hines are the weakest links." Talia lifted her chin. "I was with Monette during those years. I saw the folks she was hanging with back in the day."

"You don't *know* anything. Look what happened to Hines when Barron thought he would talk." Derrick's dark eyes flashed. "No!"

"The hearing is Monday. I'm going show up and have a little talk with Jerome Hines. I found some old hotel receipts, slips of paper Monette made notes about meeting up with Jerry. I can guess enough details to make him talk." Talia wore a tight smile.

"Please don't tell me you want to wear a hidden microphone. Even if I agreed to do it, and I won't, Hines wouldn't be so stupid."

"His back is against the wall. He's got nowhere to turn and no one to trust, not even his dear wife. I'll use the element of surprise. Neither one of them is expecting a long-lost kid to show up." Talia looked at him hard. "Are you going to help me or not?"

* * *

The large conference room in the prison administration building was packed. A contingent representing the Louisiana Victims' Rights coalition occupied two front rows. Their leader, a tall woman with black hair, wore an earnest expression. She gave comments to a reporter hovering at her shoulder. Talia gazed around the room. The guards hadn't brought Monette in yet. Three of the six parole board members sat at a long table. Folding metals chairs were set up in five rows for the audience. Another smaller table faced the parole board members. This was obviously for those who would address the board.

"I can't believe I let you talk me into this," Derrick muttered. He scrutinized everyone assembled like a well-seasoned security man. "I don't like it."

"Nothing will happen here. If I play it right, Hines will talk. You sure this thing will pick up his voice?"

Talia shifted the strap on her navy blue leather shoulder purse. A small microphone that resembled a designer emblem was attached to an outside flap. Derrick wore a pair of sunglasses with amber-colored lenses. A small receiver was hidden in the frame behind one ear. The wire appeared to be trendy cord attached to the eyeglasses.

"Yes. Remember you have to wait until the board quiets everybody down. Then—"

"Will you relax? I know the drill. I'll hang around out here and catch Hines before he goes in. They're going to review three other inmates before they get to Monette's case," Talia said. Oddly enough she felt composed.

"Yeah. I thought they'd change the agenda because of the interest in Monette's case, put her first." Derrick turned to the side as he spoke in a low monotone. "Maybe they're hoping the reporters will get bored and leave."

"Not much chance of that."

Derrick glanced at her curiously before he looked away again. "You look pretty cool considering. Acting like you've done this kinda thing before. You keeping something from me about your *real* job in D.C.?"

"What?" Talia whispered. Three prison employees studied her for several moments as they walked by. "Hi," she said to them in a normal tone. They nodded back and kept going.

"Could be you're working for the CIA or something." Derrick's handsome face was impassive. Yet there was a teasing lilt to his voice.

"Oh sure. And Monette's thinking about entering a convent." Talia checked her wristwatch. "I'm going out to be on the safe side."

Derrick didn't answer. He walked away and found an empty seat. No one around them seemed to notice they'd been quietly talking. After a few moments he took a small notebook and pen from his pocket. Dressed in a long-sleeved gray shirt and black chinos, he looked like just another reporter. Talia strolled out into the hallway. She pretended to study notes on a pad.

"Excuse me, ma'am. You got a pass?" A short, stocky female prison guard studied Talia intently.

"Sure," Talia said smoothly. She pointed to the light blue visitor's tag clipped to her jacket. "I'm waiting for someone if that's okay."

The woman looked at the tag. "No problem. Just checking."

"I understand." Talia smiled at her. The woman moved on to scan the rest of the scene.

"Thank God for public meeting laws," Talia murmured as she watched the woman leave.

Because the meetings were public, Talia and Derrick had been able to attend without arousing too much attention. She made a circle in the hall at least three times before Hines showed up. He strode toward her with a dour look on his chocolate brown face. A butterfly bandage on his left cheek and a slight limp were the only signs of the attack he'd suffered. Talia watched him approach. When he was about three feet away she glanced up from the yellow legal pad she held.

"Excuse me. Jerome Hines, right?" Talia blocked his path.

His ebony eyes narrowed. "Who are you?"

"Talia Marchand." She held out a hand.

"We've never met, and I don't talk to reporters." Hines ignored her attempt to shake hands. "I'm running late for the meeting."

"They haven't started. Monette Victor's case isn't the first one anyway." Talia didn't move out of his way despite his forbidding scowl. "And you know I'm not a reporter, Mr. Hines."

"Sorry, but I have no idea who you are, miss. Now if you'll excuse me . . ." He started to go around her, but Talia moved to head him off. Hines stared down his nose at her for several seconds. "Honey, this is flattering. Problem is I'm a married guy."

"Nobody here knows I'm Monette's daughter. Don't worry." Talia spoke in a low voice. "You called me. Does Barron know?"

Hines cast a quick glance around them. "I don't know what you've been smoking, young lady, but give it up. Now please move outta my way."

"No, he must not, or you wouldn't be able to walk," Talia went on smoothly. She marveled at her own audacity.

"Listen, little girl, don't play grown-up games. You don't know the rules." His dark eyes glittered with anger.

Talia noted the sheen of sweat forming on his top lip. "He'll stab you in the back anyway. Did you know

I was living with Monette around the time Earl Glasper disappeared? Those were some wild days. Men coming and going like buses in a busy city. Monette didn't miss a one."

Hines licked a dry bottom lip. "What are you talking about?"

"Earl was pimping for the district attorney, your boss. You know, an informant using his pals and getting paid by Barron."

"You've lost your mind. I've got no time for crazy talk from some woman I've never seen before." Despite his words Hines didn't leave. He seemed unable to look away from her.

"Didn't y'all meet around that old house on Bayou Road? Monette and Earl used to be over there all the time." Talia had spent hours dredging up memories she'd been repressing for years. She was surprised at the details that flooded back.

"I used to follow them, trying to keep up with her. Just a dirty little kid trying to get attention from my mama." Talia felt a tiny stab of pain at the grain of truth mixed in with her bluff.

"Oh yeah?" Hines breathed hard.

"Sure did. I grew up fast, had to with Monette for a mother. I learned a lot." Talia looked left and right before she went on. "I kept a lot of Monette's old papers from back in the day. Yes, I remember a lot from those days. Stuff like the house on Bayou Road, the long black car that used to come and pick Monette up. If I think hard enough, I might remember seeing you."

"To hell with this," Hines snapped, and pushed her aside.

In a panic that she'd handled him wrong, Talia grabbed his arm. "Listen, Barron has already proved he'll turn on you. Do the right thing, Mr. Hines. You were willing to before. Why the change?"

Hines stopped. He looked around, then motioned for her to follow him outside. Talia prayed the high tech microphone had a long enough range. Hines led her away from a group of three men smoking under a covered walkway. The trio put out their cigarettes after a few seconds and went back into the building.

"I don't know what your game is, but Winn Barron is a man of integrity and—"

"Skip the speech. I'm not wearing a wire." Talia took off her jacket and turned in a circle. She patted her white cotton blouse. "See?"

He stared at her hard. After taking a deep breath, he walked back and forth, rubbing his face. "He's probably got somebody about to show up any minute."

"To keep an eye on you." Talia's pulsed picked up. *Here we go.*

"Bastard!" Hines paced more. "I'm no angel, okay? But I have never set up anybody for something they didn't do. Never would."

"Then tell them what happened," Talia said with force.

"No way. Barron is really desperate. I've been waiting for him to fall out of power. He keeps climbing." Hines stood still and tapped a fist against one thigh.

"My mother has been in prison for fifteen years. She can't wait forever! You can knock Barron off that ladder." Talia walked close to him.

"Forget it. He'd step on me like a bug and still come out just fine."

"Then help me." Talia clutched his arm again.

"Barron would know it was me. Nobody else involved can or will talk. They know better. Come to that, so do I." Hines gazed up at the cloudless sky above the prison buildings. He sighed. "Sorry, but I gotta think about me."

Without another word or looking at her, he strode

back into the building. Talia bit her lip to keep from screaming. She'd done all she could. Maybe she should follow Mama Rose's advice and go home. Was D.C. truly home? Tears made the scene around her waver out of focus. She felt adrift, lost, with no clue about finding a way to a familiar place. Derrick emerged from the hallway.

"Hey, baby girl. I'm real sorry. You gave it your best shot." Derrick forgot about being cautious. He put one strong arm around her shoulder.

"I was hoping he'd give some hint, something you could track down." Talia sniffed.

Derrick went inside for a few seconds and came back. He handed her a wad of tissues. "He's a hard-ass."

Talia dabbed her eyes and blew her nose. She tossed one tissue into a nearby trash bin with an angry snap of the wrist.

"I was kidding myself, playing at detective. Barron wouldn't crack either if I tried my stupid idea with him," she said bitterly.

"Probably not," Derrick agreed. He put a hand under her arm. "Like I said, he'd get someone to scare you, and we'd never be able to connect him to it. With his influence he might even try to destroy your career."

"I hate feeling this way, Derrick," Talia blurted out. "When I was a kid, all the kids with money and status treated me like dirt. They could step on us poor kids, and the teachers would back them up. I swore nobody would make me feel like less than nothing again!"

"Nobody can without your permission. It's about feeling good, knowing who we are. I had to struggle with that for a long time. Still do on bad days," Derrick said. "You can go back to D.C. knowing you did all you could. I'm going inside. You coming?"

"In a minute." Talia gave him a weak smile.

Derrick gave her arm a squeeze. His dark eyes reflected caring and empathy for what she was going through. Talia watched his graceful stride as he left.

"Can I have a minute out here to smoke?" Monette said to the female corrections officer with her.

"Yeah, they're on the third inmate anyway. I figure you have time, but not much. Nobody came to speak about them others." The officer took a pack from her pocket. "Here ya go."

Monette took out one cigarette. The officer lit it for her. She didn't look at Talia. "Thanks."

"I'll be listening to the board." The officer strolled a few feet away. She stood where she could listen to the proceedings and still see Monette.

"I ain't goin' nowhere," Monette quipped. When the woman disappeared through the doorway, she turned to Talia. "I told you not to come. Mama Rose and Derrick should have stopped you."

"They tried, but I wouldn't listen." Talia looked away.

"Nothing you can do. I wanted to see you, but not this bad. Get out of here."

Talia ignored the command. "What about Earl?"

"If it comes out, I'll talk." Monette gave a gruff laugh that lacked humor. "Screwing up been my life's work. I got it down to a fine art.

"I can't argue with you." Talia bit back more biting words. She heaved a deep sigh. "I shouldn't have said that. Here you're fighting for your freedom, and I'm giving you smart remarks."

Monette laughed again. Her voice sounded lighter. "Hey, you ain't my daughter for nothin'. 'Sides, we both know you meant it."

Talia smiled and shook her head. "Yeah, I did. But I want you to know . . ." She couldn't go on. Without warning the tears came back.

"Derrick and Karl told me all you've done for me. You made me feel real proud, and loved, too," Monette said softly. "Ain't felt loved a lot in my life before now."

"I know." Talia clenched her teeth. She'd felt that way herself more times than she could count. What a sad inheritance.

"I didn't deserve such great kids, didn't have anything to do with it really. But I'm damn lucky to have good kids like y'all." Monette puffed on the cigarette. "Nah, it wasn't luck. It was a blessing. God had angels watchin' over my children even when I didn't."

The guard appeared in the doorway. "Hey, Monette, they just finished with Yvonne. Come on, you're the star of this show."

Monette cleared her throat. "Okay. How'd it go for her?"

"They approved her parole. Maybe they're in a generous mood," the officer replied.

"Humph! That'll change once I get in there," Monette said with dark humor. "I'll be there in a minute. Got a couple of puffs to go."

"Alright." The officer turned and started talking to someone.

"Don't hang around. I think we both know how this is gonna play out. Get on a plane and go back to the good things you earned. You stand out like a sore thumb in my world." Monette swept a gaze around the prison grounds. "Thank the Lord."

"Monette, you deserve a lot better, too." Talia tried to say more, but her voice caught.

"Thanks, baby." Monette ground out her cigarette. She grinned as she walked backward. "Love that outfit, girl. Damn, you got style!"

"I got it honest."

Talia's answering smile stretched tight across her

face. She watched Monette enter the building. As a child she'd indulged in a lot of escape fantasies, mostly from her family and especially from her mother. For the first time in years she dreamed of taking Monette with her. Monette's grin faltered when she crossed the threshold and a shadow crossed her face. The guard spoke to her, and Monette nodded though she still gazed at Talia. Then she turned abruptly and went ahead of the guard into the room. Derrick came out again.

"I'll call and tell you how they voted." Derrick glanced over his shoulder. "So far nobody knows who you are. Go, Talia."

Talia nodded. "Yes," she whispered.

Derrick touched her arm. "Honey, it's okay to leave."

She could only nod a second time. Derrick seemed about to speak. Instead he went back inside. Talia's heart pounded as she stood rooted to the spot. Every fiber of her being wanted to run. She heard the parole board chairwoman speaking into the microphone.

"Ma'am, they're about to start. You'd better come on in. We don't let folks wander in and out too much," a male corrections officer said. He gestured toward the room.

"I, uh," Talia stammered. "In a minute." Sweat rolled down her back.

"Just got two or three seats left. This next one is drawin' a crowd." He gazed at her with a mixture of curiosity and impatience. "You family?"

Talia gripped her purse as she stared at him for several moments. She nodded slowly, then walked past him into the hearing room. Rows of chairs were filled. Cameras clicked away as reporters aimed at Monette and the parole board. Larry Perrilloux sat on the first row ready to testify. Her legs felt like lead, but she put one foot in front of the other all the same. Derrick came to her.

"What are you doing?" he said close to her ear.

"I've got to be here," Talia replied.

He frowned, but let her have his chair. Derrick stood behind her. Talia was grateful for his supportive presence. The chairwoman first allowed prison officials to give information on Monette's behavior. Jim, dressed in a navy pin-striped suit, sat next to Monette. From time to time he whispered to her. Then Monette spoke. Her normally strong voice wavered a few times from nervousness. Dressed in a starched denim shirt and jeans, Monette's dark hair was pulled into a neat French twist.

"I won't go over again about being framed. Y'all heard it before," Monette said.

Jim said something to her. His expression was tense. Monette shook her head. Talia wished she could hear what he'd said.

"Monette, what are you up to now?" Talia mumbled low.

"Like I was sayin', I didn't smuggle them drugs. But that ain't the point. I've made somethin' outta myself in this institution, took advantage of opportunities. Got my high school certificate, earned almost half the credits I need for a BA degree. I got a reason and a way to make my life better than it was in the free world. I'm hopin' y'all give me a chance to prove it. That's all."

Her short speech caused a hum of conversation in the audience. A sharp tap of the chairwoman's gavel resulted in silence again. Talia glanced at Derrick, who lifted a shoulder.

"I'd like to make some comments," Jim said quickly.

"Go ahead, sir," the chairwoman said.

Jim began with a summary of the evidence used to convict Monette. He made a fervent, and in Talia's view, persuasive argument that the circumstances had not fit the sentence. Then he talked about the men who had testified against her after cutting deals with the district attorney. The reference to Barron riveted every listener. The parole board members seemed to lean forward as one in anticipation.

"My client has made a lot of mistakes in her life. The biggest one was starting an affair with a man who had the power to take away her freedom. Poor judgment? You bet. Bad choices? Too many to mention. But look at the evidence used to send her to prison for forty years to life. The entire case was built on the testimony of men who plea bargained for lighter sentences. These men had prior convictions for drug dealing. Ms. Victor had none." Jim paused and looked at each member of the board. "Not one, ladies and gentlemen. So why did she get the most harsh sentence? Revenge plain and simple. You can't give her back the fifteen years she's lost. But you can right a wrong. Until Ms. Victor can clear her name of this crime, please grant her request for parole."

One of the members cleared his throat and spoke into the mike. Talia craned her neck until she could see the nameplate in front of him. Samuel Broussard had huge shoulders and iron gray hair.

"Mr. Rand, you made a powerful presentation. Now what proof do you have that your client was framed, and by the district attorney no less?"

"We have receipts from hotels. Ms. Victor went to cities at the same time Mr. Barron attended various law enforcement conferences. Dates she was arrested and released immediately are documented with calls from Mr. Winn's office. He personally made those calls. At least two sheriff's deputies will testify." Jim started to go on when another board member, Harriet DeMille, spoke up.

"More circumstantial evidence that could mean

nothing," she said. Ms. DeMille frowned. "Still, we should consider her record in prison and the evidence about her previous life."

"I agree," the chairwoman added. "Ms. Victor has done very well in prison. But can she resist returning to her former lifestyle once released? Not only that, this is one of many dramatic stories she's told."

Talia closed her eyes tight as the debate went on. The woman from the victims' rights organization spoke about the impact of drugs on the community. Larry Perrilloux spoke next. Curiously, he only answered questions about the investigation and the prosecution. He avoided offering any opinion on the quality of the case or Winn Barron's behavior while he was district attorney.

"I can only say that there is no hard evidence to support Ms. Victor's allegations." Perrilloux closed the folder he'd consulted.

"Thank you." The chairwoman made notes.

Derrick rested a hand on her shoulder. The weight of it seemed to anchor her. She placed a hand over his and felt the heat seep through her. With a sigh she looked up at him in gratitude. Her brother Karl walked in, still wearing his dark blue work shirt and pants. He nodded to Talia.

"Family members or friends of Ms. Victor can make comments." The chairwoman looked at the audience.

Karl raised a hand. "I'd like to say a few things." He made his way to the front and sat down.

"And you are?"

"Karl Marchand. I'm her son. My mama has done a lot of bad. In prison she had a chance to do some good finally. Now you might say she didn't have no choice. But she did. Plenty folks sit in prison just doin' time. They keep right on livin' that gangsta lifestyle, only behind bars. It's gangs in here, too." Karl rubbed his hands together nervously and swallowed hard.

"Before you bring it up I'm gonna tell you. Monette didn't raise me. Fact is all her kids grew up bein' jerked from one place to another. Yeah, I'm still mad about some of what I went through. But that don't mean I want her in prison for somethin' she didn't do. Uh, thank you."

Karl got up and went to Monette. He hugged her briefly before moving on. Talia watched him walk with his head up as reporters took his picture. Except for a brief smile, Karl didn't acknowledge her. She knew why. They were all protecting her.

"Excuse me, I want to speak." Talia stood up.

"Talia, are you sure you want to do this?" Derrick said low.

She looked at him for a few seconds then took a deep breath and let it out. "No."

Talia strode forward. Hearing another set of footsteps, she looked back to find Derrick right behind her. He smiled and took her hand. In spite of her show of courage, Talia felt a flood of relief at the touch of his strong hand. They both sat down at the table. Derrick leaned toward her and put a hand around the back of her chair. Talia drew some measure of strength from his strong presence, but she had to face the past on her own.

"State your name and interest in this hearing," the chairwoman said.

"My name is Talia Marchand. I'm a consultant based in Washington, D.C. I have been working with Senator Kelvin Jackson to modify Louisiana's mandatory-sentencing laws. My interest is both professional and personal. I'm also Ms. Victor's daughter."

Video and still cameras went crazy whirring and

clicking in her direction. A hum of voices came from the spectators. Talia ignored them.

"Oh God!" Monette said softly.

"Mandatory-sentencing laws were passed with the sincere intention to protect the public. In theory it should work. Crooks are encouraged to testify against other, more dangerous crooks. These 'America's Most Wanted' are then taken off the streets. But time after time it's been found that the opposite happens. What happens is that crooks lie, something that shouldn't surprise us. In order to save their own skins they cut deals based on lies. They accuse others of the crimes they themselves committed."

"Excuse me, but if that's true then the case against these defendants would fall apart," Mr. Broussard said.

"You would think so, but not as often as you'd like to believe. Mistakes are made. Motives are not always pure on the part of prosecutors or law enforcement personnel," Talia replied. "In six months she will have served fifteen and a half years. She's changed. Please grant her request."

When she stood, Talia's legs felt weak. Derrick held her elbow to steady her. Monette rushed forward and hugged her tightly as the cameras clicked away to catch the moment.

"You shouldna done it. Now he's gonna come after you, too," Monette whispered. She wiped tears from her face, then kissed Talia on the cheek.

"I had to for me as much as you," Talia said.

"Take good care of yourself, sugar."

The female guard put a hand on Monette's arm. "I hate to do it, but . . ."

She nodded toward the stern-faced chairwoman, her gavel poised to bang on the table. Talia walked to her seat. Derrick spoke to Jim for a few seconds, then joined her. They watched as the board members put their heads together. The chairwoman covered the microphone with one hand so they wouldn't be overheard. After five minutes they all seemed satisfied.

"The board members need more time to deliberate. We're going to review the testimony, request additional documents, and report our decision within a week." She quickly adjourned the hearing and followed the others as they exited quickly through a nearby side door.

The swarm of reporters divided. One group crowded around Monette and Jim. The other half closed in on Talia. Derrick held out one long arm as they walked.

"Let us through, please. No more comments." Derrick cleared a path to the exit. The reporters left once they realized neither of them would answer any questions.

"Thanks," Talia said. She started to touch his face but restrained herself. "I owe you one. Again."

"Nah, that was a freebie." Derrick grinned at her, then became serious again. "You were really something in there. I know what it took."

"Temporary insanity," Talia quipped. She drew in a shaky breath.

"You okay to drive home?" He gazed at her intently.

"I'll be fine once I throw up a few times." She tried to smile and failed. The sick feeling in her stomach was all too real.

"Guess that's it then." Derrick looked at the ground.

"Yes, I guess so." Talia tensed against the urge to reach for him.

"I think you're going to do even better now. The craziness will die down one of these days. Then you can get back to normal."

"In another ten years or so maybe." Talia nodded toward the mass of reporters in a tight circle around Jim.

Derrick steered her farther away and out of their line

of sight. "Jim will keep them busy for a while. You go. Listen, I won't see you before you leave."

"We, I mean, the time we had together was . . ." Talia swallowed hard at the memories. Images of his brown skin in the sun, the taste of his mouth, and the scent of his hair after he'd taken a shower would cling forever.

"I know." Derrick leaned forward and gave her a prim kiss on the forehead.

Before she could react he spun around and walked away. Talia stared at him with a pounding in her veins with each step. She savored each graceful stride of his strapping legs. "Go after him!" a small voice whispered. In only a few moments he was yards away. Then he opened the door of his 4Runner. The sight nudged her to follow. Suddenly a man walked in front of her.

"Ms. Marchand, Chad Brister with Channel 6 news." The reporter stuck a microphone in her face.

Talia backed away. His words sounded like a scratching buzz in her ears. More reporters surrounded her within seconds. Jim appeared and helped her push her way through and get into her car. All she wanted was to escape.

Chapter 25

A month later Talia sat in her office staring out at the Washington, D.C., traffic. Still bumper-to-bumper at seven o'clock, headlights danced along like giant fireflies. A thick issue of the *Times-Picayune* lay on her desk. She stared at the bold headlines of the New Orleans paper. Each word reminded her of why she'd left Louisiana. The media frenzy had driven her to run once again. All the details of her childhood had been dredged up, with help from Winn Barron, of course. Monette's request for parole had been denied the next day. No one was surprised. And now this. Talia squeezed her eyes shut. Hoping to ward off another gigantic headache that threatened, she massaged her temples.

Her boss stuck his head in the door. "You holding up okay, kiddo?"

"I'm fine, Pete. I was fine the first ten times you asked me." Talia smiled at him weakly. "Thanks for asking again."

"Just checking. Go home. Working all hours isn't the answer." Pete pointed a forefinger at her. "I mean it, young lady."

"Yes, sir." Talia gave him a mock salute that he returned with a grin. He left, and still she didn't move.

Jasmine came into her office a few minutes later. "Hello, girlfriend. Let's go out for dinner. I'm craving Thai food. What do you say?"

"Pete sent you in here." Talia squinted at her.

"No, he did not," Jasmine tossed back. "You've been skipping lunches, burying yourself in work. It's not healthy."

"And some Thai food is just what I need?" Talia rolled her stiff shoulders.

"Works for me." Jasmine peered at the open newspaper.

"Uh, this thing with the bones being found, are you going back to Louisiana?"

"I don't know," Talia replied after a long pause.

She stared at the full spread devoted to Monette, Winn Barron, and the District Attorney's Office in Pointe Coupee Parish. Jasmine cleared her throat minutes later.

"This is bad, girl."

"Tell me about it," Talia replied.

"I don't mean what's happening back home." Jasmine nodded at the newspapers. "I'm worried about you."

"I'm okay." Talia avoided her gaze.

"Hey, this is me you're talking to. I hardly see you outside the office. Last week Erika and the gang were surprised you were back in town. *Nobody* sees you these days."

"I've been busy catching up after being gone so long." Talia picked up her pen and twisted it in her hands.

"Try again. You've been walking around like a zombie since you got back from Louisiana." Jasmine pursed her lips for a few seconds. "And since you left Derrick behind."

Talia opened her mouth to protest, but couldn't. "Damn, Jas! Is it that obvious?"

"Open up. You've been carrying around too much baggage, dealing with it by yourself."

"You sound like Mama Rose now." Talia smiled sadly.

"She's a very wise woman. What's going on, girl?"

Talia turned her chair enough so that she could look out the window. She shook her head and sighed. When tears threatened, she pressed her fingertips to her eyes to hold them back. For weeks she'd lost sleep. Food seemed tasteless, and no amount of sunshine could brighten her days. Work didn't offer the satisfaction it had only a few months ago. The usual round of parties and hanging out with young power brokers no longer appealed to her. There was no denying the simple truth. She missed Derrick every hour of the day. Talia ached to see his smile, hear his voice, and, even more, to feel his touch.

"Call him," Jasmine said quietly.

"And say what? He's got a right to despise me. I jerked him around by jumping in and then out of his life. All because I can't deal with my past." Talia's throat tightened as she suppressed a sob. "He deserves better. He deserves a woman he can count on. You know what I finally figured out now?"

Jasmine went to Talia and put an arm around her shoulder. "What, babe?"

"I love him and that's all that matters. Not what happened sixteen years ago or what's happening now." Talia took a deep breath and let it out. She sat straight and patted Jasmine's hand. "I'm fine now."

"Sure you are." Jasmine gazed down at her.

"I shouldn't have stayed away from my family all these years," Talia said. "We're not exactly the Brady Bunch, but they're mine, and I love 'em."

"Is that enough?"

"I'll survive." Talia forced a smile and waved a hand toward the door. "Now stop hovering and get some work done."

"Fine, but you're coming to dinner with me. No excuses." Jasmine pointed a finger at her.

"Alright. Geez, you're pushy all of a sudden," Talia grumbled.

"Call my office when you're ready to leave," Jasmine said in a firm tone.

"Okay. I—" Talia broke off abruptly and blinked hard.

Derrick seemed to have appeared out of thin air in the open doorway. Dressed in an indigo blue pullover sweater and matching denim slacks, a dark tan all-weather coat was draped over one arm. His warm nut-brown skin looked smooth and sleek against the dark colors. He towered over them when he walked in. Talia felt a rush of heat at the way his body moved. Trying to sleep for the last four weeks had been almost impossible. She'd hungered for him, burned to feel his touch.

"Hi, Talia." He smiled at Jasmine. "Hello."

Jasmine gaped at him. "Wow! I mean, hi."

"Hello, and I'm stunned." Talia stared at him.

"I was just leaving." Jasmine sprang to her feet. She pumped his hand. "Real nice seeing you again! Ahem, perfect timing," she added in a stage whisper and gave him the thumbs-up sign. She winked at Talia, then left.

"I see you know." Derrick tilted his head to indicate the headlines.

"How did Earl's body get to Wilkinson County, Mississippi?" Talia shook her head.

"You were right, Monette had help. The press doesn't know it yet, but Jerome Hines is talking. In fact, we can't get him to shut up." Derrick sat down.

"We?"

Derrick tossed his coat over the chair next to him. "I'm working as a contract investigator for the U.S. Attorney in Lafayette."

"All very secret since the reporters don't seem to have missed much."

"After those attacks on him and Monette, you better believe it's being kept quiet. Barron is sweating it out, too. He doesn't know a thing, but he suspects he's about to go down and—"

"Wait a minute." Talia got up and closed her door. She sat in the chair next to him facing her desk. "Don't tell me Monette is in even worse trouble."

"It's complicated." Derrick crossed one long leg over the other.

"Well, we are talking about Monette." Talia heaved a sigh. "Let me have it."

"On a hunch I checked on the land where they found the body. It's a stretch of woods owned by Hines's family. With that connection and a little bit of pressure he decided to cooperate. He claims Earl overdosed." Derrick shrugged. "I was sure he'd point the finger at Monette. He shocked us all, especially Barron."

"His conscience was bothering him," Talia said.

"Hines? I don't believe it." Derrick waved a hand.

"No, it's true. I talked to him at the parole board hearing. He felt bad about Monette being set up."

"Not bad enough to tell the truth fifteen years ago," Derrick said with a dubious frown. "Finding out about that property was just the first step. I found more that linked him to Earl. He started talking to save his butt."

"I didn't say he was perfect." Talia wore a wry smile.

"Anyway, he confirmed that Monette had an affair with Barron. Hines has told us just how Barron set her up when she broke up with him. A special parole board hearing is scheduled. There's not much doubt Monette will be released. Once this hits she might even get a full pardon."

"And Barron? He shouldn't get away with what he's done," Talia said with bitterness.

"He's taken a leave of absence from his office. Health reasons. The truth is he's huddling with a team of top criminal defense attorneys." Derrick wore a hard smile. "I expect he'll be on the other side of the justice system soon, as a defendant."

"So things will get even messier." Talia squeezed her eyes shut.

"Yeah. He and Hines are scrambling to dump on each other."

"One thing about it, Monette keeps life interesting. I'll bet she signs a fat book and movie deal before the year is out." Talia opened her eyes again.

"She's got an agent already. Jim's law students have received national attention. They might all end up in a movie of the week."

Talia laughed and shook her head slowly. "I knew she'd end up in show business one day. And they all lived happily ever after."

Derrick's smile melted. "Not quite." He stood and picked up his coat. "Anyway, I was in the neighborhood and decided to tell you before it came out in the news."

"You sure took the long way home from work." Talia rose and searched his face.

"Yeah, well." He avoided her gaze and started to put on his coat.

"Wait a minute." Talia stood. "Maybe I'll just happen to be in your neighborhood soon."

"Not a good idea." He didn't move.

"Since I let the dogs out, might as well face 'em. Did you really come all this way just to tell me about Hines? I thought you'd just as soon never see me again."

"Looking out for you is a hard habit to break. I might have mentioned that a few times." Derrick gazed at her. "You have a way of driving me crazy," he said softly.

"You kept digging. Barron and those crooks might have come after you, Derrick."

"I'll never learn, huh? Way too much drama with me." Derrick looked around the smart style of her corner office and smiled at her. "Good-bye, Talia."

Talia's heart ached when he walked to the door. "Derrick, wait." He turned and faced her. "I thought I needed to wipe the slate clean, leave everything from my past behind. I was wrong, so wrong."

Derrick's impassive expression shook her. They stared at each other in silence for several minutes. Talia walked back to her desk. She turned her back to him and stared out the window, unable to stand the sight of Derrick walking out of her life for good.

"Anyway, thanks for coming," she said over her shoulder. His muscular arms wrapped around her from behind.

"If you want me to stay, then say so, baby girl," he said. His lips caressed her earlobe.

Talia leaned against his solid chest and closed her eyes. "Please stay with me."

"The answer is yes." He rubbed his face against her cheek.

"What about your career? And how will we work a long-distance relationship? I can't expect you—"

"I really like D.C. A sexy lady once told me about all the opportunities around here for a guy with my expertise." Derrick pulled her tight against his body. "I think she was trying to entice me."

"I think you're right. Did it work?" Talia squirmed against him, eager to feel the warmth of his desire.

"Oh, yeah."

Talia turned in his arms and pressed her lips to his. "Very good," she murmured, her voice muffled by their kiss.